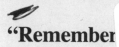

"Remember

Looking into his ~~~~~~~~~~~~~~~~~~~~~ ly long lashes, she d~~~~~~~~~~~~~~~~~~~~cause it felt as if all the air in the diner had suddenly vanished. She couldn't keep from glancing at Tom's mouth, thinking about his kisses, remembering them in exacting detail and wanting to kiss him now.

"Of course I do, but I'm surprised you do."

"I do. Why do you think I asked you out again?" he said, those hazel eyes twinkling, and she felt a tug on her heartstrings because she remembered again what fun she'd had with him.

"It was all exciting, Tom," she said with regret.

"Then don't cry about it now. Happy memories. Take the ones that were special and exciting and concentrate on them."

"Thank you," she said, smiling at him as he released her.

Right away, she missed his strong arms around her.

* * *

Reunited with the Rancher
is part of the series Texas Cattleman's Club:

REUNITED WITH THE RANCHER

BY
SARA ORWIG

First Published in Great Britain 2017
By Mills & Boon, an imprint of HarperCollins*Publishers*
1 London Bridge Street, London, SE1 9GF

© 2017 Harlequin Books S.A.

Special thanks and acknowledgement are given to Sara Orwig
for her contribution to the Texas Cattleman's Club: Blackmail series.

ISBN: 978-0-263-92812-9

51-0317

Our policy is to use papers that are natural, renewable and recyclable products and made from wood grown in sustainable forests. The logging and manufacturing processes conform to the legal environmental regulations of the country of origin.

Printed and bound in Spain
by CPI, Barcelona

Sara Orwig is an Oklahoman whose life revolves around family, flowers, dogs and books. Books are like her children: she usually knows where they are, they delight her and she doesn't want to be without them. With a master's degree in English, Sara has written mainstream fiction, and historical and contemporary romance. She has one hundred published novels translated in over twenty-six languages. You can visit her website at www.saraorwig.com.

With many thanks to
Stacy Boyd and Charles Griemsman
for working with me on this.
Thank you to Tahra Seplowin.
Also, thank you to Maureen Walters.

With love to my family—you are so special to me.

One

Tom Knox hurried down the hall of the Texas Cattleman's Club, his footsteps muffled by the thick carpet. The dark wood-paneled walls held oil paintings and two tall mirrors in wide ornate frames. There were potted palms and chairs covered in antique satin. Tom was so accustomed to his surroundings he paid no attention until a woman rounded the corner at the end of the long hall.

Tom's insides clutched and heat filled him as he looked at his estranged wife, Emily Archer Knox. Physical attraction, definitely lust, hit him as his gaze swept over her.

Wavy honey-brown hair framed her face. Her hair was always soft to touch. There was no way to shut off the memories, no matter how much they hurt or stirred him. A red linen suit with a matching linen blouse and red high heels added to her attractiveness. The red skirt ended above her knees, leaving her shapely legs bare to her ankles. His imagination filled in how she would look without the red linen. While desire ran rampant, at the same time, a shroud of guilt enveloped him. He had failed her in the worst way possible.

Each time he saw Emily, guilt gnawed at him for failing to save the life of their four-year-old son, Ryan, after a tour bus accident on a family ski vacation in Colorado. It had been five long, guilt-ridden years since then, and a chilly bitterness had settled in between them. His life had improved only slightly last year when he'd moved out of the house to the guesthouse on their ranch. They could go for weeks without crossing paths.

In many ways it was better to be apart, because then he could let go of the burden of guilt. That's why he had joined the Army Rangers for three years after the accident. After the death of his close friend, Jeremy, he wanted out of the Rangers. He couldn't be with Emily without thinking about how he had failed her and how unhappy she had been with him.

At the moment when they approached each other, Emily looked up and her green eyes widened. They avoided each other most of the time but couldn't today. He kept walking, his heart drumming while desire and guilt continued to war within him. Would he ever be able to face her without an internal emotional upheaval? Her smile was polite, the kind of smile usually reserved for strangers. When she came closer, her smile vanished before she greeted him with a quiet, "Hi, Tom."

"Good morning. You look great," he couldn't keep from saying.

Her gaze shifted to the briefcase in his hand. "Are you at the club for a meeting?"

"Yes. The finance committee. How about you?"

"I'm having lunch with a friend," she answered. How polite they were, yet a storm was going on within him. Guilt, hurt, too much loss plagued him each time he saw Emily or talked to her.

"Have a good time," he said as he passed her.

Her perfume stirred memories of holding her in his arms while he kissed her. Longing tore at him along with anger at himself. Why couldn't he let go completely? He and Emily didn't have anything together any longer. Only he knew that wasn't true. There was one thing they still had that hadn't vanished—a physical attraction that he felt each time she came into his sight. It was something he couldn't understand and didn't want to think about.

On a physical level, he knew she felt that chemistry as much as he did. She couldn't hide her reactions completely, and neither could he. But each time he encountered her, he was reminded that they both needed a chance for a fresh start, and that maybe the best thing he could do would be to give her a divorce and get out of her life completely.

After lunch at the Texas Cattleman's Club and an afternoon at her photography studio in downtown Royal, Emily drove home to Knox Acres, the cattle ranch she shared with Tom. She still couldn't stop replaying their brief encounter at the Texas Cattleman's Club. Since she first met him, she'd had a strong physical reaction to Tom. She still got tingles from just seeing him. Through good times, through the worst of times, Tom had dazzled her since they had fallen in love at sixteen. She had no comparison, but she didn't think that mattered. Tom was the best-looking, most appealing guy she had ever known.

Even so, other aspects of their marriage outweighed sheer lust. And they had lost what was essential in a marriage—that union of hearts, that joy in each other.

Their happiness had shattered the night their tour bus had skidded on an icy Colorado highway, going into a frozen pond. Tom had almost died pulling Ryan from the frigid water. Tom had ended up with pneumonia, a deep cut on his knee and a broken collarbone, broken ribs and a ruptured spleen. But in the end, he hadn't been able to save their son's life. After three days Tom could travel and they flew Tom, Emily and Ryan to a big hospital in Denver. They couldn't help Ryan, either. In eight more days, Ryan succumbed to his injuries. Somehow, amid all the grief, she and Tom composed themselves long enough to donate Ryan's organs to spare other parents the agony of losing a child.

The vacation had been Tom's family reunion, and twenty-three members of his family were on the bus. Besides Ryan, Tom's aunt died from drowning. Three other people, including two children, died in the accident, but they weren't in the Knox party.

Weeks turned into months and months into years, and her memories became more precious. In an effort to strengthen their marriage, they had tried to conceive again, but a new baby—a new start—never happened for them. Emily felt she had failed Tom in this; it was another blow to their marriage. They'd lost their son, and eventually their love, and their relationship became more strained until Tom moved out and they hardly saw each other any longer. It was general knowledge with most people they knew that they were estranged. Sometimes that still shocked her as much as everything else that had happened to them. She had been so in love with Tom when they married, she never would have believed the day would come when they barely spoke and hardly saw each other.

Hoping to put Tom out of her thoughts, she talked to her big white cat that had been a kitten given to Ryan when he was four. After feeding Snowball, she turned on her computer to read her email, and in seconds, a message caught her attention.

It was harsh, simple: Guess you weren't woman enough to hold his interest. Here's his real family, his secret family—until now. Frowning and puzzled, Emily scanned the subject: Today—for your eyes only. Tomorrow—for all of Royal to see.

She froze when she read the sender's name: Maverick. She had no idea who Maverick was. No one in Royal knew the identity of the hateful troll who'd been threatening and blackmailing people in town for the past few months. There were rumors Maverick might be the work of the three snooty stepsisters—that's how she pictured the clique of women, Cecelia Morgan, Simone Parker and Naomi Price, who seemed to think they owned the Texas Cattleman's Club and everything else in Royal these days. They always made Emily feel that she wasn't good enough to be included in their company.

Another chill slithered down Emily's spine when she opened the email attachment. It was a photograph. She stared at Tom in the picture, and shock hit her. As a professional photographer, Emily knew at a glance this picture was real. A smiling, earthy redhead with her hair fastened up in a ponytail posed with Tom, who stood close and had his arm draped around her shoulders. In front of them were two adorable children. The boy she guessed to be around four—the same age their Ryan had been when they had lost him. The little red-haired girl was pretty. In the background was a gingerbread dream house and beside the boy was a show-worthy golden retriever. They looked like the perfect family.

So this was Tom's preferred family. That made her the world's biggest fool. She and her husband had been growing apart for the past five years, and now she could see an additional reason why. Fury made her hot. There was a whole different side to Tom she had never seen— a deceitful side. She had trusted him completely. She stared at the picture, which was absolute evidence that their marriage was built on lies. Tom had another family. He was leading a double life. The realization was almost a physical blow.

If she wanted proof that their marriage was irrevocably broken, she had it now. Fresh out of excuses to delay the inevitable, heartsick and furious with Tom for his deception, she could see no other option: she planned

to file for divorce. She would give him his official freedom to stop being secretive about the family he loved.

Shaking with anger, she leaned in closer to the computer screen to study the photo intently. The woman
looked familiar, but Emily didn't know who she was.
Were she and her kids in Royal?

And was the message on target—was Emily not
woman enough to hold Tom? She shivered as she admitted to herself that the message was accurate, dead-on
accurate. She couldn't give Tom the family he wanted.

It had been Tom's idea to move out to the guesthouse.
He'd said separating would give them a chance to think
clearly about their futures. He was the one who'd said
they needed to get the physical attraction out of the way
so they could straighten out their emotions and feelings
for each other.

Knowing the real reason Tom wanted to move out of
the house, away from her, hurt Emily badly.

She looked again at the sender's email signature. She
had no idea who Maverick was. Could the rumors be
right, that Cecelia Morgan, Simone Parker and Naomi
Price were behind the nasty emails and the blackmail?
Those three were successful businesswomen, so it didn't
seem likely in a lot of ways. They might be snooty, but
that didn't mean they were this evil.

Someone intended to make Tom's secret public to
people in Royal. When that happened, Emily knew she
would be viewed with pity and there would be laughter
behind her back. That was insignificant next to the pain
that consumed her over Tom's deception. How could he

have been so duplicitous? It seemed totally unlike the man she knew and loved.

Would Maverick write Tom and threaten to go public? Had he—or she—already tried to extort money from Tom for silence? Emily could easily imagine Tom telling Maverick to go to hell first.

Emily couldn't stop her tears as her growing fury overwhelmed her. All this time, Tom had had a wife to love, to love him in return, precious children and a home. No wonder she couldn't get back together with him.

She intended to confront Tom with the truth. Their marriage was over. Completely finished. She needed a divorce to go on with her life. She had lost their son, and evidently, she'd lost Tom long ago, too. He was a lying, two-faced man she hadn't ever really known. She had never suspected that side of Tom. She had never even had a hint of it before now. Tom had seemed totally honest, kind—how he had fooled her! She wanted to scream at him and tell him how deceitful and hurtful he was. She wanted him out of her life, and this would ensure that happened.

She spent a sleepless night and drove into Royal the next day. Angry and hurt, she filed for divorce. Tom was now home from the military after his tour of duty with the Rangers, and he had taken over running the ranch. She had her photography studio and had just inherited her uncle Woody's old home in Royal. She and Tom could go their separate ways.

After work later that day, she went by the three-story house she had inherited from her uncle, the man who had raised her. The house was all she had left of family, so she intended to hang on to it and restore it so she could live there. She would be close to her photography studio and off the ranch, away from Tom. She didn't want to live in the palatial house on the ranch that they had built before Ryan was born anymore.

Tom drove back to the guesthouse after working outside all day on first one job and then another. Hard physical labor was the best way to drive the hurtful memories away, at least temporarily. It was early March, and the days were growing longer and warmer. It was spring—a time that used to be exciting and filled with promise. Now one day was like another and he spent time thinking over how he should plan his future.

At the present moment he wanted a shower and a beer and wished he had someone, a friend, to spend the evening with. Nights were long and lonely, and weekends were the worst.

As he pulled up, he saw a car parked in front of his house. It surprised him even more when he realized it was Emily's.

Why was she here? She never came to see him. Worried something might have happened to a friend, he frowned. Emily really had no family—only older cousins she didn't see. He parked and stepped out, slamming the pickup door behind him. He watched her open her car door to get out. She wore stiletto heels with black straps on her shapely feet. Her jeans fit her tiny waist snugly and were tight enough to emphasize her long, long legs. She wore a pale blue short-sleeved sweater that hugged her lush curves. In jeans, high heels and the sweater, she looked stunning. Her hair fell loosely around her face—the way he liked it best.

When his gaze raked over her, his pulse jumped. In spite of all their troubles, he was as physically drawn to her as ever. She was a good-looking woman—he'd always thought so and he still did. At the sight of her, memories tormented him, moments when he'd held and kissed her and wanted her with all his being. They'd had steamy nights of sexy loving, exciting days filled with happiness—a time that seemed incredibly far away and impossible to find ever again. He had failed her in the biggest possible way and now their love had ended. They had been through too much upheaval and loss to ever regain what they'd had.

Even so, desire for Emily was intense. He remembered that silky curtain of honey-brown hair spilling over his bare shoulders. Thoughts of kissing her haunted him. Memories of her softness, her voluptuous curves and her hands fluttering over him made him hot. She stood only a short distance away, pure temptation, and he wanted to reach for her…until he thought about all the problems between them. And it had to be a problem of some kind that brought her to see him. One glance in her big green eyes and he knew she was angry.

"Hi," he said. "What brings you here?"

Glaring at him, Emily waved papers in his face and then shoved them into his hand while she snapped, "You're welcome."

Startled out of his fantasy, Tom focused on her. "What am I welcome for? What are these papers?" he asked, looking down and turning over the official-looking forms in his hands before he looked up at her again. Puzzled, he met her fiery green eyes that flashed with fury.

"You can thank me now, because I've given you what you want—your freedom. You're free to marry the mother of your children."

"What the hell are you talking about?" She was rarely in a rage, but he could see she was boiling.

"Your secret is out, Tom," she said, her voice quivering with wrath. "You hid your family well. Have you paid Maverick to keep your secret? Or has it already spread all over Royal?"

Mystified, he saw that while she was shaking with rage, she was also fighting to hold back tears. "What the hell are you talking about, and what are these papers? And why are you talking about Maverick? What do you know about Maverick?"

"I think you know the answers to some of those questions," she said in a tight voice. "You have your divorce papers. You'll be free to be with your other wife."

"Other wife?" Stunned, Tom repeated the words as he frowned. "Emily, what are you talking about? There is no other wife—"

"Oh, please. I have proof. I've seen the picture of you and your family." She started to turn away.

Tom reached out to take her arm. As she yanked free of his grasp, the pain of her rejection made him hurt from head to toe. In three long strides, he caught up with her and held her arm more tightly this time.

"Emily, I don't understand what you're talking about.

Mother of my children? You're not leaving until you tell me what's going on."

"You can drop the lies and false front now that I know the truth," she snapped, twisting away to head back to her car.

Shocked, he went after her again with long strides that closed the distance between them. He grasped her shoulder to turn her to face him. "I have no idea what you're talking about or what brought this divorce on so suddenly without us talking about it."

"We're through and you know it. Your other family is what brought it on. I got an email from Maverick about them." She yanked free from him again and turned to open her car door.

He closed her door and stepped between her and the car. In minutes she would be gone and he wouldn't have any answers. He placed his hand on her shoulder. "You can't pop in and tell me we're getting divorced and then leave. Tell me what the hell all this is. And tell me about this email from Maverick. That troll who's blackmailing people in town? When did you get that?"

She twisted free again. "Get out of my way."

"Like hell I will. You're not going until you tell me. There is no secret family. That's nonsense."

"Oh, no? Tom, how could you be so deceitful?" she asked, sneering at him as she fumbled in a pocket to pull out a wrinkled piece of paper and wave it in front of him. "Here's proof, Tom. Here's your picture with your family. You have your arm around your secret wife. How could you lie to me like this?" Tears filled Emily's eyes, her cheeks were red and her voice was tight with anger. "How could you do this?" she repeated. "You've hurt me again, but this will be the last time."

"Give me that," he said, taking the paper from her to smooth it out and look at it. As he did, she wiggled away and opened her car door.

Determined to get answers from her, Tom reached out to push the car door closed again, stepping close with his hip against the door so she couldn't get inside while he smoothed the paper more to look at it. "Don't go anywhere, Emily, until we get this straightened out."

"Don't you dare tell me what to do," she said in a low voice that was filled with rage.

He paid no attention to her as he focused on the computer printout. Startled, Tom realized it was a copy of a very familiar snapshot.

Two

"Emily," he said, his anger changing to curiosity, "you got this in an email? This is Natalie Valentine and her kids. She's Jeremy Valentine's widow, who owns the Cimarron Rose Bed-and-Breakfast. Why have you filed for divorce over Natalie Valentine?"

Wide-eyed, Emily looked up at Tom and then glanced at the picture. "Jeremy Valentine?" she repeated, sounding dazed. "That's his wife? You told me about his death."

"That's right. I told you how he died on a mission and my promise to him to take care of his family if he didn't make it back."

"I remember that," Emily said, sounding stunned and confused. "She looked vaguely familiar, but I was in so much shock, I just didn't put anything together." She sagged against the car.

"Jeremy was shot," Tom reminded her. "We were on a mission in Iraq to rescue three hostages and Jeremy was shot twice. I promised him if he didn't make it, I'd take care of his family," Tom said, momentarily lost in remembering the battle, the blood, the noise of guns and men yelling. Tom looked at Emily, who had grown pale. Her eyes no longer held anger but uncertainty; he was sure she remembered him telling her about Jeremy's death.

"He was so worried about his family because he didn't expect to make it. I told him I'd be there for them if he couldn't." Tom held out the picture. "This is Natalie, and she's doing a great job being brave and upbeat and pouring herself into taking care of their two kids."

"Heavens, Tom," Emily whispered, shaking her head. "Those kids are Jeremy Valentine's? I've made a terrible mistake."

"Jeremy was their dad. They're really sweet kids. Colby is four—just like our Ryan when we lost him. Colby has autism. He's gotten accustomed to me and he's pretty relaxed around me. Lexie is two and thinks she's seventeen. She's pretty and cute. I just try to help out, because there's always something that needs fixing at the B and B. I try to be a man in the kids' lives and do things around the place or with the kids that Jeremy would do. Jeremy was one of the best."

Emily focused on him with a piercing look. "Tom, have you slept with Natalie?"

"Never," he answered with a clear conscience. "That isn't what this is about. I'm helping Natalie out, for Jeremy. That's all there is to it. He was a buddy and he died for his country." Tom gazed into Emily's green eyes and wondered whether she believed him or not. "It would be a good idea if you two met. Natalie has a sweet family."

"Oh, Tom," Emily said. She looked as if she'd been punched in the gut. Her shoulders sagged and she frowned. She ran her hand across her brow. "I've made a big mistake then," she repeated.

"I think you did," he said quietly. "But not one that can't be fixed."

Emily nodded. "I owe you an apology, because I believed this, even though it was so unlike you. The picture really shocked me."

"Forget that. We've got this ironed out between us now as far as I'm concerned, and I'll arrange for you and Natalie to meet."

"You never told me about seeing them. If it was just to be a help and do this for Jeremy, why didn't you tell me? I could have done some things for them, too."

He felt a ripple of impatience. "You haven't been interested in anything I've done for a long time. We don't keep up with each other any longer. I don't know any more about what you're doing than you know about what I'm doing. We're out of each other's lives now." He looked down at the papers in his hand. "This divorce was inevitable."

Clamping her lips shut, she nodded. "That's true. I can see why you didn't tell me." She frowned. "So this troll just sent the message to upset and hurt me," Emily said quietly, as if more to herself than to Tom, but he heard her.

"You got this from Maverick?"

"Yes."

"Damnation," Tom said, his temper rising as he thought about someone hiding behind a fictitious name, sending hateful messages to try to hurt Emily, who had already suffered the worst possible losses. He had failed Emily in the worst possible way before, but he wasn't going to fail her this time. "There's too much damn hate in this world and we don't need this going on in Royal. Maverick." He said the name with distaste. "Someone has hurt you once, but I damn well can see that he doesn't hurt you again. First of all, unless you've already called him, I'm calling Nathan Battle and letting him know about this," Tom said, pulling his phone out of his pocket.

"Sheriff Battle?"

"Yes. This week it's a hateful message to you. Who knows what this might escalate into next or how much this troll might hurt someone else? For some reason, he or she or they want to hurt you or you wouldn't have received that email. But I can't imagine you have an enemy in this world."

"Frankly, Tom, I didn't think about calling the sheriff. I was thinking more about us."

"I'm glad to hear you say that. If you get another message from Maverick, call me the minute you do."

"You saw the message—it was on target," she said quietly, and his anger increased at hearing the pain in her voice.

"It was a lie meant to hurt you. I'll call Nathan right now."

Tom's anger boiled and he was frustrated not to be able to take more direct action. When Nathan answered, Tom quickly told him about the email. After a minute or two, he turned to Emily. "Nathan wants to come pick up your CPU. He knows it most likely won't do any good, but he doesn't want to overlook anything."

"I don't mind if he checks the CPU and the email," she answered. "Goodness, I have nothing to hide. I'm going back into town, so I can drop it off at his office."

Tom smiled, then went back to talking to the sheriff for a minute before ending the call. "We'll go by his office. I'll help you get your CPU."

"That's fine. How do you suppose someone got that picture? Do you remember who took it?"

"There was some guy, about seventy years old, staying at the bed-and-breakfast. He was taking pictures. I'm sure he didn't know any of us."

"Well, then, how did Maverick get the picture?"

"The guy was using a camera. Maybe he got the prints made at a store. Those can be handled by several people. It wouldn't be hard to get a copy." He tilted his head to look at her. "Do you have plans tonight?"

"Not at all," she answered.

"Good. Because I'm moving back in," Tom announced in an authoritative voice that she assumed he'd developed in the Rangers. "I want to stay close, because no one knows Maverick's ultimate intentions."

Startled, Emily stared at him. "I appreciate your offer but it's not necessary. I'm not staying on the ranch any longer. I'm going to restore Uncle Woody's house and move in there. I've put a cot in a bedroom and I'm already living in Royal."

"You've moved off the ranch?" Tom said, frowning. "Look, Maverick isn't getting the reaction from us that he, she or they expected, which will increase the hatred and anger toward you. Move back to the ranch until this Maverick gets caught. You'll be safer here."

She might have been tempted to do what he asked, except he was asking for the wrong reason. She wasn't moving back because of an email message. And now that she knew the truth and Tom still was the same Tom she had always known, she had lost her anger toward him. But they still had all the problems they'd had for the past five years. She was going to move into town and Tom wasn't going to stop her.

As she calmed down, the feelings and responses she had always had began to return, including noticing his thick black hair that was a tangle over his forehead but always looked appealing to her. She could remember running her fingers through his hair. Her gaze slid down and she thought about his strong arms holding her against his rock-hard chest.

She sighed, because the memories were a torment and she couldn't keep them from happening. The breeze caught locks of his hair and blew them slightly. Everything about him made her want to walk into his arms and hold him close. She had always thought he was good-looking, and as the years went by, he seemed more handsome than ever. Or did she feel that way just because he was more off-limits than ever? She wasn't staying on the ranch no matter what he said, because they had been too unhappy together there. There were too many bad memories in the big house on the ranch.

"I'll be fine in town," she said, knowing that was the best place for her to be. "I'm working at my studio four days a week now, and the other days, I can work on the house."

"Okay, I'll get a sleeping bag and stay with you in Royal. You don't know if you're in any danger from this troll. Just because nothing's happened in the past doesn't mean it won't in the future."

Startled, she stared at him. "You can't live in Royal—you have a ranch to run," she blurted, feeling a sudden panic that they would be in close quarters. No matter what problems they had, when they were together, the physical attraction was impossible to resist. She had been trying to get over him and build a new life. If they lived together, she wouldn't be able to resist him.

"You don't need to spend all that time driving back and forth every day from Royal to the ranch," she said. She was pleased that he was concerned and had made the offer, and overwhelmingly relieved to discover that the troll's message hadn't been true and Tom was still the same trustworthy person she had always thought he was, but her panic about spending nights under the same roof again began to revive. She gazed into his thickly lashed hazel eyes, which made her get a tightness low inside and think about his kisses that could melt her.

"If you're in danger and something happened to you in Royal while I'm out here on the ranch," he said, "I couldn't live with it. You'd do the same if the situation were reversed."

She had to smile at the thought of being a bodyguard for Tom. "That's such a stretch of the imagination, I can't picture it. Don't even think about moving to Royal, but thank you for the offer, which is nice of you," she said, running her fingers along his forearm, feeling the solid muscles. She had meant it as a friendly gesture of gratitude, but the minute her fingers touched his arm, a sizzling current spiraled in her and she thought again of having his strong arms around her.

As she drew a deep breath, she saw his eyes narrow. Either he felt something, too, or he knew that she had—or both.

She dropped her hand instantly and stepped back. "Thanks anyway," she said, dismissing his offer.

"Give some thought to this. For all we know, you might be in danger. The safest possible place would be in the guesthouse. I can protect you the easiest there."

"I don't think that's necessary at all. According to the rumors I've heard, Maverick hasn't done anything except send terrible messages, trying to blackmail Royal citizens and stir up trouble. I need to work in town and I don't want to drive back and forth. I'm staying at my uncle's. Thank you for your concern, but you don't need to stay with me," she said firmly.

"I've already lost one of the most important people in my life," he said in a tight voice. "I don't intend to let anything happen to you." His hazel eyes looked darker, as they did when he was emotional or making love. "I'm going to ask Nathan to have someone drive by Natalie's and check on her to make sure she and her family are protected and okay." Tom removed his phone from his pocket again. Emily wondered who he was calling now until she heard him say hello to their foreman.

"Hey, Gus. I need to be away from the ranch for a while."

Even as she stepped in front of him and shook her head, trying to discourage him, she knew the futility of her efforts. Tom had made up his mind that she should have protection and she wouldn't be able to stop him. She threw up her hands and walked away as he gave instructions to Gus. How was she going to be able to resist Tom if they were under the same roof? Maybe he would stay downstairs and she could stay upstairs, or vice versa.

"There, now," he said when he finished talking to the foreman. "I'll bring my sleeping bag and stay in the old house with you. I won't be in your way, and I can help you with the restoration."

Exasperated, she stared at him. While she was annoyed, she knew this alpha male attitude was part of why she had been drawn to him in the first place. He was decisive and got things done. In high school it had been part of his appeal. Now she was glad he could make a decision and solve problems, but this time she really didn't want him interfering in her life by taking charge. Each time she thought about being back under the same roof with him all night, her heart pounded. If he was going to help with the restoration of the old house, they would be working together. And she couldn't trust her physical response to Tom. He would stir up all those latent longings again. Tom had a virile, sexy body. He was superbly fit from the Rangers and from ranch work.

Tom turned to her. He had his hands on his hips and he stood close. He had the shadow of stubble on his face and his tangled hair added to his disheveled attraction. He looked more appealing than ever in a rugged, sexy way. She realized where her thoughts were drifting and tried to pay attention to what he was saying.

"Nathan told me that Case Baxter, president of the TCC, plans to have an emergency meeting this coming week. Case agrees with Nathan that Maverick has to be stopped. To do so, they need to learn Maverick's true identity. I'm going to that meeting, and I'd like you to come with me."

"Sure, I'll go. But I don't think I can help in any way."

"It won't hurt, and the more of us who are informed and keep in touch with Nathan, the more likely he'll be able to catch Maverick. If you go, remember, Maverick may be sitting in the audience."

She shivered. "That's creepy."

"Hopefully, his emails and threats on social media won't escalate into violence, but no one knows right now. What he's doing now is bad enough. He hasn't really hurt us, but he could have, and he can hurt others badly."

After a pause, Emily steered the conversation to an equally unpleasant topic. "Tom, when we've waited a bit, we need to sit down and talk about the divorce and how we'll divide things. I was so angry when I filed. The picture was so convincing."

He nodded. "I don't think we'll have a problem dividing up the ranch, the house, the cars or the plane."

"You can definitely have the plane," she remarked, and he gave her a fleeting smile that made her smile in turn.

"I'll sign the divorce papers. We're there anyway, and you can have a life."

She turned away before he saw tears in her eyes. He was right. They were as good as divorced now, and she couldn't give him children. Their marriage had such devastating memories. Even so, it still hurt when divorce became reality; she had filed and the papers were in his possession. It was one more big loss in her life and this one she took responsibility for because she'd been unable to get pregnant again. If she had been, it would have held them together. She'd wanted so badly to give Tom another child like Ryan. There was adoption—Tom had been willing—but it wasn't the same and she was against it. She wanted to have another child like Ryan.

Now she and Tom were estranged, and if they got divorced, they could each go ahead with life. But it was difficult to imagine ever loving another man.

And it didn't help that Tom had proved Maverick wrong and was trying to help her. It was easy to file for divorce when she was so angry with Tom because she thought he had deceived her. To know that he was still the same guy she had always admired and trusted made the divorce hurt.

"Emily?"

She blinked in surprise, turning to face him again. His eyes narrowed, and he studied her intently. "I'm sorry, Tom. My thoughts drifted back to Maverick," she said, her cheeks burning with embarrassment. She suspected he could guess exactly why she hadn't heard him.

"You said you're going back to Royal from here. Let me grab a sleeping bag and a few things. I'll take you."

She opened her mouth to protest, but before she said a word, he waved his hand. "I'm taking you to Royal. Tomorrow we'll come back and get your car. I'd just as soon let everyone see us together—it'll give me pleasure. Hopefully, the damned troll will see us and realize that email did no harm. Far from it. How's that for a plan?"

She shrugged. "I have a feeling if I didn't like it at all, I would still end up doing it. I think you're right about letting Maverick see us together. That gives me a sense of getting even with the troll."

"We can flaunt that we're getting along. It doesn't take long for word to get around Royal."

"I agree. While it's good to be seen together, you don't need to stay with me," she argued again. "I'll be in town, where I can call for help at any hour and someone will be right there."

"I'm staying, Emily. This is someone with a grudge and you're on the list. That was a damn hateful message you received. Look at the results. You filed for divorce. If rumors started, they could have hurt Natalie, which in turn would have hurt her kids. Frankly, I'm not ready to divorce you when it's because of a bunch of lies from a vengeful creep."

"You have a point, Tom," she said, wishing he had said he didn't want the divorce for other reasons, yet knowing he was right. "And while we've been talking, I've been thinking—Maverick has to be somebody who lives in Royal, or has lived in Royal until recently, to know this about you and Natalie and to know to send the picture to me."

"That's right." He looked down at his dusty boots, his mud-splattered jeans. "Can you have a seat inside and let me take a quick shower? I can be speedy."

"You were never speedy when I showered with you," she teased and then blushed. "I don't know where that came from," she said. "Forget it."

"Hell, no, I won't forget it," he said, his voice getting soft. "You were teasing like you used to, and that's allowed, Emily. We can have some fun sometimes—let it happen. We've got too much of the sad stuff. At this point in our lives, it really isn't going to change anything to have a laugh or two," he said.

She nodded. "I suppose you're right," she said quietly, thinking he was the way he used to be before the bad times set in. Relaxed, kind, understanding, practical, sexy. He had been fun, so much fun, so sexy. She waved her hand at him. "Go on, Tom. Shower. I can go get the CPU while you're in there."

"Nope. I want to be with you. This Maverick bothers me, I'll admit. I can't imagine why you're on anyone's hit list. That's worrisome. You're softhearted, generous—"

"Oh, my! We've turned into a mutual-admiration society, thanks to a troll."

"It's not thanks to the damned troll. It's time we have something between us again that isn't sad, even if it's just for five minutes."

"Tom, I agree with everything you just said. For just a few minutes, it was sort of the way it used to be, at least a tiny bit," she said, suddenly serious, thinking it was a lot better than not speaking and avoiding each other. "I know we can't turn back the clock, but we can at least be civil to each other."

"Damn right. Don't disappear while I go shower," he said, starting inside and holding the screen door. He paused, looking over his shoulder at her. "Unless you want to come inside and join me."

She shook her head. "No, thank you."

He grinned. "After your remark, I had to try." He let the door slam shut behind him and disappeared.

"Don't make me fall in love with you all over again," she whispered, and wound her fingers together, trying to think of seeing Nathan Battle, of her appointments tomorrow, of anything except Tom in the shower.

In less than ten minutes Tom reappeared, his hair slightly damp. He wore a clean navy T-shirt, fresh jeans, black boots and a black hat. He carried a rolled-up sleeping bag and a satchel. "I'll put up my truck and get the car and we'll go get the CPU."

"Sure," she said, walking out with him and waiting on the porch until he pulled up in a black sports car. He was out and around the car by the time she got to it. He held the door for her, and as she passed him, she glanced up and received another scalding look. She was close, her shoulder brushing his arm as he held the car door open. Their gazes met and she couldn't catch her breath. For just a moment, she forgot everything except Tom, pausing to look into his thickly lashed hazel eyes that immobilized her. The differences between them fell away, and all-consuming lust enveloped her.

It took an effort to tear her gaze from his. In that brief moment, she had wanted his arms around her and his mouth on hers.

"Thanks," she said, hating that it came out breathlessly. She slipped into the passenger seat and gazed ahead as he closed the door. He strode around the car. Handsome, purposeful, filled with vitality, he would be married again after their divorce, she was certain. Tom was too appealing to live alone, and he liked women. The idea of Tom marrying hurt even though they had no future together and no longer had the joy and happiness of their first years together.

She rode in silence as they drove the short distance from the guesthouse to the mansion they had shared. Now it stood silent and empty. They had been happy in the sprawling, palatial two-story house until they lost their son. She didn't want to live in it alone. It was too big, too empty without Tom. He'd seemed to fill it with his presence when he would come home. When they had Ryan, his childish voice and laughter had also seemed to fill the big house. At present, she found it empty, isolated and sad. She didn't like living alone in it and she didn't intend to ever again. This wasn't the place for her any longer.

The house had a somber effect on her and Tom seemed to react the same way. They both were quiet as they walked to the door. Tom still had a key and opened the door to hold it for her. She walked through into the spacious entryway, switching on lights as she went, although it wasn't dark outside yet.

She suddenly thought about Ryan running around in front of the house when he was so small. Tears came and she wiped them away quickly. Pausing, she glanced over her shoulder at Tom, and he looked stricken. She guessed that he, too, was thinking of Ryan and hurting because he hadn't been in the house in almost a year. He rubbed his eyes—the tough, decorated Ranger who had been in combat, been wounded, been a prisoner until he escaped. She couldn't bear his grief, which compounded her pain. When she turned away, crying silently while she tried to get control of her emotions, Tom put his arm around her.

"Come here," he whispered. Sobbing, she turned to him and they held each other. His strong arms around her felt wonderful and she tightened her hold on him as if she could squeeze out some of his strength, transferring it from him to her. He was a comfort and she hoped she was for him. She stroked his back, relishing holding him. It had been so long since she had been in his arms.

"I'm sorry, Tom. Sometimes I just lose it and I guess you do, too. Having you here helps," she said, wiping her eyes with a tissue.

He looked down at her, easing his hold on her slightly. "I'm glad I'm here for you. It helps me. Grieving is part of it that we can't escape." She nodded as he released her. She missed his strong arms around her.

"I'm okay now. Thanks."

They went through the house to the large room that

was her office. "I'll get the CPU out for you, Emily," he said and strode past her. "I'm sure this is futile, but it would be ridiculous for Nathan not to check it out."

"While you do that, Tom, I'll pick up a few things to take to Royal."

"Where's that white cat of yours?"

"Your cook has Snowball until I get settled in Royal. You don't care, do you?"

"No, I don't care where your cat is."

It seemed natural to be in the house with Tom again. She watched him hunker down to disconnect the CPU, the fabric of his jeans pulling tightly over his long legs. Desire swept through her, and she turned to leave the room abruptly to get away from him.

In less than half an hour they were on their way to Royal. They rode together in silence. She knew he was bound in his own thoughts as much as she was in hers, and they had little to say to each other. While they didn't talk, she was acutely conscious of him. She hadn't been around him this much in a long time. And their time together was just starting. How could she live under the same roof with him again without being in his arms and in his bed and back on an emotional roller coaster?

She glanced at his hand on the steering wheel. He had a scar across the back of it that had healed long ago. He had scars all over his body from his time in the military.

His hands were well shaped, nails clipped very short, veins showing slightly. Too easily she could remember his hands drifting over her when they had made love—strong hands that could send her to paradise.

She realized her thoughts were carrying her into a place she didn't want to go. "I think you're right about the divorce. We'll get it—that's inevitable—but I don't like getting a divorce because of Maverick, either."

"Let's table the divorce for now. I'll try to find out how much effort Nathan is devoting to catching this troll. The meeting Monday at the club may shed more light. If we don't divorce and we both stay at the house in Royal—"

"Maverick will know you've become my bodyguard," she said, shaking her head.

"Not necessarily. If I help you restore the old house, it'll look as if we're back together. For all anyone knows, we're fixing it up for you to sell. For a few weeks, maybe we should keep quiet that I'm worried about your protection and that we're not really together anymore."

"That's fine with me. Anything to defeat Maverick. Frankly, I'm still amazed I'm a victim. I'm not the sweetest person, but I usually get along with people I know and work with, neighbors, church friends."

"I'll ask you the question that Nathan is going to ask—do you have any enemies? Anyone who doesn't like you or you've angered?"

She laughed softly. "Tom, I may have people who don't like me, but if so, I don't know anything about it. I don't have enemies. I can't think of anyone."

"The whole world loves you," he remarked. "That's what you'll hear from Nathan, I'll bet."

"The one person I've made the most unhappy is you," she answered quietly, and he glanced quickly at her and back at the road. When she looked again, she saw his knuckles had tightened on the wheel.

"Hell, Emily, I loved you with all my being, but we've just had so much happen between us there is no way we can go back to that life we had. When I ask if you have angered anyone, I'm talking real enemies."

"I know you are," she said, hurting inside because she'd answered with the truth. There was no one who had been as hurt by her or more at odds with her or more disappointed by her than Tom. "We're not real enemies and you're a good guy."

"Thanks for that much, Em. Think about it. Think if there is anyone you've crossed who might hold a grudge."

She gave a small laugh. "Darla from our class in high school. Oh, did she have a crush on you. Now if this had happened when we were sixteen instead of now when we're thirty-two, I'd give out her name in a flash, but the last I heard she's married and has three kids."

"I hate to say this, but I don't even remember the person you're talking about."

"One of your groupies."

"I didn't have groupies."

"Every cute football captain has groupies."

"May have seemed so to you, but I didn't. And I haven't been called cute since I was five."

"You were cute. That was the general consensus with all the girls. Ooh, long eyelashes, broad shoulders, cute butt, sexy, to-die-for—"

"Stop it." He laughed. "If I had only known then—you didn't tell me all that when we were in school."

"Of course not. It would have just gone to your head—or elsewhere."

"Oh, damn, we should have had this conversation long ago," he said, grinning at her. And once again, for just an instant, she was reminded of old times with him.

"Kidding aside, Emily, keep thinking. It's important. Could it have to do with your business?"

"I take pictures of kids and families—there's nothing in my work that should anger anyone. I've never had an irate customer."

"I'm sure you haven't—you're a damn good photographer."

"The result wasn't what Maverick intended, so let's not worry too much about it right now," she said, placing her hand on Tom's knee in a gesture that at one time would have been casual. It wasn't now. He turned to stare at her, and she saw his chest expand as he took a deep breath.

She removed her hand and looked out the window, turning from him and trying to make light of the moment. She was thankful he couldn't hear or feel her racing heart.

"I'll try to think, but I'm blank. I know I'm overlooking something or I wouldn't have received that email."

"That's right, so work on it," he said, and they lapsed into silence as they drove toward Royal.

She thought over what Tom had said. What enemies did she have? "Tom, maybe Maverick was getting at you through me."

"That occurred to me, and I've been trying to think

of anyone in these parts I could have really annoyed. Frankly, Emily, I can think of some. I've fired cowboys who didn't want to work. I was in the military—there are people in the area who don't like that or what I did. Politically, they don't agree with me. There are guys I competed with in college and high school sports. There are guys I've competed with in rodeos. I'll talk to Nathan about it. He's got to catch this troll. It has to be someone really low-down mean to hurt you after what you've been through."

"I haven't been through any more than you have," she said, and he was silent. His jaw was set and she suspected he was frustrated and angry.

"You have been through more than I have," he said quietly. "You lost Ryan, you lost your uncle, your dad split when you were two, your mom died when you were nine, the man who raised you and the last close member of your family died this past year and you haven't had another child. You don't need more anguish, much less to get hassled by a rotten coward."

It hurt to hear Tom say that she couldn't have more children, but everything he said was the truth. As their conversation trailed off, she was acutely aware of him so nearby. She had been doing fairly well when she didn't see him or talk to him on a regular basis, but now to be with him, to joke around with him, even just this tiny bit, drew her to him. And the memories were tormenting her. They had been so wildly in love when they were dating and first married. Her world had crashed and would never again be the same. She had been slowly adjusting to life without Tom, and now he was coming right back into it. Would she be able to cope with living in the same house again? Could she resist the intense, scalding attraction she always felt for him? What would happen if he tried to seduce her?

The questions came at her constantly, and there were no answers.

Three

When they got to town, Tom parked in front of the sheriff's office and carried the CPU inside. Nathan greeted them and shook Tom's hand. "We don't have much in the way of good leads and I don't expect to get anything from your computer, but I need to check it out. I hope both of you will go to the meeting Monday."

"We plan to," Tom said. "I'll help in any way I can. Just let me know."

"Thanks," Nathan said. The sheriff was tall and had friendly brown eyes. "I'd like to talk to each of you, one at a time. Emily, want to go first?"

"Sure," she answered, smiling at him. He was slightly older than Tom and she, but she knew him and his wife, Amanda, who owned the Royal Diner, which was a town fixture.

Emily went into his office and tried to answer his questions. She was with him only a short time and then he talked to Tom. Their session was also brief.

Soon both men came out of Nathan's office. "If either one of you think of anything to tell me, just call, no matter what the hour is. I want this Maverick caught."

"I think most of the people in Royal probably want him caught quickly," Emily said.

"Sorry we weren't more help, Nathan," Tom said. "I'll keep thinking about any possibilities."

"Sure. Both of you try to make the meeting Monday. I'm shocked that Emily was a target. And it could have been to get at you, but why you? You don't have any real enemies around these parts."

"You never know—you can aggravate someone without even knowing it. Since there are several people now who've received these Maverick messages, I'd say this is a sour character who has a lot of grudges."

"You're right. I want to catch him—or her. I'm sure Emily's computer will be the same as the others—we can't trace where the messages originated. Maverick may be mean, but he's not stupid."

Nathan followed them outside, and the three of them stood for a moment in the late-afternoon sun. "Emily, since you've moved into your uncle's house here in town, if you need us at any time, just call. I'm glad Tom is there now, because that takes away some worries."

"We'll keep in touch," Tom promised as he took Emily's arm lightly. He was saying goodbye to the sheriff, paying little attention to her, but with each of Tom's touches, the contact was startling. How could he still do this to her when they were no longer in love and headed for divorce? They had no future together, she was annoyed he had taken charge of her life and was staying with her, yet the slightest contact was electrifying. She hoped her reaction didn't show.

They told Nathan goodbye and walked to the car. As they drove away, Tom glanced at her. "Let's stop at the diner and get a burger."

"Sure," she answered, knowing Tom was probably hungry, but suspecting he wanted people in Royal to see them together.

Everything they did reminded her of old times with him, which made her sad, but at the same time, she couldn't keep from enjoying his company.

They drove the short distance down Main and stopped at the Royal Diner for burgers. Too many things she did with Tom reminded her of their life when everything was exciting and they were in love. The reminders hurt and made her realize how her expectations had been destroyed and there wasn't any putting their marriage back together. They might fool Maverick, but it was going to cost her peace of mind to have Tom hovering around.

They sat down in a booth upholstered in red faux leather. "How many times have we eaten burgers or had a malt here?" she couldn't resist asking Tom.

He smiled at her. "Too many to keep track, but my mind was never on the burgers or the malts."

"I doubt mine was, either," she said, remembering

how exciting he was to her. "This is the first place you asked me to go with you—to get a malt."

"I remember," he said, focusing on her with a direct gaze that made her warm. "After you ran into my car."

"That was one of the first times I ever took the car. I just didn't see you when I pulled out of the school parking lot. It's a good thing you had quick reflexes, because it would have been a worse wreck if you hadn't put on your brakes."

"That seems so long ago. Your uncle Woody was understanding about the whole thing. His insurance paid for my car and he had faith in you. He knew you'd learn to drive, and I guess he figured you'd be more careful after hitting my car."

"I was definitely more careful."

"It was worth it to get you to pick me up every morning and take me to school while my car was being fixed," Tom said, smiling at her.

"I thought so, too," she said, loving to see him smile. The sad times they'd experienced had taken away smiles and laughter, but before that she had always had more fun with Tom than anyone else. "I liked picking you up, except it was embarrassing, too, because everyone in school knew what I'd done."

He leaned across the table, and his voice dropped as he spoke softly. "Remember our first kiss? I do."

She looked into his bedroom eyes and drew a deep breath. But it felt as if all the air in the diner suddenly vanished. She couldn't keep from glancing at Tom's mouth, thinking about his kisses, remembering them in exacting detail and wanting to kiss him again.

"Of course I do, but I'm surprised you do."

"I do. Why do you think I asked you out again?" he said, those hazel eyes twinkling.

"It was all exciting, Tom," she said, full of regret.

"Then don't cry about it now. Happy memories. Take the ones that were special and exciting and concentrate on them."

"Thank you, Doctor," she said lightly, smiling at him.

Their burgers came. She ate half of hers, reflecting on how she didn't want Tom staying with her but finding no way to avoid it, especially after Nathan said it was a good arrangement.

They left and she felt certain they would never eat burgers together in the Royal Diner again. She glanced up at Tom as she walked beside him. He was still exciting to her, which was something she didn't want to feel, because they had no future and all too soon they would officially be divorced. Why did that hurt so badly when it was what they both wanted? Now with him moving in to stay in the same house with her, was she going through another emotional upheaval that would be more difficult and painful to get over than the last time?

"Want to make a quick stop and see my studio?" she asked impulsively. "It isn't something you have to do."

"No, I'd like to see it."

"Turn at the next corner." She gave him directions and they drove just two more blocks and parked in front. She was sandwiched in between a law office and a popular bakery that had delicious bread. He paused to look at the pictures of babies and dogs and families on display in her front window.

"Very nice, Em. You've turned your hobby into a good business. You're very good."

"Thank you," she said, feeling he was being polite.

"I think I may just stand out here and smell the bread," Tom remarked.

"It's fantastic. We can pick up a loaf to take with us. They have specialties. Come in. This is tiny, but big enough for me."

He walked around the waiting room, looking at more pictures on the walls. Some of the people he recognized, a lot he didn't, especially the children. Then he came upon a large framed picture of their son when he was two years old.

"Em, this is a wonderful picture of Ryan. I want a copy."

"I'll get you one. I'm glad you like it. It makes me happy to see his picture when I come to work."

Tom continued looking at the framed photographs. There was one from when the tornado hit Royal, of the damaged town hall with three floors destroyed and the clock tower left standing. "You're very good at this," he said, moving to another picture of a black horse in a pasture, the wind blowing its tail, sunlight spilling over its satiny black coat. Tom glanced at her.

"This looks like my horse Grand."

"It is. He's photogenic and cooperative."

"Wow. I'd like a copy of that picture, too." He leaned closer. "I don't see a price on these."

"You're special. You can have that picture compliments of the house."

"You don't need to do that."

"I want to," she said, smiling at him.

"Thanks. It's a great picture of him."

"Come see where I take pictures and my desk."

He walked around and bent down to look through a camera set on a tripod. Across from him was a backdrop of a field of green grass.

"Tom, let me take your picture."

He grinned at her. "You're kidding. You know what I look like."

She took his arm. "Come stand and let me have a picture of you. I might want it on cold winter nights when you're not with me."

His smile faded. "You're serious. All right, I will if you'll let me take one of you on my phone."

She laughed. "Sure I will."

"And promise you won't stick me out there in the window."

"I wouldn't think of it," she said. "Your picture will go home to my bedroom," she said, expecting a laugh or sexy reply, but he stood quietly looking at her and she wondered what he was thinking. "You stand right here," she said, motioning to him.

Behind the camera, she adjusted the settings and took a picture. "Now turn slightly and look over your shoulder a little at me and smile."

"Em, I feel silly."

"Smile and cooperate. I'll buy you a loaf of bread when we leave."

"You're really good at this bribery business." He turned and smiled and she snapped some more.

"Now, want to see your pictures? I can get proofs for you while we go get that loaf of bread."

"I don't really care about seeing my picture, but I definitely care about that bread. You don't have to buy it. I'll go get it and you get your proofs or whatever you do. What kind do you want me to get?"

"I love the sourdough."

"Sourdough, coming up. I'll be back." He left and she worked quickly on the proof. She was examining them when she heard the bell in front. She scooped up the proofs, turned off lights and hurried to meet him.

"I have two loaves of bread and they smell almost too good to wait to eat. Ready to go?"

"Yes, look. You take a very appealing picture."

She held a couple of proofs out for him to see. He barely glanced at them but smiled at her. "I'm a very appealing subject," he said and she smiled.

The sun was low in the west when they left her shop. As soon as they were in the car, she turned to him slightly. "When we leave here, get ready for a shock. The house is in terrible condition. At the last, Uncle Woody was so ill—"

"Emily, I've meant to tell you that I'm sorry I missed being at his funeral."

"There wasn't any reason for you to fly back from your business trip in Wyoming. I never asked you if you bought the ranch," she said, realizing how far apart they had grown. In times past he would have been at her side for her uncle's last hours and through the service. She would have known whether Tom bought another ranch in Wyoming and he would have discussed his decision with her before he did anything. They were moving farther apart and the divorce was inevitable, but right now, she didn't want to give any satisfaction to Maverick and neither did Tom, so they'd stay together.

"No, I didn't buy it. If I buy another ranch, it'll be in this part of the country," he said. "I'm beginning to rethink getting someone else to run it. I have to be hands-on with a ranch."

She was quiet when they turned on the street where she had lived from the time she was nine years old until she had married Tom. Big sycamores and oaks lined the road. Tiny green leaves covered some branches, but many had bare limbs. The aging sidewalk was pushed up by tree roots. Tom slowed in front of the three-story house and turned onto a driveway where grass filled the cracks of aged concrete that had disappeared beneath a cover of weeds.

Tom parked beside the back corner of the aged house. "I want the car out here where it can be seen. If anyone has been watching you, whoever it is will know this isn't your car. I want Maverick to know I'm here with you, that the email didn't work and didn't hurt either one of us."

"It gives me the shivers to think someone might be watching me," she said. "I never even thought of that."

Tom gave her a look and smiled. "You're trusting."

He cut the engine while he gazed at the house, and she studied it with him. Long ago it had been painted white, but now the paint was peeling. There were gables on the front and west sides with a shingled roof that needed replacement. The large round tower on the east side had broken windows and all the ground floor windows were broken. The house had a wraparound porch with wooden gingerbread decoration that had shattered through the years and ornate spindles that were broken.

She sat a moment looking at the dilapidated condition: peeling paint, shutters hanging awry or gone, broken windows, concrete steps crumbling. She remembered one night when Tom had brought her home and parked on the drive. They had gotten out of his car and he had kissed her beneath the mulberry tree. A kiss became kisses and then he asked her to marry him. They both had a year of college left and they'd talked about waiting, but that night was the night he proposed. Before she went in, they agreed they wouldn't do anything official until they finished their senior year.

"What are you thinking about?" he asked.

Startled, she turned to him and wondered if he had guessed that being with him at the house had triggered memories. "I have a lot of windows to repair," she said.

"Yeah," he said in a gruff voice, and she wondered if he remembered the same moments she had. "So this is where you want to live instead of the house on the ranch. This is going to be a job and a half," Tom said, looking at it in the dusk as the last sunlight slipped away into darkness. "It's also the least secure place you could pick to stay."

"I'm in Royal, which is a peaceful town."

"A peaceful town that has a hateful troll spreading grief."

"I know I have a lot of work to do here, but I work in town now and the house is my only tie to my past and my family. The ones I was really close to are all gone. I hardly know my cousins, and they live in Oregon and Vermont. I never see them. This house is my tie to Mom and Uncle Woody."

"It's a fine old home, but your uncle couldn't keep up with it and it'll be an expense for you."

"He didn't want me to hire anyone to work on it, so I did what he wanted."

"Honoring his wishes was probably more important. Well, we can fix it up and hire people to do some of the work."

"It's not a *we* thing, Tom. This isn't where you'll live. It's not your house and it's not your problem," she said. "You don't need to be concerned with it, and I still think you could go back to the ranch."

He frowned, his jaw clamped shut. The happy moments they'd had disappeared with her request for him to leave. Jolted by regret, she reminded herself it was for the best. She didn't need Tom staying with her, and it would complicate both their lives—he had a ranch to run and she didn't need him hovering.

"People will have seen us together and your car here and they'll talk about it. You don't need to stay longer," she added when he didn't say anything.

"You may not want me, but I'm staying," he said in a gruff tone. "Think of me as a bodyguard and maybe you can tolerate my presence. You might need me."

"Suit yourself," she said, still wondering how she would get through the night with him in the house.

She reached for the door handle and he placed his hand on hers.

Startled, she looked up at him.

"I don't feel right about you walking into this big empty house. Anybody could be in there, because there is not one lick of security here. They could step in through any one of downstairs windows. Do you even lock the doors?"

"Actually, no. What's the point with windows broken out?"

"You just wait here in the car while I check the place. Keep the car keys and give me your house key."

"Tom—"

"I know I'm being cautious, but it only takes minutes and we have time. I'll feel better. Now you stay locked in this car, and if you see anyone call me instantly. And if anyone tries to get in the car—"

"I'll just run over them," she couldn't resist saying, because she thought he was being ridiculous.

He didn't laugh. "Emily, I've seen a guy walk into a house and get his throat slashed. I know we're in Royal, but I don't see one damn reason to take a chance."

"Ah, Tom. Sorry," she said. "I know you're trying to help, but this isn't a war zone, it's Royal, and so far, Maverick has only sent emails." She waved her hand. "I'll do as you say. You check out the house." She knew his warrior background had kicked in and there was no use arguing.

Nodding at her, he stepped out of the car and closed the door quietly.

She couldn't imagine any danger, but then she had

never expected to receive such a hateful message from Maverick, either. And so now she was under the same roof with Tom again—that seemed the biggest threat, but it was a threat to her heart when she was just pulling herself together and beginning to establish a life without Tom in it.

He vanished into the house. It was still dusk. She could still see outside, but inside the old house, darkness would prevail. She could imagine Tom checking out each room. He would be thorough and silent.

Her nerves were on edge by the time the lights were switched on in the house and she could see him coming through the kitchen. As she took in his broad shoulders and purposeful stride, she knew she would feel totally safe with Tom in the house. In the past she had always felt completely safe when he was around, but then, in the past, she hadn't worried about any kind of threat.

He passed by the windows and a light went off in what Uncle Woody called his front parlor. Next the hall light went off and she realized Tom was going to turn off all the lights and leave the downstairs in darkness.

She didn't even see him coming when he tapped on the car window.

He opened the door for her, pushing a button to keep the car light off. "Thanks for humoring me. I feel better about the house now." She stepped out and closed the door. He reached to help her, taking her arm. It was casual, something he obviously wasn't thinking about, but like any physical contact with him, she was intensely aware of his touch.

"Emily, you have no security here. You don't have

one damn window covering except in a bathroom downstairs, and anyone watching can see where you are in the house at any time. We've got some work ahead of us. Do you have curtains or sheets here?"

"I have sheets."

"Okay, come on. Let's get moving. We need some windows covered, and you need to move upstairs."

"I don't suppose there is any point in arguing with you about moving upstairs."

"No, there isn't," he said. "That's what you're going to do."

"When did you get so take-charge?"

"When someone threatened you. You're on that troll's hit list, and until he or she is caught, don't forget that for a moment. You've crossed someone in some way and they want to get even. It could be me they're after, but if it is, that's a damn roundabout way to get at me. Just remember someone wants to hurt you."

"I don't think you're going to let me forget it."

They walked around to the back door and entered the dark house. Night had fallen and there was no moon. She realized he hadn't left any lights on in the back hall entrance.

Tom took her arm and, again, the minute his fingers touched her, she had the usual tingles from head to toe. How would she live with him in the same house, work with him to restore it? How would she get through this one night? She was always attracted to him, but she needed to resist him now. She couldn't bear to go through all the emotional upheaval she had in the past. There were no solutions to their problems, and their divorce would be finalized as soon as this threat from Maverick ended.

"Tom—"

In little more than a whisper, his breath warm on her ear, he said, "Wait until we're upstairs."

Four

They moved silently in the dark through the back hall into the breakfast room and then the main hall. When they stopped for a second, Emily collided with him.

Tom slipped his arm around her waist. The minute he did, everything changed. He became aware of her softness, the faint trace of perfume, her hair spilling across his hand. He held her lightly. Her soft blue sweater fit snugly and he could feel her warmth, her lush curves, her soft breasts pressing against his arm. Desire was sudden and intense.

Off balance, she grabbed his arm, but he held her and she wasn't going to fall. It took an effort to hold her lightly, to keep from wrapping his arms around her and kissing her until she responded. She was soft, alluring, warm.

Time disappeared and took along with it memories of the bad times and the loss. At the moment memories of holding her and kissing her consumed him, making his heart race. He tightened his arms to pull her close, feeling her slender arm slide around his neck.

"Some things between us haven't changed," he said quietly. He shifted, fitting her against him, still holding her close. The pounding beat of his heart was loud and he fought to keep control. Even though he knew the trouble it would cause, he wanted to hold her, to kiss her, to make love to her all night long.

"We can't do this, Tom," she whispered.

He couldn't answer. He was hot, hard and he wanted her. It was physical, a hungry need because he had been alone so long. He had to let her go and get upstairs, but he didn't want to release her. It had been so damned long since he had held her, kissed her or even just touched her.

He released her slightly, still holding her arm. "Are you okay?"

"Yes, I'm fine. I just stumbled," she answered. She sounded breathless and tense, and that just added to his desire. He tried to focus on the situation and stop thinking about kissing her.

"I don't want to turn on a light. You have all these damn windows. With your sunroom, you have thirty-two windows downstairs that are not covered, and anyone looking in can see what you're doing. Let's take this gear upstairs."

"I know this house even in the dark," she said. They talked in quieter tones, but he wasn't sure he was making sense, because all he could think about was kissing her. He was already tied in knots over her. Even while they talked, he continued to hold her arm and she had hers on his shoulder.

"I'm glad you know this house. We won't have to turn on lights until we're upstairs. Can you get up the steps in the dark?" he asked.

She leaned closer to his ear, her breath warm on his neck. "How many times do you think I turned out all the lights downstairs and tiptoed upstairs in total darkness after you brought me home from a date later than I was supposed to stay out? I can't recall you worrying then whether I could get up the steps in the dark."

Her words eased some of his tension and he chuckled softly. "Okay, you go ahead and I'll follow."

Reluctantly, he released her. Today, there had been moments when tension fell away. It was the way things used to be. This was a bubble in their lives—when they could live together again while Nathan and others tried to discover Maverick's identity.

Tom stayed right behind her as she silently went up the steps in the dark, leading him to a large bedroom at the back of the house. "We're in my room, Tom. I'm going to turn a light on now."

"Go ahead. I've checked out the house and we're the only ones in it. I've been in the attic and basement. No wonder these old houses are in scary movies. Plunk one of these in a scene and you already have atmosphere before you even start."

"I love this old house and there isn't anything scary about it, including the basement."

"I'm glad to hear you say that. Let's start hanging sheets and get you some privacy. Tomorrow you buy whatever you want—shutters, shades, curtains. Get something that will be easier to deal with than sheets on the windows for these upstairs rooms. Downstairs we can hang sheets and leave them."

Lost in thoughts about Emily, Tom worked fast. He was tall enough to hang sheets in front of a lot of windows without getting on a ladder, but he needed a stepladder for others.

"This place doesn't have an alarm system. You should go ahead and get one tomorrow and make arrangements to have it installed as soon as possible. I can recommend a good one. The guy who has the franchise is an ex-Ranger and a friend. He'll do a rush job."

"You're getting really bossy," she said. Her voice was light and he knew she was teasing.

Tom got hot working, so he yanked off his shirt. When he turned around to reach for another sheet, he glanced at Emily. She stood transfixed as her gaze danced over his chest. Her cheeks were pink, her breathing fast, and desire filled her expression as she stared at him. She looked up and met his gaze, making his pulse speed up.

Without breaking eye contact, he crossed the room to her. The temperature in the room climbed and memories tugged at him—of holding her, of kissing her, of making love. Desire intensified as he looked down into her green eyes. He slipped his hand behind her head, feeling her soft hair, looking at her mouth. Memories tore at him of kissing her and how soft her mouth was.

She looked up at him with a dazed expression as she shook her head.

"No," she whispered. "Tom, I was just getting adjusted to being on my own—I don't want to do this."

He could barely hear her over his pounding heart. "The hell you don't." His voice was low and gruff. "Emily, it's been so long. A kiss won't change anything. We can kiss and walk away." He was fighting to control desire because he wanted her more than he had dreamed possible. He hadn't made love to her in so long and there had been no other women. He was hard, ready, with visions taunting him of Emily naked in his arms. Memories poured over him of how she responded, of her scalding kisses and her hungry zest for making love.

He pulled her to him and kissed her passionately, wanting to take her now, hard and fast, yet knowing when she agreed to sex, he should take his time. And he felt she would agree. One look into her big green eyes and he could tell she was as ready as he was. Maybe not tonight, but soon, so soon. Heat filled him at the thought.

He bent over her and continued the kiss, dimly aware that her arms were wrapped around him and she held him tightly, rubbing against him, moaning with pleasure.

She was soft, warm, luscious in his arms. He slipped his hand over her breast and felt he would burst with hungry need to just take her now. Fighting for control, he caressed her. Her softness sent his temperature soaring. She wriggled out of his embrace and stepped back, gulping air.

"I can't do this. I just can't. It's emotional turmoil and I get too worked up and torn up. We're not good for each other. We're getting divorced."

He turned away, trying to control his desire and emotions. She wanted him out of her life. "I'll be downstairs," he said, yanking on his shirt and leaving the room, knowing he had to get that divorce and move on, let go of Emily because he made her unhappy.

He went down the steps, moving quietly, his gaze adjusting to the darkness as he reached the first floor. He looked over his shoulder and saw the light in the hall that spilled from her upstairs bedroom. She had been right—how were they going to stay in the same house, live together and not constantly hurt each other?

He wanted her, but the damned attraction between them that had been so exciting, sexy and fantastic in the early years was now an albatross for both of them.

Yet he had to stay with her. He couldn't walk out of here and leave her alone in this big rambling house that came straight out of a horror movie. She had zero security. She might not want him here any more than she had in the big house on the ranch, but he had to stay until she repaired the windows and installed alarms. Maverick scared him. What could either of them have possibly done to make someone so angry?

Tom stepped outside, letting his eyes adjust to the dark. Was anyone watching Emily? Was she in any danger?

He looked up at the house. The second story in front was as dark as the downstairs. Tom walked back to the porch and sat in the dark, trying to cool down, to stop thinking about her kiss or how soft she was. To stop thinking about divorcing Emily. It still seemed impossible.

He remembered that night on the bus in Colorado. They'd spent the day on the ski slopes near a new lodge with an indoor water park. By the time they started back to the hotel where they were staying, the weather had changed and the driver said they would skip the planned stop for dinner. In a short time, it had turned into a blizzard.

On a curve on the side of a mountain, the bus hit ice and slid off the road. Going down the mountainside, the bus crashed into trees and then rolled. Seat belts gave way and people and belongings were tossed into the aisle. The sounds of screams, yelling and crying rose above the howling wind. Emily had screamed to him to get Ryan. He wanted to protect both of them, but she was right that he had to focus on trying to help their son. Tom had tried to hold Ryan in his seat and protect him as the bus crashed down the mountain. Ryan kept crying, "Daddy! Daddy!" until his screams went silent.

Something had struck Tom, causing pain to shoot across his shoulder and arm as the bus slid on one side. Another blow brought oblivion. Seconds—or minutes—later, he'd come to and fought to stay conscious. The headlights were still on and Tom had seen a sheet of gray ice illuminated in the bus's headlights and fading into darkness—and he'd realized the momentum was carrying the bus to a frozen pond.

To Tom's horror, Ryan and the seat he had been buckled into were gone. "Ryan!" Tom's shout had been lost

in all the chaos and noise. His cousin appeared and
Tom yelled to Jack to look for Emily. People screamed
and children cried. Most chilling of all, he couldn't
hear his son's voice, and in the darkness he hadn't been
able to see.

The front of the bus had lurched as it slid onto the
frozen pond. At the same time, he'd heard the loud crack
of ice breaking. The bus tilted and in seconds the bus
slid partially underwater. Water gushed into the bus
through gashes ripped in the sides and windows broken during the slide down the mountain. He'd had only
minutes to find Ryan and get them both to the surface
before the bus slipped deeper into the water.

It probably only took a minute for him to find his
son, but it had seemed like forever. Holding Ryan's un-
conscious body against his chest and with his own lungs
about to burst, Tom fought to get out of the wreck and
to the surface. When he finally broke through, he swam
the short distance to shore, where someone hauled him
up onto the ground.

Red-and-blue lights flashed, sirens sounded, people
were crying and yelling and screaming. To his relief
there were already ambulances, and Tom had fought to
get Ryan on one and climbed in with him when Jack appeared with Emily. Tom hauled her into the ambulance.
An attendant started to say something to him, looked at
Tom and merely nodded. The paramedics hovered over
Ryan after a cursory look at Tom and Emily.

She had a head wound with blood streaming over
her face and into her hair. Tom collapsed in the ambulance. He had broken bones, sprains, a ruptured spleen,

deep cuts and pneumonia. He and Ryan each ended up in surgery. Tom was moved off the critical list after a day, but Ryan lived eleven days on life support.

Tom would never forget the day they'd returned to the ranch and walked into the empty house. Emily had started sobbing. He had embraced her, holding her while she cried quietly, and he'd felt as if his heart was shattering. He couldn't console her. All he could do was tell her he was sorry.

"You couldn't save him. I couldn't save him. We've lost our baby," she cried.

Tom couldn't keep back tears and his throat was raw. He held her close and stroked her head and knew there were no words to console her.

It was a crushing loss they would have to live with all their lives. Her words—"You couldn't save him"— would also be with him the rest of his life.

As he reflected on the difficult times, Tom wiped his eyes, then ran his hand over the scar on his knee. He would always have scars on his body and his heart from that night. Tom put his head in his hands. He should have been able to save Ryan. It was his fault and he had failed Emily.

He was beginning to get some peace in his life from working on the ranch, beginning to be reconciled to their separation, when Maverick sent the message to Emily.

Now Tom was back with her, and there was no way he could stop their attraction. She was irresistible, yet when they were together, it conjured up all the old hurts.

Tonight was the first time he had kissed Emily since

he moved out of the house last year. It had stirred his desire and probably ruined his chances of sleep for the night. How long would they be together? Was she in danger, or was Maverick just a coward who would go away after a while?

Until Tom knew, he wasn't going to leave her alone. He should have saved Ryan. He damn well wasn't going to let Emily get hurt.

He just hoped Nathan caught Maverick soon so life would settle down and he could try to pick up the pieces of his torn-up life again and move on.

He sat for an hour on the porch, gazing into the night, listening for any strange noises. He heard the sound of a frog croaking somewhere nearby. There was a slight breeze. There were no cars on the residential street. He dozed and woke and finally decided he should be closer to Emily, so he went inside. Emily had kept some odd pieces of her uncle's furniture, like the kitchen table and a rocker, but she'd gotten rid of the beds and sofas, leaving nowhere to sleep except the floor or his sleeping bag. Or with Emily.

"Damn," he whispered, thinking he had to get her out of his thoughts or he would not have another peaceful night until they caught Maverick. Then he went upstairs quietly and crossed the room adjoining hers with a door between them left open. He stretched out on his sleeping bag. He was asleep instantly. Twice in the night he stirred and went back to sleep, only to wake before sunrise.

He showered and dressed and went to the kitchen, where he cooked oatmeal.

As he poured orange juice, he heard footsteps and then Emily appeared. He was unable to resist letting his gaze drift to her toes and back up again. His breath caught in his chest.

"There goes peace and quiet for today," he said. "What are you trying to do to me, Emily?"

"What? I'm not doing anything except getting ready to fix breakfast and go to work on this house. What are you talking about?" she asked.

He walked closer and put his hands on his hips to look at her. She wore a blue cotton shirt tucked into cutoffs, ankle socks and tennis shoes. His gaze roamed over the V-neck of her blouse, down over her tiny waist and her long, long shapely legs. When his gaze slowly drifted up again, she shook her head.

"That's ridiculous. You've seen me like this hundreds of times."

"I'm used to being on the ranch with a bunch of cowhands."

"I think you better work. This place needs a lot done, and you insisted on being here."

"I'll try to concentrate on painting. Right now, I have a pot of oatmeal waiting. There are blueberries, strawberries, orange juice. Let's partake and then I'll work at the opposite end of the house."

She laughed. "You're being ridiculous," she said.

He couldn't smile. By nightfall, she would have him tied in knots. "I hope I can get my hands on this Maverick for just a few minutes," he said quietly. She heard him and smiled, shaking her head because she probably thought he was joking.

As they ate, Tom sipped coffee and looked around. "I sent a text to my friend and he'll be out this morning to look at the house and give you an estimate on the cost of the alarm. I told him it's a rush."

"That's fast, Tom."

"I'm a very good customer. I send a lot of business their way by telling friends and other ranchers about them."

"You're taking charge again."

"I'm just helping you get organized and telling you what I can do to help. I can do other things," he said, unable to resist flirting with her. When she walked into the room, she brought cheer and sunshine that drove away his demons from the night. "We're eating together and we'll work together."

"We'll work together. With you here, I don't know why I need an alarm. Now if you're planning on leaving—" she said cheerfully before he interrupted.

"I'm not leaving you. I'll take you with me if I need to. I'm here until they get Maverick. This place is going to take a whole lot to fix," he said, looking around.

"It's all I have," she answered quietly, looking at the high ceiling in the kitchen. "It's a tie to Mom and Uncle Woody and, really, a tie to when we first got married and after Ryan was born. Uncle Woody was always so happy to see Ryan."

"I remember staying here with you after we married when your uncle went to Chicago to his Shriner convention."

"I remember, too, and all we did was stay in bed. But we're not going to reminisce about that."

"Might be more fun than painting the house," Tom said, and she smiled as she shook her head.

She stood and leaned forward over the table. "You're so good at giving orders. Well, so am I. You clean the kitchen while I get out the paint and brushes."

"Where did Uncle Woody keep his paintbrushes?"

"In the workshop at the back of the garage."

"I think I'll go with you to get them and then I'll clean the kitchen."

"Tom—"

"We've been over this. You don't know how angry Maverick is. Besides, you'll enjoy my company."

"Too bad you don't have more confidence."

He walked around the table as they both carried their dishes to the sink.

"You win," she said with a sigh. "Let's both clean the kitchen and then we'll both go get the paint and brushes."

He worked fast, glancing at her. He had been teasing, but what he'd said to her was the truth. He had been dealing with guys who worked for him, cattle, horses, dusty fields and new calves. To work with her dressed in shorts and a cotton shirt was dazzling, and it was going to be difficult to keep his mind on anything else. Emily was good-looking, and it seemed to him she had gotten more so in the past year. He turned to watch her.

He thought about their kiss yesterday and just as quickly knew that was the way to disaster. He needed to think about getting the house safe. He needed to think about anything except kissing or making love to her. He turned again to look at her, taking his time because her back was still to him. She couldn't reach a shelf to put a bowl away. He crossed the room, took the bowl from her and placed it on the shelf, turning to her.

"Thank you," she said. Her words came out breathless and he knew he should walk away quickly.

He stopped at the door. "Ready to go get paint?"

"Sure. I think we better get to work," she said, heading for the kitchen door. He crossed the room to follow her out. They were kidding and flirting—something that hadn't happened in an incredibly long time, since before he moved out.

Did she want to make love? The thought made the temperature in the room rev up several notches. Did he want the emotional storm again? Looking at her legs and thinking about yesterday's kiss, he realized he did. If he had a chance, he'd take it even if it meant hurting later when they said goodbye. And he knew they would say goodbye no matter what they did during this time while Maverick was on the loose. Their problems were unsolvable and permanent. They had lost their son, and Emily could not get pregnant again and would not adopt because she had wanted a child exactly like Ryan, with their blood in his or her veins. And she blamed him for Ryan's death. Tom knew he had failed her, failed Ryan, and there was never a day that passed that he didn't think about it.

None of that could stop this lusty desire to seduce her, though.

Tom held the door for her and they walked to the garage, which was dark and stuffy. Tom took one look at the ladder and shook his head. "No way."

"Here we go again. Are you going to tell me I can't use that ladder?"

"I sure as hell am." He stepped on the bottom rung and put all his weight on it. It snapped in two and he dropped to the ground.

"Want to fall today? I'll be glad to catch you. Go ahead and try."

She shook her head. "Okay. You made your point—a new ladder."

He looked around. "Em, you need new paint, new brushes and a new ladder. When was the last time you or your uncle used this stuff?"

"Probably when I was seventeen. I don't remember." She laughed again. "You win that one. Let's go."

He placed his hand on her waist and she stopped instantly, looking up at him. "This reminds me of when we dated. I remember being out here once with you."

She blushed again. "I think we better go."

"Want to know how to make work a little bit fun? Do you remember being here with me?"

"Yes, I remember every single second. You know full well what you can do to me," she answered and this time she was breathless. They might both have regrets, but right now he thought she wanted to kiss as much as he did. Sliding his arm around her waist, he leaned down to kiss her.

The minute his mouth touched hers, he lost the casual, playful attitude he'd had. His tongue went deep as she stood on tiptoe, wound her arms around his neck and pressed against him. She kissed him in return, setting him on fire with longing. He might be sorry tomorrow, but right now, he wanted to kiss her for the rest of the day and the night.

He wound his fingers in her thick, soft hair and ran his other hand down over her enticing bottom. He could easily get his fingers inside her tiny shorts. She gasped and moaned with pleasure, thrusting her hips against him. He wanted her and he was hot, on fire, melting from her kisses and from touching her intimately.

She finally stepped out of his arms and gasped for breath. "We're going to have regrets," she said and turned, walking away swiftly. "You close up," she said over her shoulder and kept going.

He wanted to seduce her. Even knowing that it would cause a world of pain later and complicate his life, that he would have regrets because nothing was going to change between them, he wanted to make love to her all night long.

He'd known when he told her he was going to stay with her until they caught Maverick that he was walking straight into more heartache. He kicked one of the paint cans and it rolled across the floor and hit a wall. Why did she have to be so damned sexy? She'd always appealed to him, and that had never changed no matter what kind of heartaches they had between them.

And she wanted to make love. She was at war with herself and trying to maintain control, but he could tell what she wanted. When he touched and kissed her, her response was instant and intense.

He looked at the ladder; it was a piece of junk. He

gathered it up along with the paint cans and took them out to the big trash barrel. He went back to close the garage door and fasten the lock. As he walked back to the house, he wondered if he could seduce her. He had a sleeping bag and she had a cot. He didn't care if he had to stand on top of the car, he wanted her. "Stay away from her," he said aloud. "Leave her alone. She's trouble. Pure trouble," he added.

He didn't find her downstairs, but before he could go up to the second floor to look for her, she appeared at the top of the stairs. She wore a long-sleeved T-shirt and jeans and had her hair in a pigtail.

She came down fast and paused on the bottom step. "Now I should look much more ordinary and unappealing. Less…something."

"Go ahead and say it—less sexy. You'll never look unappealing to me and there will never be a time you are not tempting. But I know we have things to do, so I'll try to avoid looking below your chin or at your cute butt when you walk away. I'll warn you, no matter how you dress, my thoughts are wicked and sinful."

"I believe that one," she said, smiling, and he smiled in return.

"I'm glad we can still get along, Emily."

"Time helps," she said, and she sounded earnest. All the playfulness left her voice. He felt as if there was a very thin veneer of joy and fun and sex appeal, of what they used to have together, and in this rarefied atmosphere, they could enjoy each other's company again. But beyond that, nothing had changed—their close, loving relationship had ended long ago.

Tom's friend came from the alarm company and Tom joined her while they settled on the alarm system with the stipulation that it would be installed Monday...

At noon, they decided to take a break from their errands and went to the Royal Diner again for another burger.

"Yesterday when we left here, I didn't think I would ever be here again to eat a burger with you. Here I am less than twenty-four hours later. I didn't think that would be possible," Emily said.

"Just goes to show, expect more and maybe you'll get more."

"Right."

After a few minutes, he smiled at her. "I'm glad your photography is going well."

"I like it and I'm getting customers from other towns. I may just move to Dallas if business continues to grow. I'll keep Uncle Woody's house—"

"Em, it's your house now. You can stop calling it Uncle Woody's," Tom said, but his thoughts were on her moving to Dallas. When she said that, he felt another stab of loss. Instantly, he knew that was ridiculous because when their divorce went through, he and Emily would go their separate ways. He tried to avoid thinking about the future and pay attention to what she was saying to him.

"It's difficult to remember that this is my house now. Frankly, it's still Uncle Woody's to me even though I own it." She sipped her malt and after a few minutes asked, "Do you miss the military?"

Tom shook his head. "No. I've served and I'm glad

to be on the ranch now. Life hasn't turned out the way I expected it to, but I love the ranch. Frankly, Em, losing Jeremy took it out of me. That one hurt more than the others. Maybe it's because of losing Ryan and because I'm older now, but I've had enough of death and my buddies getting hurt"

"You were patriotic serving your country," she said, placing her hand on his. Instantly, he inhaled. She blinked and started to jerk her hand away, but he covered it and held it between his.

"That's nice. Don't pull away," he said softly.

"We're both doing things that will make it worse. We'll be hurt all over again because our future hasn't changed and isn't going to."

He felt a pinch to his heart and released her hand. "You're right," he said. "If I pass the sheriff's office and Nathan is there, I'll see what I can find out. I'm sure nothing eventful has happened or we would have heard something."

"We'll have the meeting at the TCC Monday morning."

"I hope this balmy spring weather holds, because we can keep the house aired out as we paint." He nodded and they lapsed into silence as they finished their burgers and then left to get her painting supplies.

When they returned to the house, she propped the front door open. "Tom, the paint fumes will be awful. There's an attic fan that will draw fresh air through and take out the fumes. I want to open the windows that are left and turn it on."

"That's fine with me. Another thing—I'll do the ceilings. Let me do the high stuff and you stay off the ladder."

"There's no end to your orders. You're no longer in the military, remember?"

"And you never were in it and you don't take orders worth a damn," he said, smiling and shaking his head.

"That definitely isn't so. Here you are, staying with me. I didn't think that one up. I'm not getting on the ladder. I didn't make that decision. I'm getting an alarm because of you. I've moved upstairs because of you."

"You won't let me kiss you. I have to catch you by surprise and then you run me off," he said, moving closer and looking into her big green eyes.

"Not so," she said, smiling. "You kiss me every time you decide you want to and you know it," she said, poking his hard stomach with her forefinger as if to emphasize what she was saying. "Mmm, that's impressive," she said, poking him again.

"Let's see if you'll let me kiss you just any old time," he said, wrapping his arms around her and leaning over her. His mouth covered and opened hers, his tongue going deep as he leaned farther until she clung to him and kissed him in return and he forgot their silly conversation. Holding her tightly, he straightened up and his arm tightened around her waist while he slowly ran his hand down her back and over her bottom. Then his hand drifted up and he unbuttoned her blouse as he kissed her. He caressed her breast, pushing away her bra.

She finally caught his hand and held it. "Tom, wait. Don't complicate our lives. You know where we're headed—for more hurt," she whispered, looking up at him. He gazed at her intently. He was aroused, hard and ready. He wanted her and he didn't think she would argue. As he gazed at her, he thought about the rift between them and knew she really didn't want his loving.

"You're right. We've hurt each other enough," he said softly. "I'll get the windows open and start painting downstairs."

Five

Tom stood on the new ladder, painting the front parlor ceiling, while Emily painted upstairs in one of the big bedrooms. He'd been at it for hours. At a certain point, he had changed to cutoffs and a sleeveless T-shirt because the air-conditioning was off since the house was open.

As Tom worked he thought about her living in the big house all alone. She might be thinking the same thing about him on the ranch, but he never felt alone there. He worked with guys all day and he could go find someone whenever he wanted to. And when they divorced he would be able to get a date when he wanted. But at this point in his life, he couldn't imagine wanting to go out with someone. The thought of Emily doing so was another deep hurt.

His estrangement from Emily had left Tom numb and hurting, and his life would have to change a lot before he would ever want to get involved with someone again. He was surprised how well he was getting along with Emily, because it really hurt to be together and he knew it hurt her. Their divorce had merely been tabled until later but definitely loomed in the near future.

He thought about the big, expensive mansion they had built on the ranch. He didn't want to go back to it, yet it was a tie to Ryan—it was where they'd brought him home from the hospital. Where they'd rocked him to sleep and read to him, sung him songs.

What could Tom do with the house? He had no idea, and he didn't intend to worry about it now.

He wiped his sweaty forehead and tried to concentrate on his brushstrokes and keep working steadily. When he finished this side of the room, he was taking a break and going to find Emily.

After another hour of work, Tom ordered pizzas for dinner. When they were done with their break they returned to painting.

It was after 11:00 p.m. when he went to find her again in the front parlor. She was on her knees, painting the baseboard, and his gaze roamed over her trim, very sexy ass. He inhaled deeply and knocked on the open door.

Emily looked up and sat back on her haunches as Tom entered. "You're just in time. I'm getting tired of this and I think the paint fumes are getting to me even with the windows open and the fans blowing."

"Let's knock off for tonight, sit on the porch and have

hadn't planned on that. I'd like to meet them. Once again, I hope whoever Maverick is, word gets back that we're all having a good time together."

"The way word gets around Royal, I suspect it will. You'll like Natalie. After her loss, she understands ours in a way some people really don't. Jeremy was a great guy. We were close—he was almost like a brother to me. Sometimes the stuff you go through when your life is at stake creates a real bond."

"I should have known you wouldn't have a secret family."

"As you said, the picture was convincing."

They sat quietly in the dark while she sipped her raspberry tea and Tom drank his beer. She watched the shifting shadows on the lawn. "I still think you should go back to the ranch. I can get this done."

"Nope. I'm staying, and you should let me do the high stuff in every room."

"Oh, my. If you're volunteering to paint the ceilings in this old house, I will take you up on that with joy. I figured I would hire a painter to do the ceilings, but if you're sure, that fun task is yours. I'm thrilled because I can't do them."

"I'll start on the ceilings and see how far I can get. When and if they catch Maverick, I'm gone. You know that."

"Of course. I know you didn't move in permanently."

"Somehow I can't imagine you here permanently."

"I don't know why—I lived here when we met. We were together in this house lots of times."

"I was just noticing how dark it is out here. The

branches of these big oaks almost touch the ground, and they give a lot of privacy. When I move out, I think you should have yard lights and motion detectors installed."

"By the time you get through, I'll have a chain-link fence with razor wire at the top and spotlights. You were in the Rangers too long and in scary, violent situations too much. This is Royal, Tom. All the precautions aren't necessary. We're safe here. And no one cares what we're doing behind the branches of the oak tree."

"You think?" he asked, setting down his bottle of beer. "Well, if we have privacy and no one cares what we do, I think I'm wasting a really good night by sitting over here alone." He stood and she wondered what he was up to now.

He leaned over to pick her up and then sat down again with her on his lap. She gasped in surprise and started to protest, but she liked being in his arms again, so she closed her mouth and wrapped her arm around his neck instead. "It's as dark as a cave out here tonight. I can't see you," she said quietly. "What brought this on?"

"Why not? We've got privacy to do what we want— you just said so. Why not forget our problems for ten minutes and enjoy each other's company and a few kisses besides? Or more."

She smiled as she ran her fingers through his hair. "You really have a one-track mind."

"No, I've been alone for a long time," he replied. "And now I'm with you. That's the biggest part of it."

His voice was low, the way it got when he was lusty. She was aware of being in his arms, on his lap. Even more, she was aware of his arousal. He flirted and teased the way he used to, so it was fun to be with him.

"You're not only a good guy. You're a very sexy guy."

"Is that right? On a scale of one to ten, where do I rate?" he asked, nuzzling her neck.

"Somewhere around one hundred," she said, her words coming out breathlessly and as if she barely thought about what she said. "But I'm not going to let you complicate my life tonight. I've spent the past year picking up the pieces and I'm on a shaky foundation—"

"This will get you on something solid."

"You're naughty, Tom," she replied as he trailed kisses across her neck and ran his tongue around the curve of her ear.

"But, oh, so sexy. You just said so." He kissed away her answer. His mouth covered hers, his arm tightening around her as he leaned her against his shoulder. She clung to him, kissing him in return. His kisses sizzled, making her want more loving from him.

He raised his head and yanked off his shirt, tossing it aside while she said, "For just a minute more, Tom. That's all we—"

He leaned close to kiss her again and end her talk. And she didn't care. She clung to him, thinking he was the most exciting man on earth and trying to avoid thinking about all the painful things that had come between them.

He caressed her breast and then slipped his hand beneath her shirt. His hand was warm, his palm rough and callused. He unfastened her bra easily and pushed it away. She moaned with pleasure as her breast filled his hand. His thumb circled the taut peak and she shifted her hips closer against him—as close as possible while she arched her back and gave him more access to caress her further. For the moment she was lost to the sensations he stirred up. His hands on her, his mouth on her—it seemed natural and right and made her want more. But the memories of past heartache were still strong. Suddenly she thought back to the last time they'd made love—he'd moved out immediately after.

"Tom, wait." She paused to look at him as she placed her hand on his jaw and felt the short stubble beneath her fingers and palm. "You're going to bring back all that we're trying to get away from."

"Live a little, darlin'. We should just let go and enjoy each other and the night. You can't tell me you don't like this."

"You know I love everything you do," she said, "but we've tried every way possible to work things out and haven't even come close." She wiggled away and slipped off his lap. "It's time for me to go upstairs."

He didn't answer. She left her drink and turned to hurry inside. She wanted to be in his arms, ached to have him carry her to bed and make love to her all night long. But if he did, morning would come and with it painful choices. They would go back to the way they were and it would hurt more than ever. She couldn't stay on that seesaw of hot sex and then estrangement. He couldn't have it both ways. Besides, she knew the night he moved out to the guesthouse, he had meant it to be for good.

She rushed upstairs, fighting with herself silently

every second because she really wanted to go right back to him. But it would be futile and lead to more hurt. She grabbed clothes and went to her shower, hoping he didn't come upstairs until she was asleep.

Finally she was settled beneath the sheets on her cot. The house was still open, the windows flung wide, but Tom would take care of everything downstairs and lock up. She didn't have to worry about any of it. What she had to worry about was Tom causing her to fall in love with him again.

She rolled over on her back and stared at the open windows. Her thoughts were on tonight and Tom. She couldn't fall in love with him again. She wasn't going through what they had before. She couldn't get pregnant and give him another son. Or a daughter. It wasn't going to happen. It had hurt to tell him over and over that she was not pregnant.

It was more than an hour later when she heard a board creak and then all was quiet. She closed her eyes and lay still, wondering if he would come see if she was asleep. She couldn't deal with him again tonight. She was torn between wanting to pull him down on the cot with her and avoiding any physical contact. His love-making could take her out of the world, but then later, regret would consume her.

The next morning she showered and dressed, pulling on a sleeveless pale blue cotton dress to wear to church. She brushed her wavy hair that fell loosely around her face. Stepping into blue high heels, she picked up her envelope purse, took a deep breath and went downstairs to breakfast.

When she entered the kitchen, Tom came to his feet and her heart lurched as her gaze ran over his white shirt, red tie and navy suit. "You look handsome enough to have breakfast with," she said. "Oh, my."

"You look gorgeous, Em," he said in a husky voice. "I fixed cheese grits with shrimp. Your orange juice is poured."

"Thank you," she said. She had already left her purse on a folding chair in the front room. She crossed the room to pour coffee. "Let me guess—you're going to church with me because of Maverick."

"That and because you're the best-looking, sexiest woman in the county."

She laughed and turned toward him. He took the coffee from her hand and set it on the counter, and her pulse raced. His arm circled her waist and she placed her hand lightly against his chest. "You'll wrinkle me," she said, trying to ignore the heat building inside her.

He dropped his hand, leaned forward and placed his mouth on hers without touching her anywhere else. She was as lost in his kiss as she would have been if he had embraced her. Desire rocked her, and she wrapped her arms around him, stepping close to hold him tightly while she kissed him in return and forgot about wrinkles and her dress.

He made a sound deep in his throat and his arms wrapped around her tightly, holding her against him. His kiss was demanding, making her want to kiss him back and shower kisses on him the rest of the day.

Instead, she stepped away and gulped for breath. "Do you do that just to see if you still can? If that's why, I'll tell you that yes, you can turn me to mush and set me on fire at the same time." She stared at him a moment and then walked away quickly. "I'm going to church."

"Come eat your breakfast. You have time and I'll get out of here," he said and left the room.

She closed her eyes momentarily, trying to get composed. Her lips tingled and she wanted to make love. She ate a few bites of the cheese grits, drank some orange juice and coffee and left it all until later to clean. She hurried upstairs and brushed her teeth. When she came back downstairs and grabbed her purse, Tom was nowhere around. She had already decided it would be a good day for her to walk.

She opened the door to leave, and as she crossed the porch, he stepped up to walk beside her. "I'll drive you there."

"I was going to walk."

"Let's take the car. You'll be a few minutes early. When you walk, you may be as safe as money in the bank vault, but humor me. I don't like you getting a message from Maverick and I can't relax about it."

"I understand," she said, trying to be patient but thinking he was being overly protective.

"You win the prize for the correct answer."

"I'm trying, too, Tom. I know your background makes you think the way you do and I know this will end. Maverick will be caught or stop sending messages and disappear. Before long we'll go our separate ways," she said, feeling a tightness in her chest when she said those last words.

"We'll get the divorce as soon as this is over," he said, sounding tense. "I've been thinking about that. We can work it out ourselves, turn it over to our attorneys."

"I think we can work this out. I know you'll be not only fair but generous, because that's the way you are."

"Thanks," he said in a flat voice that indicated this was hard for him. He held open her car door, closing it after she was seated.

As he drove away from the house, he glanced at her. "I've thought about our divorce. We can get a dollar figure on what the ranch and livestock are worth and I can buy you out. We can add the vehicles and the plane to that estimate and I'll pay you for those. You keep your car. We won't count it."

His hands gripped the steering wheel tightly. She knew him well, and knew by his tone of voice that he was unhappy.

"We don't have to decide yet," she said.

"We might as well make the decisions and be ready. When the time comes, it'll be easier and quicker and then we can say goodbye." He drew a deep breath and she hurt inside.

When he parked at the church, he walked around the car to open the door for her.

"Thank you," she said as she emerged into sunshine.

"Smile. We don't know this troll's identity, but I want Maverick to see that his damned email didn't do anything except get us together." She smiled and he took her arm. She thought they probably looked like a happy couple. She hoped the person hiding behind the name Maverick thought they were happily together again. Then she recalled how shocked she had been looking at the picture of Tom and the Valentines. Next Saturday she would meet them, and she was looking forward to it. She glanced up at Tom, sorry she had doubted him. He was a wonderful guy who had been a good dad and husband. That's what hurt so badly.

After church he took her to eat at the Texas Cattleman's Club, and afterward they drove back to her house to paint again. It was the first Sunday in March and it was a perfect spring day. She pulled on cutoffs and another T-shirt.

She found him downstairs in the front parlor, prying open a can of white paint. Plastic drop cloths covered the hardwood floor. The ladder stood to one side and he had papers spread with brushes and stir sticks laid out.

"Calm yourself, because you've seen me in shorts and less plenty of times," she said when she joined him to get the can of paint he had opened for her.

He straightened, turning to look at her.

"Although I think I'm the one who might not be able to concentrate," she amended, fanning herself as her gaze roamed over him. Tom was all muscle, in excellent physical shape and incredibly strong. She tried to avoid memories of making love and how exciting he could be. As her gaze drifted over him again, she looked up and met his hazel eyes.

"We could put off painting," he said in a husky voice.

She shook her head even though she didn't want to. "Did you open a can of paint for me?" Her voice was raspy and she couldn't stop looking at his broad shoulders.

He stepped over the paint cans and approached her. She threw up both hands. "I'm going to work. Give me the paint. I have to get this house painted, and you're here now and can help."

"What room? I'll carry it for you," he said.

"The front bedroom," she said, turning to go. He walked beside her. "We've already lost the morning and part of the afternoon. I want to get something done today." She felt as if she was babbling. In the bedroom she waved her hand. "Thanks. I'll start here and work my way around."

He put the can on the floor, turned to her, stepped close and caught her chin lightly in his fingers. "You want to kiss and so do I."

"I'm trying to be sensible and not complicate our lives more. Not to mention getting my house painted."

"See which you like best," he said and drew her close, leaning down to kiss her. She stood in his arms for about two seconds before she hugged him back, sliding her hand over his broad shoulders and down one arm over rock-hard biceps. Then she wrapped her arms around his narrow waist. It always amazed her how narrow his waist was and how flat his stomach. She finally stopped him and stepped back, trying to catch her breath, pulling her T-shirt down.

"We could make love and get that out of our systems."

She smiled at him. "Good try."

He grinned and shrugged. "It's definitely worth a

try. I might bring that up again after you've painted for seven or eight hours and the sun goes down."

"You can try me and see," she said in a sultry voice, unable to resist flirting with him.

Something flickered in the depths of his eyes, and a faint smile raised the corner of his mouth. "Ah, I think I'm on the right track. I will try again. That's a promise." He stepped close and touched the corner of her mouth. "It's good to see you smile and laugh. We used to have lots of smiles and laughs and it's nice to share them again."

"It's temporary, Tom. Nothing has changed," she stated, hurting because of all they had lost and still stood to lose.

His smile faded. "I know."

"Now, it's time for you to go to work, too, and make yourself useful. You insisted on this," she said, picking up a brush.

He leaned close and placed his hand on her shoulders. She looked into his eyes and was aware his mouth was only inches away. She drew a deep breath, wanting to kiss him and knowing she should not.

"I can make myself not only useful, but indispensable," he said as he ran his hands so lightly along her bare thighs, then sliding them to the insides of her legs.

She placed a paintbrush in his hand. "You go paint and stop with the seduction scene."

"I thought I was doing pretty good."

She leaned forward so her nose almost touched his. "You know you're doing damn good, so you have to go or this house will never get painted," she said.

"Suit yourself, darlin'. I'm ready, willing and able."

"Ready, willing and able to pick up a brush and paint? Great. Go do it and I will, too. Goodbye, Tom." She turned away and bent over to pick up the paint can and received a whistle of appreciation from him. She straightened up and spun around, but he was already going out the door. Smiling, she shook her head. It was all a lot of foolishness, but if she had taken him up on any of his offers they would be making love now, and that made her hot and tingly and wanting him back holding her close.

She dreaded going through the divorce. It would be another wrenching, painful loss, but it was inevitable. They had tried to stay married, but it didn't work and just hurt more as time passed.

She got busy painting, a routine chore that left her thoughts free. And Tom filled them. Before Maverick's email, she'd thought she was beginning to achieve some peace. She'd been adjusting to life without Tom, as well as the realization that he would be out of her life for good when they divorced. Life on the ranch, which she had loved in so many ways, would also be gone. But she was beginning to find a life for herself as a photographer. She had made the move from the ranch to Royal. Now she had been thrown a curveball when Tom came to stay with her. They were flirting, laughing together—something that didn't happen after they lost Ryan. A week ago she wouldn't have guessed that they could be this relaxed together again. Maybe it was because they had lost everything they'd once had between them. Now the worst had happened and she didn't feel as tense. Maybe she had worried too much about disappointing Tom, and the fear was a self-fulfilling prophecy. It was fun to tease and flirt again. She missed what she'd once had with Tom.

Whatever the reasons, working with him on the house now reminded her of old times together when they could flirt and kiss and laugh. It was also going to hurt a lot more to tell him goodbye after being here together.

It was almost midnight when they settled in the rocking chairs on the porch. Tom had his cold beer and she had her raspberry tea and they sat quietly rocking.

"I remember when Uncle Woody would come out here and mow the lawn. He'd wave to anyone who passed and talk to neighbors who walked by."

"Your uncle was a friendly man. I liked him. When you and I dated, sometimes he gave me a look and I wondered if he was going to tell me to get lost and leave you alone."

"No. Uncle Woody liked you and thought you were good for me."

"That's nice to hear."

"I'm glad he didn't know about our divorce. I think losing Ryan is what—" She paused, because she hadn't ever voiced aloud her theory about her uncle's death. Tears threatened and she was grateful for the dark.

"Was what?" Tom asked and his voice had changed, deepened and become serious.

"I think he just died of a broken heart. He wasn't well, but he wasn't that ill. He had a heart problem, but when Ryan died, part of Uncle Woody died and there was never a time I saw him after that when he didn't cry over Ryan. It broke his heart. So I lost them both."

Tom sat in silence and she wondered what was going through his mind. She wiped her eyes, gradually regaining her composure.

"I'm going for a walk around the place. I have my phone if you want me," he said tersely. Then he faded into the darkness.

Tom walked around the property, staying in shadows, moving without making noise and taking his time.

Emily's revelation about her uncle's death hurt. Tom had no doubt that Woody had blamed him for his failure to save Ryan. He felt equally certain Woody had blamed Tom for Emily's unhappiness. He was just one more person who was important to Tom that he had failed.

He finally decided to rejoin Emily on the porch or just sit there alone if she had gone inside. But when he got back to the front of the house, she was still there. He climbed the steps to sit by her.

"You're back. This is nice, Tom. I'll miss us out here together when you go," she said quietly.

"Maybe I'll come visit and we can sit and talk. I like this, too. This is peaceful, and I can always hope I might get a kiss or two or get you to sit on my lap."

"No," she said, a note of sadness in her voice. "After our divorce, you'll go out, fall in love and marry again. You'll have a family, because that is what you were meant for. You're wonderful with kids. You and I will go our separate ways and our marriage will just be memories that fade into oblivion." She stood. "I'm going inside."

He came to his feet swiftly and wrapped his arms around her to kiss her, a hard, possessive kiss that took only seconds before she responded.

When he slipped his hand beneath her shirt and caressed her, she moaned softly, holding him until she suddenly stepped away.

"I can't go there. We'll just hurt each other more. I've disappointed you in the past and I don't see any future. Making love just binds us together for more heartache. I'm going in." She swept past him and he let her go.

She didn't want him in her life. He had failed her, disappointed her, hurt her. He needed to let her go and keep his distance and hope they caught Maverick soon. He couldn't live under the same roof with her much longer without making love, and he had no doubt that he could get her to agree, but afterward, their relationship might be worse than ever because that wasn't what Emily wanted. She wanted him out of her life. She was moving to Royal, taking up photography, finding a new life for herself, and he should do the same. He should find happiness with someone he hadn't failed and hurt and disappointed.

He stepped off the porch to circle around the big yard, wishing he could catch the troll and end his worries about Emily once and for all.

Six

Monday morning they drove the short distance to the Texas Cattleman's Club for the emergency meeting about Maverick.

Tom parked and they walked together toward the front door. Emily looked at the dark stone-and-wood clubhouse. In recent years, the TCC had voted to include women. It still hurt to walk in the front door and see the children's center where she had taken Ryan occasionally.

She waited while Tom checked his black Stetson. He wore a tan sport coat, a white dress shirt open at the throat and dark jeans, and just looking at him, her heart beat faster.

He turned and his gaze swept over her, and for another moment, she forgot everyone around them and saw only Tom. She took a deep breath. She would soon be divorced from him. Their marriage was over. Life was changing, and it was difficult to worry about Maverick when she had lost Ryan and now was losing Tom. Their happy marriage had been gone a long time, though, even if the past few days with him had reminded her of how it used to be.

Looking back now, she realized she had made a big mistake with Tom in being so desperate to get pregnant. That had made her tense and nervous on top of the grief they both dealt with daily.

Now she realized she had driven Tom away. For the past few days, she hadn't had her old worries about her inability to get pregnant, and she was relaxed with him.

At the time she hadn't realized what a mistake she'd made with him, and now it was too late to undo it.

"You look pretty," he said when he walked up to her. He leaned close to speak in her ear. "When you get home, take your hair down."

She smiled at him as she reached up, unfastened the clip that held her hair and shook her head. Her wavy, honey-brown hair fell around her face and on her shoulders.

"I like that," he said softly. He took her arm. "Let's get a seat." He turned and she walked beside him. They went through the foyer lined with oil paintings of past members. The motto of the club from its early days—Loyalty, Justice and Peace—was emblazoned on the wall in big letters for all to see.

They went past a lounge, and Emily saw a boar's head hanging above a credenza that held a crystal decanter on a silver tray. Some members wanted the

stuffed animal heads removed. But they'd had been fascinating to Ryan, and as far as Emily was concerned,
they could stay because other little kids might find them
just as interesting.

She and Tom greeted friends as they walked through
the club. Taking in her surroundings, she couldn't believe the club was more than a hundred years old. It had
been founded around 1910 by Henry "Tex" Langley
and other local ranchers. Tex wouldn't recognize a lot
of things about the club now, particularly that women
had been accepted as members, which had resulted in
a child-care center where the billiard room once was.

They finally arrived at the large meeting room and
settled in near the back. She had an eerie feeling when
she thought about how Tom had said Maverick might
be present at the meeting. As the room began to fill,
she wasn't surprised to see the mean girl trio, Cecelia,
Simone and Naomi, arrive and take seats near the front.
Could the three women be behind the emails and blackmail? That was the rumor. But Emily couldn't imagine
them doing something that wicked and then coming to
this meeting. They were members of the TCC and had
had background checks, friends in the club and people
to vouch for them. They might be snooty, but she didn't
think any one of them would do something criminal.
She'd heard that Maverick blackmailed Brandee Law-
less. And why would they have come after her, sending
her that photo of Tom with the Valentines? How would
they have even gotten such a photo?

"There's Nathan," Tom said and she glanced around
the room. Sheriff Battle stood to one side, leaning

a cold drink, and just relax. It's do-nothing time." He crossed the room to her and took her brush. "I'll clean the brushes."

"And I'll get the drinks," she said, standing and looking at the painting she had done. Tom put the lid on her paint can and then picked up the other brushes.

"Let's get out of here. We need fresh air and I want a cold beer."

"I want a drink, too. See you on the porch."

She got there first and sat in one of the big wooden rocking chairs. She had brought beer for Tom and iced tea for herself. It was cool on the porch, and in minutes her eyes adjusted to the darkness. Tom came out and picked up a small table with their drinks to place it slightly in front of their chairs and then moved his rocking chair closer to hers.

"Now the view is better here," he said when he sat down.

"Liar. You can't enjoy the view in all this darkness. You just wanted to sit closer together," she said, amused by him. "It's nice out here."

"Yes, it is, and it's nicer closer together."

"It's wonderful you've been helping the Valentines. You're a good guy and I still feel so foolish for believing that email. That was a huge mistake."

"Forget that, Em. We worked it out, and Natalie invited us to a picnic in the park next Saturday, if you want. I told her I'd call her after I talk to you."

"Saturday's fine."

"Can you skip painting long enough for a picnic?"

"Of course. I have your help with painting and I

against the wall, looking as if he wasn't paying attention, but she knew he probably wasn't missing anything that was happening in the big room.

At the stroke of the hour, Case appeared. Whenever she saw him, he looked in a hurry. Often he talked fast. His brown suit matched his short dark brown hair, and he looked as if he hadn't shaved for a couple of days.

"Good morning and thanks for coming," he said, holding a mike and stepping out from behind a podium they had set up for him.

People in the audience answered with an enthusiastic, "Good morning."

"Everyone here knows why we're having this meeting. We have a problem in Royal. Someone going by the name of Maverick is harassing and blackmailing people using social media and email. We need to put a stop to it." Case paused to allow for applause.

"I'd like to form a TCC committee to investigate, coordinating with the sheriff to back up his department's work. We're not law enforcement—just a group of concerned club members, citizens of Royal, who will make a big effort to keep their eyes and ears open for anything that might aid Sheriff Battle. You can sign up at the door and you'll be notified when we'll have our first meeting.

"Also, Chelsea Hunt has asked if she may speak. She has some ideas of her own that should help. Chelsea, why don't you come up here?"

Wearing head-turning designer jeans with a tucked-in white silk shirt and a leather vest, Chelsea walked up to join Case, amid more applause. Her high-heeled ankle boots made Chelsea appear to be the same height as the club president.

"Here comes the tech genius. She'll get things moving," Tom said quietly as he applauded. Emily knew that Chelsea was considered the cyber expert in Royal, so she was a good one to have at the meeting.

"I'm glad all of you are here today. I'm fully committed to the TCC's grassroots investigation into these cyber attacks. I'll have a tablet here at the front, so when the meeting is over, if you have computer skills and want to help me with the technical aspects of the investigation, please sign up. There has to be a way to find Maverick. There will be a trail of some sort, and I think if we pool resources, we can trace these messages."

Everyone applauded again and Chelsea thanked Case and sat down.

Tom stood and Case turned to him. "Tom?"

"I think we need to get word out to citizens in Royal. If they get a message from Maverick, they need to let Sheriff Battle know, even if there's blackmail involved. We can't do anything if we don't know who Maverick is targeting."

"I think we can all work on getting that message out," Case said, nodding. "Thanks." Tom sat back down.

Emily wondered how many people already knew she had received an email. She knew Tom and Nathan would only tell people on a need-to-know basis, so she suspected that not many were aware of her situation.

"Simone," Case said, recognizing Simone Parker, one of the mean girls triumvirate. There was instant quiet. Simone's striking looks, her blue eyes and long black hair usually commanded everyone's attention.

"I think we should have another meeting here in a month so the committee can bring the rest of us up-to-date on what's been done. The more informed TCC members are, the better we can deal with what's happening."

"We can do that," Case said. "If there are things Sheriff Battle thinks should not be made public, then they won't be, but otherwise, we'll meet again next month. Unless Maverick is caught in the meantime."

As Emily listened to the other speakers' suggestions, she looked over the club members in attendance. Once again she couldn't help wondering if the troll was in the audience.

How would they ever catch Maverick? What had she done to make herself a target of this troll? She still couldn't imagine someone being so angry with her that they would send that nasty message with the picture.

Finally, the meeting was over and Tom left her side to sign up for the committee. When he was done, he found Emily and took her arm to lead her out. His touch was as electrifying as ever. Why did he have that effect on her after all they had been through?

"I hope that meeting helped," she said as they drove back to her house. "Tom, shouldn't you go back to the ranch and check on things?"

"I will later this week. I talk to Gus several times a day and I'm available. This isn't the first time I've been away from there, and it hasn't been long yet. We're just getting started on this. It may take a long time to catch this Maverick character, but I have high hopes in Chelsea. If I were the troll and had Chelsea after me, I would be worried. Nathan, too. Nathan is quiet and easygoing, but he's tough and he doesn't miss a thing."

"I hope they can discover something soon," she said, wondering if living with Tom much longer would make it even more difficult to part again.

"I hope so, too," he said, but he didn't sound too happy about it.

"Stop at the grocery and let's pick up what we need to make sandwiches for lunch. It's a pretty day and we can eat on the porch. I don't even have a table."

"Take some furniture from the house at the ranch. The guys will move it for you. Just tell me or Gus what you want."

"Thank you. There are a few things I'd like, but in general, I don't want to move much from the ranch. Your cook likes Snowball so much, I may leave him with her because he likes the ranch."

"That's fine with me."

They bought groceries and when they were back in the car, he turned to her. "Why don't you buy a bed while I'm with you—"

She started laughing. "You've always been a little more subtle in your approach than this. Getting tired of your sleeping bag, or do you think you're going to coax me into bed?"

He raised his eyebrows. "Now that's a thought. I might give that one a try. Seriously, I suggested a bed because I can help you get it moved where you want it. You can get one delivered and set up, but they aren't

going to move it around while you make up your mind
where you would like it. As I recall on the last bed, I
moved it until I wanted to put wheels on it."

"It wasn't that bad," she said, knowing he was teasing her. "When I get a bed, I'll probably go to Dallas
or Midland. Though Royal has a good furniture store,
so I suppose we can look here."

"Good. Let's look on the way back to the house.
You can wait a few more minutes for lunch, I'm sure."

"Okay. We'll get a bed, Tom, but I still think you
have at least one other motive besides helping me move
it around," she said, watching him drive and wishing
they could be like this all the time.

He smiled. "I might. We'll see if you object."

"You usually get what you want," she said, wanting
to reach over and touch him just to have a physical connection. At one time she wouldn't have hesitated, but
again, those times were over.

"That's interesting. Why do you think I get my way?"

"It's your good looks, your charm, your incredibly
sexy body and your seductive ways, of course," she said
in a sultry voice, teasing him.

"I may wreck the car. Now I know you need to hurry
up and buy that bed."

"Don't rush me."

"I wouldn't think of rushing you to bed. This is
something that will take some testing and touching to
see if it feels right," he drawled in an exaggeratedly
husky voice.

"Stop it," she said, smiling. "I never, ever guessed
you and I would go shopping for a bed again."

"Life's full of surprises, and this is a damn fine one."

"I agree," she said, turning toward him as much as her seat belt would allow. "This is like our lives used to be."

"I told you before and I'll tell you again—we can still enjoy each other even though there are some terrible times behind us and some rough times up ahead."

"I've made big mistakes, and I can't undo them. But I'm glad you forgave me for the mistake I made believing Maverick's message. I'm thankful for that."

"We've both made mistakes," he said, suddenly serious, and she wondered what he felt he had done wrong. "Here we are," he said, stopping to park in the shade in front of the furniture store. He stepped out of the car and the moment for discussing their past was gone.

They shopped for almost an hour before she finally pointed to a fruitwood four-poster with a high, intricately carved headboard.

"I like this four-poster. And I like that sleigh bed. What do you think?" she asked, too aware that his opinion didn't matter because she would not be sharing the bed with him.

"I think the four-poster is great. Sleigh beds—even king-size sleigh beds—are too short. There is a tiny off chance I might get into this bed sometime."

"Shall we take bets on how many hours after purchase?" she asked sweetly and he grinned. "A sleigh bed is never too short for me," she said, studying the two frames. "Okay, I guess I'll get the four-poster."

"That's an excellent choice. Let's find the mattresses."

"You're very anxious to get a bed in my house," she said.

"I want you to be comfortable. You never know when you'll really want a bed. I'm sure you're enjoying your cot as much as I'm enjoying my sleeping bag," he said and then frowned slightly. "What's wrong, Em?"

"I started to say I should get a bed for the guest room now, too, but I don't have family. Uncle Woody was the last except the cousins, and I never see them. My family is gone. You and I will get our divorce and you'll be gone. I don't need a guest bed."

He put his arm around her shoulders. "You'll have a family soon enough. I know you'll marry again. You can wait and get another bed for the guest room some other day, but you need one for yourself now."

She felt the tears threatening. "What happened to us, Tom?"

He pulled her around to hug her. There was no one in that corner of the store and he really didn't care if there was. "We had the most devastating loss, and we just made too many mistakes dealing with that. But maybe some of them can be fixed," he said, holding her close.

She pulled away and wiped her eyes. "We're in public. I'll pull myself together. It's just a little scary to know I'm alone."

"You're not alone. Look, you can call me anytime you want."

She smiled at him. "Sure, Tom. I'm sure your next wife will just be thrilled to hear that you told your ex to call you anytime."

"Don't marry me off so fast. Let's get the bed, a mattress and springs, and go home and eat. Then they'll deliver the bed and mattress and we can try it out," he said, licking his lips and looking at her.

She smiled, shaking her head.

As they drove to the house, he went through what they had already done to the house, what they had lined up to do and what else should be added to the list. "Now I know you need a new roof, and I know a really good roofer. I'll call and get you a couple of estimates."

"Tom, I don't want to pay for all this at once. I have lots of windows. I'm having a security system installed. I've bought a lot of paint. I'll have bills and more bills."

He kept his attention on his driving as he talked. "Em, put all of this on the ranch expenses. We're still married. We're still a couple and we'll pay it out of the ranch budget."

"That simply means you'll pay it all," she said, looking at him in surprise. "You're divorcing me. Why would you pay for all this?"

He reached over with his free hand to squeeze hers. "You're my wife right now, and this divorce is not out of anger. Don't fuss. I'll just add it to the ranch tab. You forget about it."

She was surprised he would do that, but was more lost in his remark about how their divorce was not out of anger. But what difference did that make? They had made mistakes and hurt each other and soon would part.

"You're worrying. Don't. It's taken care of. Uncle Woody's house, which is now Emily's house, is getting a makeover."

"Thank you, Tom."

He reached over to give her hand another squeeze. "Sure. I intend to do some things right."

"You do a lot of things right," she said. She was amazed that he would do this for her. She rode the last two blocks in silence wondering what Tom really felt and wanted.

When they got home, they had to deal with the first window company. They were so impressed, they decided to skip getting the other estimates and go with this firm.

It was two in the afternoon before they ate lunch and she washed her new sheets. Then they went back to painting. As she painted, her thoughts were on Tom.

He worked fast and efficiently. He'd already taken care of the alarm system. The downstairs windows would be installed in two weeks, which was a rush job for custom-made windows. Going ahead without discussing it, Tom had also hired a professional outfit to paint the outside of the house and they had started this morning. And now he was going to pay all her repair bills.

Tom got things done, and with his help, it was going to take her far less time to finish restoring the house. How long would he stay? Trying to catch Maverick, if it was even possible, could take a long time. So far, she didn't think anyone had come close to learning the true identity of this monster. Maybe she would be the last victim—but how long would Tom feel she might need protection?

In some ways they were getting along better than they had, or maybe she had just relaxed about being with him. She was looking forward to meeting the Valentines Saturday. Tom liked them and his voice softened when he talked about them.

Like shifting sands beneath her feet, she felt as if her world was changing again, slight changes that might make a big difference later. She thought about Tom holding her in the store and telling her she wasn't alone. She expected Tom to eventually get the divorce and they would no longer be in each other's lives. He probably expected to marry again and she was sure he would. He probably expected her to marry again and she was sure she would not. She still wanted the divorce and she was certain he did. As great as Tom was, they could not have happiness together. Tom needed a family, and she couldn't give him his own kids.

The following day after the store delivered the bed, she got out her new sheets and Tom helped. He wore cut-offs, boots and another T-shirt with the sleeves ripped away, and it kept her tingly and physically aware of him every second they were together.

They made the bed and she spread a comforter on top with some new pillows. She stood back to admire it. "I think it's beautiful."

"I agree," he said, picking her up. His voice had lowered. "Let's try it out. I've been waiting for this moment."

"Aw, Tom, don't get me all torn up when I'm getting over what we went through," she said, but at the same time, joy rocked her and she loved being in his arms.

She put her arm around his neck and he carried her to the bed, placing his knee on the mattress to lower her.

While she wanted to kiss him, she didn't want to get tied up in emotional knots again. "Tom, we can't do this."

"Sure, we can. Try me and see," he said, stretching beside her and holding her in his arms as his mouth covered hers. She felt as if she were in free fall, the world spinning around her as his tongue stroked hers and he ran his hand over her breast and down to slip beneath her T-shirt. She tightened her arms and thrust her hips against him and felt his hard erection. Pushing aside her bra, he caressed her, his hand warm against her skin.

For a moment, she thought, *just for a moment*... She ran her hands over him, beneath his shirt as he had done, feeling his smooth back, the solid muscles. But she knew she was getting into deep trouble and would get hurt all over again. She slipped out of his embrace and stepped off the bed, shaking her head.

"I can't go through all that pain."

He gazed at her solemnly. She wanted to go right back into his arms, but she knew the futility of that, because it would lead straight to more unhappiness with nothing solved between them.

She turned and went downstairs and outside, trying to find something she could work on far away from him, away from the new bed that had been one more big mistake. The thought of sleeping in a comfortable bed instead of a narrow cot night after night had seemed so marvelous, but a bed and Tom—the mere thought made her hot and tingly.

He still could melt her with a look. She was headed for more heartbreak if she wasn't careful and didn't keep up her guard. Tom was a wonderful, sexy man, but they had no future together. She needed to stay aware of that all the time with him. They had relaxed now and had fun a lot of the time. But with hot sex and fiery passion, she would soon want him back on a permanent basis and then the problem of her inability to have children would come crashing down on her again and Tom would say goodbye.

She returned to her painting, working fast, focusing on her task and trying to avoid thinking about Tom. Then around four o'clock he stepped into the room. She heard his boot heels as he approached the open door and stepped inside.

"How're you doing?"

"Painting away and getting a lot done. You're an inspiration," she said, trying to keep things light and impersonal again, where they seemed to get along the best.

"I'm glad to hear I inspire you. And I'm glad you're okay. Shall I get carryout or do you want to go to a restaurant, or what?"

"I think carryout will be perfect."

"You had your chance to go out to dinner." He turned and was gone and she went back to painting. It was a couple of hours later when he sent her a text that he was leaving and taking orders. Smiling she sent him a reply and kept painting.

Half an hour later, she heard a loud whistle. Startled, she smiled and put down her brush. She went into the hall to look over the banister. He stood below with his hands on his hips and his hair in its usual tangle.

"I'm here and dinner's here, so come on down."

"I have a brush full of paint. You should have given me a warning."

"Bring your brush and I'll take care of it." He turned away without waiting for an answer. Smiling, she picked up her paintbrush and went downstairs.

They ate salads, barbecued ribs and corn bread on the porch and then went back to painting. It wasn't until ten o'clock when they sat back down together on the porch. As usual, she had raspberry tea and he had his cold beer.

"I'm amazed how much you've gotten done. I don't recall you being that fast before."

"I'm getting better as I age."

"Maybe we both are," she said, smiling in the dark.

They sat and talked until midnight and then walked up the stairs together. "Now you sleep tight in your big, cushy new bed while I crawl into my sleeping bag on the floor."

At the top of the stairs as they started down the hall, he put his arm across her shoulders. She smiled. "I will remind you, you insisted on staying here. I told you there was nowhere for you to sleep."

"Not quite true now. If you get lonesome, just whisper. I'll hear you."

She laughed. "Good night, Tom. You can have my cot."

"No, thanks. I'll wait for your invitation." He switched off the lights and she could hear him rustling around and then all was quiet. She suspected it would be a long time before she would get to sleep.

What would it be like when he went back to the ranch

and she was in this big old house all by herself? She knew she was going to miss him badly.

In the night a clap of thunder rattled the windows and jolted her awake. She could hear the wind whistling around the house outside and felt the cool breeze coming through the open windows. She got out of bed and slipped on flip-flops to go turn off the attic fan.

Brilliant flashes of lightning illuminated the interior of the room, so she could see as went out into the hall. She bumped into Tom, who steadied her. "Did the thunder wake you?" she asked, aware of his hands still on her arm and waist.

As if to emphasize her words, thunder rumbled again and a flash of lightning cast a silvery brilliance in the hall and was gone, followed by the hiss of a sudden downpour.

"I hoped you'd be scared of thunder and jump into my arms. You can get in my sleeping bag and be cozy."

"Are you trying to wrangle an invitation to sleep in my new bed?"

He ran his finger lightly over her collarbone. "My darlin', if I get an invitation to get on your new bed, I will not sleep. I can think of wonderful ways to try out that new bed." Lightning flashed and she gazed up at him. "Damn, I want you, and it's been a hell of a long time and we're still married." He drew her to him and leaned close to kiss her on the threshold of her bedroom. "You know you want to kiss," he whispered. "Live a little, Em."

Seven

Emily's breath caught as her arms slipped around his neck. Common sense went with the wind. Tom was right. She wanted him, it had been a long time and they were married.

She relished being in his strong arms, held tightly against his virile body that for an hour or two could drive every problem into oblivion.

His hand roamed over her, caressing her breasts, sliding down over her bottom and drifting over her, setting her on fire with wanting him. "Why do we have this effect on each other?" she whispered, more to herself than to him.

"I can't answer your question," he said between kisses. His tongue followed the curve of her ear and then he tugged away the T-shirt she slept in, drawing it over her head and dropping it to the floor. He cupped her soft breasts in his callused hands while his thumbs caressed her, drawing circles so lightly, making her shake and gasp with pleasure.

"I can't resist you. I never could." She sighed.

He framed her face with his hands. "That's damn mutual. You would have been free of me a long time ago if we could walk away from each other, but we can't. You take my breath away, Em. I dream about you. I still want you even when I should let you go."

She didn't reason out what he said to her. Instead, she kissed him and stopped all conversation. His arms tightened around her and he peeled away her pajama bottoms, tossing them aside while holding her tightly.

It had been too long, aeons, since they had made love, and his body beneath her hands was fit and strong. She wanted that strength, his passion for life, hot kisses and lovemaking that could shut out the pain of loss.

He was an exciting man, and all the things she couldn't be—physically strong, a decorated warrior, tough, sexy. Her world had been caring for her aging uncle, raising her baby, taking pictures of families and children and pets.

For right now, Tom's kisses drove away the heart-breaking problems between them. At the moment nothing was as important as Tom. Making love tonight would not satisfy anything except carnal lust, but she wanted him and he was here with her. If they made love, maybe she could be more relaxed with him, less sexually responsive to even the slightest touch—although that had never happened in the past. Sex with him had always had just the opposite effect, as she knew it would tonight. If they made love, she would want to make love again soon. She would want more instead of less because making love with Tom was fantastic.

She ran her hands over him. Her fingers shook as she peeled away his briefs.

His dark hair was tangled, falling on his forehead. She ran her hands over his broad, muscled shoulders, letting her hand slide down over his flat stomach, his narrow waist.

He was hard, ready to love, and she caressed him, wanting him, wanting to take her time. They hadn't made love in a year and now that they'd started, she couldn't stop and she was certain Tom didn't want to stop. He picked her up and moved to her new bed. He lay down, holding her against him while he stroked and kissed her and moved over her.

He showered kisses on her, starting at her ankle, and then stretched beside her and drew her closer, his leg moving between hers, parting her legs as he caressed her intimately.

She held him tightly, kissing him, the pressure building while desire intensified. Her hips moved and she arched against his hand, straining for release.

His fingers drove her, and then his mouth was on her, his tongue sending her over the edge as she thrashed and burst with release and need for all of him.

She moved over him to kiss him, taking him in her mouth, using her tongue and hands while she rubbed her breasts against him.

With a growl deep in his throat, he rolled her over and moved between her legs to look down at her.

"You're beautiful. I'll be right back," he said, starting to leave.

"I don't need protection," she replied, the moment changing as reality invaded the passionate idyll they had created. "I can't get pregnant, Tom."

He kissed her again, another devastating kiss that made her want him inside her and drove her wild with need. Shifting away swiftly, she got on her knees.

"We're doing this, so let's take our time. I haven't been loved by you in so very long. Take the night and drive away our sorrows. Let's grab joy here and hold it tight. I'm going to make you want me like you never have before," she said, her tongue stroking his thick manhood. "Turn over."

She caressed the backs of his legs, her hands trailing lightly over sculpted, hard muscles. She slowly ran her tongue, hot and wet, up the backs of his thighs, her fingers moving between his legs, her hand playing over his hard butt. Then he rolled back over, pulling her on top of him to kiss her passionately.

As she looked down at him, she wondered why he dazzled her so much and always had. "I can't resist you," she said.

"That's my line," he replied solemnly. "You have it all mixed up—I'm the one who can't resist."

She swung her leg over him to kneel beside him, running her tongue over him again while her fingers stroked and toyed with him. He fondled her breasts, his hands warm, his fingers brushing her nipples. Then he shifted, turning to take her breast in his mouth and run his tongue over the taut peak.

She tried to caress and kiss every inch of him until Tom knelt between her legs, putting her legs on his shoulders, his hands driving her to more heights.

"Come here," she demanded, tugging his hip with one hand, holding his rod with her other. "I want you inside me."

He shifted, coming down to give her a deep kiss that made her heart pound as she clung to him. "Tom, love me. I want you more than you can imagine."

He entered her slowly, filling her and almost withdrawing, moving with slow strokes that drove her wild as she tugged at him. She locked her long legs around his waist, clinging to him, wanting to consume him and for both of them to reach ecstasy and release.

He kissed her as he took his time, driving her wild with need. And then he thrust deep and faster, pumping and taking her with him as tension built until she climaxed, bursting with release, rapture, crying out.

"I love you," she gasped without thought.

Tension gathered swiftly again, built, and she achieved another orgasm. Tom kept up his relentless thrusts, and in minutes, his shuddering release came as she gasped and cried out with another. They clung tightly to each other and gradually her breathing slowed to normal. Then they were finally still, locked in each other's arms.

He showered light kisses on her temple, her ear, her cheek while he finger-combed her long hair away from her face.

Shifting, he held her close and kept her with him as he rolled to his side and faced her, all the while continuing to brush light kisses on her body and lips.

She knew when she let him go and the idyll ended, their problems would emerge, as omnipresent as ever. The problems they had between them would last a lifetime. Nothing could take them away. The moments of lovemaking only briefly blocked everything else out.

Feeling sadness seep back, she held Tom. She couldn't give him more children and he didn't want to stay married.

"You have to be the sexiest man ever."

One corner of his mouth rose in a slight smile. "I don't think you have a lot of experience to compare, but I'm glad you think that," he said gently. "Em, there aren't words for how much I wanted to make love to you."

"We didn't solve anything tonight," she said, voicing aloud her thoughts. "I don't care. I wanted you to kiss me. I wanted to make love." He was damp with sweat, his hair a tangle. She wound her fingers in it, running them down over the stubble on his jaw. Then her fingers played over the red lightning bolt tattoo on his right shoulder. She stroked his back, sliding her hand over his butt, down to the back of his thigh.

His arm tightened around her waist, pulling her closer against him. "You're right. It didn't change anything, but I wanted to hold you and kiss you again. Let me stay here with you a bit. You have the rest of your life to get away from me," he said. And that hurt. Reality was coming back and she couldn't stop it.

"Sure, Tom," she said, holding him, staying in his arms as they remained quiet. She couldn't have regrets for their lovemaking.

She finally shifted slightly. "You can stay here in my bed tonight."

Turning, he drew her against his side. "This seems right in so many ways."

She kissed his shoulder lightly in agreement and felt a pang, wishing they could go back to where they could love each other freely. Where they could feel they were doing right by the other person and their marriage was good. For tonight it was an illusion and she could pretend, but tomorrow, she would have to live with the truth.

He held her close and she clung to him, her arm wrapped around his narrow waist. She wished she could go back a couple of years and have a second chance, because she could see how she had driven Tom away. She ran her finger along his jaw and tried to think about the present, tonight, about loving him and having him in her arms, and forget everything else for now. Tomorrow the problems would all be right there for her to live with and try to cope.

With morning he drew her into his arms to kiss her awake. It was two hours later before they showered together and more than another hour before they went their separate ways to dress.

After breakfast they mopped up where the rain came in last night.

"You have a working alarm system now, in the house and in the yard."

"You've put motion-detector lights all over the place. The door locks all work. If you need to go to the ranch even for just a few days, go ahead."

"If I have to go, I'll tell you. Otherwise, I'm here for a while longer." He turned to face her. "I'll work outside now, so if you want me, I'll be on the east side of the house."

"I'll paint inside," she said and left him.

As Emily painted, she thought about living with Tom.

How would she cope when he walked out of her life? Would they say goodbye and never see each other again? Maybe she would see him at the Texas Cattleman's Club. But if she didn't like living in the old house she had inherited, she would move to Dallas. She would move if she got enough clients and business from the area. If she lived there, she didn't think she would ever see Tom. There were questions about her future that she couldn't answer.

Now, looking around her at the house she had inherited, the smell of fresh paint still filling the air, she thought about her future, when she would have to deal with another parting with Tom. This time a permanent one.

Saturday morning sunshine spilled in through the open windows and Tom was eager to wake Emily. Today was their picnic with the Valentines and he was excited. She'd told him to act as her human alarm clock if she slept past six thirty. It was ten seconds past six thirty now.

He stood beside her bed for seconds, looking at her sleep, her hair spread on the pillow, the sheet down to her waist, her breasts pushing against her T-shirt. He slipped beneath the sheet and pulled her into his arms.

She stirred, wrapped an arm around his neck and rolled over. He couldn't resist. He kissed her. He started out in fun, expecting her to wake instantly, the way she usually did. But the minute he was in bed with her and had her in his arms, all playfulness left him and he wanted to make love to her. He knew he was weaving a web of trouble that would ensnare both of them when they moved on in their lives.

By eleven, after they'd made love, showered, dressed and had breakfast, they were ready to go. Tom was in jeans and a navy T-shirt while she wore capri pants and sandals with a red-white-and-blue-striped cotton blouse. Tom had spent the past half hour packing the truck with provisions for the picnic. Then they locked up the house, setting the new alarm, and left for Royal's big park by the Texas Cattleman's Club.

When they got to the park, Tom noticed Emily's expression as she gazed out the car window. "Look at all the new trees," she said. "They've replaced a lot of the ones that were destroyed by the tornado."

"This is a great park. We could have gone to the Cattleman's Club, but a lot of people there would have wanted to join us. Another time, that would be fun, but I want you to meet and get to know the Valentines when it's just us and them."

Emily had been chatting, but as he wound slowly alongside a silvery pond toward where he and Natalie had agreed to meet, she became silent, and he knew she was remembering the last time she had been in the park. "This is the way we used to come when we brought Ryan," she said softly.

Tom glanced at Emily and pain stabbed him. She had her head turned away from him. He changed course and drove to a deserted parking area. He stopped the car, unfastened his seat belt and placed his hand on her shoulder. He hurt, and his pain was greater because he knew she felt it, too. She put her head in her hands. "I'm sorry."

A knot in his throat kept him from answering and tears burned his eyes. He braced for her to tell him to leave her alone as he pulled her into his arms as much as he could in his pickup. She put her arms around his neck and clung to him, which made him feel better because he had expected her to shove him away.

"I'm sorry, Tom. I thought I could do this without tears. It's a happy occasion and I've looked forward to meeting Natalie and her family and I really mean that—" Emily couldn't finish. She cried while he held her tightly, stroking her head.

"This is the first time I've been back in the park since Ryan was alive," she said between pauses to cry. She spoke so softly he could barely hear her. "We all came here together, remember?"

"I know it, darlin', and I wondered if this would tear you up. I've been here with Natalie and the kids once. This is the main park in Royal and where the Valentines always go. The kids love it here just like Ryan did."

"Then it's a good place to come. I'll be all right in a minute."

"I knew you might have difficulty, and I'm not surprised." He buried his head against her, holding her tightly while she clung to him and they cried. "It hurts like hell, Em, but we don't have a choice. I figure there's a little angel in heaven who loves us as much as we love him."

"Why is life—" She couldn't finish through her tears.

"So damn hard?" he offered. "I don't know. There aren't answers for some questions. When I'm ninety— if I make it that far—I'll cry for my son. As long as I live, I'll miss him."

"I will, too. Why aren't we more of a comfort to each other?"

"I don't know. I guess because that loss is a mountain of sadness and blame and guilt between us. It hurts, so go ahead and cry," he said quietly.

She looked up at him while tears still ran down her cheeks. Tom pulled out a clean, folded handkerchief and dabbed at her cheeks as they gazed at each other.

"You're a comfort to me now. I wish I could be for you, but I can see in your eyes that I'm not."

"Shh, Em. There's a point where it's just too much pain. Over our baby I should have saved. Guys that should have made it home and didn't."

"You just seem to go somewhere where I can't reach you."

He pulled her close again and held her tightly.

She stopped sobbing and became quiet. Raising her head, she wiped her eyes. "I'm making us late."

"If there is anyone on earth who will understand

people stopping to grieve, it's Natalie. She and Jeremy were so in love. Take your time. The kids will play and Natalie will be fine. I'll call her. We're only a minute or two from where we're going. She'll understand, believe me." Tom continued to stroke Emily's head lightly, wishing he could do more but knowing he couldn't.

"I'm sorry Natalie is widowed, but I'm glad we'll be with someone who will understand if I lose it again. That doesn't usually happen when I'm out with people, but this is different."

"I know it is, and sometimes the memory of losing Ryan just comes at you out of the blue."

When she shifted to brush a light kiss on his cheek, he looked down at her. "You're a great guy, Tom. I've been lucky."

He frowned, studying her intently. "Thanks, Em. That makes me feel better. We've had some rough times and we'll have more. I want to help, not be part of the problem."

She looked straight ahead. "You are a help. We got through the rough times until now, so hopefully, we'll get through what's ahead," she said. Her voice held a sad note, and he wondered if she dreaded the divorce or wished they could go ahead sooner and get it now.

He put his hand behind her head and pulled her close to kiss her lightly, tenderly, hoping he conveyed the bond he knew they would always have. Even after they divorced and went their separate ways, memories of Ryan would always be there between them.

She moved away from him and he let her go. "I'm

ready. She'll know I've been crying, but you said she would understand."

"She definitely will, and I told her this might be tough for you. It was for me the first time I was in the park after the wreck."

"Let's go meet them. I'm pulled together. Thanks for being patient and understanding."

"I feel the same as you do, so it's damn easy to be understanding."

He pulled out and returned to the main drive, winding through the park beneath tall oaks until he got to another parking spot near the pond, where a picnic table was already spread.

"There they are—including their dog," Tom said. "Miss Molly is a well-trained golden retriever and as long as we're the only folks out here, she's okay running free, because she sticks close to the kids. She loves those kids. If other families come out, Natalie has a lead she can put Miss Molly on.

"I told you about Colby. He's standoffish, but he'll warm up. He knows me well now, so he's usually responsive around me. I try to not push him," Tom said as he parked. "They're really great kids."

Emily lightly placed her hand on his arm. "You sound happy. You like being with a family and kids. That's what you need, Tom, your own family, your own kids. The sooner we divorce, the sooner you'll have that life."

Frowning slightly, he parked and studied her. "If you marry again, would you be willing to adopt a child?"

"I've never thought about that. I suppose I would,

because the only reason I didn't want to with us was I wanted another Ryan for you," she replied. "The only way we could have a child who would be like you would be if you fathered the child. That's why I held out to not adopt. I kept expecting to get pregnant. If I marry someone else—that wouldn't matter, so yes, I'd adopt."

He had decided long ago they would each be better off if they divorced. Now he knew they would. Emily would have a family and the life she wanted.

He needed to call Nathan and see if they had found any more clues about Maverick. Because Tom felt more strongly than ever that he needed to get out of Emily's life.

Eight

Emily got out when Tom did and they both gathered all they picnic supplies they could handle. Tom carried a big cooler loaded with ice and bottled drinks. He slung a tote bag on his shoulder, with pinwheels and kites sticking out of it. Emily carried a big sack with two beach balls. Two little wooden flutes were in the bottom of the sack. Tom also had an electronic toy for Colby and a little box containing a tiara, a feather boa, bangles and a beaded purse for Lexie to play dress-up. Before he picked up the cooler, he waved and Natalie waved back.

Miss Molly saw them and came bounding over. She went to Tom, but was too well behaved to jump all over him. He put down everything he carried to pet her and scratch her ears. It was obvious the dog loved him and it was mutual. She looked at Emily, who held her hand out, and Tom stepped closer to her. "Here's Miss Molly. She's friendly and has been through obedience school, so she's well trained."

Miss Molly sniffed Emily's hand and looked up expectantly. Tom took a doggie treat from his pocket and handed it to Emily. "Give her this and she will love you forever."

"That's a bribe."

"And it works beautifully. Try," he said.

She held out the treat, which Miss Molly politely took and ate, wagging her tail. She moved closer and looked up at Emily expectantly.

"See, you have a friend now," Tom said, picking things up to carry to the picnic spot.

Emily smiled as she petted Miss Molly and retrieved what she had been carrying. Miss Molly ran to catch up with Tom and walk beside him, moving around to his left side.

Natalie was sitting at the picnic table with a little redheaded girl on her lap. "Lexie is a little doll," Tom said. "At two, Lexie is too young for outdoor games, so I brought some toys and musical instruments. And I have two beach balls and two kites, but we'll need more wind than this. I have some pinwheels, too."

"You're a walking toy store. No wonder they're excited to see you."

As they drew close, Natalie set Lexie on the ground. The minute her feet touched the grass, she ran with her arms out. Tom put down his things and scooped her up, laughing as he said hello. He looked around and walked over to pick up Colby with the other arm. "Hi, Colby," he said easily. "Isn't this fun? We're at the park and I brought some toys and some things to do." The children were both talking to him and he laughed, setting them on their feet.

"Wait a minute. I need to mind my manners. We have someone new with us. Emily, meet Lexie and Colby. This is my wife, Miss Emily to you two." He looked at Emily. "Lexie's still a toddler, so no telling what you'll be called."

"Whatever she settles on, it'll be fine."

Emily greeted them with a smile while they politely said hello. She barely heard Colby, who shyly looked away.

"We'll get to what I brought, but first, I want to talk to your mama," Tom told them.

As they approached the picnic table, which already had a red-and-white-checkered plastic tablecloth covering it, Emily saw Natalie Valentine turn and come forward to greet them, smiling.

"Emily, I'm Natalie. I'm glad to finally meet you."

"I'm glad to meet you," Emily answered politely, amazed Tom hadn't fallen in love with Natalie, who was pretty with huge green eyes.

Natalie held out her hands. "Let me carry something."

"Here's a cake you can carry," Emily said, handing a covered pan to the other woman.

"Lexie woke up an hour earlier than usual this morning because she was so excited about the picnic today. The kids love to see Tom. He's wonderful with them and he's good to share his time. Jeremy picked the right guy to be friends with, and I know why."

"He's good with kids," Emily said, watching him hunker down to let Lexie and Colby look in the sack he'd brought and pull something out. They each got a pinwheel and stepped away to swing them through the air and make them spin. It was obvious they had played with them before.

"Tom has been a lifesaver for us," Natalie continued. "Last month he installed two new motion-detector lights outside at the B and B. And then I had an appointment to take Colby to the dentist and Miss Molly had an appointment at the groomer at the same time—both hard to change—so Tom took Lexie with him to get Miss Molly to be groomed while I took Colby to the dentist. He even took Lexie to the pediatrician when she had to get a tetanus shot because she cut her foot on a rusty piece of metal. He held her hand while she got her shot, took her for ice cream and then to the bookstore."

Emily continued to listen to Natalie talk about how much Tom had helped her. She was so effusive in her praise for Tom, talking about all the things he had done for her and her family, that Emily realized she had pushed Tom away and hadn't let him take care of her when that was probably what he needed to do.

It was what he was doing now, but she had been fighting him on it every step of the way, while Natalie accepted his help and was grateful for it.

In the past Emily had robbed him of his need to be her protector, a need she decided after listening to Natalie that was as essential to his life force as breathing.

He had tried in the days after they lost Ryan, but she had wrapped herself in a shell and withdrew from him. She hadn't relied on him then and she wouldn't have now, but he'd simply taken charge because of worrying about what Maverick might be intending to do.

She thought about Tom telling her that he had lost Ryan, but he wasn't going to lose her to a troll.

She watched him with the kids and wondered if part of the reason they were getting along so much better now was because he felt he was helping her and doing things for her. If so, she had made really big mistakes by shutting him out of parts of her life after Ryan's death.

"I know you and Tom have been estranged in the past," Natalie said quietly. "I don't want to intrude, but it looks as if you might be getting back together. I just want to say you have a wonderful husband who has been so good to us and a marvelous substitute for Jeremy with the kids."

"Tom loves kids. He's got six nieces and nephews, but this past year we haven't seen them often, because all three of his brothers have moved farther away."

"Jeremy picked well when he got Tom for a friend. But Tom's gone through a lot at home and abroad. Jeremy told me about some of what they did and it was rough. Tom's a tough guy, but losing his son has really been hard on him. Just as I know it's hard on you. That's something we all share. But enough about our lives."

As Emily started to unpack the things they'd carried from the car, her thoughts were on all Natalie had said.

The more Emily thought about it, the more she realized that pushing Tom away after Ryan's death, doing things herself and shutting him out had been disastrous. But now she was accepting his help, and they both seemed to be thriving. He was getting the house in shape far faster than she would have been able to do. And since Tom appeared, she hadn't had any more messages from Maverick.

At least this part was good. She was happy to meet Natalie and the kids, who'd made her realize that it would have helped Tom heal more after they lost Ryan if she hadn't shut him out. He needed her to rely on him, to need him—which was something he had found with the Valentines.

Emily wondered if it was too late for her. Was having Tom working on Uncle Woody's house and staying with her for protection enough to meet the need he had to be a provider in her life and in the marriage?

Natalie watched as the kids played with the beach balls. Tom patiently helped Lexie, who was too little to keep up with her brother or do much of anything with her beach ball except toss it around and let Tom bring it back and roll it to her.

As soon as Emily and Natalie were done unpacking everything, the kids started dancing around Tom, asking him to create bubbles for them to pop.

"They'll keep him busy," Natalie said, turning to look at Emily. "Tom told me about the hateful email you got. It's terrible, but I'm so glad you two got it straightened out between you." She gave a faint smile and shook her head. "Tom's secret family. He is so good to us. I would have been sick if I thought all he's done for us would cause you both pain. Tom is a wonderful person."

"Yes, he is, and he thought your husband was. He told me about Jeremy, but that was a while ago. When I saw that picture, I didn't put it together and think about your husband. I just accepted the email as truth."

"I hope they catch this person before someone else gets hurt."

"I hope so, too. I'm sorry, Natalie, about Jeremy. Tom thought so much of him."

"Thanks," Natalie said. "I'm sorry for your loss. Tom is good to always spend time with the kids. Both kids love him. He's so patient with them and good for Colby."

"He's good with kids because he really likes them," Emily said quietly, hurting as she watched Tom play with Lexie and Colby. "And he's patient," she said, thinking again if she could have gotten pregnant, they might not be getting the divorce. Tom had been wonderful with Ryan.

"We've both lost so much," Natalie said quietly. "I hope you and Tom can work things out, because he should have his own family, his own kids."

"I agree with you about that and I know we have a mutual bond in losing someone we love deeply." She looked around. "We better start getting food ready, or there will be other kinds of tears shed."

"Indeed, there will be," Natalie said, smiling. "Before you and Tom arrived, they were coming to me every five minutes to ask when you'd get here and how soon we'll eat. Let's get some of this set up and then we can go join them and play for a short time. If you don't want to, that's okay," Natalie said.

"It'll be fun. Look at Tom. He has to be having a good time."

They paused a moment and watched Tom open a bottle, dip a wand inside and then wave it, leaving a stream of big bubbles. Laughing, both kids began to chase and pop bubbles while Tom kept producing more.

Another pang struck Emily as she looked at Tom. Wind tangled his hair. He was agile and strong, playing with the kids and obviously enjoying it. This was a fun few hours, but their lives were not a constant picnic with kids included. Their marriage was over and that was one more thing she had to accept and learn to live with. Tom was handsome, so appealing—she turned from watching him, focusing on the kids and laughing at their antics.

"Your children are wonderful."

"Thank you," Natalie answered. "They have their moments, and Colby has special needs and special abilities. They're good kids and I love them with all my heart."

Looking at both kids, Emily hurt because she wanted her own. She wanted to run and join the fun and play with them, too, but she didn't want to leave Natalie and they didn't need three adults mixing with the bubbles. "Lexie is so cute."

Natalie laughed. "She thinks so. She would love to have my shoes and makeup. I can't imagine what I'm in for when she's a teen."

Emily smiled. Tom glanced their way and said something to Colby and Lexie. He turned to walk toward Emily and Natalie.

"Hey, when do we get to eat around here?"

"We can any time you want to fire up that grill and do burgers," Natalie said.

"I'll tell Colby and Lexie and go to work at the grill."

"I'll tell them," Natalie said. "You get the food. Emily and I can play with them while you cook. I think we have everything else out and ready."

"Good deal," he answered.

Emily spread a blanket and gave each child a new box of crayons and tablets of plain paper so they could draw.

Natalie joined her and after a few minutes, Emily left to help Tom with the cooking and getting last-minute things on the table.

When they all sat down to eat, she felt as if she were part of the family. Natalie was easy to get to know and Emily already loved the kids. Colby was quiet, sometimes a little withdrawn, but he liked all the toys and gadgets Tom had brought. She took pictures of them and of everybody.

They had homemade strawberry ice cream for dessert along with chocolate chip cookies Natalie had made. As they sat in the shade and ate ice cream and cookies, Miss Molly stretched out at Tom's feet. Tom ran the toe of his boot back and forth behind her ear and she looked serenely happy.

When they put things away after the picnic, Lexie ran up to grab Tom's hand and tug. Colby stood back, holding one of the beach balls. "Back to work," Tom said, getting up to join the kids again. "Don't carry anything to the cars. I can do that later."

"I'll go with you," Emily said, smiling at Natalie. "Take a break and sit in the shade. We'll play with Lexie and Colby. It'll be fun."

Natalie smiled. "Thanks. Stop whenever you've had enough."

Tom and Colby moved yards apart while Emily stood near Lexie, who was too little to play but wanted to participate. The adults tossed the beach ball first to one child and then the other. Lexie couldn't catch it, but she chased it to bat it and Emily helped.

By late afternoon, Lexie was sitting on a blanket alternately playing with a doll and drawing while Colby played with the electronic game that Tom had brought. The three adults sat in the shade and talked.

Emily enjoyed being with all of the Valentines. Lexie brought over her drawing and scrambled up onto her lap. Emily held her, admiring her drawing and talking to her about making another picture. The minute she climbed on her lap, Emily thought of Ryan. She looked down at Lexie's red hair, thinking she was an adorable child. She took the crayons to draw. As she drew, Lexie listened attentively while Emily made up first one story and then another to go with the pictures. When she finished, she asked Lexie to draw a story and watched and listened as the little girl spoke of a mouse and an elephant and drew unrecognizable creatures. But she was happy with her story and her drawings.

"Emily, you don't have to do that the rest of the evening," Natalie said, smiling. "I think you've served your time."

Shaking her head, Emily smiled. "I'm having a good

time, too. As long as she wants to. When I want to stop, I will."

Lexie tugged on her hand. "Let's do another one," she said.

"Do you want to tell another story?" Emily asked, looking at Lexie and thinking how wonderful it was to have a little child in her lap again.

Lexie's eyes sparkled as she nodded. "I have a story about a kitty and a butterfly."

Emily listened, smiling and smoothing Lexie's hair, thinking Natalie had a wonderful family. She glanced up to see Tom watching her. Their gazes met and she wondered what he was thinking.

The sun was below the treetops in the west when Natalie announced they needed to pack things up and get home. She called to Miss Molly, and the big dog loped to her side.

"We'll follow you home and I can help carry things inside," Tom said.

"You don't need to do that," she said, smiling at him. "Emily told me how you're helping her get her house painted. I know how big a job that can be. Besides, I have four couples at the bed-and-breakfast, just getting away from city life for a weekend. The guys carried the things out for me this morning and have already told me they would carry the stuff in when I get back. Their reward will be the strawberry ice cream," she said, smiling at them.

"Come see me," Lexie said, taking Emily's hand. Her tiny hand felt so small, and Emily's heart lurched when she thought about Ryan holding her hand.

"I'd love to see your room and Colby's, too," Emily said, and Lexie's smile broadened.

"We'll be happy to have you come visit," Natalie said.

They let Miss Molly jump into the back of the SUV and then the kids climbed in and buckled into their car seats, with Natalie checking on Lexie's. Natalie got into the front and Tom closed her door.

Tom draped his arm across Emily's shoulders as they walked to the pickup. She wondered if he even gave any thought to what he was doing, but she was aware of it. The minute he put his arm across her shoulders, she was reminded of old times with him. And then she became aware of how close they were. All day he had looked virile, filled with energy, strong and incredibly appealing to her. How much would it tear her up to go back to the house and sleep with him? The thought of making love tonight made her draw a deep breath; she just couldn't suppress her eagerness.

Tom held the pickup door open and she climbed inside. He got in and waited while Natalie backed out and turned to drive away. Then he followed.

"They look like the all-American family, Tom. Especially with the dog hanging out the window," Emily said.

"Except the all-American dad was shot dead on foreign soil, defending his country so we can go on picnics. He's not in that car with his wife and kids and dog."

Emily wanted to reach for Tom's hand, just to hold it. At one time in her life that's what she would have done, but not now. Now they were going their separate ways soon and reaching for him would be almost like reaching to hold a stranger's hand. "You knew that when you joined the service," she said.

"I know I did, but sometimes when I'm with Natalie and the kids, it gets to me, because Jeremy should be with them instead of me."

"You've really kept your promise to Jeremy. She's so grateful for all you've done for them."

"I'm trying," he said. "When I think of the sacrifice he made, there's never enough I can do."

"You're a good guy," Emily said, and meant it. Tears threatened because she had lost Tom and there were moments it hurt badly. After a few minutes, she pulled herself together. "Natalie appreciates everything you've done and it's obvious the kids love you. You should have your own kids," she said quietly. He shot her a quick, startled glance but said nothing.

She felt another wave of sadness that she couldn't give Tom another little boy. If only she had been able to get pregnant, they might have had a chance to save their marriage. But that wasn't what had happened.

"They are cute kids. Lexie knows she is," Tom said, smiling. "That little girl can steal the show when she wants to. I'm glad you and Natalie met. I should have done that long ago, but you and I have been out of each other's lives for a long time now."

"I'm glad to meet her. I understand her loss and she understands mine—actually, ours."

"Yes. She's done well, but she has moments. She keeps a good front for the kids' sakes, so that helps in a way."

Emily thought about how all three of them—she, Natalie and Tom—had been targets of Maverick in a way. But Maverick's hateful lies had backfired, bringing them closer together instead of driving them all apart.

When they got back to her house, she was astonished again by the difference only a week had made. The new coat of paint was beginning to transform the house into the home she remembered and loved and always thought was so beautiful. Tom had started working on the yard because the days were getting warmer. He'd made two beds ready for spring planting. Filled with energy, Tom got things done, but she always had been impressed by his strength and vigor.

"It's just been a week and you've made a giant difference. It doesn't look like the same house."

"I'm glad you noticed, and you sound happy with it."

"I am happy with it. It's done and it looks nice and thank you."

"Good. It's a hell of a lot safer and more secure, too," Tom said. He parked at the side of the house, leaving the pickup so it could be seen from the street.

"You're not getting out of the pickup," she said, looking at him sitting still, staring straight ahead.

"No, I'm looking at the garage."

"Oh, heavens, what now, Tom? There must be something I need to fix."

"There sure as hell is. Emily, that garage is as old as this house. That big mulberry tree with giant roots is pushing the garage over and the driveway up."

"You want me to get rid of the garage?"

"Yes. You need to get estimates—I'll do it—on a

new driveway and a new garage and come into this century. Or even come into the last half of the last century. That thing is simply going to collapse someday soon and you don't want to be in it when it does."

She looked at the old garage and the cracked slabs of concrete driveway that had been pushed several inches into the air.

"Do you remember when your uncle Woody stopped using it?" Tom asked.

"I was probably about twelve. Okay. You're right about the garage."

Tom smiled. "So I'm finally right about something concerning this house."

"You're right about everything concerning this house. Tom, it is definitely better. It would have taken me months to get done what you've done. I'm grateful for your help," she said.

"I'll get your estimates on a driveway and the cost for a new garage. This will be a garage today's car will fit into," he said, grinning and shaking his head. "That thing was built for a Model T."

Together they carried the picnic things into the house. "It's a pretty Saturday night," he remarked. "After we get through putting the stuff away, let's sit on the porch, have a drink and enjoy the evening."

"Sure," she said, knowing if they did that many more times, she would miss having him here when he returned to the ranch. "But I need a shower first—I've been outside all day, in the grass, petting the dog—"

"Right. I know one thing that would make taking a shower better—"

"It's not going to happen tonight."

He grinned. "I have to keep trying. I can really be fun to take a shower with, or maybe you remember. I remember you're lots of fun to shower with. It would make this a superspecial Saturday."

"Will you stop?" she said, laughing and shaking her head. "No, we don't shower together. What would you like to drink? Let me guess—a cold beer."

"Ah, you know me too well. All the mystery is gone."

"There's plenty of mystery about you—I'm surprised you haven't fallen in love with Natalie Valentine. She is so sweet and has a wonderful family. And you love that dog."

He came back to put his hands on her shoulders and she wondered what chord she had struck. Was he falling in love with Natalie? She gazed into his seductive hazel eyes.

"I'll tell you what, darlin'. I don't fall in love with someone because of their dog. Or their kids—and those are adorable kids. Natalie is beautiful, but she's Jeremy's widow and she still loves him. And he was my buddy."

"You're a good guy, Tom," she said, turning back to her task.

When they were done putting things away in the kitchen, she turned to him. "I'm going upstairs to shower—alone. I'll meet you on the porch. The first one done can get drinks. See you in thirty minutes."

"Fine. I'll go upstairs and shower, too." At the head of the stairs he turned to her. "The invitation is still open."

"I'll have to admit, I'm tempted—"

"Oh, darlin'," he said, holding his arms out. "Come

join me. We'll have a shower you'll never forget." She laughed and he laughed with her. "See, I told you I can be fun in the shower," he said. "We're not even there yet and I have you laughing."

"You are fun, you devil," she said, squeezing his jaw and looking into his mischievous eyes. "As fun as you are, I'm going to shower all by myself and then enjoy sitting with you on the porch," she said.

He placed his arms casually on her shoulders. "We can still enjoy each other's company. It's been a good day."

"It has. The Valentines are wonderful."

"Yes, they are, but the good time today wasn't just because of the Valentines. You and I can laugh and enjoy each other. We haven't totally lost it," he said with so much confidence she felt a thrill.

"I know we can as long as we stay away from real life and the serious stuff."

"I'll settle for what we can get. We can do a lot of things together," he said, his voice changing, becoming deeper while his hands slid down to rub her bare arms lightly.

"I know we can."

Her heartbeat raced as his gaze lowered to her mouth. Her lips parted.

"Tom," she whispered, his name an invitation. She might have huge regrets very soon, but at this moment she wanted to kiss him. What would one kiss hurt?

When his mouth covered hers, she opened to him and felt on fire. Their tongues mingled as he wrapped his arm around her and pulled her tightly against him.

She hugged him around his waist and ran one hand over his muscled back.

She had no idea how long they kissed, but when she felt his hand on her breast, she placed her hand over his. "Wait," she whispered, looking up at him. "I want to shower and sit on the porch and talk and maybe kiss again—okay?"

He inhaled deeply and nodded. "Okay." He caressed her nape and tugged lightly on her braid. "Take your hair down."

"I will. I'll see you on the porch." She walked away, hearing his boots as he went into the room where he kept his things. Now what would she agree to after her shower? She better think before she brought pain and regret crashing back down on them.

When she came down, he was already on the porch. She wore navy capri pants, flip-flops, a pale blue sleeveless cotton blouse and a clip in her hair to hold it behind her head. The minute he saw her, Tom stood up. His gaze drifted over her from her head to her toes, making her tingle. She took in tight jeans, his black boots and short-sleeved navy T-shirt. To her, he was still the most handsome man she knew. And definitely the sexiest. She strolled to the empty chair beside him and picked up the drink he'd prepared for her.

He stepped closer and smiled at her, making her heart race as she gazed into his eyes. "You look as good as a million dollars."

"Thank you. You look rather good yourself." She didn't want to admit how appealing he did look to her.

"Let's fix this," he said, reaching over to take the clip out of her hair and placing it on the table. She smiled at him as she shook her head, letting her hair fan out over her shoulders.

As they rocked and talked, she felt as if she was standing on the edge of a high cliff and a misstep could mean ruin. She thought about what she should do and what she wanted to do. She wanted to be in his arms, making love again. How much would that hurt later? It wouldn't change anything. It just might mean more heartache.

"Think you'll stay in Royal or move to Dallas after our divorce?" he asked after a long silence.

"Right now, after a fun day together, I don't want to think about the divorce." She gazed into the darkness and sipped her tea. "I'll probably stay in this area unless some opportunity with my photography comes up and causes me to move on. We'll cross paths, I'm sure."

With his feet propped on another chair, Tom was silent. While he sipped his beer, he idly rubbed one knee and she remembered how he ran and played with the kids. She also remembered how badly his knee was hurt in the bus wreck and the big scar he still carried.

"Does your knee hurt?"

He looked around. "Not really. I guess rubbing it sometimes has gotten to be a habit from when it did hurt."

"That's good. It used to bother you some after a long day like today," she said.

"I don't think about it much any longer. We'll both carry that night with us in our memories forever, but the pain isn't as constant as it was."

"I agree. I'm sorry that you got hurt so badly. I was scared I'd lose you both," she said, thinking about all they had been through.

"I'm sorry I made it and Ryan didn't," he said quietly.

"Tom, don't ever apologize because you survived," she said, turning to stare at him. "I didn't want to lose either one of you," she said. "I was terrified when they told me you were on the critical list along with Ryan. I called your brother and that's why you were on so many prayer lists, because he got the word out. Don't ever apologize for surviving."

"I figured you wished I had died instead of Ryan," Tom replied. Stunned, she stared at him in the darkness while she clutched his hand.

Nine

"If one of us could have lived and one couldn't, I would rather it had been Ryan, too," Tom continued.

Shocked, she shook her head. "Tom, I never felt that way," she said, staring at him in the dark. "That's dreadful. I never for one second wanted to lose you."

He didn't answer and she wondered if he doubted her. "It has never occurred to me you could have thought I wished it had been you. I loved you. I loved you so much." When he still didn't answer her, she hurt to think he had been carrying that idea around all this time. "I was so scared you wouldn't make it. I stayed awake all through that first night praying for you and Ryan."

Setting her glass of tea aside, she got up and stepped over to sit in his lap. She framed his face with her hands so she could look into his eyes even though it was dark on the porch. "I never wished you had died instead of Ryan. Not for one part of a second. Oh, how I loved you."

His arms tightened around her and he shifted, cradling her against his shoulder as he leaned over to kiss her, a possessive kiss that made her insides seize up. She kissed him back as if she could erase all the heartaches and differences with their kiss. She leaned away again and cupped his chin in her hand.

"Don't ever think or say that again. With my whole heart I wanted you and Ryan, both of you, to survive." Holding him tightly, she resumed their kiss.

Minutes later, she raised her head. "Tom, I never for one second wanted you to die," she said.

He gazed intently at her and started to say something, but she stood, taking his hand. She pulled lightly and he came to his feet to sweep her into his arms.

If she couldn't convince him with words, she wanted to show him with her loving, with kisses and caresses to give him all the sensual pleasure possible. As if he knew what she wanted, he carried her inside. Holding her close, he climbed the staircase and switched on the light in the upstairs hall.

In her bedroom beside the new bed, he stood her on her feet and kissed her. The instant his mouth covered hers, she trembled with desire. She stepped back to take off her blouse, moving slowly while he watched her. When she had her blouse off, she stepped forward to pull off his shirt and rake her hands over his chest and shower kisses there, running her tongue over the flat, hard nipples, tangling her fingers in his thick chest curls.

He caressed her breasts, cupping them and stroking her nipples lightly with his thumbs while she peeled away her capri pants. She unfastened and pulled off his belt as they kissed. Then she unfastened his jeans and pushed them down his legs.

Tom paused to kick off his boots and pull off the rest of his clothes and her lace panties. He placed his hands on her hips and stepped back to look at her. "You're beautiful. I've dreamed about you and spent hours remembering." His fingers again drifted over her breast, a faint brush of his hand that was as electrifying as his hungry gaze.

His look was as sexy and stimulating as his touch, making her quiver. She twisted and turned, rubbing her warm, naked body against him, all the while caressing him, touching him, stroking his thick manhood.

"Ah, Em, this is good with you, so good." He leaned down to take her nipple in his mouth and circle the tip with his tongue. Intense sensation shot through her from each hot brush of his tongue and she gasped with pleasure.

"Tom, my love," she whispered. Her fingers trailed over his scars, some new, most old and familiar. She followed with her tongue.

Reaching for her, he watched her expression as he cupped her breasts again.

She clung to his shoulders, closing her eyes and drowning in sensation. "I want to take all night to give you pleasure, to show you how wrong you were."

He kissed her fiercely, holding her tightly as if it might be their last kiss, and she clung to him.

When he released her, he gazed into her eyes. "Tonight is for memories of the good times, for a day well spent, to celebrate being alive."

Emily tangled her fingers in his chest hair as she kissed him. He stood with his eyes closed as she knelt to lick and kiss and stroke him, until he picked her up and placed her on the bed. He propped himself up on an elbow beside her, watching her, and then leaned down to shower kisses and caresses over every inch of her.

He pushed her over onto her stomach, his tongue trailing down her spine, over her smooth, round bottom, lower between her legs and then over the backs of her legs while his hands were everywhere caressing her.

She moaned softly, her hands knotted in the sheets on the bed. She turned to face him, her gaze raking over his muscled body and thick manhood. He stretched out beside her to pull her into his arms and kiss her hard while his hand was warm between her legs, rubbing her, driving her to new heights. She arched against him and ran her hand over his legs, over his thick rod that was hot and hard and ready for her.

With a murmur deep in his throat, he stepped off the bed and picked her up. They looked into each other's eyes while he pulled her up onto her toes. He looked fierce, desire blazing in his expression.

As he kissed her, he braced himself. She locked her long legs around his waist and he lowered her onto his thick shaft.

Gasping with pleasure, she dug her nails into his muscled shoulders and then wrapped her arms around him, clinging tightly to him She wanted his lovemaking to drive her to oblivion, to make love until pain and hurt and loss were mere shadows that couldn't affect her.

And then all thought was gone as she rode him. He thrust hard and fast, driving her to a brink and then over. She cried out with ecstasy before kissing him again, a kiss of love, of longing and of rapture.

Time and hurt didn't exist. She was wrapped in his arms, one with him, and for this moment it felt as if she was enveloped in his love once again.

When she finally slid down to stand, she gazed into his eyes that looked filled with love. For this moment they had recaptured the past. Gently, he picked her up to place her on the bed and stretched out beside her. She lay in his arms, exhausted, pressed against his hard length. Tom held her close against him, slowly combing his fingers through her hair. "This is good, Em," he said in a raspy tone.

She placed her hand on his cheek. They lay quietly, holding each other, touching, stroking each other gently, and she wished the night would stretch into eternity.

"We're way ahead of the schedule for fixing the house, aren't we?" he asked, his deep voice soft in the silent night.

"Yes, thanks to you and your dynamo energy."

"How about going to the ranch for a few days to get a break? You've already blocked off time from your photography. Honestly, I can use a little time on the ranch. Would you do that? A little break won't hurt."

She gazed at him as she thought it over. "Just a few days?"

"Sure. Just a break. I think we've earned one. I've

hired a company to get these hardwood floors back in shape for you."

"Tom—you didn't tell me. Are they putting in new floors?"

"No. It's a cleanup and polish, that sort of thing. If you want something more, though, now is the time to say so."

"No, that will be wonderful. That's all I intended to do. Thank you."

"You're welcome. Let's go to the ranch tomorrow and I'll call and tell them to come do the floors. I know the guy that owns the company, and we can trust him with the house key."

She laughed. "Sure. What's to steal here?" she asked, looking around at an empty room. "Very well. Yes, I'll go to the ranch—what? A week, four days, two days?"

"How is four days?"

"Four days it is. Thanks. I'll make arrangements and we'll go after lunch."

"Where are we staying?"

He leaned close. "Let's try the main house together. Our house. I can stay in a separate bedroom if you want, but four days—let's try, Em."

"You can always get your way with me. You know all you have to do is look at me, touch me or even just stand close and I'm putty."

"Very sexy putty, I'd say."

"Don't try to butter me up now," she said, smiling at him.

"Ah, butter. That's something we haven't tried. Maybe I will butter you up one night."

She laughed and hugged him. "Why can't it stay this way?"

"I can't answer that one."

The next afternoon, they were packed, had the house locked up and were in the car by two o'clock. On the ride back to the ranch, they reminisced about their high school days and dating. Emily wondered if they could maintain their relaxed, friendly attitude on the ranch, where so many painful memories came up day after day.

She would soon know. They moved into the big house and she had a chill run down her spine because she had a feeling they were making a big mistake by coming back when they didn't have to. Standing in the entryway beneath the Waterford crystal chandelier, she looked around.

"Tom, I'll take the guest bedroom on the far west side."

"Good idea. I'll take the one next to it unless you'll just let me move in with you from the start."

She laughed. "Let's see how we're doing by nightfall. We don't have a good track record in this house."

He took her hand and stepped close in front of her. With his other hand he caressed her nape lightly. "We had the best track record possible until that bus wreck. That's when it all went to hell. But we've been doing pretty well together in town these past weeks."

She nodded but still had the feeling of foreboding.

"I need to go see Gus and check on some things. I'm sure you can entertain yourself, and if nothing else, just take a four-day vacation."

"That sounds awesome," she said, smiling at him. "You get going and my vacation will start. I may go swim."

"Better check the pool over first for critters. No one has been here except a skeleton garden and cleaning staff."

"Oh, yes. I look before I jump in."

"So you do." He smiled at her. "See, we're doing pretty well. Kiss me and we'll see if we are still speaking to each other."

She laughed, but she really didn't feel lighthearted. He stepped close to embrace and kiss her, startling her for one second, and then she held him and returned his kiss, wondering if he would still want to kiss her in four days.

In minutes, he picked her up and carried her to a downstairs bedroom, setting her down only to yank the covers off the bed.

"Tom—" she protested.

"We're alone. What I'm going to do can wait. This can't," he rasped. In seconds, their clothing was gone and he picked her up as he kissed her. She locked her legs around him and he spread his feet apart, letting her slide down on his thick rod while they kissed.

Emily held him tightly, moving on him, her cries of ecstasy smothered by his kisses. She moved fast with him as he thrust deeply and groaned when he reached a shuddering climax.

She finally sagged against him, placing her head on his shoulder as he placed her in bed and then stretched out beside her.

"You are fantastic and leave me frazzled and in paradise at the same time."

She smiled. "You're never frazzled. We'll shower soon, but for a minute I want you close to me. This is a good way to start our current life here."

They talked softly, stroking each other, and he seemed to enjoy the moment as much as she did until he finally rolled over.

"I hate to go, but I have several things to do. First I'm going to talk to Gus. Then I'm going to my office in the guesthouse, because I need to find some old records for our accountant to do the taxes. No one will be here today except me, so do whatever you want. We should have dinners in the freezer and a couple in the fridge. I won't be gone long."

"I hope not. I don't do well in this big house by myself."

Something flickered in his gaze. "We had a lot of good years here and really good memories. We both need to try to remember to hang on to those times."

She leaned close to kiss him tenderly. "You've been my world since I was sixteen. Then, when the crash happened—"

"A day at a time," he said solemnly. "I'm going to shower and see you later. You find something in that freezer to thaw for us."

"Sure will." She watched him get up and leave the room. He was naked, handsome, all muscle. He had scars, but she barely noticed them. Desire stirred and she wondered if there was any hope for them to have a future together. Was the sex between them blinding them to the problems they faced—or was it helping to work those problems out?

Sex for them had always been good, but they couldn't stay married on that alone, and they really hadn't solved any problems between them. Or had they? There was her discovery that Tom thought she wished he had died instead of Ryan. They'd been able to clear the air about that. And she realized how tense and uptight she had been about getting pregnant, and how that might have driven him away from her. So maybe they were making progress.

After she showered and dressed, she walked through the house, closing off some rooms because she wanted to avoid seeing them.

As she set a casserole out to thaw, she received a call and didn't recognize the number, but then she saw the name Jason Nash on the caller ID and her breath caught.

She answered the call and heard a lilting female voice. "May I please speak to Emily Knox?"

"This is Emily Knox," Emily answered, barely able to catch her breath and feeling as if her heart was being squeezed by a giant fist. She gulped air, trying to calm.

"Mrs. Knox, this is Becky Nash. I'm Polly's mother. I'm sure you remember us."

"Yes, I do," she said, instantly recalling the discussion with the doctor who'd first told them about the Nash family after the bus accident. "How is Polly?" Emily asked, holding her breath and wondering why she was receiving this call.

"Polly is fine," Becky Nash said. "We'll be passing

through Texas, and we thought we could stop by if you would like to meet our daughter."

For a moment Emily couldn't answer. Tears filled her eyes and she felt a mixture of emotions—dread at revisiting all the pain from those days when Ryan was in the hospital, but also a thrill to get to meet the little girl who had received Ryan's heart. Their Ryan had given part of himself to another child who would have lost her life. Now their Ryan's heart kept Polly Nash alive.

"We'd love to meet her, Mrs. Nash."

"Please, call me Becky. We can come by your house if you'd like. Royal isn't too far from where we'll be on the interstate. I know this is rather short notice, but we changed some plans and now we'll be driving where we can stop by next Tuesday if that is convenient. Would Tuesday afternoon be possible?"

"Yes, that would be perfect. We're at Knox Acres Ranch, just outside town. I can tell you how to get here."

They finished making the arrangements and ended the call. Emily remembered the young mother—a pretty blue-eyed blonde in her early twenties. Jason Nash, her tall brown-haired husband, was an accountant with a big company in Denver. One of the doctors had approached them about the transplant, and later, after they agreed, they met the parents. But Emily and Tom had never met Polly. Now that was going to change on Tuesday afternoon.

She started to call Tom to tell him, but she decided she'd rather tell him in person. And she was curious about the guesthouse. She hadn't been inside since he'd moved there after their separation. She didn't know if he had changed it, spreading out and making a new home for himself. Or maybe he'd just left it the way it was.

She basked in the sunshine as she made the short walk across the yard and wide driveway. The guesthouse was a much smaller, far simpler house than the mansion, with a friendly warmth to it that she'd never felt the large house had. When she arrived, she crossed the porch to the open door. The screen door was closed, so she knocked on that.

"Come in," Tom called.

She stepped inside. "Where are you?" She looked around the living room that looked exactly like it always had after visitors had come and gone. The front room was immaculate and did not appear lived in.

"I'm in my office."

She had no idea where he had made an office, but she followed the sound of his voice and then saw him in the big master bedroom. He was on a ladder in the closet rummaging around on a shelf. Boxes and papers were strewn at his feet.

"I'm glad to see signs of someone living in here since you've been doing so for the past year. But you don't have much in the way of excess anything."

"I don't need much."

"Can you come down from there? I want to talk to you."

He paused and looked at her, and then came down a step and jumped the rest of the way.

He frowned as he faced her. "This must be something serious."

"It is. I need to talk to you."

He held out his hand. "Let's go in the living room and we can sit."

"I don't know that we need to sit to talk," she said, walking back into the front room and turning to face him. "I got a phone call. And I'm worried this might bring up some painful memories for us."

"Who called? This sounds important," he said.

"It is important. It was from Becky Nash."

Ten

Tom's hand stilled. "Why did she call us? Is the little girl all right?" he asked.

"Yes, she's fine. Her mother called because they are driving through Texas and asked if we would like to meet Polly. They are going to stop by here next Tuesday afternoon."

He looked away, his jaws clamped shut while he was silent. Finally he faced her again. "That is a big deal. We're going to meet the little girl who has our son's heart."

Silence stretched between them again, and Emily had a sinking feeling that a lot of their old problems were about to return, ending the fragile friendly truce.

"Would you rather I had told them not to come?"

He flinched and shook his head. "No. You did the

right thing. We should meet her. I just keep thinking that part of Ryan is still a living organ, that there's part of him still here."

"And keeping another child alive. Tom, Ryan has given life to this little girl."

Tom wiped his eyes. "I know that. And that's what we wanted and it's good, but it doesn't make our loss lighter or lessen the hurt of losing Ryan one damn degree. It brings the loss all back in a way. We should meet her, but that doesn't make it easy." He turned his back to her and she knew he wiped his eyes again.

And she knew she couldn't comfort him and he didn't want her to try. He had turned his back on her and was shutting her out of his life.

She hurt more than ever and suspected the last little vestige of her marriage was shattering.

In spite of their time together, the quiet hours spent on Uncle Woody's porch just talking about each other's plans, Emily could tell that this reminder of their loss had thrown them back to the way it used to be. To when they had been estranged and avoided each other.

She knew he didn't want her there, so she walked quietly out of the guesthouse and crossed back to the main house, barely able to see for her tears.

It was definitely over between them. She could tell when Tom turned his back on her that had been a final goodbye.

She had been wrapped in a false sense of happiness when he had lived in the old house with her and helped her get it back in shape. That was over and all the hurt over the bus wreck and loss of their son had returned.

And it would always come back. There would be reminders through life and she and Tom needed to let go and try to rebuild their lives.

She loved Tom and she couldn't imagine ever loving anyone else, but her marriage to him was over. She suspected she would not see him again until the Nashes arrived on Tuesday.

She cried as she walked back to the mansion. But she felt she had known all along the day would come when they would go back to avoiding each other and Tom would sign the divorce papers.

She decided that she would pack and choose what she wanted to have moved to her house in Royal so she could go as soon as the Nashes left.

She entered the empty, silent house, wanting to be back in town and away from so many painful memories here.

She thought of the fun times she and Tom had had over the past days. The evenings they'd spent on the porch, just talking. They had found joy in each other again and she was beginning to have hope. Tom was the most wonderful man she had ever known and she had fallen in love with him all over again. And now she was hurting all over again.

She didn't feel like having dinner and Tom didn't show, so she put the casserole back in the refrigerator and went out to the sprawling patio to sit where she could look at the spring flowers in the yard and the big blue swimming pool with its sparkling fountain. It was a cool March evening and she would rather sit outside.

She would borrow one of the ranch trucks to take

some furniture back with her. Tom wouldn't care what she took or what she left. She doubted whether he would ever live in the main house again, and she didn't want to.

She put her head in her hands to cry. She had lost them both—Ryan and Tom.

She cried quietly as she sat there in the dusky evening, looking at the fountain and feeling numb. She gazed beyond the pool. Silence enveloped her. Occasionally she could hear the wind, a soft sound, the only sound. As if the entire world was at peace. She knew better. It wasn't, and neither was her little corner of it. But the illusion was nice.

"Did you eat dinner?"

She heard Tom's deep voice from the doorway and turned around. He stood in the door with his hands on his hips.

"No. Do you want any?"

"No. I'll stay at the guesthouse tonight."

"I thought you probably would. I'll get my car tomorrow so I can take it back to Royal when I go."

When he didn't say anything else, she finally glanced over her shoulder to see if he stood watching her. She was alone. He had gone, and she wondered if they would ever again be relaxed and compatible the way they had been these past weeks.

Long after dark she went inside and began to gather scrapbooks and small things she wanted to take to Royal. There was nothing to hold her here at the ranch.

She propped up the pillows in her bed and sat against

them on top of the covers to look through the old scrapbooks. But they made her sad, so she finally scooted down in bed to go to sleep.

Tom lay awake in the dark. As long as he and Emily were together, there would be reminders of their tragic past, some little moments and some big ones, like the Nashes' visit. Their visit would tear Emily up. It would probably tear him up just as much. He wanted them to come by, but it was going to hurt and be difficult to deal with. It also brought all the memories swarming back, the pain, the fear, the terrible wreck and panic that had consumed him. His inadequacy, his failure to protect the two he loved most—that's what always tore him up.

He couldn't ever forget carrying his son's little body, holding Ryan, which was like holding ice, against his heart, praying for him, unaware of his own injuries until much later. And then the decision to donate Ryan's organs to save another child—to save other parents from going through what they'd suffered.

Tom wiped his eyes. As long as he and Emily were together, they would always have moments when the memories and pain would return full force.

The loss was devastating and it didn't get easier. They had moved on, but the hurt of missing little Ryan...that never changed. Tom knew that if he lived to be one hundred, he would still shed tears over his baby.

The Nashes' upcoming visit complicated the healing process for him. In a way, it was a stark reminder that he had failed Emily when he failed to save Ryan. He had loved her with his whole heart and still loved her in so many ways, but he just didn't know how to make it up to her. Tom was certain Emily would be better off without him in her life.

If they both started with new friends, new homes, new everything—new loves in their lives, even—maybe each day wouldn't be filled with pain and loss and sorrow.

Tuesday would be tough. He dreaded the day, but if he had taken the Nashes' call, he would have done the same thing Emily had and agreed to meet with them. Even though he knew it would be more heartache, he wanted to see the little girl who had Ryan's heart beating in her chest and giving her life.

Just the thought caused a knot in his throat. After Ryan, he had never been able to handle death and dying as well. Maybe it added to his heartache to have Jeremy's death so soon after losing Ryan.

Sleep wasn't going to come easily, probably not at all, but it wouldn't be his first sleepless night. Tom put his hands behind his head and looked out the open window at the stars. The divorce hung over them, and he wanted to go ahead and get it over and done with.

This living together in the same house again was gearing up to cause another big hurt for both of them. He ought to get out and let her go on with her life.

All the basic things were lined up to get done on Emily's old house. Nathan would send someone around to check on her, just like they were doing for Natalie. He and Emily needed to go ahead with their divorce.

Divorce was going to hurt because Emily was part

of his life and it was like cutting into himself, but it would be best for both of them, definitely better for her.

Would seeing Polly Nash tear them both up? Ryan's heart still beat—that was the most amazing thing. Little Polly Nash could live because she had Ryan's heart. They would meet her Tuesday afternoon—and for just a little while part of Ryan would once again be with them, at the only home Ryan had known. Tom stared through the window. It would be another day he would remember as long as he lived. So would Emily.

On Tuesday morning, Tom showered and got dressed in a navy Western-style shirt, jeans and his best black boots. When he was finished, he combed his hair and left the guesthouse.

At noon, he walked over to the mansion and rang the bell. When Emily didn't come to the door, he stepped inside.

"Emily?" he called. He heard her heels as she approached in the hall. Then she entered the room and he couldn't get his breath as he looked at her. Her wavy honey-brown hair fell loosely around her face. She wore little makeup, but had a natural beauty he loved. She wore a sheer pale blue top over a pale blue silk cami and white slacks with high-heeled blue sandals.

"You take my breath away, you look so beautiful."

"Thank you," she said quietly. "I think that should be my line, only substitute 'handsome' for 'beautiful.' You're the one who is dazzling."

"I'm not sure you have ever realized how beautiful I think you are."

"It's nice to hear you say that to me. I won't forget."
She smiled, but there was a sad look in her eyes.

"I want to do this, and at the same time, I know it's
going to hurt like hell."

"I know," she whispered. "You might as well come
in and sit. You're a little early, and they may have trouble finding the ranch."

They walked into the formal living room and she sat
in a dark blue wing chair while he went to the window
to look out at the drive.

"This week I think we should go ahead with the divorce," Tom said quietly. "I think each of us will be
better off. Reminders like today will always bring the
pain back, and I just don't think we're equipped to deal
with it together."

"I think we're dealing with it okay, Tom. Some things
will fade as the years go by."

"We're better off just starting anew." He turned to
face her. "You said you don't need me to stay with you
in Royal, so I've talked to Nathan and he'll send someone around to check on you."

"Thank you."

"Will you be all right there alone?"

"Yes, I will," she said, smiling, sitting back in the
chair and crossing her long legs, which momentarily
captured his attention and made him forget everything
else.

"I told you I'd deal with the roofers, and I think I
can get them out by the first of next week. How's that?"

"It will be fine. Thank you."

He gazed at her, thinking she was being very polite,

which meant she was keeping a tight rein on her feelings. She was probably upset about meeting the Nashes' daughter. He turned back to the window. He needed to get through meeting Polly Nash. Get through the divorce. Maybe then he would find some peace in life.

He saw a car approaching and he doubled his hands into fists. Once again, he asked himself why he hadn't died in place of his son. Emily might not have wanted that, but he did. And why hadn't he died instead of Jeremy, who was within yards of him when he took the enemy fire? Jeremy had had so much to live for.

Frowning, Tom watched the car approach, wondering about those two situations that he had survived. He had better do something useful with his life to make up for the fact that Ryan's and Jeremy's had been cut short.

Emily followed Tom to the front porch and they stood waiting to greet the family as they stepped out of their gray van. A slender woman with straight hair got out as her husband walked around the car to her. He was in tan slacks and a tan knit shirt. He held the door as his daughter stepped out. Polly Nash was a pretty little girl with brown hair and hazel eyes with thick brown lashes—the same coloring as Ryan. She stood politely with her mother and held a wrapped package in her hands.

"Mr. and Mrs. Knox, we're so glad to see you again. This is our daughter, Polly," Becky Nash said by way of greeting.

"Please just call us Tom and Emily," Emily said.

"And you can call us Becky and Jason," Polly's mother replied.

"Come inside," Tom said and held the door.

When they were all in the formal living room, Emily invited them to take a seat. "Thanks for calling us. Are you vacationing?"

"Yes," Jason Nash said. "We're on our way back to Colorado now and thought we'd stop because we were passing so close by."

"Polly has something for you," Becky said and nudged her daughter, who smiled shyly and took the present to Emily.

"Thank you, Polly," Emily said, smiling at the little girl. "How old are you?"

"I'm eight. I'm in the third grade."

"That's great. Third grade is a good year. Tom, come open this with me."

The package was wrapped in light blue paper with a big silver-and-blue ribbon tied in a huge bow. Tom slipped it off the package and Emily carefully undid the pretty wrapping paper. "Did you wrap this, Polly?"

"No, ma'am. Mom did," she said, glancing at her mother, who was smiling.

When they unwrapped the package, there was another in brown mailing paper and tape addressed to a school. Emily handed it to Tom, who took out his pocketknife and carefully cut into the brown paper. When he was done, he pushed the paper away and held up a framed picture of a schoolroom with a picture of a plaque on the wall. The plaque had a picture of Ryan in one corner.

Looking more closely at the plaque, Emily read aloud. "'This Jefferson music room is built, furnished and maintained in loving memory of Ryan Knox of Royal, Texas.'"

"We've done that in your son's memory at Polly's school in Colorado."

"Thank you so much," Emily said. "That is touching and kind of you."

"We want to express our thanks to your son and to you folks in some way that's permanent. You gave our Polly back to us, gave her a chance at life."

"That's a fine memorial," Tom said. "Thank all three of you."

Emily gazed at Ryan's smiling picture. "This is a lovely memorial, and it means so much to Tom and me. Hopefully, we'll get to visit the school and see this," she said, smiling at the Nashes.

Tom turned to Polly. "Do you have a music class?"

"Yes, sir," she answered politely. "I'm learning to play the violin and I take piano lessons. I like my books and I like my piano lessons," she said, smiling.

"She has lots of friends at school, too," Becky added.

"Have you ever been on a ranch?" Tom asked.

Polly shook her head. "No, I haven't."

"Want to see the barn and the horses?"

She looked at her parents. "I think that's a yes," her dad said and stood. "I'll go with you and we'll look a little." He held out his hand and Polly took it. It reminded Emily of how she used to hold Ryan's hand, and she felt a tug on her heart.

Tom walked out with them, sounding friendly and

cheerful, telling Polly about the ranch, but Emily wondered what his cheer was costing him.

"She's a sweet little girl," Becky said. "And I can't say enough how thankful we are—you've given our little girl life," she said, getting tears in her eyes. "That memorial is just a token gesture. We're looking into a college scholarship. Whatever we do, you'll be notified. We wanted to come here to show our gratitude in person."

"We're thrilled that Ryan's heart is giving her life," Emily said.

"I pray for you and your husband every day, and I give thanks that we are blessed to have our little girl. We just owe all of that to you and your husband."

"It's a miracle of science, and I'm thrilled we could help. Polly seems so sweet and bright."

Emily sat and talked to Becky until the others came back, Polly skipping ahead of the men. Emily's heart clutched again as she watched her.

After Polly told her mother about the three horses she had seen, Becky looked over Polly's head at Emily. "We have a lot of miles and should go, but before we do, would you like to feel her heartbeat? We've talked to her about it and she knows where she got her heart and she's happy for you to feel it beating."

Emily stood and crossed the room. "Is it all right if I touch you, Polly?"

Polly smiled and nodded. Emily put her hand on Polly's chest and felt the steady beat of the heart that had given life to her son. For an instant she experienced a renewed tie to her child. Tears filled her eyes.

Emily turned away, wiping at her tears. "Tom," she said. He stood close, and she took his hand and placed it on Polly's small chest.

"That's part of Ryan," he whispered and turned away. Becky wiped her eyes, too.

"We can never tell you what your gift has meant to us except that our Polly wouldn't be here with us today if it hadn't been for your Ryan. We're sorry for your loss. We are so grateful for your gift of life for Polly."

Emily looked into Polly's hazel eyes. "Thank you," she said softly. "Polly, thank you. You share a special tie with our little baby. Thank you." Emily moved away.

She and Tom went out with the Nashes to see them off. Standing on the drive waving as they drove off, Emily knew they would not see each other again.

Without waiting for Tom, she turned and went inside, walking to the kitchen to get a drink of water. She put her head in her hands and cried.

When she felt composed, she went back to the formal living room but found it empty. She walked out to the porch, but Tom was nowhere around. She looked at the guest cottage down the drive and saw no sign of him, but she suspected he was already there and she wouldn't see him again today. She had seen Tom's tears and knew he would be hurting badly.

Once again, she thought about her losses—of her son and her husband, the only man she had ever loved or ever would love. But he was as lost to her as Ryan. Next would come the divorce, and then she didn't know if she would ever see him again.

She felt as if she was losing him for the second time,

but this time, it would be permanent. She went to the bedroom where she was staying.

Soon Tom would be out of her life. She would have to make her own life.

She walked through the house to go upstairs and movement caught her eye. She realized Tom was outside in the back. He was standing on the patio, looking at the pool or the yard or something beyond him. She went out.

"I thought you had gone home."

"Not yet, but I'm going. I wanted to wait until the Nashes were gone." He wiped his eyes. Once again, there was a time she would have gone to him and put her arms around him. Now she knew he really wouldn't want her to do that. The wall was back between them.

He turned around to face her. His eyes were red, and she guessed hers probably were, too. "I think it's time for that divorce. We'll each be better off."

"I know, Tom. It's all right," she said. She looked at his broad shoulders and wondered if he was right. "I'll go back to Uncle Woody's tomorrow. If you can get someone to help me, I'd like to move a few things from here. Can I borrow a pickup?"

"Don't ask stuff like that. Do whatever you damn please. We share this ranch. I'll get two guys to help and you take anything and everything you want. You know how much this house means to me."

That hurt, because this house was where they had spent some wonderful years and it was the only home Ryan had known except Uncle Woody's.

"Thank you for all you did for me in Royal."

"I'll keep up with the window guys, also the floor people and the roofers. The floors should be done in two weeks. I'll check and let you know." He stood looking at her. "I'm going back to the guesthouse. What time do you want the guys here tomorrow?"

"I should be ready at about ten o'clock. I'll take some things. I may want to come back and get some more."

"Sure. Do what you want. Let me know if you need help." He looked at her a long time and turned away, passing her and going inside. She suspected he walked straight through and out the front and was headed to the guest cottage.

She went in, walking to the window to watch, and saw she was right. He walked with that straight back that people in the military develop. With each step he was walking out of her life.

She thought about Ryan's heart beating in Polly's chest. Her baby's heart—still beating, giving life to another child. Longing for Ryan, to hold him again and hear his laughter, swamped Emily. Longing for Tom quickly followed, to have his strong arms around her, his solid reassurance. She put her head in her hands and cried, aware she was losing Tom now even though she still loved him with all her heart. They'd had unhappy moments and she thought their love had crumbled, but she realized that was one more mistake. She loved him and she always would.

When she had calmed down, she locked up and went upstairs to sit on the balcony of the big master bedroom and cried some more. She hurt over both of them and she knew she would continue to hurt.

* * *

The next day she called Tom and didn't get an answer. She selected furniture she wanted and called their foreman, Gus. He already knew she was taking furniture to the house in Royal and he had three guys to help and two pickups and they were ready when she was.

Wondering where Tom was, she told Gus to send the men over. In a short time they were on the drive by the back door. She knew all three—Bix Smith, Ty Green and Marty Holcomb.

She showed them which pieces of furniture to pack up. Tom didn't want anything to do with the house, so she took what she wanted.

She drove her car to Royal behind the two pickups and they spent the morning unloading furniture. The men left before noon, and when she was alone, she looked around, remembering Tom in every room and the happiness she'd had while they worked on the renovations together. The time had been good, but why couldn't life ahead be filled with a lot more good times? They had been through the worst. She stood gazing down the hall, seeing Tom there, smiling, flirting with her, making her laugh. Why were they getting a divorce when they had so much between them that was wonderful and fulfilling?

Thinking about their future, she drove down Main Street, turning on the block where her studio was located. As she stepped out of her car, the enticing smell of baking bread assailed her and she remembered Tom buying two loaves and eating half of one himself that night. She went into the bakery and bought two more loaves. She could always freeze them if she didn't eat them.

She went into her studio to pick up her mail and saw two other proofs of Tom's pictures on her desk. She picked one up and looked at him. "I love you," she whispered.

And that's when it hit her.

"We can't give up what we have," she said. "We're not going to get a divorce, Tom Knox, because life with you is too awesome. It's way too marvelous to give up." She sat there staring at his picture. She didn't want a divorce. They'd had wonderful moments in the past weeks they were together. They had weathered the worst and survived and they still could enjoy each other's company.

She was going back to the ranch to find Tom and tell him she didn't want the divorce. She still had clothes at the ranch, so she didn't have to go home and get anything.

As she drove back to the ranch, she missed Tom and thought about the happiness they'd had together. Their love had moments when it was so great. She also thought about their lovemaking, which had been exciting and bound them together closer than ever. She wasn't ready to give up on their marriage. Not after the time she had spent with him.

But there was still the question of children. She thought about Tom as a father. He needed children in his life. She did, too. He was willing to adopt and he was right—they both would love any child in their lives. Why had she been so opposed to adoption? If she'd only agreed to adopt, this divorce wouldn't be looming in her life. Another big mistake she had made. But mistakes could be fixed sometimes. She hoped it wasn't too late.

As soon as she turned onto the ranch road, she called Tom, but he didn't answer. She didn't see his pickup at the guesthouse when she passed it, so he must be out on the ranch.

She decided to stay at the mansion until she reached him. She tried the rest of the day and that night, but when she still didn't get him at midnight, she wondered if he had stopped taking her calls.

She slept little that night, pacing the floor and thinking about Tom, their past and their future.

By morning she was firmly set in her opinions about their future.

She didn't intend to walk away and lose him, because for the past few weeks, he had acted like a man in love. And she was definitely in love with him. She had fallen in love with him when she was sixteen and she had never stopped loving him.

She had made mistakes that might still cost her the marriage—like being so uptight about getting pregnant. Tom was right and they should just adopt. He was wonderful with any kids he was ever around.

Had he already signed the divorce papers?

It didn't matter. They could marry again. She wasn't giving up, because the days they had spent together had been a reunion for them, binding them together stronger than ever. He thought when they were together, they compounded the hurts. They might sometimes, but they definitely did not compound the bad times often.

Life had rough times, and Tom was tough enough to weather them. And so was she. Together they would do better at getting through them.

She showered, brushing out her long wavy hair and pulling on a red T-shirt, jeans and boots. She left to find him, walking to the guesthouse. He wasn't there, so she had called Gus, who said he hadn't seen Tom but thought he was still on the ranch.

She stood in front of the guesthouse and then she thought about where she might find him. She drove to the most beautiful spot on the ranch, a gradual slope that had a winding, shallow stream along the bottom. There were big oaks planted inside the small area that had a white picket fence around it. It was the plot of land she and Tom had picked out together for the cemetery where Ryan was buried, with a marble angel standing beside the marble headstone and a bank of blooming Texas Lilac Vitex on either side. Tom stood in the shade of one of the oaks with his pickup parked outside the fence.

When he saw her coming, he turned to face her and waited as she came through the gate.

He had on his black Stetson and a black cotton shirt, along with jeans and black boots. He looked wonderful to her.

"I was just about to leave to find you. I figured I'd have to drive to Royal. I thought you went back to town."

"I did, but I came back. I thought I would find you here at the family cemetery. This place holds so much meaning for us."

"It's quiet out here and I can think about Ryan and

about us, the past, the present—these days we've spent together. Think about this miracle of another little child having Ryan's heart that is givng her life."

"I know you used to come out here and just stay for a while."

"For me, it brings up so many good memories. Working on your house together, we added some more good moments."

As he stepped closer, he raised an eyebrow. "Why were you looking for me?"

A breeze tugged at her hair as she faced him.

"Will you come home with me?"

She saw the flare of surprise in his eyes. "I love you, and I don't want a divorce," she said. "Ever since I received the email from Maverick, you have acted like a man in love. We've had a lot of love between us, and I'm not ready to give up on this marriage." She hugged him tightly. "I know I've made mistakes, Tom, but we can work through the problems."

He wrapped his arms around her to kiss her, a kiss that was an answer by itself. Trembling, she clung to him and kissed him back while joy filled her because he would never kiss her this way if he was going to divorce her.

He released her slightly, letting his hands rest on her shoulders again. "Before we go any further, there's something I have to say." His expression was solemn and suddenly she wondered if she had guessed wrong, that his possessive and responsive kiss was goodbye.

Cold fear wrapped around her again. "What is it?"

"Ah, Em, I'm so sorry. I failed you both, you and

Ryan. I couldn't save him. I failed you then in the worst way," Tom said, looking beyond her.

"You didn't fail me. You didn't fail him, either. Don't blame yourself when you are blameless."

"Yes, I did. I should have saved him."

"You couldn't. The doctors said he died from the trauma caused by his injuries in the bus," she said. "You didn't fail me or Ryan, because you did the very best you could. All of Ryan's life, you were an amazing father, and Ryan wanted to be just like you."

"I've always felt I failed you both. I don't know, Em—"

"Well, I know what I want and what I need. Our marriage has been good again—joyous, sexy, productive. We've been best friends and enjoyed each other's company, helped each other. We can do this. I'm not giving up on our marriage," she said, squeezing him tightly as if by holding him she could keep him from doing anything to end their union.

She looked up at him and he brushed her hair from her face to gaze into her eyes.

He stepped back and reached into his jeans pocket, struggling to pull something out. "That's why I was going to town. I wanted to find you and tell you that I don't want the damn divorce. I love you with all my heart and I need you in my life."

Tears of joy filled her eyes as she hugged him. "I love you. We can get through life together. Tom, I love you so."

Wrapping his arms around her, he kissed her again and this time her heart pounded with joy. He leaned away.

"You were always so strong," he said. "Too strong. I didn't think you needed me anymore."

"Yes, I do. I need you desperately. I'm unhappy without you. And I'm complete when we're together. Tom, there will be problems, but we can work through them. I love you. I need you." She looked into his hazel eyes that she loved, eyes that could melt her and at other times give her strength. "There will always be problems. That's life, but we're better at handling them when we're together. I love you and I need you."

"I love you more than you'll ever know and I want to spend my life trying to show you." He released her and held out his hand. "I got this for you after we saw the Nash family."

Surprised, she examined the small velvet box. She couldn't imagine what he was giving her. She looked up at him and he smiled.

"Are you going to see what your present is?"

"Yes," she said, taking the box to open it. Inside was a tangle of a piece of jewelry. She picked it up and gasped as a necklace shook out in her hand. It was a golden heart pendant on a thin gold chain that was covered with diamonds.

"Oh, my heavens, Tom. It's beautiful."

"It's because of Ryan giving life with his heart to little Polly Nash. That holds meaning for both of us. It's a locket."

"Let me see. This is gorgeous—" She gasped when she opened the locket. "Tom, this is wonderful. I'll treasure this always," she said, hugging him again and kissing him longer this time while he held her tightly in his embrace.

She leaned away and held the locket up so they could both look inside at the picture of Ryan smiling into the camera. "You selected this locket for me. You must have changed your mind right after you told me we should go ahead with the divorce."

"It didn't take long. I've spent a year living in the guesthouse alone and then we've had this fantastic time together. No matter what we go through, I want you with me. I thought about it and I've loved you always. You're the only woman for me for the rest of my life. I love you. I'd give my life for you. I've loved you since you ran into my car when we were sixteen. And, Em, you worry so about having my child—"

"We can adopt. You're right. I watched you with the Valentine kids and I played with them and if we adopt, we'll love them like our own. We both would love any child we raised. Whatever you want to do. We can go without kids. There are loads of kids we can help without raising them—through reading programs, starting a ranch camp for kids, playing ball, you know, things you can help with and so can I."

He studied her. "You've got this all figured out, haven't you?"

"I'm desperate. I don't want to lose you, because I love you with all my heart. And you have never failed me, Tom. Never. You couldn't save Ryan. I couldn't save Ryan. The doctors couldn't save him. But you didn't fail me. You tried all you could."

"You're sure?" he asked.

"With all my heart. Please put my locket on me." She handed him the necklace and turned so he could fasten it at the back of her neck. "You really got this since we saw the Nashes?"

"I have a jeweler in Dallas. I sent a text, he sent me pictures of what he had. I picked out this one and told him I wanted it delivered yesterday."

"Oh, my word. Someone from the jewelry store drove this to you?"

"That's right. I didn't want to wait. We've been separated way too long, my love."

She turned to face him. "This is wonderful, Tom, but most of all is knowing you'll be in my life."

"Baby, you're all that I need, and I'll spend the rest of my life making that clear to you. Em, I've thought all this time that you were angry because I failed you—"

"Never. We've both made big mistakes, but we've survived them and some of them we're able to let go and try to forget. They're not part of our lives any longer." She slipped her arms around him. "I'm so happy. I love you with all my heart. I know we'll be all right."

"I know we will. But how the hell do you undo a divorce?"

"I'm leaving that one to you. Oh, how I love you. I'll show you, too. It's time to leave here and go home. Oh, my heavens, we don't have a home," she said, frowning as she looked up at him. "You can't be a rancher and live in Uncle Woody's house in Royal. Neither of us wants to live in the mansion. We're not both living in the guesthouse."

Tom held her with his arms around her waist as he smiled at her. "It's just another problem we'll work out. What do you think about finishing your Royal house? Then that will be our town house and you can still work in town part of the week if you want. And maybe it's time for a redo of ranch house. Or we can demolish it if you want and start over."

"We'll talk about that one—I vote for the redo because we have good memories there. I'll live on the ranch with you and maybe drive into town and keep the studio open by appointment only. But come home with me now," she said. "I've got two new loaves of bread for you in the car. How's that? And maybe some fun in the bedroom?"

"You've got a deal." Laughing, he pulled her into his embrace. "But I don't want to wait to show you how much I've missed you. We're not driving to Royal now. We're going to live in the guesthouse for a little while. I'll tell Gus we're going to Royal and he's in charge, but today, I don't want to drive any farther than our guesthouse. I have plans for us and that bread."

She laughed, looking into his eyes and seeing the happiness mirrored there that she felt.

"Tom, I'm not sure I felt this excited on our wedding day."

"It's a bigger deal now, Em. We know what we lost, what we almost lost and what we have. Our love is the essential part of our lives and we have our memories of Ryan to share. I want to spend every day of the rest of my life trying to show you how much I love you."

His words thrilled her as much as the look in his

eyes. She stood on tiptoe and he leaned closer to kiss her while he embraced her.

Joy poured into her that there wouldn't be any divorce. She loved him—always had and always would. As she returned his kiss, she thought their future was filled with promise and hope.

* * * * *

*August 2017: TEMPTED BY THE WRONG TWIN
by* USA TODAY *bestselling author Rachel Bailey.*

*September 2017: TAKING HOME THE TYCOON
by* USA TODAY *bestselling author Catherine Mann.*

*October 2017: BILLIONAIRE'S BABY BIND
by* USA TODAY *bestselling author
Katherine Garbera.*

*November 2017: THE TEXAN TAKES A WIFE
by* USA TODAY *bestselling author Charlene Sands.*

*December 2017: BEST MAN UNDER THE
MISTLETOE by* USA TODAY *bestselling author
Kathie DeNosky.*

* * *

*If you're on Twitter, tell us what you
think of Mills & Boon! #mills&boon*

"We're going to be awesome parents."

"The best," he agreed. "And don't worry about the wedding expenses. I'm going to pay for everything."

"You don't have to do that."

"I want to." He touched her cheek, then lifted his hand away. "But what am I going to do during the part of the ceremony where I'm supposed to kiss my bride?"

She wet her lips, a bit too quickly. "You'll have to kiss her, I guess."

"She's going to have to kiss me back, too."

Her pulse fluttered at her neck, as soft as a butterfly, as sexy as a summer breeze. "Yes, she will."

As they both fell silent, she glanced away, trapped in feelings she couldn't seem to control. She didn't want to imagine what the wedding kiss was going to be like.

Still, she wondered how it would unfold. Would he whisper something soft and soothing before he leaned into her? Would their mouths be slightly open, their eyes completely closed? Would she sigh and melt against him, like a princess being awakened by the wrong prince?

Just thinking about it felt forbidden.

* * *

Paper Wedding, Best-Friend Bride
is part of the Billionaire Brothers Club series—
Three foster brothers grow up, get rich…
and find the perfect woman.

PAPER WEDDING, BEST-FRIEND BRIDE

BY
SHERI WHITEFEATHER

MILLS & BOON

HarperCollins
PUBLISHERS
Since 1817

First Published in Great Britain 2017
By Mills & Boon, an imprint of HarperCollins*Publishers*
1 London Bridge Street, London, SE1 9GF

© 2017 Sheree Henry-Whitefeather

ISBN: 978-0-263-92812-9

51-0317

Printed and bound in Spain
by CPI, Barcelona

Sheri WhiteFeather is an award-winning, bestselling author. She writes a variety of romance novels for Mills & Boon and is known for incorporating Native American elements into her stories. She has two grown children, who are tribally enrolled members of the Muscogee Creek Nation. She lives in California and enjoys shopping in vintage stores and visiting art galleries and museums. Sheri loves to hear from her readers at www.sheriwhitefeather.com.

One

Lizzie McQueen emerged from a graceful dip in Max Marquez's black-bottom pool, water glistening on her bikini-clad body.

Reminiscent of a slow-motion scene depicted in a movie, she stepped onto the pavement and reached for a towel, and he watched every long-legged move she made. While she dried herself off, he swigged his root beer and pretended that he wasn't checking out her perfectly formed cleavage or gold pierced navel or—

"Come on, Max, quit giving me *the look*."

Caught in the act, he dribbled the stupid drink down his chin. She shook her head and tossed him her towel. He cursed beneath his breath and wiped his face.

The look was code for when either of them ogled the other in an inappropriate manner. They'd agreed quite a while ago that sex, or anything that could possibly lead to it, was off the table. They cared too much about each other to ruin their friendship with a few deliciously hot romps in the sack. Even now, at thirty years old, they held a platonic promise between them.

She smoothed back her fiery red hair, placed a big, floppy hat on her head and stretched out on the chaise next to him. Max lived in a 1930s Beachwood Canyon mansion, and Lizzie resided in an ultra-modern condo. She spent more time at his place than he did at hers because he preferred it that way. His Los Angeles lair was bigger, badder and much more private.

He returned the towel, only now it had his soda stain on it. She rolled her eyes, and they shared a companionable grin.

He handed her a bottle of sunscreen. "You better reapply this."

She sighed. "Me and my sensitive skin."

He liked her ivory complexion. But he'd seen her get some nasty sunburns, too. He didn't envy her that. She slathered on the lotion, and he considered how they'd met during their senior year in high school. They were being paired up on a chemistry project, and, even then, she'd struck him as a debutant-type girl.

Later he'd learned that she was originally from Savannah, Georgia, with ties to old money. In that regard, his assessment of her had been correct, and just being near her had sent his boyhood longings into a tailspin. Not only was she gorgeous; she was everything he'd wanted to be: rich, prestigious, popular.

But Max had bottomed out on the other end of the spectrum: a skinny, dorky Native American foster kid with a genius IQ and gawky social skills, leaving him open to scorn and ridicule.

Of course, Lizzie's life hadn't been as charmed as he'd assumed it was. Once he'd gotten to know her, she'd revealed her deepest, darkest secrets to him, just as he'd told her his.

Supposedly during that time, when they were pouring their angst-riddled hearts out to each other, she'd actually formed a bit of a crush on him. But even till this day, he found that hard to fathom. In what alternate universe did prom queens get infatuated with dorks?

She peered at him from beneath the fashionable brim of her pale beige hat. Her bathing suit was a shimmering shade of copper with a leopard-print trim, and her meticulously manicured nails were painted a soft warm pink. Every lovely thing about her purred, "trust fund heiress," which was exactly what she was.

"What are you thinking about?" she asked.

He casually answered, "What a nerd I used to be."

She teased him with a smile. "As opposed to the sexy billionaire you are today?"

"Right." He laughed a little. "Because nothing says beefcake like a software designer and internet entrepreneur."

She moved her gaze along the muscle-whipped length of his body. "You've done all right for yourself."

He raised his eyebrows. "Now who's giving who *the look*?"

She shrugged off her offense. "You shouldn't have become such a hottie if you didn't want to get noticed."

That wasn't the reason he'd bulked up, and she darned well knew it. Sure, he'd wanted to shed his nerdy image, but he'd started hitting the gym after high school for more than aesthetic purposes. His favorite sport was boxing. Sometimes he shadowboxed and sometimes he pounded the crap out of a heavy bag. But mostly he did it to try to pummel the demons that plagued him. He was a runner, too. So was Lizzie. They ran like a tornado was chasing them. Or their pasts, which was pretty much the same thing.

"Beauty and the brainiac," he said. "We were such a teenage cliché."

"Why, because you offered to tutor me when I needed it? That doesn't make us a cliché. Without your help, I would never have gotten my grades up to par or attended my mother's alma mater."

Silent, Max nodded. She'd also been accepted into her mom's old sorority, which had been another of her goals. But none of that had brought her the comfort she'd sought.

"The twentieth anniversary is coming up," she said.

Of her mom's suicide, he thought. Lizzie was ten when her high-society mother had swallowed an entire bottle of sleeping pills. "I'm sorry you keep reliving it." She mentioned it every year around this time, and even now he could see her childhood pain.

She put the sunscreen aside, placing it on a side table, where her untouched iced tea sat. "I wish I could forget about her."

"I know." He couldn't get his mom out of his head, either, especially the day she'd abandoned him, leaving him alone in their run-down apartment. He was eight years old, and she'd parked him in front of the TV, warning him to stay there until she got back. She was only supposed to be gone for a few hours, just long enough to score the crack she routinely smoked. Max waited for her return, but she never showed up. Scared out of his young mind, he'd fended for himself for three whole days, until he'd gone to a neighbor for help. "My memories will probably never stop haunting me, either."

"We do have our issues."

"Yeah, we do." Max was rescued and placed in foster

care, and a warrant was issued for his mom's arrest. But she'd already hit the road with her latest loser boyfriend, where she'd partied too hard and overdosed before the police caught up with her.

"What would you say to your mother if she was still alive?" Lizzie asked.

"Nothing."

"You wouldn't tell her off?"

"No." He wouldn't say a single word to her.

"You wouldn't even ask her why she used to hurt you?"

Max shook his head. There wasn't an answer in the world that would make sense, so what would be the point? When Mom hadn't been kicking him with her cheap high heels or smacking him around, she'd taken to burning him with cigarette butts and daring him not to cry. But her most common form of punishment was locking him in his closet, where she'd told him that the Lakota two-faced monsters dwelled.

The legends about these humanoid creatures varied. In some tales, it was a woman who'd been turned into this type of being after trying to seduce the sun god. One of her faces was beautiful, while the other was hideous. In other stories, it was a man with a second face on the back of his head. Making eye contact with him would get you tortured and killed. Cannibalism and kidnapping were among his misdeeds, too, with a malevolent glee for preying on misbehaving children.

The hours Max had spent in his darkened closet, cowering from the monsters and praying for his drugged-out mother to remove the chair that barred the door, would never go away.

He cleared his throat and said, "Mom's worst crime was her insistence that she loved me. But you already know all this." He polished off the last of his root beer and crushed the can between his palms, squeezing the aluminum down to nearly nothing. He repeated another thing she already knew. "I swear, I never want to hear another woman say that to me again."

"I could do without someone saying that to me, too. Sure, love is supposed to be the cure-all, but not for…"

"People like us?"

She nodded, and he thought about how they tumbled in and out of affairs. Max went through his lovers like wine. Lizzie wasn't any better. She didn't get attached to her bedmates, either.

"At least I have my charity work," she said.

He was heavily involved in nonprofits, too, with it being a significant part of his life. "Do you think it's enough?"

"What?" She raised her delicately arched brows. "Helping other people? Of course it is."

"Then why am I still so dissatisfied?" He paused to study the sparkling blue of her eyes and the way her hair was curling in damp waves around her shoulders. "And why are you still stressing over your mom's anniversary?"

She picked up her tea, sipped, put it back down. "We're only human."

"I know. But I should be ashamed of myself for feeling this way. I got everything I ever wanted. I mean, seriously, look at this place." He scowled at his opulent surroundings. How rich and privileged and spoiled could he be?

"I thought your sabbatical helped." She seemed to be evaluating how long he'd been gone, separating himself from her and everyone else.

He'd taken nearly a year off to travel the world, to search for inner peace. He'd also visited hospitals and orphanages and places where he'd hoped to make a difference. "The most significant part of that experience was the months I spent in Nulah. It's a small island country in the South Pacific. I'd never been there before, so I didn't really know what to expect. Anyway, what affected me was this kid I came across in an orphanage there. A five-year-old boy named Tokoni."

She cocked her head. "Why haven't you mentioned him before now?"

"I don't know." He conjured up an image of the child's big brown eyes and dazzling smile. "Maybe I was trying to keep him to myself a little longer and imagine him with the family his mother wanted him to have. When he was two, she left him at the orphanage, hoping that someone would adopt him and give him a better life. She wasn't abusive to him, like my mother was to me. She just knew that she couldn't take proper care of him. Nulah is traditional in some areas, with old-world views, and rough and dangerous in others. It didn't used to be so divided, but it started suffering from outside influences."

"Like drugs and prostitution and those sorts of things?"

"Yes, and Tokoni's mother lived in a seedy part of town and was struggling to find work. She'd already lost her family in a boating accident, so there was no one left to help her."

"What about the boy's father?" she asked. "How does he fit into this?"

"He was an American tourist who made all sorts of promises, saying he was going to bring her to the States and marry her. But in the end, he didn't do anything, except ditch her and the kid."

"Oh, how awful." Lizzie's voice broke a little. "That

makes me sad for her, living on a shattered dream, waiting for a man to whisk her away."

It disturbed Max, too. "She kept in touch with the orphanage for a while, waiting to see if Tokoni ever got a permanent home, but then she caught pneumonia and died. The old lady who operates the place told me the story. It's a private facility that survives on charity. I already donated a sizable amount to help keep them on track."

She made a thoughtful expression. "I can write an article about them to drum up more support, if you want."

"That would be great." Max appreciated the offer. Lizzie hosted a successful philanthropy blog with tons of noble-hearted followers. "I just wish someone would adopt Tokoni. He's the coolest kid, so happy all the time." So different from how Max was as a child. "He's at the age where he talks about getting adopted and thinks it's going to happen. He's been working on this little picture book, with drawings of the mommy and daddy he's convinced he's going to have. They're just stick figures with smiley faces, but to him, they're real."

"Oh, my goodness." She tapped a hand against her heart. "That's so sweet."

"He's a sweet kid. I've been wanting to return to the island to see him again. Just to let him know that I haven't forgotten about him."

"Then you should plan another trip soon."

"Yeah, I should." Max could easily rearrange his schedule to make it happen. "Hey, here's an idea. Do you want to come to Nulah with me to meet him?" He suspected that Lizzie could manage her time to accommodate a trip, as well. She'd always been a bit of a jetsetter, a spontaneous society girl ready to leave town on a whim. But mostly she traveled for humanitarian causes, so this was right up her alley. "While we're there, you can interview the woman who operates the orphanage for the feature you're going to do on your blog."

"Sure. I can go with you. I'd like to see the orphanage and conduct an in-person interview. But I should probably spend most of my time with her and let you visit with Tokoni on your own. You know how kids never really take to me."

"You just need to relax around them." Although Lizzie championed hundreds of children's charities, she'd never gotten the gist of communicating with kids, especially the younger ones. A side effect from her own youth, he thought, from losing her mom and forcing herself to grow up too fast. "For the record, I think you and Tokoni will hit it off just fine. In fact, I think he's going to be impressed with you."

"You do?" She adjusted her lounge chair, moving it to a more upright position. "What makes you say that?"

"In his culture redheads are said to descend from nobility, from a goddess ruler who dances with fire, and your hair is as bright as it gets." Max sat forward, too, and leaned toward her. "He'll probably think you're a princess or something. But you were homecoming queen. So it's not as if you didn't have your reign."

Her response fell flat. "That doesn't count."

He remembered going to the football game that night, sitting alone in the bleachers, watching her receive her crown. He'd skipped the homecoming dance. He wouldn't have been able to blend in there. Getting a date would have been difficult, too. As for Lizzie, she'd attended the dance with the tall, tanned star of the boys' swim team. "It counted back then."

"Not to me, not like it should have. It wasn't fair that my other friends didn't accept you."

"Well, I got the last laugh, didn't I?"

She nodded, even if neither of them was laughing.

Before things got too morose, he reached out and tugged on a strand of her hair. "Don't fret about being royalty to me. The only redhead that influenced my culture was a woodpecker."

She sputtered into a laugh and slapped his hand away. "Gee, thanks, for that compelling tidbit."

He smiled, pleased by her reaction. "It's one of those old American Indian tales. I told it to Tokoni when he was putting a puzzle together with pictures of birds." Max stopped smiling. "The original story involves love. But I left off that part when I told Tokoni. I figured he was too young to understand it. Plus, it would have been hypocritical of me to tell it that way."

She took a ladylike sip of her tea. "Now I'm curious about the original version and just how lovey-dovey it is."

"It's pretty typical, I guess." He went ahead and recited it, even if he preferred it without the romance. "It's about a hunter who loves a girl from his village, but she's never even noticed him. He thinks about her all the time. He even has trouble sleeping because he can't get her off his mind. So he goes to the forest to be alone, where he hears a beautiful song that lulls him to sleep. That night, he dreams about a woodpecker who says, 'Follow me and I'll show you how to make this song.' In the morning, he sees a real woodpecker and follows him. The bird is tapping on a branch and the familiar song is coming from it. Later, the hunter returns home with the branch and tries to make the music by waving it in the air, but it doesn't work."

Lizzie removed her hat. By now the sun was shifting in the sky, moving behind the trees and dappling her in scattered light. But mostly what Max noticed was how intense she looked, listening to the silly myth. Or was her intensity coming from the energy that always seemed to dance between them? The sexiness that seeped through their pores?

Ignoring the feeling, he continued by saying, "The hunter has another dream where the woodpecker shows him how to blow on the wood and tap the holes to make the song he'd first heard. Obviously, it's a flute the bird made. But neither the hunter nor his people had ever seen this type of instrument before."

She squinted at him. "What happens with the girl?"

"Once she hears the hunter's beautiful song, she looks into his eyes and falls in love with him, just as he'd always loved her. But like I said, I told it to Tokoni without the romance."

She was still squinting, intensity still etched on her face. "Where did you first come across this story? Was it in one of the books you used to read?"

"Yes." When he was in foster care, he'd researched his culture, hoping to find something good in it. "I hated that the only thing my mom ever talked about was the scary stuff. But I'm glad that Tokoni's mother tried to do right by him."

"Me, too." She spoke softly. "Parents are supposed to want what's best for their children."

He met her gaze, and she stared back at him, almost like the girl in the hunter's tale—except that love didn't appeal to either of them.

But desire did. If Lizzie wasn't his best friend, if she was someone he could kiss without consequence, he would lock lips with her right now, pulling her as close to him as he possibly could. And with the way she was looking at him, she would probably let him kiss the hell out of her. But that wouldn't do either of them any good.

"I appreciate you coming to Nulah with me," he said, trying to shake off the heat of wanting her. "It means a lot to me, having you there."

"I know it does," she replied, reaching for his hand.

But it was only the slightest touch. She pulled away quickly. Determined, it seemed, to control her hunger for him, too.

A myriad of thoughts skittered through Lizzie's mind. Today she and Max were leaving on their trip, and she should be done packing, as he would be arriving soon to pick her up. Yet she was still sorting haphazardly through her clothes and placing them in her suitcase. Normally Lizzie was far more organized. But for now she couldn't think clearly.

She hated it when her attraction to Max dragged her under its unwelcome spell, and lately it seemed to be getting worse. But they'd both learned to deal with it, just as she was trying to get a handle on how his attachment to Tokoni was making her feel. Even with his troubled past, being around children was easy for Max. Lizzie was terribly nervous about meeting the boy. Kids didn't relate to her in the fun-and-free way they did with him. Of course her stodgy behavior in their presence didn't help. But no matter how hard she tried, she couldn't seem to change that side of herself.

After her mother had drifted into a deathly sleep, she'd compensated for the loss by taking on the characteristics of an adult, long before she should have.

But what choice did she have? Her grieving father had bailed out on parenthood, leaving her with nannies and cooks. He'd immersed himself in his high-powered work and business travels, allowing her to grow up in a big lonely house full of strangers. Lizzie didn't have any extended family to speak of.

Even after all these years, she and her dad barely communicated. Was it any wonder that she'd gone off to Columbia University searching for a connection to her mom? She'd even taken the same journalism major. She'd walked in her mother's path, but it hadn't done a bit of good. She'd returned with the same disjointed feelings.

Her memories of her mom were painfully odd: scattered images of a beautifully fragile blonde who used to stare unblinkingly at herself in the mirror, who used to give lavish parties and tell Lizzie how essential it was for a young lady of her standing to be a good hostess, who used to laugh at the drop of a hat and then cry just as easily. Mama's biggest ambition was to be awarded the Pulitzer Prize. But mostly she just threw away her writings. Sometimes she even burned them, tossing them into the fireplace and murmuring to herself in French, the language of her ancestors.

Mama was rife with strange emotions, with crazy behaviors, but she was warm and loving, too, cuddling Lizzie at night. Without her sweet, dreamy mother by her side, Elizabeth "Lizzie" McQueen had been crushed, like a bug on a long white limousine's windshield.

After Mama killed herself, Dad sold their Savannah home, got a new job in Los Angeles and told Lizzie that she was going to be a California kid from then on.

But by that time she'd already gotten used to imitating her mother's lady-of-the-manor ways, presenting a rich-girl image that made her popular. Nonetheless, she'd lied to her new friends, saying that her socialite mother had suffered a brain aneurysm. Dad told his new workmates the same phony story. Lizzie had been coaxed by him to protect their privacy, and she'd embraced the lie.

Until she met Max.

She'd felt compelled to reveal the truth to him. But he was different from her other peers—a shy, lonely boy, who was as damaged as she was.

The doorbell rang, and Lizzie caught her breath.

She dashed to answer the summons, and there he was: Max Marquez, with his longish black hair shining like a raven's wing. He wore it parted down the middle and falling past his neck, but not quite to his shoulders. His deeply set eyes were brown, but sometimes they looked as black as his hair. His face was strong and angular, with a bone structure to die for. The gangly teenager he'd once been was gone. He'd grown into a fiercely handsome man.

"Are you ready?" he asked.

She shook her head. "Sorry. No. I'm still packing."

He entered her condo. "That's okay. I'll text my pilot and tell him we're running late."

Lizzie nodded. Max's success provided him the luxury of a private jet. She'd inherited her mother's old Savannah money, but she was nowhere as wealthy as he was. He wasn't the only Native American foster kid in LA who'd made good. He remained close to two of his foster brothers, who'd also become billionaires. Max had been instrumental in helping them attain their fortunes, loaning them money to get their businesses off the ground.

He followed her into her room, where her suitcase was on the bed, surrounded by the clothes she'd been sorting.

He lifted a floral-printed dress from the pile. "This is pretty." He glanced at a lace bra and panty set. "And those." Clearly, he was teasing her, as if making a joke was easier than anything else he could think of doing or saying.

"Knock it off." She grabbed the lingerie and shoved them into a pouch on the side of her Louis Vuitton luggage, glad that he hadn't actually touched her underwear. As for the dress, she tugged it away from him.

"Did you really have a thing for me in high school?" he asked.

Oh, goodness. He was bringing that up now? "Yes, I really did." She'd developed a quirky little crush on him, formed within the ache of the secrets they'd shared. But he'd totally blown her away when she returned from university and saw his physical transformation. He'd changed in all sorts of ways by then. While she'd been hitting the books, he'd already earned his first million, selling an app he'd designed, and he hadn't even gone to college. These days, he invested in start-ups and made a killing doing it.

"It never would have worked between us," he said.

Lizzie considered flinging her makeup bag at him and knocking him upside that computer chip brain of his. "I never proposed that it would."

"You were too classy for me." He gazed at her from across the bed. "Sometimes I think you still are."

A surge of heat shot through her blood. "That's nonsense. You date tons of socialites. They're your type."

"Because you set the standard. How could I be around you and not want that type?"

"Don't do this, Max." He'd gone beyond the realm of making jokes. "You shouldn't even be in my room, let alone be saying that sort of stuff."

"As if." He brushed it off. "I've been in your room plenty of times before. Remember last New Year's Eve? I poured you into bed when you got too drunk to stand."

She looked at him as if he'd gone mad. But maybe he had lost his grip on reality. Or maybe she had. Either way, she challenged him. "What are you talking about? I wasn't inebriated. I was coming down with the flu."

"So you kept telling me." He gave her a pointed look. "I think it was all those cosmopolitans that international playboy lover of yours kept plying you with."

Seriously? His memory couldn't be that bad. "You were tending bar at the party that night." Here at her house, with her guests.

"Was I? Are you sure? I thought it was that Grand Prix driver you met in Monte Carlo. The one all the women swooned over."

"He and I were over by then." She wagged a finger at him. "You're the one who kept adding extra vodka to my drinks."

"I must have felt sorry for you, getting dumped by that guy."

"From what I recall, it was around the same time that department store heiress walked out on you."

"She was boring, anyway."

"I thought she was nice. She was hunting for a husband, though."

"Yeah, and that ruled me out. I wouldn't get married if the survival of the world depended on it."

"Me, neither. But what's the likelihood of us ever having to do that, for saving mankind or any other reason?"

"There isn't. But I still say that you were drunk last New Year's, and I was the gentleman—thank you very much—who tucked you into this very bed." He patted her pillow for effect, putting a dent in it.

"Oh, there's an oxymoron. The guy feeding me liquor is the gentleman in the story?"

"It beats your big-fish tale about having the flu."

"Okay. Fine. I was wasted. Now stop taking it out on my pillow."

"Oops, sorry." He plumped it back up, good as new. "Are you going to finish packing or we going to sit here all day, annoying each other?"

"You started it." She filled her suitcase, stuffing it to the gills. She only wished they were going on a trip that didn't include a child she was nervous about meeting.

"Are you still worried about whether or not Tokoni will like you?" he asked, homing in on her troubled expression. "I already told you that I think you're going to impress him."

"Because he might regard me as a princess? That feels like pressure in itself."

"It'll be all right, Lizzie. And I promise, once you meet him, you'll see how special he is."

She didn't doubt that Tokoni was a nice little boy. But that didn't ease her nerves or boost her confidence about meeting him. Of course for now all she could do was remain by Max's side, supporting his cause, like the friend she was meant to be.

Two

Lizzie awakened inside a bungalow, with a tropical breeze stirring through an open window. Alone with her thoughts, she sat up and stretched.

Yesterday afternoon she and Max had arrived at their destination and checked in to the resort he'd booked for their weeklong stay. They had separate accommodations, each with its own colorful garden and oceanfront deck, equipped with everything they needed to relax, including hammocks. The interiors were also decorated to complement the environment, with beamed ceilings, wood floors, cozy couches and canopy beds.

Nulah consisted of a series of islands, and the sparsely populated island they were on was a twenty-minute boat ride to the mainland, the main island within the nation, where the capital city and all the activities in that area were: the airport, the orphanage they would be visiting, shopping and dining, dance clubs and other tourist-generated nightlife, nice hotels, cheap motels, burgeoning crime, basically what you would find in any city except on a smaller scale.

Of course at this off-the-grid resort, things were quiet. Max had stayed here before, during his sabbatical, and now Lizzie understood why it appealed to him.

With another body-rolling stretch, she climbed out of bed. She suspected that Max was already wide awake and jogging along the beach. He preferred early-morning runs. Typically, Lizzie did, too. But she'd skipped that routine today.

She showered and fixed her makeup and hair, keeping it simple. She didn't want to show up at the orphanage looking like a spoiled heiress. Or a princess. Or anything that drew too much attention to herself.

Returning to her bedroom, she donned the floral-printed dress Max had manhandled when she was packing yesterday, pairing it with T-strap sandals.

Lizzie made a cup of coffee, with extra cream, and headed outside. With a quiet sigh, she settled into a chair on her deck and gazed out at the view—the pearly white sand and aqua-blue water.

She closed her eyes, and when she opened them, Max appeared along the shore, winding down from his run. For a moment, he almost seemed like an apparition, a tall, tanned warrior in the morning light.

He glanced in her direction, and she waved him over. But before he strode toward her, he stopped to remove his T-shirt, using it like a towel to dry the sweat from his face and chest. Lizzie got a sexy little pulse-palpitating reaction from watching him. He'd already told her that his shower was outside, located in a walled section of his garden. He'd requested a bungalow with that type of amenity. So now she was going to envision him, naked in the elements, with water streaming over his sun-bronzed skin.

"Hey." He stood beside her chair. "What happened? I was expecting to see you out there. I figured you would've joined me at some point."

"I wasn't in the mood to run today." She glanced past him, making sure that she wasn't ogling his abs or giving him *the look*. Instead, she checked out a foamy wave breaking onto the shore. This island was a certified marine reserve, allowing guests to snorkel off the beach from the front of their bungalows. Lizzie hadn't been in the ocean yet, but according to Max there were heaps of fish, clams and coral reefs.

"You look pretty," he said.

His compliment gave her pulse another little jump start, prompting her to meet his gaze. "Thank you."

"I like your hair that way."

All she'd done was tie a satin ribbon around a carefully fastened ponytail, creating a girlish bow. "It's nothing, really."

"I think it gives you an interesting quality. Like a socialite trying to be incognito."

So much for her plan to be less noticeable. She changed the subject. "You must be hungry by now. I can get us something and bring it back here." Although room service was available, there was also an eat-in or takeout breakfast buffet. She didn't mind packing up their food to go. The restaurant and bar that provided their meals was a short walk along the beach.

She waited while he balled up his sweaty T-shirt and pondered her suggestion.

Finally he said, "I'll take bacon and eggs and a large tumbler of orange juice. Last time I was here, they served seafood crepes in this mouthwatering wine-cheese sauce, so fill my plate with those, too. I'm pretty sure they'll have them again. It's one of their specialties."

Apparently he'd worked up an appetite. "Anything else?"

"No. But I have to shower first."

Damn, she thought. The outdoor shower she shouldn't be thinking about. "Go ahead, and I'll see you in a few."

He left, and she watched him until he was out of sight. She finished her coffee, then headed for the buffet.

As she made the picturesque trek, she admired the purple and pink flowers she passed along the way. They flourished on abundant vines, growing wild in the sandy soil. The garden attached to her bungalow was also filled with them, along with big leafy plants and tall twisty palms.

After she got their food, she set everything up on her patio table. Inspired by the flora that surrounded her, she used a live orchid from her room as the centerpiece.

Max returned wearing a Polynesian-print shirt, board shorts and flip-flops. His thick damp hair was combed away from his face, but it was already starting to part naturally on its own. He smelled fresh and masculine, like the sandalwood soap he favored. Lizzie had used the mango-scented body wash the resort gave them.

He said, "This looks good." He sat across from her and dived into his big hearty breakfast.

For herself, she'd gotten plain yogurt and a bowl of fresh-cut fruit. But she hadn't been able to resist the crepes, so she was indulging in them, too.

He glanced up from his plate and asked, "Do you want to see a picture of Tokoni? I meant to show it to you before now. It's of the two of us."

"Yes, of course." She waited for him to pull it up on his phone, which took all of a second.

He handed it to her. The photo was of an adorable little dark-haired, tanned-skinned boy, expressing a big toothy grin. Max looked happy in the picture, too. She surmised that it was a selfie, snapped at close range. "He's beautiful."

"He's smart as a whip, too. Kindergarten starts at six here, so he isn't in school yet. But they work with the younger ones at the orphanage, preparing them for it." He took the phone back and set it aside. "I'm glad that you'll get to meet him today."

"What time are we supposed to be there?"

"We don't have an appointment. Losa said we can come any time it's convenient for us."

"That's her name? Losa? The woman who runs the orphanage?" The lady Lizzie would be interviewing today.

He nodded. "The kids call her Mrs. Losa."

"So is that her first or last name?"

"Her first. It means Rose in their native tongue."

That seemed fitting, with all the other flowers Lizzie had encountered today. "Is there a mister? Is she married?"

"She's widowed. She started the orphanage after her husband died. They were together for nearly forty years before he passed away."

She couldn't imagine being with the same person all that time. Or losing him.

"She has five kids," Max said. "They had three of their own, but they also adopted two from their village, orphaned siblings whose extended family wasn't able to care for them. But those children weren't adopted in an official way. Losa and her husband just took them in and raised them."

"Really? That's legal here?"

"Yes, but mostly it's the country folks, the traditionalists who still do that. They live in small communities where the people are tightly knit, so if there's a child or children in need, they band together to help. Losa and her husband used to be farmers. But she sold her property and moved to the capital to open the orphanage when she learned how many kids on the mainland were homeless. Her entire family supported her decision and relocated with her. All of her children and their spouses work there, along with their kids. She has two grown granddaughters and three teenage grandsons."

"They must be quite a family, taking on a project like that. Do they have any outside help?"

"At first it was just them, but now they have regular volunteers. And some who just pitch in when they can." Max drank his juice. "I volunteered when I was here before. That's how I spent the last three months of my sabbatical, helping out at the orphanage."

Lizzie hadn't realized the extent of his commitment. She'd assumed he'd merely visited the place. "No wonder you know so much about it."

He offered more of his knowledge by saying, "Nulah didn't used to allow international adoptions. But they finally decided it was in the best interest of the children. Otherwise, finding homes for these kids would be even more difficult. There aren't enough local families who have the means to take them. The older folks are dying off, and most of the younger ones are struggling to raise their own children."

He paused to watch a pair of colorful seabirds soaring along the shore. Lizzie watched them, too, thinking how majestic they were.

Then he said, "Not all of the kids at the orphanage are

up for adoption. Losa is fostering some of them, keeping them until they can return to their families. But either way, she devotes her life to the children in her care, however she can."

"She sounds like a godsend."

"She is. She spent years lobbying for the international adoption law here. Without her, it might never have happened."

Clearly, Losa had strength and fortitude, seeing things through to the end. "When we're on the mainland, I'd like to stop by a florist and get her a rose."

"You want to give her a flower that matches her name?"

"Mama always taught me that you should bring someone a gift the first time you visit." She paused to reflect. "I should bring something for the kids, too. Not just for Tokoni, but for all of them. How many are there?"

"The last time I was here, it was around thirty. It's probably still about the same."

"And what's the age range?"

"It varies, going from babies to young teens."

"That's a wide margin. I'm going to need a little time to shop for a group like that. We should leave for the mainland soon." Lizzie was anxious to get started. "We can take the next boat."

He grinned. "Then maybe we should eat a little faster."

She knew he was kidding. He'd already wolfed down most of his meal. Hers was nearly gone, too. "It's delicious." She raised her fork. "These crepes."

"This island is paradise." He stopped smiling. "If only everything on the mainland was as nice as it is here."

"Yes, if only." She'd caught glimpses of the capital city yesterday and had seen how poverty-stricken some of the areas were, the places where the kids from the orphanage had come from. And if anyone could relate to their ravaged beginnings, it was Max. He'd been born in South Dakota on one of the poorest reservations in the States, before his mother had hauled him off to an impoverished Los Angeles neighborhood.

As lonely as Lizzie's childhood had been, she'd never known the pain and fear of being poor. But that hadn't stopped her and Max from becoming friends. They'd formed a bond, regardless of how different they'd been from each other.

Trapped in emotion, she said, "Thank you."

He gave her a perplexed look. "For what?"

For everything, she thought. But she said, "For inviting me to take this trip with you."

"I'm glad you're here, too."

Their gazes met and held, but only for a moment.

Returning to their food, they fell silent, fighting the ever-present attraction neither of them wanted to feel.

Max and Lizzie got to the mainland around eleven, and he hailed a cab. Taxis weren't metered here, so they had to agree on the price of the fare before departure. Max arranged to keep the taxi at their disposal for the rest of the day. Their driver was a big, broad-shouldered twentysomething with a brilliant smile. As pleasant and accommodating as he was, he drove a bit too fast. But tons of cabbies in the States did that, too. As for the car, it was old and rickety, with seat belts that kept coming unbuckled. But it was better than no transportation at all, Max thought.

As they entered the shopping district, the car bumped and jittered along roughly paved roads. The still-smiling cabbie found a centrally located parking spot and told them he would wait there for them. To keep himself occupied, he reached for his phone. Max, of course, was consumed with technology, too. It was his world, his livelihood, his outlet. But he never buried his face in his phone when he was with Lizzie. She hated it when people ignored each other in favor of their devices, so he'd made a conscious effort not to do that to her.

Behaving like tourists, they wandered the streets, going in and out of small shops. Some of the vendors were aggressive, trying as they might to peddle their wares. But Max didn't mind. He understood that they had families to feed. He went ahead and purchased a bunch of stuff to ship back home, mostly toys and trinkets for his nieces—his foster brothers' adorable little daughters.

Lizzie wasn't faring as well. Although she'd already gotten a stack of baby goods for the infants and toddlers at the orphanage and placed them in the taxi for safekeeping, she couldn't make up her mind about the rest of the kids.

Finally she said, "Maybe I can put together a big box of art supplies that all of them can use."

"That's a great idea. Tokoni would appreciate it, too, since he loves to draw. There's an arts and crafts store around the corner. They also have a little gallery where they sell works by local artists. I always wanted to check it out."

"Then let's go." She seemed interested in the art, too. "But first I want to get what I need for the kids."

They walked to their destination. The sun was shining, glinting beautifully off her ponytailed hair. He'd teased her earlier about her looking like a socialite who was trying to go incognito. In his opinion, Lizzie wasn't the type who could downplay her breeding. She'd already spent too many years perfecting it, and by now it was ingrained into the woman she'd become.

When they came to the arts and crafts store, they went inside, and she gathered paints, brushes, crayons, markers, colored pencils, paper, blank canvases and whatever else she could find. She added crafts, too, like jewelry-making kits and model cars. The man who owned the shop was thrilled. He was a chatty old guy who introduced himself as George. Max figured it was the English translation of his birth name.

After Lizzie made her purchases, she and Max browsed the work that was for sale in the gallery section. George followed them. Hoping, no doubt, that Lizzie was an art collector.

Only it was Max who got curious about a painting. It depicted a ceremony of some sort, where a young couple was cutting pieces of each other's hair with decorative knives. In Native American and First Nations cultures, shearing one's hair was sometimes associated with death and mourning. But the people in this picture didn't appear to be grieving.

While he inspected the painting, Lizzie stood beside him. George was nearby, as well.

"What are they doing?" Max asked him.

The owner stepped forward. "Preparing for their wedding. It's an old custom, chopping a betrothed's hair. Doing this symbolizes their transitions into adulthood."

Max frowned. "I'd never do that."

"Do what? Cut your lady's hair?" By now George was gazing at Lizzie's bright red locks.

"I meant get married." Max shook his head. "And she isn't my lady. She's my friend."

"Hmm." George tapped his chin. "Is this true?" he asked Lizzie. "You're only friends with this man?"

"Yes, that's all we are," she assured him.

"It's different for me," he said. "I have a wife." He

took her hand and tugged her toward the other side of the gallery. "You come, too," he told Max. "I'll show you something else."

As soon as Max spotted the painting George wanted them to see, he stopped to stare at it. The nearly life-size image depicted a wildly primitive young woman on a moonlit beach, dancing with a male partner, only he was made completely of fire. She swayed in his burning-hot arms, with her long slim body draped in a sparkling gold dress. Her flame-red hair blew across her face, shielding her mysterious features from view.

"It's called *Lady Ari*," George said.

Max sucked in his breath. "After the royal goddess of fire." He hadn't known her name until now.

"Yes," George said. "With hair like your friend's." He glanced over at Lizzie.

Max shifted his attention to her, too, but she didn't acknowledge him. She continued looking at the painting. Was she as captivated by it as he was, or was she focusing on the picture so she didn't have to return his gaze?

He couldn't be sure. But the feverish feeling *Lady Ari* gave him was too overpowering to ignore. "I'm going to buy it." Now, he thought, today.

With a sudden jolt, Lizzie jerked her head toward his. "And do what with it?"

"I'll hang it in my house." He considered where to put it. "Above the fireplace in my den."

"You already have a nice piece of artwork there."

"So I'll replace it with this one."

She fussed with her ponytail, as if she was fighting its brazen color, and he realized how uncomfortable his attraction to *Lady Ari* was making her. But he simply couldn't let the painting go.

As they both fell silent, Max noticed that George

was watching the two of them, probably thinking what strange friends they were. But nonetheless, the older man was obviously pleased that he'd just made a significant sale.

"The artist would be enchanted by you," George told Lizzie. "You would be charmed by him, too. He's young and handsome." He then said to Max, "A lot like you."

Lizzie raised her eyebrows at that, and Max shrugged, as if the artist's virility was of no consequence. But it made him feel funny inside, with George making what seemed like romantic comparisons.

Still, it didn't change his interest in buying it. The need to have it was too strong. Max arranged to have the painting shipped home, as he'd done with the items he'd bought for his nieces.

After the transaction was complete, they said goodbye to George and returned to their taxi, piling the art supplies Lizzie had purchased into the trunk.

She scowled at Max and said, "I still have to get Losa a rose."

"Okay, but don't be mad about the painting."

"I'm not."

Yes, she was, he thought. She didn't like the idea of him owning a picture that could be mistaken for an untamed version of her. But he wasn't going to apologize for buying something he wanted.

"Do you know where the florist is?" she asked him.

"No." He didn't have a clue. He checked with their driver and was informed that it was close enough to walk, so they set out on foot again.

The florist offered a variety of exotic plants and blooms. Max waited patiently while Lizzie labored over what color of rose to buy.

She decided on a pale yellow, and they returned to the

taxi and climbed into the car. The driver started the engine and off they went, en route to the orphanage.

After a beat of silence, she said, "I wonder who modeled for it."

For it. The painting. Obviously her mind was still on *Lady Ari*. "I assumed that the artist had created her from his imagination."

She sat stiffly in her seat, clutching the rose. "I should have asked George, but I didn't think of it then. I'd prefer that she was a real person."

"Why? Because then she would seem less like you and more like the model? Just think of how I feel, knowing the artist is a handsome guy who's supposedly a lot like me."

She narrowed her eyes at him. "It serves you right. I mean, really, what were you thinking, buying something like that?"

He defended himself. "You ought to be glad that I did."

"Oh, yeah? How do you figure?"

"Because now I can lust over the painting and forget that I ever had the hots for you."

"You wish." As they rounded a corner, he leaned into her. She shoved him aside. "And stop crowding me."

Max cursed beneath his breath. He wasn't invading her space purposely. The force of the turn had done it. He wanted to tell the driver to slow down, that this wasn't the damned Autobahn. Instead he said to Lizzie, "You're nothing like Lady Ari. It's not as if you'd ever dance that way in the moonlight."

"Gee, you think?" She waved her arms around, willy-nilly. "Me and a male heap of burning fire?"

"That was the worst sensual dance I've ever seen."

"That was the idea."

"To suck?"

The taxi came to a quick halt, stopping for a group of pedestrians. Max and Lizzie both flew forward and bumped their foreheads on the seats in front of them.

He turned to look at her, and she burst out laughing. He did, too. It was impossible to keep arguing in the midst of such absurdity.

"I'm sorry for giving you a hard time," she said. "You can buy whatever artwork you want."

"I'm sorry, too." He leaned toward her and whispered in a mock sexy voice, "I didn't mean what I said about forgetting that I have the hots for you. Even if you can't dance like her, you're still a temptress."

She accepted his flirtation for what it was. But she also pushed him away from her again, keeping him from remaining too close.

Then…*vroom*! The car sped off, taking them to the grassy outskirts of town, where the orphanage was.

Three

The orphanage was in a renovated old church, large enough to accommodate its residents and perched on a pretty piece of land with a cluster of coconut trees.

A short stout lady greeted them on the porch. With plainly styled gray hair and eyes that crinkled beneath wire-rimmed glasses, she appeared to be around seventy. Max introduced her as Losa.

After they shook hands, Lizzie extended the rose. "This is for you."

"Thank you. It's lovely." The older woman accepted it with a gracious smile. Although she gazed at Lizzie's fiery red hair, she didn't comment on it.

Thankfully, that made the painting Max had bought seem less important. For now, anyway. No doubt *Lady Ari* would keep creeping back into Lizzie's mind, along with Max's sexy little joke about Lizzie tempting him.

Clearing her wayward thoughts, she said, "I also

brought gifts for the kids." She gestured to the boxes Max had placed beside the door. "I got blankets and bottles for the babies and art supplies for the rest of them."

"That's wonderful." Once again, Losa thanked her. "You seem like a nice girl."

"She is," Max said. "We've known each other since high school. We've been proper friends a long time."

Proper friends? Was that his way of making sure that Losa didn't mistake them as lovers, the way George had done? That was fine with Lizzie. She preferred to avoid that sort of confusion.

Losa invited them into her office, a simply designed space that was as understated as she was. Max brought the boxes inside and put them next to a metal file cabinet.

Losa offered them iced tea that had been chilling in a mini fridge and slices of homemade coconut bread that were already precut and waiting to be served.

They sat across from her with their food and drink, near a window that overlooked the yard.

Lizzie noticed a fenced area with picnic benches, occupied by groups of children who appeared to be between the ages of two and five. Two colorfully dressed young women watched over them.

Losa followed her line of sight and said, "The older children are in school and the babies are in the nursery. The others are having lunch, as you can see. Tokoni is among them. You can visit with him afterward."

Lizzie didn't ask which child was Tokoni or try to recognize him from the photo Max had shown her, at least not from this distance. She was still nervous about meeting him, especially with how much Max adored him.

"So," Losa went on to say, "you want to interview me for your charity blog?"

"Yes," Lizzie quickly replied, "I'd like to feature the

orphanage. To provide whatever information you're willing to give." She removed her phone from her purse. "Also, may I get your permission to do an audio recording? It's more accurate than taking written notes."

"Certainly," Losa said. "It's good of you to help. It was kind of Max to donate to us, too. He was very generous." She sent him an appreciative smile.

Although he returned her smile, he stayed quiet, drinking his tea and allowing Lizzie to do the talking.

Once the recording app was activated, she said to Losa, "Max told me that you and your family founded this orphanage after your husband passed."

"He was a dear man." Her expression went soft. "He would be pleased by what we accomplished here."

Lizzie stole another glance at the window. "Are those your granddaughters? The young women tending to the kids?"

"Yes. They're good girls, as devoted as I am to keeping this place going and matching our children in waiting with interested families. Tokoni is especially eager to be adopted. He chatters about it all the time."

Lizzie nodded. Max had said the same thing about him. "I'm hoping that my article will raise more than just money for your cause. That it will bring awareness to the kids themselves and how badly they need homes."

"We work with international adoption agencies that provide pictures and information of our children in waiting. You're welcome to post links to those websites."

"Absolutely." Lizzie intended to be as thorough as possible. "Will you email me that information, along with whatever else you think will be helpful?"

"Actually, I can give you a packet right now." Losa went to the file cabinet and removed a large gray envelope. She resumed her seat, slid it across the desk and said, "In the United States, intercountry adoption is governed by three sets of laws—the laws of the child's country of origin, your federal laws and the laws of the US state in which the child will be adopted."

"How long does the process typically take?"

"In some countries, it can take years. For us, it's between three and six months."

"Wow. That's fast." Lizzie leaned forward. "Are you the only country that's been able to expedite it that way?"

"No. There are others in this region. Small independent nations, like ours, with less red tape, as one might say."

"Will you tell me about your guidelines?"

"Certainly," Losa replied. "We don't have residency requirements, meaning that the applicants don't have to live here before they adopt. But we do require that they study our culture through the online classes we designed. Prospective parents may be married or single. They need to be at least twenty-five years of age and demonstrate a sufficient income. But what we consider sufficient is reasonable. We're not seeking out the rich. Just people who will love and care for these children. Honorable people," she added. "Their character is what's most important to us."

"Did you help develop these guidelines when you lobbied for international adoption?"

"I worked closely with the authorities, giving them my input. But in some cases, the requirements are modified to accommodate a family member's request. For example, Tokoni's mother asked that he be adopted by a married couple. She didn't want him being raised by a single parent." The older woman softly added, "So I promised her that he would be matched with the type of parents she envisioned, a young romantic couple who would devote their hearts to him, as well as to each other."

Lizzie considered Tokoni's mother and how terribly she'd struggled. Apparently she wanted her son to have a warm, cozy, traditional family, which was what she'd longed to give him when she dreamed of marrying his father.

Losa said, "Most of our applicants want girls. Studies show this to be true in other countries, as well. Unfortunately, that makes it more challenging to find homes for the boys. If Tokoni were a girl, he might have been placed by now."

Lizzie's chest went heavy, tight and twisted, in a way that was beginning to hurt. "I hope the perfect parents come along for him. But you never really know what hand life will deal you. My mom died when I was ten, and my dad raised me after she was gone. But I hardly ever saw him. He was wealthy enough to hire nannies and cooks to look after me."

"I'm sorry that your father wasn't available for you," Losa said. "It shouldn't be that way."

Lizzie noticed that Max was watching her closely now. Was he surprised that she'd offered information about herself?

After a second of silence, he said, "I told Losa about my childhood last time I was here. Not all the sordid details, but enough for her to know that I came from an abusive environment."

"So much sadness." Losa sighed. "Perhaps spending a little time with Tokoni will cheer you up. He's such a vibrant boy."

Lizzie glanced out the window. By now the children had finished eating and were playing in the grass. She watched them for a while, analyzing each one. Was Tokoni the boy in the green shirt and denim shorts? He appeared to be about the right age, with a similar haircut to that of the child in Max's picture, with his bangs skimming his eyes. He was laughing and twirling in the sun, like the happy kid he was supposed to be.

"Their recess is almost over," Losa said. "And as soon as they come inside, you can meet him."

"Yes, of course." Since the interview was coming to a close, Lizzie turned off the recorder on her phone and gathered the packet she'd been given. "I'm looking forward to it."

"Splendid." Losa stood. "You can chat with him in the library. We use it as an art room, too, so that's where the supplies you brought will be kept." She said to Max, "You know where the library is, so you two go on ahead, and I'll bring Tokoni to you."

Lizzie put on a brave face, but deep down she was still concerned that Tokoni would find her lacking. That he wouldn't take to her the way he had with Max.

But it was too late to back out. She was here to support Max—and the orphaned child they'd come to see.

The library was furnished in the typical way, with tables and chairs and shelves of books, but as Lizzie and Max stepped farther into the room, she spotted a seating area in the back that she assumed was designed for guests.

Max led her toward it, and they sat on a floral-printed sofa. She folded her hands on her lap, then unfolded them, attempting to relax.

"It feels good to be back," he said, far more comfortable than she was. "I miss volunteering here."

"What kinds of things did you do?" she asked, trying to envision him in the throes of it.

"Mostly I read to the kids or told them stories. But sometimes I helped in the kitchen. I fixed the plumbing once and mopped the floors in the bathroom when one of the toilets overflowed. Tokoni got in trouble that day because he caused the problem, flushing a toy boat down there."

She bit back a laugh. Apparently sweet little Tokoni had a mischievous side. "I guess your donation didn't make you immune to the grunt work."

"I didn't think it was fair for me to pick and choose my tasks. Besides, as much as Losa appreciated the money, she understood that I needed to be useful in other ways, too."

"The kids must have gotten used to having you around."

He smiled. "Yeah, they did. That's how Tokoni and I got so close."

Just then Losa entered the library, clutching the boy's hand. He was the kid in the green shirt and denim shorts Lizzie had noticed earlier, and up close he looked just like the picture Max had shown her, with full round cheeks and expressive eyes. As soon as Tokoni saw Max, he grinned and tried to escape Losa's hold. But she wouldn't let him go, so he stood there, bouncing in place.

Max came to his feet. Lizzie followed suit, and her nerves ratcheted up a notch.

Tokoni tried to pull Losa toward Max, but the older woman wouldn't budge. "If you want to see Max, you have to be good," she warned the child. "And then I'll come back to get you."

"Okay." He promised her that he would be "very, very good." A second later, he was free and running straight to Max.

Losa left the library, and Lizzie watched as man and child came together in a joyous reunion.

"Hey, buddy," Max said, scooping him up. "It's great to see you."

"Hi, Max!" He nuzzled the big, broad shoulder he was offered, laughing as Max tickled him.

Once the kid calmed down, he gazed curiously at Lizzie. This strange woman, she thought, who was just standing there.

She tried for a smile, but feared that it might have come off as more of a grimace. He just kept staring at her, *really* staring, to the point of barely blinking. She could tell it was her hair that caught his attention. Her dang Lady Ari hair.

With Tokoni still in his arms, Max turned to face her, too. At this point, he'd become aware of how the five-year-old was reacting to her.

"Is she a goodness?" the child asked.

"You mean a *goddess*?" Max chuckled. "No. She's just a pretty lady with red hair. But sometimes I think she looks like a goddess, too. She's my friend Lizzie."

Tokoni grinned at her and said, "Hi, Izzy."

"Hello." She didn't have the heart to correct him. But Max did.

"Her name is Lizzie," he said. "With an *L*. Like Losa. Or lizard." Max stuck out his tongue at her, making a reptile face. "I always thought her name sounded a little like that."

"Gee, thanks." She made the same goofy face at him, trying to be more kidlike. But truth of the matter, he'd nicknamed her Lizard ages ago. Just as she sometimes called him Mad Max.

Tokoni giggled, enjoying their antics.

Max said to him, "So you think we're funny, do you?"

"Yep." The child's chest heaved with excitement, with

more laughter. Then he said to Lizzie, "Know what? This is an orange-fan-age."

She smiled, amused by his pronunciation of it.

"Know what else?" he asked. "My real mommy is gone, but I'm going to get 'dopted by a new mommy. And a daddy, too."

Overwhelmed by how easily he'd rattled that off, she couldn't think of anything to say. She should have been prepared for a conversation like this, knowing what she knew about him, but she couldn't seem to find her voice.

But that didn't stop him from asking her, "Why are you at the orange-fan-age?"

"Because Max wanted me to meet you."

Tokoni reached out to touch her hair, locating a strand that had come loose from her ponytail. "How come?"

"Because of how much he likes you." She released the air in her lungs, realizing that she'd been holding her breath. "And because I'm going to write a story about the orphanage and the kids who live here."

"Can I be a superhero in it?"

Oh, dear. "It's not that kind of story."

He was still touching her hair. "It could be."

No, she thought, it couldn't. She wasn't good at writing fiction. She'd always been a reality-type gal.

"Come on, buddy," Max said, redirecting Tokoni's attention. "Let's all go over here." He carried him to the sofa and plopped him down.

Lizzie joined them, with Tokoni in the middle. She fixed her hair, tucking the loose strand behind her ear.

"I made a book of the mommy and daddy who are going to 'dopt me," he said to her. "I can show it to you."

"Sure," she replied, trying to be as upbeat about it as he was.

Tokoni climbed off the sofa and dashed over to a plastic bin that had his name on it. There appeared to be personalized bins for all the children, stacked in neat rows.

He returned and resumed his spot, between her and Max. He showed her a handmade booklet, consisting of about ten pieces of white paper with staples in the center holding it together.

He narrated each picture, explaining the activity he and his future parents were engaging in. On page one, they stood in the sun. On page two, they swam in the ocean. In the next one, they were going out to dinner, where they would eat all of Tokoni's favorite foods.

Everyone had red smiles on their faces, black dots for eyes and no noses. Dad was the tallest, Mom was wearing a triangle-shaped dress and Tokoni was the only one with hair. His folks were completely bald.

Lizzie assumed it was deliberate. That Tokoni hadn't given them hair because he didn't know what color it should be. He obviously knew that he might be adopted by people who looked different from him. Blonds, maybe? Or even redheads?

She fussed with her hair, checking the piece she'd tucked behind her ear, making sure it stayed put.

"Your book is wonderful," she said. "Your drawings are special. The best I've ever seen." She didn't know much about kids' art, but his work seemed highly developed to her, with how carefully thought out it was.

He flashed a proud smile and crawled onto her lap. She went warm and gooey inside. This child was doing things to her that she'd never felt before.

He said, "You can color inside my book if you want to."

Heavens, no, she thought. As flattered as she was by his generous offer, she couldn't handle the pressure that would cause. "That's very nice of you, but I don't think I should."

He persisted. "It's okay if you don't color very good. I'll still let you."

Her skills weren't the problem. "I just don't—"

Max bumped her shoulder, encouraging her to do it. Damn. Now how was she supposed to refuse?

"All right," she relented, her stomach erupting into butterflies. "But I'm going to sit at one of the tables." Where she could concentrate. "And I'll need some crayons." She didn't mention that she'd brought new art supplies for Tokoni and his peers, because it was up to Losa to distribute those.

After Tokoni got the crayons, he scooted next to her at the table, directly at her elbow and making it difficult for her to work. But she didn't tell him to move over. He was so darned excited to have her do this, almost as if she really was a goddess.

Max joined them, only he didn't have to draw. He got to kick back and watch. Lizzie wished she hadn't gotten roped into this. What if she ruined the boy's book? What if he didn't like what she did to it?

She opened the first page: the depiction of Tokoni and his family on a sunny day. She used an orange crayon and added more rays to the giant sun, giving it an extra pop of color. That seemed safe enough.

Tokoni grinned. What Max had told her about the boy was true. He smiled all the time.

"Do something else," he told her.

She put grass beneath the people's feet and glanced across the table at Max. He shot her a playful wink, and her pulse beat a bit faster.

Returning to the picture, Lizzie drew multicolored

flowers sprouting up from the grass. "How's this?" she asked Tokoni.

"That's nice." He turned the page for her. "Do this one."

It was the ocean scene. She embellished it with bigger waves and a school of fish. She added sand and seashells, too.

Tokoni wiggled in his seat and went to the next page, where the family was going out to dinner. He said, "Make the mommy look more like a girl."

Lizzie contemplated the request. She certainly wasn't going to give the female a bust or hips or anything like that. So she detailed the mommy's dress, making it more decorative. She also gave her jewelry, a gold necklace and dangling earrings.

"That looks pretty," Tokoni said.

"Thank you." She drew high heels onto the mommy's feet.

But the poor woman looked incomplete, all dressed up with her bald head, so Lizzie included a hat with a flower poking out of it.

"Put stuff on her mouth," Tokoni said.

"Lipstick?"

He nodded.

She reached for a pink crayon. "How about this?"

"Okay." He moved even closer, eager to see the transformation.

She reshaped the mommy's lips, making them fuller but still retaining her smile.

"I think the mom needs some hair coming out from under her hat," Max said. "The dad could use some, too. Unless he's the shaved-head type."

Seriously? Lizzie could have kicked him. With all the months he'd spent here, getting close to Tokoni, he should have known what the hairless parents were about. But sometimes men could be downright clueless, even the sensitive ones like Max.

And now poor little Tokoni was mulling over the situation, looking perplexed. "What color?" he asked Max.

Realization dawned in Max's eyes, and Lizzie squinted at him, wishing he hadn't opened this can of worms.

After a beat of outward concern, Max said, "Any color." He quickly added, "Blue, green, purple."

Tokoni laughed. "That's silly."

Max laughed, too, recovering from his blunder. "Not as silly as you think. There are people where I live who dye their hair those colors."

"You should do yours," the boy said to him.

Max ran his fingers through the blackness of his hair. "Maybe I will."

Tokoni laughed again. Then he said to Lizzie, "But not you."

She tapped the tip of his nose. As cute as he was, she couldn't seem to help herself. "You don't want me to dye my hair a funny color?"

"No. I want it to stay red."

The hair discussion ended and the mommy and daddy in Tokoni's booklet remained bald.

A short while later, Losa returned. Tokoni didn't want to go with her, but he didn't have a choice. It was naptime. All the younger kids had to nap in the middle of the day. Or at least rest their eyes and stay quiet.

"Will you and Max come back tomorrow?" he asked Lizzie.

"Yes, absolutely," she replied. "Maybe we can volunteer for the rest of the week and see you every day, if that's all right with Losa."

The older woman readily agreed, and Lizzie's heart

twirled. She wanted to spend as much time with Tokoni as she could before their trip was over. She was certain that Max did, too. He seemed pleased with her suggestion. But he'd already told her that he missed volunteering there.

"See you soon, buddy." Max got on bended knee to say goodbye to the boy, and they hugged.

Lizzie was next. Tokoni held her so warmly, so affectionately, she nearly cried. This child needed a family, and she was going to do everything within her power to help him get one.

Four

While dusk approached the sky, Lizzie and Max walked along the beach at their resort. Collecting her thoughts, she stopped to gaze at the horizon.

Reflecting on the day's events, she said what was on her mind, what she'd been consumed with since they left the orphanage. "I want to help Tokoni get adopted."

An ocean breeze stirred Max's shirt, pulling the fabric closer to his body. "You're already going to try to do that with your blog article."

"Yes, but I want to do more than just write an article that *might* help. I want to actually—" she stalled, trying to make sense of what it was she thought she was capable of "—find the perfect parents for him."

"How?" he asked. "How would you even begin to go about doing something like that?"

"I don't know." All she'd ever done was raise money for children's charities. She'd never set out to find an orphaned kid a home. "But with all my resources, with all the people I know, there has to be a way to make it happen."

He looked into her eyes, almost as if he was peering into the anxious window of her soul. "You're really serious about this."

"Yes, I am." She couldn't help how eager she was, how attached she'd already become to Tokoni. "You were right about how special he is. And I want to make a difference in his life."

His gaze continued to bore into hers. Did he think that she was getting in over her head?

Then he smiled and said, "I'll help you, Lizzie. We can do this. Both of us together. We can find him a home."

Her pulse jumped, her mind raced. Suddenly the beach seemed to be spinning, moving at a dizzying pace.

She pushed her toes into the sand, steadying herself. "Thank you, Max." He was the one true constant in her life. The person she relied on most, and if he was onboard, her quest seemed even more possible.

He kept smiling. "I loved watching you with him today. You were amazing the way you interacted with him."

She breathed in his praise. "I can't wait to see him again. But at least we've got the rest of the week."

Max's smile fell. "I can't believe how I screwed up, saying what I did about his drawings. I should have been aware of the hair thing before now."

"It's all right. When he gets adopted by his new mommy and daddy, he can add their hair and anything else that will identify them to him."

"He was certainly fascinated with your hair. But I figured he would be."

"That made me uncomfortable at first."

"I know. I could tell." His voice went a little rough. "It sure looks wild now."

"It's just the wind." She tried to sound casual. But it wasn't easy. Before they'd ventured out to the beach this evening, she'd removed her ponytail, and now her hair was long and loose and blowing past her shoulders, probably a lot like Lady Ari's in the painting he'd bought.

Before the moment turned unbearably awkward, she redirected his focus and hurriedly said, "We're going to have to talk to Losa about our plan, since she's the one who will be approving Tokoni's prospective parents."

"In a way, we will be, too, with the way we'll be searching for them." He stooped to pick up a shell at his feet and study its corkscrew shape. He returned it to the beach and asked, "Are we really going to know, Lizzie?"

"Who's right for him? I think we will. Besides, we have the guidelines his mother set."

A hard and fast frown appeared on his face, grooving lines into his forehead. "A young romantic couple, devoted as deeply to each other as they'll be to him? That's out of our league."

A heap of concern came over her. "You're starting to sound as if you don't want to do this. Are you having second thoughts?"

"No. But I don't want to choose the wrong people. Or send the wrong applicants to Losa or whatever."

"I agree, completely. We're not going to run right out and grab the first wannabe parents who come along. Besides, we haven't even figured out the best way to approach this yet."

"You're right. Once we research the possibilities and explore our options, I won't be as worried about it."

"Whoever his parents are going to be, they need to encourage his artwork. I think he's going to excel at art.

His cognitive skills blow me away, too, with the way he analyzes everything. I doubt many five-year-olds are as advanced as he is."

Max grinned. "That's exactly how I felt when I first met him. And with as happy as he is all the time, he makes everybody around him smile."

She laughed. "Gosh, do you think we're biased?"

He laughed, too. "With the way we're both singing his praises, you'd think he was our kid." His mood sobered, his handsome features going still. "But he's not."

"No, he definitely isn't." She couldn't get over the loss of her own mother, let alone become one herself. "But that isn't something we need to think about. No one is going to suggest that we adopt him."

"We couldn't even if we wanted to."

"No, we couldn't." They weren't married or in love or anything even remotely close to what Tokoni's mother had requested. "Not that you wouldn't make a great dad. It's being a husband that you would fail miserably at."

"You've got me there." He shrugged, reaffirming what they both already knew. "I definitely couldn't handle that, any more than you could cope with being a wife."

"That's for sure. I've never even dated anyone for more than three months, which is weird, when you think that someone could actually adopt Tokoni within three to six months." She added, "But that should help our cause with a couple who's eager and ready to adopt."

"You're right, Lizard." He turned playful, kicking a bit of sand at her ankles. "It should."

She kicked a bigger pile at him, some of the grains making it all the way to his knees. "Don't mess with me, Mad Max."

"Ooh, check you out," he teased her. "I should dunk your ass in the water for that."

She shot a glance at the ocean. Dusk was still closing in, painting the sky in mesmerizing hues. Bracing to get wet, to splash and frolic, she said, "If you do, I'm taking you down with me."

Yet when she turned back to gauge his reaction, a look of common sense had come into his eyes. He'd obviously thought better of it. Then again, why wouldn't he?

The only way for him to dunk her in the water would be to pick her up and carry her there, and that wouldn't be a good idea, not with how intimate it could get. Goofing around was one thing; creating intimacy was quite another.

Foolish as it was, she actually wished that he would lift her into his arms and haul her off to the sea. But that was just a side effect of the yearnings between them. Lizzie knew better than to want what she shouldn't have or push the boundaries of their attraction. But darned if he didn't affect her in ways she was struggling to control.

"You know what I could use about now?" He gestured in the direction of the resort's palm-thatch-roofed restaurant. "A pineapple smoothie at the bar. Do you want to join me?"

"They serve smoothies?"

He nodded. "Along with the usual spirits. But I'd rather skip the alcohol and have a smoothie."

"Then I'll have one, too." A sweet, frothy concoction that would go down easy—and help her forget about the troubling urges he incited.

The bar was dimly lit, with a tiki décor and a spectacular view of the ocean. Music played from an old-fashioned jukebox. Pop tunes, mostly, from eras gone by.

Max drank his smoothie in suffering silence. Being sexually attracted to his best friend was a hell of a burden to bear. But at least the feelings were mutual and Lizzie was suffering right along with him. They'd been dealing with this for years, so tonight was just more of the same—except for their pledge to find a family for Tokoni.

"Did you really mean what you said about me making a great dad?" he asked, breaking the silence with an emotional bang.

"Yes, I meant it." She stirred her smoothie with her straw. "You've always had a natural way with kids. It's a wonderful part of who you are."

"Thanks, but I've never actually considered being a father, not with the loner life I've chosen to lead. Now it seems sort of sad to think that I might never have kids." He glanced out the window at the darkness enveloping the sea. "But I guess being around Tokoni is making me feel that way."

"You could still have children someday if you wanted to."

"Yeah, right." He struggled to fathom the idea. "And who am I supposed to have these kids with?"

"You could adopt and become a single dad."

"I don't think that's very common."

"No, but it's still possible in this day and age, depending on the circumstances. Now, me..." She heaved a heavy sigh. "I'm not cut out to be a mom."

"You could've fooled me, with how beautifully you engaged with Tokoni."

"I'd be scared to death to be responsible for a child, to give him everything he needs."

He knew that she was referring to emotional needs. "You've always been there for me when I needed someone to lean on."

"I'm your friend. That isn't the same as being someone's mom."

"No, but it's still a testament to who you are. And so is your commitment to Tokoni. Truthfully, I'm starting to think you'd make an amazing mom."

"I don't know about that." She shook her head. Her hair was still windblown from the beach, as gorgeous as ever. "But thank you for saying it."

"I meant it." He honestly did. "Of course all that really matters is for Tokoni to have the parents he longs for."

"Does he know that you were once eligible for adoption?"

"No. I've never told him anything about my childhood, and thankfully he's never asked. But I was just one of many. About half the kids who enter the foster care system are eligible for adoption. Even now there are over a hundred thousand children in waiting." Max knew the numbers well. He helped run a foster children's charity that he and his brothers had founded. "Typically, foster kids are adopted by their foster parents. Or by extended family. That's the most common scenario."

She sighed. "Not for you, it wasn't."

Max nodded. His extended family had been as bad as his mother. He'd even had a bitter old grandmother back on the reservation who used to call him an *iyeska*, a breed, because she believed that he was half white, spawned by one of the Anglo men Mom used to mess around with in the border towns. Mom, however, had insisted that he was a full-blood and his daddy was a res boy. Till this day, he didn't have a clue who'd fathered him. He'd never been accepted by his grandmother, either. She'd died a long time ago.

"I never wanted to be adopted, anyway," he said.

"Not even by any of your foster parents?"

"I preferred being left alone. Besides, I got shifted

around so much in the beginning I never got close to any of them. Of course when I met Jake and Garrett, things got better." Two other misplaced foster boys, he thought, who'd become his brothers. "But you already know that story."

"Yes. I do." She relayed the tale. "Jake was leery of you at first because he thought you were a dork. Garrett, however, was your protector from the start and would fight off the kids who bullied you."

"Garrett saved my hide more times than I can count. But Jake came around, too, and accepted me."

"It's strange how I don't know them very well, even after all these years. I see them at fund-raisers and whatnot, but that's as far as it goes."

Max had never considered how superficial her relationship with his foster brothers was. Was that his fault for not bringing her together with them in a closer way? Probably, he thought. But he wasn't good at family-type ties. Sometimes he even shielded himself from his brothers. He'd cut everyone off during his sabbatical, including Lizzie.

"I missed you," he said, blurting out his feelings.

She blinked at him. "What are you talking about?"

"When I was gone. When I was traveling." Was that a stupid thing for him to admit? Or even think about now that she was here with him?

She gazed at him from across their rugged wood table. "I missed you, too. It was a long time for us to be apart."

"I needed to get away. It was just something I had to do."

"It's okay. I didn't feel abandoned by you. I knew you were coming back. And look how it turned out. You found Tokoni on that trip."

"And now we're going to work toward finding him the parents he dreams about," he said, confirming their plans once again.

And hoping they could actually make them come true.

Lizzie and Max's week of volunteering at the orphanage went well. And now, on their very last day, Lizzie was making banana pudding, Tokoni's favorite dessert, for all the children to enjoy. She was using a recipe that Losa's oldest daughter, Fai, had given her. Fai was the primary cook at the orphanage, but she was staying out of the kitchen today.

Nonetheless, Lizzie wasn't doing this alone. Max and Tokoni were helping her. She'd put Tokoni on banana duty, sitting him at a table where he could peel the 'nanas, as he called them. Max was seated across from him, slicing the fruit and dumping the pieces into a bowl. Later, they would be layered into casserole dishes.

"Come on, buddy." Max spoke gently but firmly to the boy. "If you keep doing that, there won't be anything left for me to cut."

Tokoni had already squished the banana that was in his hand. He could be quite the mischief maker when he wanted to be. Lizzie laughed as Tokoni stuffed a small glob of it into his mouth and ate it.

"Don't encourage him," Max said to her.

"Sorry. But after my mom was gone, my revolving-door nannies would bring me into the kitchen so I could observe our chefs preparing their masterpieces, except I always had to sit quietly and observe, like the proper little lady that I was." She glanced at the mess Tokoni was making. "It's nice to see a kid goofing around."

"Okay." Max smiled at her. "Then you're forgiven. You, too," he said to Tokoni. "Only maybe I better get you cleaned up a bit." Max got up and wet a towel at the sink. He returned and wiped the child's face and hands.

Afterward, Tokoni asked Lizzie, "What are 'volving-door nannies?"

Oh, goodness. She should have known better than to say that. Tokoni was a highly observant boy, picking up on just about everything around him.

"Nannies look after children, sort of like teachers and nurses. I had lots of them when I was young, so that's why I said revolving door. They never stayed at my house for very long."

"How come?"

"Because it wasn't a very fun place to work."

"How come?" he asked again. He was prone to do that, to keep asking until he got an answer that satisfied him.

Lizzie glanced at Max. He was silent, watching her, obviously waiting to see how she was going to handle this.

"I didn't smile and laugh all the time, like you do," she told Tokoni.

"Were you sad?"

She wasn't going to lie. "Sometimes, yes."

"'Cause your mommy was gone?"

Well, there you go. He'd picked up on that, too. "Yes."

"Is she gone like my mommy is gone? Is she in heaven?"

Lizzie turned down the heat on the mixture that she'd been stirring, letting it simmer on its own. Leaning against the counter, she said, "Yes, that's exactly where my mommy is." Only she couldn't tell him that her troubled Southern belle mother had chosen to be there.

"I don't 'member my mommy, but Mrs. Losa says that she loved me."

Lizzie fought back a glaze of tears. No way was she going to cry in front of this sweet, comforting child. "Losa told us about your mommy, too."

"I don't have any pictures of her. Do you have pictures of your mommy?"

"Yes, they're in an album at my house." Photos that Lizzie rarely looked at anymore.

He tilted his head. "Was her hair like yours?"

"No, it was blond. Yellow," she clarified, "and always all done up." She made an upswept motion. "She wore fancy clothes and lots of jewels, too." Lizzie had inherited her mother's diamonds and pearls. She lowered her hands. "My dad is a ginger, though, like me."

"Ginger?"

"That's what some people call redheads."

Tokoni peeled another banana, neatly this time. "Is Ginger the name of a goodness? I mean a goddess?" he corrected himself, peering at her with his big brown eyes.

Max was looking at her, too. He stood beside the table with the damp towel still in his hands.

She replied, "No. Ginger isn't a goddess. In some places, it's been used to make fun of redheads. But now lots of redheads are claiming it as their own and making it a good thing. Ginger is a spice that people cook with that gives food a reddish tinge. There was also a character on an old TV show named Ginger who had red hair. I've heard that it might have come from her, too, but I'm not sure."

"What was she like?" Tokoni asked.

"She was a movie star who got stranded on an island with some other people when the boat they were on was caught in a storm. It sounds serious, but it was a funny show."

Max was smiling now. "The island wasn't like this

one. It was uncharted, meaning that no one knew where it was. They built their own huts and ate lots of coconuts."

"We eat lots of coconuts here!" Tokoni got excited.

Lizzie replied, "Yes, you most certainly do." Losa's grandsons tended to the trees. They had a vegetable garden on the property, too. "But if we don't get back to the pudding we're making, it's never going to get done."

"We better hurry," the boy said to Max.

"You bet." Max returned to his seat and pretended to cut the bananas really fast.

Tokoni exaggerated peeling them, too. Then he said, "I wish this wasn't your last day."

"I know. Me, too." Max cleared his throat. "But we'll come back and see you again." He looked at Lizzie. "Won't we?"

"Yes, we definitely will." They couldn't tell Tokoni that they were going to try to find a family for him in the States. They discussed it with Losa, of course, and she was open to the idea, as long as they understood the challenges associated with it. Lizzie wasn't expecting it to be easy. But she wanted to stay as positive as she could.

Immersing herself in her task, she turned away to beat egg yolks in a bowl and add them to the mixture she was cooking. Lots of pudding for lots of kids, she thought. She couldn't imagine cooking regularly for this crowd.

"Is your mommy in heaven, too?" Tokoni asked Max suddenly.

Lizzie spun around. So far, Max had gotten away with not having to tell Tokoni about his childhood. But now he'd been put on the spot. He certainly couldn't claim that his mean-spirited mother had bypassed heaven and gone straight to hell, even if that was the answer buried deep in his eyes.

"Yes, she's gone," he said.

"Do you any have pictures of her?"

"No." He quickly added, "But I have pictures of my brothers on my phone that I can show you. I have two brothers, and they both have kids. Jake's daughter is a baby, and Garrett is adopting a little girl who belongs to his fiancée, the woman he's going to marry."

"He's 'dopting a kid?" Tokoni wiggled in his chair, gratification written all over his face. "He must be a nice guy."

"He is. Very nice. Both of my brothers are. After my mom went away, I became a foster kid. I lived in other people's homes because I didn't have anywhere else to go. Sort of like the foster children who stay here."

Tokoni nodded in understanding.

Max continued, "And that's where I met my brothers. Jake lost his parents, too, and Garrett's mommy was too sick to take care of him. But she got better. Or as well as she could."

"Better enough for him to go back to her?"

"Yes."

"Did you or your other brother ever get 'dopted?"

"No, neither of us ever did."

Max exchanged a glance with Lizzie, and she thought about how he hadn't wanted to be adopted. Of course he wasn't about to reveal that to Tokoni.

"I'm going to get 'dopted," the boy said. "I know I will."

Lizzie smiled, encouraging his dream. "I know you will, too."

Tokoni beamed, and her heart swelled, especially when he came over to her and wrapped his arms around her middle, giving her an impromptu hug. She reached down and smoothed his bangs, moving them out of his eyes, and for one crazy, beautiful moment, she believed what Max had said about her was true: that she would make an amazing mom.

But she shook off the feeling. This wasn't about her maternal stirrings, no matter how incredible they seemed. This was about uncovering the parents Tokoni was meant to have.

Five

Max and Lizzie were home, seated across from each other at a hectic little sandwich shop. They'd both gotten the same thing: turkey and Swiss clubs, side salads and lemonade. She looked tired, he thought. For the time being, he was exhausted, too.

They'd been back in LA for a month, working nonstop on their goal of finding Tokoni a family, using every resource they could think of. She'd written and posted her original blog article, along with a special feature on Tokoni. She'd also crafted tons of articles as a guest blogger on international adoption sites. Max had created a slew of social media accounts dedicated to their cause, and today, before stopping for this quickie lunch, they'd met with an adoption attorney to give him a packet about the orphanage in case he had any clients who might be interested in a boy Tokoni's age. This wasn't the first attorney they'd spoken to nor would it be their last. They had a checklist a mile long.

"You seem discouraged," Lizzie said. "But we knew this wasn't going to be easy."

"I'm not discouraged. I'm just—" he searched his befuddled mind for the right word and came up with "—worried."

She shifted in her chair. "About what?"

"The way I feel. How this is affecting me. How it's draining you. How it's making zombies out of us."

She furrowed her brow. "I'm doing fine."

"Are you? Are you really?" The late-afternoon light from a nearby window showcased the pale lavender circles beneath her eyes. "I think it's taking an emotional toll on you."

"So what are you saying? That you want us to slow down?" She frowned directly at him. "Or quit and leave that poor little boy in the orphanage? I can't do that. It'll break my heart not to try to give him the family he deserves."

"I'm not suggesting that we stop or slow down. I'm—" Once again, he faltered, struggling to say what he meant.

"You're what?" She picked at a corner of her sandwich, eating it like a bird.

"I've been thinking a lot about us lately. You and me. And how we would be better parents for Tokoni than these strangers we keep searching for. So far, no one else has even taken an interest in him. And even if someone does, are they going to care about him as much as we do?" *There.* He'd said it. He'd admitted the true reason for his exhaustion. Max wasn't physically tired. It was his heart that was working overtime.

"Oh, my God." She released a jittery breath. "Do you hear what you're saying?"

"That I wish we could adopt him? Yes, I'm hearing

it." From his own parched lips. He grabbed his drink and took a swig.

"It's impossible. You know Losa would never let us adopt him. We don't meet his mother's requirements. We aren't who she envisioned for him."

"I know, but it shouldn't matter that we're single. We'd still make the best parents he could ever have."

She picked at her food again. "Do you really believe that? Even about me? Am I really the best mom he could have?"

"Yes, you are. Look what you're going through to find him a family. There isn't another woman on earth who's fighting for his happiness the way you are." Max still hadn't taken a bite of his sandwich yet. But he was watching Lizzie, sweet, delicate, ladylike Lizzie, dissect hers.

"On our last day at the orphanage, when we were making the pudding, I was starting to feel like a mom." She tore at a slice of tomato. "But I knew better than to focus on it."

"It isn't fair that his mother set such strict requirements. Every other kid in that place is allowed to be adopted by a single parent. And in our case, Tokoni would be getting two single parents, a mom and a dad, who would raise him with as much love and care as he needs."

"Except that we would be parenting him from separate households," she pointed out.

"There's nothing wrong with that. Our friendship is stronger than most marriages, anyway."

"I agree, completely. But Losa is bound by their laws to follow his mother's instructions. She couldn't let us adopt him, even if she wanted to." Lizzie's voice rattled. "She already told us how imperative it was for him to be adopted by a married couple."

Max made a frustrated rebuttal. "Do you know how many people get divorced and fight over their kids or use them as pawns? What if that happens with Tokoni's future parents? What if their relationship turns bitter and he gets caught in the cross fire?"

"That's out of our control. Or Losa's or anyone's. All any of us can do is try to find him the parents his mother wanted him to have and pray for the best. I don't want to think the worst. It makes me too sad." She tore at her sandwich again, looking as if she might cry. "I need to believe that everything will work out."

"I'm sorry. I shouldn't have put such a negative spin on it. We'll just keep going, moving forward to find him a family." Even if it hurt, he thought. Even if he was convinced that he and Lizzie were the parents Tokoni needed. He went quiet for a moment, collecting his thoughts. "Speaking of adoption, Garrett called me this morning and said that Ivy's adoption was finalized today." Ivy was the toddler who belonged to Garrett's fiancée. The child he'd told Tokoni about. "He's officially her father now."

"Oh, that's wonderful. I'm happy for him. But do you think that's part of the reason you've been hit so hard about not being able to adopt Tokoni?"

"I don't know. Maybe." He hated to think that he was comparing his life to his brother's. "Garrett and Meagan are having a party to celebrate. A big bash they're planning for the Saturday after next. Do you want to come with me?"

"Yes. I'd love to go. I've never even met little Ivy."

"Then here's your chance."

"I haven't met Meagan yet, either."

Damn, he thought. He should have introduced her to Garrett's fiancée by now. But at least he was making up for lost time. "I think you'll like her."

"I can't help being curious about her, especially with her shaky past and how she stole from Garrett. And from you and Jake, too," she quickly added.

Max nodded. Meagan had embezzled from the three of them when she worked for their accountant. Her former boyfriend had talked her into committing the crime and then ditched her after she'd gotten caught. Meagan didn't even know she was pregnant until after she went to prison. "It's awful to think that she gave birth while she was incarcerated and that the father wanted nothing to do with her or Ivy."

Lizzie blew out a sigh. "It's sort of like what Tokoni's dad did."

"Only he can't try to come back into the picture." According to the adoption laws in Nulah, he'd relinquished his parental rights when he abandoned the boy and his mother. Even his name had been removed from the birth certificate. "Ivy's dad tried to make a claim on her."

"He did? When?"

"Soon after Garrett and Meagan got together. But he wasn't interested in his daughter. It was money he was after."

Lizzie made a tight face. "What a jerk."

"Totally. But you know what? Garrett paid him off, anyway. He just wanted to get rid of the guy so he could adopt Ivy."

"And now Garrett's her new daddy." She softened her expression. "I'm looking forward to the party. Thanks for inviting me to go with you."

"It's going to be a princess theme. Ivy was named after a princess in a children's book."

"Oh, that's cute."

"And just think, a princess theme is right up your alley, with you being a royal goddess and all."

She tossed a crumb of bread at him. "Smart aleck."

He smiled, trying to stay as upbeat as he possibly could. But that didn't change how troubled he felt inside or how much he wished that Tokoni could become their son.

The party was being held in one of the ballrooms at the luxurious beachfront hotel and resort Garrett owned. Lizzie was running a bit late, so she'd told Max that she would meet him there, and by the time she arrived, the festivities were well underway.

Everyone had the option of donning a complimentary crown. A table at the entrance of the ballroom was filled with them, in all sorts of shapes, colors and sizes. Lizzie chose a tiara decorated with green gems because it complemented her emerald gown. The attire was formal. Costumes were encouraged, too. Girls posing as Cinderella, Snow White and the Little Mermaid ran amok. Prince Charming and knights in shining armor were favorites among the boys.

Games, party favors, face painting, lessons on how to be a prince or a princess. You name it, this party had it. There was a magnificently crafted wooden castle/playhouse for the kids, which was also big enough for the adults. Even the food appeared to be fit for royalty, with a spectacular buffet.

Lizzie scanned the crowd for Max. She found him near the castle, holding a toy scepter. He wore a black velvet tuxedo with a tailcoat, and his big, bold medieval-style crown sat high atop his head, making a strong statement.

As she approached him, she noticed that he'd forgone the customary shirt and tie. Instead, he'd paired his tux with a Princess Leia T-shirt. Lizzie smiled to herself. Max was and always would be a *Star Wars* nerd.

"Look at you," she said.

"And you." He waved his scepter at her. "Your dress is hot."

"This old thing." She laughed. Along with the long silk gown, she'd draped herself in diamonds. "I see that you found a way to sneak in your favorite princess." She poked a finger at his T-shirt. "That was clever."

"I figured it would work. This is quite the kiddy soiree, isn't it?"

"I'll say. Where's the newly adopted girl?"

"In there." He motioned to the castle.

"Are you on guard duty?" A wonderfully offbeat king, she thought, behaving like a knight.

"For now I am. I told her parents that I would hold down the fort so they could grab a bite to eat. They'll be back from the buffet soon. You should have seen Ivy when she was first announced to her guests, under her new last name. We stood in a receiving line so she could greet us."

"I'm sorry I missed that. I can't wait to meet her."

"Hold on and I'll get her for you now." Max put the scepter on a gilded ledge of the castle exterior and went inside.

He returned with a dark-haired toddler dressed in a puffy pink dress, rife with taffeta and lace. Her face was painted with glitter, and multicolored gems embellished her sparkling gold tiara.

Max scooped up her up and said, "This is Ivy Ann Snow, the belle of the ball."

Ivy gazed at Lizzie and said, "Garry do this."

Garry, she assumed, was Garrett. And "this" was most likely a reference to the party, unless it meant the adoption.

Either way, Lizzie told her, "You look beautiful, like a princess should."

The child said, "Tank you," for "*Thank* you."

Lizzie smiled. Apparently Ivy had a bit of trouble with her pronunciation. But Tokoni mispronounced some of his words, too. "I know a five-year-old boy who would have liked to be here. But he lives too far away."

"What's him name?"

"Tokoni."

"Where him live?"

"In an island country called Nulah," Lizzie replied. Ever since Max had lamented that they should be the ones to adopt him, making her long for the impossible, she missed Tokoni even more.

"Do Maddy know him?"

Maddy? It took Lizzie a second to realize that Ivy was taking about Max. "Yes, he knows him."

"Maddy my uncle."

"Your favorite uncle," he said, tickling Ivy and making her laugh.

A few giggles later, she tried to wiggle out of his arms, her attention span waning. "I go now."

"Okay, Princess." He put her down, and she dashed off, back into the castle to play with her friends. Or her subjects. Or whoever she was holding court with.

"I didn't know she called you Maddy," Lizzie said.

"When I first met her, I told her my name was Mad Max, and she turned it into Maddy."

"I like it. Maybe I'll start calling you that, too, since I started the Mad Max handle to begin with."

"Go ahead, pretty Lizard. I don't mind." He reached out to touch one of her diamond drop earrings. "Are these new?"

"No, they're from my mother's collection." She went a little breathless, having him standing so close to her. "Vintage Harry Winston."

"And this?" He skimmed her necklace. "Was it your mom's, too?"

She nodded. "Yes, except it's early Cartier." She lifted her wrist to showcase her bracelet. "And here we have Tiffany and Company." Normally she kept her mother's jewelry in a safe-deposit box at the bank. "I got into the vault, so to speak."

"What made you decide to do that?"

"They remind me of when I was a little girl, so wearing them to a child's fancy party felt right somehow." She tempered her emotions, trying to keep her voice from cracking. "Mama used to let me play with her jewelry when I was young. She would dress me up and stand me in front of the mirror, giving me the history of each piece."

"I'll bet your mother would have loved this party."

"Yes, I'm sure she would have." She took a step back, away from him. But what she really wanted was to move straight into his arms and be held by him, soothing the ache of them not being able to become Tokoni's parents.

"Hey, you two," a masculine voice said from behind them.

Lizzie and Max turned simultaneously. The man who'd spoken to them was Garrett. He stood tall and trim and polished, his jet-black hair slicked straight back, his classic tuxedo sharp and crisp. He wasn't sporting a crown. But he'd probably removed it after the opening ceremony.

Next to him and holding his hand was his fiancée. Meagan was a lovely brunette with almond-shaped eyes and waist-length hair. She wore a powder-blue gown and a silver tiara.

Garrett introduced Lizzie to Meagan, and the women smiled and greeted each other.

Afterward, Lizzie said to Garrett, "Congratulations on the adoption. I met your new daughter. She's beautiful." To Meagan, she added, "She looks like you."

"Thank you." Meagan leaned toward Garrett. "She certainly adores her new daddy."

As if on cue, Ivy poked her head out of the castle, saw her parents and ran over to them. She grinned at everyone, her puffy dress askew. Then she said, "Come," to Garrett and tugged him toward the playhouse. With her other hand, she grabbed Max, pulling him in the same direction.

Meagan laughed. "Apparently the men have been summoned."

Lizzie laughed, too. "So it seems." She watched them disappear into the castle, with the toddler leading the way.

After a stretch of silence, Meagan said, "I saw you once before. It was at a fund-raiser at the park. But it was a while ago, before Garrett and I had gone public with our relationship. So no one introduced me to you. You were off in the distance, with a group of other women."

"Was Max there, too?"

"Yes. It was the first time I met him. Later that day, Garrett told me about you and how close you and Max were. I've wondered about the two of you ever since."

Lizzie's heart went bump. "What do you mean?"

"If you were more than friends—" The brunette stalled. "I hope it was all right that I just said that."

"You're not the first person who's been curious about us." And she wouldn't be the last, Lizzie thought. "It happens all the time."

"Then you must be used to it."

Was she? At the moment, she wasn't so sure.

Meagan said, "When Garrett and I first got together, we told everyone we were just friends, when we were actually having a secret affair. So I thought maybe that's what you and Max had been doing. That at some point, your friendship had turned into more. But Garrett insisted that wasn't the case. Still, I wondered how anyone, outside of you and Max, could know the absolute truth."

"The truth is that we're just friends." Friends who wanted each other, she thought. Being painfully honest, she added, "But I'm not denying that there's an attraction between us. That we…" That they what? Wished they could be lovers, but were afraid it would ruin their friendship?

"I'm sorry. I wasn't trying to pry." Meagan made a face. "Well, maybe I was. But only because of how fascinated I was by you and Max when I first saw you."

"I've been fascinated by you, too, and your history with Garrett. You've had a lot to overcome."

"That's why we kept our relationship a secret at first. I didn't want anyone to know that I was dating one of the men I embezzled from. But Garrett convinced me that we needed to come clean."

"He's a forthright guy."

"Yes, he is. I love him so much I could burst."

Lizzie couldn't relate. So far, her experience with love hurt something fierce: the loss of her mother, the pang of not being close to her father. And now she'd begun to love Tokoni, a child who wasn't even hers.

Determined to keep a rein on her emotions, she asked, "Did Garrett happen to mention the boy that Max and I are trying to find a home for?"

"Yes, he did. If there's anything I can do to help, just let me know."

"Thanks, I will." Lizzie gestured to their surroundings, her mother's Tiffany bracelet catching the light. "I told Ivy that Tokoni would have enjoyed coming to this party. It's hard not to think of him in a setting like this."

"Oh, I'm sorry that he couldn't be here." Meagan watched her with sympathy. "You must be really attached to him."

If she only knew how attached, Lizzie thought. "Max and I both are. He's a special kid."

"It's sad to think of kids living in orphanages and foster care. My brother, Tanner, raised Ivy when I was locked up, or else she would have been placed in the system. Tanner is here tonight, with his wife. My other brother and his wife and son are here, too. They flew in from Montana."

"Sounds like you have a wonderful support group."

"I couldn't have gotten through my struggles without them. Garrett's mom has been amazing, too. And of course, Garrett's brothers. Jake and Carol were here earlier with baby Nita, but they left already. Nita was getting fussy and needed to go home for her nap. Do you know Carol? Have you seen the baby?"

"I met Carol before Jake married her, when she was working for him as his personal assistant. But I don't know her very well. I haven't seen the baby yet. I sent a gift when she was born. But she must be about four or five months old by now."

"I didn't know Carol very well at first, either. But I'm becoming really close to her and the baby. Ivy adores them, too. She thinks her cousin Nita is the most wonderful being on earth."

"It's nice that you and Carol formed a bond and that your children will grow up together." Lizzie wanted Tokoni to have that type of family, too, the loving, caring kind every child should have.

"Maybe you could join us for lunch sometime."

"You and Carol?"

"Yes."

"Thank you. I'd like that." After they exchanged numbers, programming them into their phones, Lizzie asked, "Have you and Garrett set a wedding date?"

"Not yet. I want to complete my parole first. But Garrett didn't want to wait to adopt Ivy, so he started those proceedings months ago."

Lizzie smiled. "It sure seems to have worked out."

Meagan smiled, as well. "It definitely has."

Just as their conversation came to a close, Max and Garrett returned with Ivy in tow. Garrett was carrying her. He approached Meagan, and the child leaned forward to kiss her mommy.

Lizzie's heart ached from the sweet sight.

After the smooch ended, Garrett and Meagan took their leave, hauling their little princess over to the dance floor, where a kid-friendly band prepared to play Disney tunes.

In the moment that followed, Lizzie said to Max, "Meagan invited me to have lunch sometime with her and Carol."

"That's nice. I'm glad she included you in the girly stuff."

"She's easy to talk to. We discussed all sorts of things." She quickly added, "But I didn't tell her what you said about wishing that we could adopt Tokoni. There was no point in saying anything about that."

"I haven't told anyone that, either, not when there's no way to make it happen." He bumped her shoulder with his, his jacket grazing her arm. "Unless we suck it up and get married."

Her jaw nearly hit the floor. "Please tell me that you're kidding. That you didn't mean that."

"Of course I was kidding. You didn't really think…" He hesitated, frowned, blew out a choppy breath. "Besides, in order for something like that to work, we'd have to fake everyone out and pretend to be a real couple."

Lizzie's tiara was starting to feel uncomfortably heavy. "Meagan wondered if we were having a secret affair."

His voice turned grainy. "Yeah, people sometimes wonder about that. But in order for this to work, we would have to split up after the adoption with an amicable divorce. That way, we could co-parent Tokoni and still hang out as friends."

She couldn't believe what was coming out of his mouth. "Listen to yourself, Max. You're plotting the details. You're actually starting to think about it."

"I'm just thinking out loud."

"About us faking a marriage." Confused, she shook her head. "Do you know how crazy that sounds?"

"You're right." He cleared the roughness from his throat. "I shouldn't have mentioned it."

Lizzie shifted her gaze to the parents and kids and happy festivities. Everywhere she looked, she saw what she and Max were missing. But no matter how badly it hurt, entering into a phony marriage wasn't the answer.

Was it?

Six

At 1:45 a.m. Lizzie was still awake, alone in the dark, staring at the red digits on the clock.

She couldn't stop thinking about Ivy's party and the conversation she'd had with Max.

About marrying him.

Or not marrying him.

Or adopting Tokoni.

Or not adopting him.

She wasn't supposed to be letting that discussion spin around in her brain. Yet she couldn't seem to get it out of her mind.

Her only solution was to work even harder to find prospective parents for Tokoni. To sleep tonight and get up tomorrow, refreshed and ready to go. But that was easier said than done. She would probably be up for the rest of the night, fighting this battle.

And it was all Max's fault. If he hadn't tossed that

fake marriage idea out there, she wouldn't be in this insomnia mess.

Just as she cursed him, her cell phone rang.

She jumped to attention. Was it Max, having the same wide-awake struggle as her? God, she hoped not. He was the last person she wanted to talk to.

She reached for the blaring device, where it sat on her nightstand. Sure enough, it was him. His name flashed on the screen, way too bright in the dark. But instead of ignoring him, like she should've, she answered the damned call.

"What do you want?" she asked.

"I knew you would be up," he replied, undaunted by her frustration. "I can't sleep, either. Can I come over?"

She switched on the lamp beside her bed and shot a pissy glance at the clock. Three minutes had passed since she last looked at it. "Do you know what time it is?"

"Yeah, it's almost two. And I'm going to lose my freaking mind if you don't let me come over."

"All right. Fine." She gave in. If she didn't, she would only lie awake, even more embattled than before. "But you better bring some donuts. I need some comfort food."

"I'll stop by a convenience store on the way over and get a package of the powdered kind, the mini ones you used to eat when we were kids. Those always made you feel better."

"Get two packages." If she was going to pig out on itty-bitty donuts, she might as well do it right.

"Sure thing. I'll see you soon."

He ended the call, leaving her staring at the phone. What had she just gotten herself into, agreeing to entertain Max in the wee hours of the morning?

She got dressed, climbing into the nearest jeans and

T-shirt. She certainly wasn't going to answer the door in her short little satin chemise. Lizzie always wore fancy lingerie to bed. Her mom used to do that, too. But she shouldn't be likening herself to her mother right now. She'd already draped herself in Mama's diamonds earlier.

Hoping that a cup of tea would help soothe her nerves, she entered her bright white kitchen and filled an old-fashioned teakettle with water. She'd bought it at an antiques store, intending to use it as a flowerpot on her patio, but changed her mind and kept it on her stove top instead.

Anxious about seeing Max, she riffled through the tin container where she stored her tea bags and chose a fragrant herbal blend.

She sat at the chrome-and-glass dining table in the morning room, adjacent to the kitchen, and waited for the whistle.

Finally, when the kettle sang its song, she removed it from the flame and fixed her tea. She put an empty cup on the counter for Max, in case he wanted some, too.

He arrived with the donuts. He handed them to her, and she offered him the tea. He opted for orange juice, getting into her fridge and pouring it himself. He was attired in the same *Star Wars* T-shirt he'd worn to the party, only he was wearing it with plaid pajama bottoms instead of a velvet tuxedo.

"I can't believe you went out of the house like that," she said.

"What can I say? I'm still the same dork I always was." He grinned and toasted her with his juice.

"Stop that." It was bad enough that he was here, rumpled from bed; she didn't need him smiling like a sexy loon.

"Stop what?"

"Nothing. Never mind." She couldn't tell him how hot he looked. Better for him to assume that he looked like a dork.

He finally stopped grinning. "I can't quit thinking about us adopting Tokoni, Lizzie."

"I know. Me, too." She carried the donuts into the morning room, where she'd left her tea. She brought a stack of napkins, as well, certain she would need them.

Max followed her, and they sat across from each other. The blinds on the window that normally bathed the table in natural light were closed. Typically, Lizzie used this room for breakfast, not for middle-of-the-night snacks.

She tore into the donuts and ate the first package, right off the bat. They tasted like the processed junk they were, cheap and stale, but satisfying, too.

"Do you want one?" she asked him.

He shook his head. "Do you think we should just do it?"

"Do what? Adopt Tokoni?" She grabbed a napkin and wiped her mouth with shaky hands. "We can't."

"We could if we followed my plan."

"And get married?" Her hands shook even more. "Then divorced later? That's cheating."

"So you're suggesting that we should stay married instead? Cripes, Lizzie, that wouldn't work."

"No." Absolutely, positively no. "I'm saying that faking a marriage is cheating and that we shouldn't do it at all. It's not fair to Tokoni's mother."

"But we'd be good parents. The best we could be to her son."

"That still doesn't give us permission to bend the rules. And what about Losa? How are we supposed to convince her that our ruse is real?"

"We'll just tell her that our quest for finding Tokoni

a home created feelings for each other that we never knew we had."

She opened the second package of donuts. "Feelings?"

"Yeah, you know." He made a sour face. "We'll tell Losa that we've fallen head-over-stupid-heels in love."

"Gee, what a nice, romantic way to put it. And if your sickly expression is any indication of how in love you are, this story you cooked up is never going to fly."

"Stop giving me such a hard time. You look miserable, too."

"That's because I don't want to get married."

"I don't, either. But I want to be Tokoni's father, and I want you to be his mother. And I don't know how else to make that happen."

Heaven help them, Lizzie thought. He sounded so beautifully sincere, so deep and true, that a marriage based on a lie was beginning to seem like the right thing to do. "Do you really think we could pull this off?"

"Yes, I do. But we would have to fake it with everyone, even friends and family. We couldn't let it slip that we're only doing it for Tokoni or that we plan to get divorced later."

"Won't the divorce seem suspicious, so soon after the adoption?"

"Not if we say that we misunderstood our feelings for each other and mixed it up with our love for the boy. Besides, when people see how amicable our divorce is and how easily we've remained friends, there shouldn't be any cause for concern."

She imagined having Tokoni as her forever son, of sharing him with Max, of seeing this through. "I want to be his mom as much as you want to be his dad."

He leaned forward, lifting the hind legs of his chair off the floor. "Then let's go for it."

She looked into the vastness of his eyes. By now she could barely breathe. But she agreed, anyway.

"Okay," she said. "But what's our first step?" Besides sitting here, losing the last of their sanity? Her heart was pounding so fast she feared she might topple over.

He wasn't grounded, either, not with the way he was tipping his chair. "I think we should start by talking to Losa."

"Should we go see her?"

"Truthfully, I'd rather call her with the news." He dropped his chair back onto the floor with a thud. "In fact, we can do that later today."

Lizzie wasn't ready. "I need more time than that."

"What for?"

"To work on a script for us to follow."

"Winging it would be easier for me."

"I'd prefer to research what I'm going to say." She always prepared herself for proper speeches. "I can't just spout it off the top of my head."

"And I can't refer to something you drummed up. It'll sound canned."

She blew out a sigh. Already they were having problems, and they weren't even an official couple yet.

He glanced at the darkened window. "Maybe I should do it alone. It isn't necessary for both of us to call her, and it'll probably make me more nervous to have you there, anyway, with your handy-dandy script."

Lizzie considered his point. Lying to Losa was bad enough, but doing it together might make it worse, especially if they were out of sync. "All right, but you should go home now and try to get some rest. It won't help your cause if you're half asleep when you profess these phony feelings of ours."

"Okay, but you better not change your mind about marrying me between now and then."

"I won't." Because as afraid as she was of becoming Max's temporary wife, she was more afraid of losing the child they so desperately wanted.

Max did it. He'd talked to Losa. And now he was back at Lizzie's house, sitting on her artfully designed patio, with its built-in barbecue and portable bar, preparing to tell her how the discussion went. He glanced around and noticed that the greenery seemed far more tropical than he recalled it being in the past, as if she'd gotten inspired by their trip to Nulah and the private gardens at the resort where they'd stayed. But this wasn't the time to comment on her plants and flowers.

"I think Losa believed me," he said.

"You *think* she believed you?" Lizzie's blue eyes locked on to his. "What's that supposed to mean?"

"It means that I told her everything I was supposed to tell her, and it seems like she bought it. Of course I felt like I was going to have a panic attack when I got to the part about how we'd fallen in love during our search to find Tokoni a family. But I played up how long you and I have known each other and how close we've always been and all that. I tried to make it sound plausible." Even now his heart was roaring in his ears, the panic he'd endured still skirting through his blood. "Luckily, I didn't have to fake the part about how much we wanted Tokoni. That was easy to say."

Lizzie looked as nervous as he felt. "Is she going to let us adopt him?"

"She said that she can't make that determination until after we're married and start the process, like any other applicants would have to do. Legally, she can't promise him to us until we meet the requirements. But she did seem eager for us to come back after the wedding, so we can all meet in person again and discuss the specifics."

She appeared to relax, her shoulders not nearly as tense. "That seems like a positive sign."

"I thought so, too. I told her that we're planning on having a traditional ceremony. I didn't want her to think that we were going to elope or exclude our family and friends. To me, that didn't seem like what a happily engaged couple would do. I did stress, however, that we were eager to be together and bring Tokoni into our lives, so the wedding would be sooner than later."

"Sounds like you did a good job of presenting us as the type of parents Tokoni's mother wanted him to have."

He'd sure as hell tried. "Thanks. But now we really do need to hire a wedding planner and get this thing going."

"Maybe Garrett can recommend one of the events coordinators his hotel uses."

"I'll have to talk to him about it. But first I need to tell him and Jake the same story I told Losa." Only this time Max would be lying to his brothers, something he wasn't looking forward to.

"I need to tell my friends, too. And decide who is going to be part of my bridal party. I've been a bridesmaid before, so I have an inkling of what it entails."

Max nodded. He was also experienced in that regard. He and Garrett had shared the responsibility of being the best men in Jake's wedding.

She made a pained face. "What should I do about my dad? If we're having a traditional ceremony, should I adhere to protocol and ask him to walk me down the aisle?"

"I don't know, Lizzie. That's up to you." He couldn't make that determination for her. Nor did he want to.

"Damn, there's so much to think about, so much to do. I'm already getting overwhelmed."

"Me, too." She smoothed the front of her button-down blouse, fussing with the starched material, almost as if it were the lacy bodice of a wedding gown. "What about our living arrangements? Am I supposed to move in with you after we're married?"

"That makes the most sense. My house is bigger, and you can use one of the rooms in the guest wing, without anyone being the wiser."

"What about your maid service? Won't they notice that we're not staying together?"

"We can stage the master suite to give the impression that you're sleeping there. We can stage your room, too, so it appears as if we have a female visitor, a reclusive celebrity or someone that they're never going to see. They're not going to suspect it's you. Besides, it's a highly secure company, with housekeepers who are screened to work with wealthy clients and protect their privacy."

"If I move into your mansion, what should I do about this place?"

"You can say that you're going to rent it out for vacationers and whatnot, keeping it furnished the way it is. It would be an ideal condo for that."

"Except that I won't actually be renting it. I don't want out-of-towners staying in my home."

"That part doesn't matter. No one is going to delve that deeply into your business affairs." He considered another aspect of the plans. "If we're going to announce our engagement, then I need to hurry up and buy you a ring."

"You're right. Everyone will be asking to see it. Whenever one of my friends gets engaged, that's the first thing that comes up."

He didn't doubt it. "I'll arrange for a jeweler to bring

some rings by for you to choose from. We can meet at my house, maybe later in the week."

She frowned at her left hand, where the bauble was going to go. "I'll be sure to return it to you after the divorce."

He shook his head, refusing her offer. "I don't want it back."

"But you could resell it."

"I'd rather that you kept it. You can lock it away with the jewelry your mom gave you, as a keepsake or investment or whatever."

"What about a wedding band for you?"

"I'll have the jeweler bring those, too. We can do it in one fell swoop. And hopefully with the least amount of fanfare possible." But even as he said it, he knew it wasn't going to be a casual process, not when it involved a ritual created for people who were supposed to be in love.

Although Lizzie had been to Max's house more times than she could count, she'd never expected that she would be living there. Yet that was what would be happening, soon enough.

The three-story mansion had a spiral staircase in the center of the home that curved with an air of mystery. There was also a large entryway, a woodsy den, a formal drawing room and a screening room. On the third floor was a ballroom with a wraparound balcony, designed for glamorous parties. The original owner was the head of a movie studio, way back when.

The servants' quarters were located on the first level, directly off the kitchen, but Max didn't have a live-in staff. The maid service he used kept things tidy, and when he wasn't eating out, he cooked for himself. A chef wasn't necessary.

The mansion itself probably wasn't necessary, either, Lizzie thought. But Max had bought it to console the poor battered boy he'd once been, fascinated by its rich 1930s charm.

Today she and Max occupied the den, waiting for the jeweler to arrive. While she sat on an art deco settee, he stood beside the fireplace, with the painting of Lady Ari showcased above it. She couldn't deny how nicely the artwork complemented the spot he'd chosen for it.

Was this really happening? Was she actually going to become his bride?

"I'm getting stage fright," she said.

"About picking out rings?"

"About all of it. It's weird, but I wish my mom was here to help me through it. She loved big fancy occasions."

"I'm sorry you have to face this without her."

As much as her mother's suicide hurt, Lizzie couldn't bear to hate her for it. "She would have liked you, Max. This house would have impressed her, too."

"I've been thinking that we could have the wedding here, that we could do the ceremony outside, on the lawn, and then head up to the ballroom for the reception."

She studied him: his tall, trim physique, his shiny black hair falling just shy of his shoulders. He'd never had a picnic on his lawn, let alone a wedding. He'd never used his ballroom before, either. He wasn't keen on entertaining, even if his house was wonderfully suited for it. "Are you sure you're comfortable with that?"

He shrugged. "At this point, I'd rather do it here than somewhere else. Plus it'll be easier than trying to book another venue. I'd like to set the date for two months from now. I don't want to hold up the adoption any longer than that."

"Me, neither. But we'd better be prepared for a nonstop venture, if we're going to get everything done by then."

"We'll just have to find a wedding planner who's able to speed through it."

"I'll have to put a rush on finding a dress, too." But for now she didn't have a clue what type of gown she was going to wear. "Gosh, can you imagine how strange it's going to be, with you and me, reciting vows? Talk about being nervous."

He scowled, hard and deep. "They're just words, Lizzie."

"Words about love and commitment and things that don't pertain to us."

"We're committed to Tokoni, and that's all that matters."

"You're right. I need to try to relax and go with the phony-wedding flow."

"Yes, you do. And so do I." He pasted a smile on his face. "This is supposed to be a joyous occasion. We don't want the jeweler to think there's something wrong with us."

She smiled, as well, practicing her bride-to-be expression. "This will be a good test of how we're supposed to behave."

He glanced at a cuckoo clock on the wall, a quirky old timepiece from the same era as the house. "He should be here soon."

"I wish he would hurry." She was eager to get the ring thing over with. But thank goodness they had the luxury of the jeweler coming to them, instead of them having to go to him.

Max's gaze roamed over her. "You look pretty, by the way."

"Thank you." She was attired in a stylish tweed ensemble with her hair twisted into a neat chignon. "I tried to keep it classy."

"You always do."

"I noticed that you donned a jacket."

"Yeah." He smoothed the lapels of his sleek black sports coat. "I've got Batman on underneath, though." He opened his jacket and showed her his T-shirt.

"At least you didn't sleep in it." She gave him a double take. "Or did you?"

He laughed. "I'll never tell."

She laughed, too. "My fiancé is weird."

"Your fiancé, huh? Look who's trying out the lingo."

"After today, it will be official." Her ring would seal the deal. "So I better get used to calling you that."

"Until you have to start calling me your husband."

"Then my ex-husband." She turned serious. "Are you going to draw up a prenup for me to sign?"

"Why would I do that?"

"To protect your money. Typically, that's what rich people do when they're getting married, and you have a lot more to lose than I do."

"I don't need to protect my assets from you." He came over and sat beside her. "You're the person I trust most in this world."

"Me, too. With you." And that was precisely why they were adopting a child together. "We're going to be awesome parents."

"The best," he agreed. "And don't worry about the wedding expenses. I'm going to pay for everything."

"You don't have to do that."

"I want to." He touched her cheek, then lifted his hand away. "But what am I going to do during the part of the ceremony where I'm supposed to kiss my bride?"

She wet her lips, a bit too quickly. "You'll have to kiss her, I guess."

"She's going to have to kiss me back, too."

Her pulse fluttered at her neck, as soft as a butterfly, as sexy as a summer breeze. "Yes, she will."

As they both fell silent, she glanced away, trapped in feelings she couldn't seem to control. She didn't want to imagine what the wedding kiss was going to be like.

Still, she wondered how it would unfold. Would he whisper something soft and soothing before he leaned into her? Would their mouths be slightly open, their eyes completely closed? Would she sigh and melt against him, like a princess being awakened by the wrong prince? Just thinking about it made her feel forbidden.

Sucking in her breath, she shifted her gaze to his. She saw that he was studying her, as if he sensed what was going on in her head. Uncomfortable in her own skin, she clasped her hands on her lap. She'd been fighting these types of urges for what seemed like forever, and now the ache had gone warm and rogue.

Brrrrinng.

The security buzzer sounded, alerting them that the jeweler had arrived at the front gate.

What timing.

Max jumped off the settee and took his phone out of his pocket. He punched out a key code and opened the gate with an app he'd designed. When he glanced up, he studied her again. "You okay, Lizzie?"

She nodded, even if she wasn't. He'd certainly recovered much easier than she had. But he wasn't the one who'd drifted into la-la land. "I'm fine."

"All right, then. I better go." He headed for the door.

"I'll stay here." And collect her composure.

While he was gone, she opened her purse and removed

her compact, checking her lipstick. Nothing was out of place, of course. Max's mouth hadn't come anywhere near hers.

He returned with an older gentleman, formal in nature, who introduced himself as Timothy. The three of them gathered around a nineteenth-century mahogany card table, a focal point in the den, where Timothy could set up his portable cases. He started with the engagement rings, sweeping his hand across the impressive display once it was ready.

The diamonds were big and beautiful and dazzling. Enormous rubies, emeralds and sapphires dazzled the eye, too. But Lizzie struggled to focus. She was still stuck on that future kiss. She even bit down on her bottom lip, trying to inflict pain as a conditioned response to keep her mind off it.

Her method didn't work. Biting her lip just made her hungrier for the man she was going to marry.

"Wow. Check this out." Max lifted a ring from its slot. An oval ruby with two perfectly matched half-moon diamonds surrounding it. He said to Timothy, "This one is downright fiery." He glanced at Lizzie. "Like her hair."

His comment made her skin tingle. But she was already immersed in all kinds of heat.

Timothy glanced at her, too. Then back at Max. With a smile, he said, "Rubies are often associated with fire and passion. That particular stone is six carats and is a star ruby, a rare variety. See the starry points in the center? How they magically glide across the surface? It's an optical phenomenon known as asterism."

Lizzie finally spoke up. "It's stunning," she said about the ring. The ruby, the star, the diamonds, every glittering aspect of it.

"Try it on," Max said.

She placed it on her left hand and held it up to view. It felt right. Too right. Too beautiful. Too perfect.

Both men watched her, silent in their observations. She glanced at the painting of Lady Ari. And for a jarring instant, it almost seemed as if the goddess was watching her, too.

"That's the one, Lizzie." Max spoke up, pulling her attention back to him.

She nodded. "It is, isn't it?" She couldn't refuse the ring, no matter how much she wanted to.

Timothy suggested a petite pavé diamond band to go with it, and her bridal set was complete. Pavé was a French word, and in this context it meant that the ring was paved with diamonds, creating an unbroken circle of sparkle and light.

When Timothy presented the men's wedding bands, Max's demeanor changed. He wasn't as self-assured as when he'd been examining rings for her.

Lizzie took the liberty of choosing a design for him—a simply styled, highly masculine piece dotted with black diamonds. There was a ruby among the gems, too. Just one, she noticed, the same fiery color as hers.

When he put it on, he frowned.

"You don't like it?" she asked.

"No, I do. Very much."

Maybe too much? she wondered. Well, at least she wasn't suffering alone. They were in this torturous situation together.

And now they would both have bloodred rubies to prove it.

Seven

Max took his brothers out for a steak dinner and ordered a fancy gold bottle of Cristal. He did everything he could to make it a celebratory occasion and tell them his news, repeating the same tale he'd told Losa. At this stage of the lie, he had it memorized.

Jake accepted it easily, lifting his glass in an immediate toast. But that was Jake for you, with his half-cocked smile, fashionable wardrobe and stylishly messy hair. He'd probably never given Max's relationship with Lizzie more than a passing glance. Either that or he'd assumed the platonic part was bogus and they'd been sleeping together for years. Prior to settling down, Jake had been a playboy, dating actresses and models and whoever else caught his roving eye.

And then there was Garrett, with his protective personality and proper ways. He'd joined in on the toast, too, but now that it was over, he appeared to be analyzing Max. Was he questioning the validity of his story? Did he suspect the truth?

Max frowned. He didn't like being judged and especially not by a man who'd helped him fight his childhood battles. "Why are you looking at me like that?"

"Because I want you to say it one more time," Garrett replied.

"Say what?"

"That you're in love with Lizzie."

Shit, Max thought. *Shit.* He grabbed his champagne and took a swig, needing the buzz. "Why are you goading me to repeat myself?"

"I'm not goading you, little brother. I just want to hear you say it."

"I already did." And it had taken every ounce of strength inside him to rattle off those phony feelings. Topping it off, he was immersed in images of how Lizzie had looked when they talked about kissing at the wedding. Rubies and diamonds and dreamy musings. How was he supposed to deal with all that?

Jake put down his fork. He'd been enjoying his big old rib-eye steak, but now he watched Max and Garrett like a tennis match.

Garrett turned to Jake. "Does Max look like he's about ready to jump out that window to you?" He gestured to the view. The restaurant was on the tenth floor, overlooking the city.

"Actually, he does." A slow grin spread across Jake's face. "But I was like that, too, when I first realized how I felt about Carol."

"Ditto," Garrett said. "About Meagan."

Now Max wanted to wring both of their necks. Apparently, Garrett had only been kidding around, setting Max up and pulling Jake into it, too.

Max shook his head. Typically, Garrett wasn't a jokester. "When did you get to be such a wise guy?"

"Since you brought us here and told us you were getting married. But in all seriousness, I was surprised to hear it. I never thought you and Lizzie were anything more than friends." Garrett sat straight and tall in his chair, impeccable, as always. "But you already explained that the adoption brought you closer."

Just in case the lies weren't clear, Max reiterated, "We're not getting married because of the adoption. But it is part of the reason we scheduled the wedding so soon."

Jake interjected, "I had a short engagement, too. But that's what sometimes happens when children are involved."

Max managed a smile. "Oh, that's right. While I was on my sabbatical, searching for the meaning of life and volunteering at an orphanage, you were at a wild party in the Caribbean impregnating your assistant."

Jake chuckled. "It was just that one weekend. Speaking of which, are you and Lizzie planning a big family? Maybe more adoptions? Or a few seedlings of your own?"

Max all but blinked. They hadn't even gotten the first kid and already they were being prodded to have more? "We're just going to focus on Tokoni for now." It was as good an answer as any and certainly more diplomatic than admitting that they would be divorced long before the possibility of other children ever came up.

"I was panicked at first about becoming a dad." Jake returned to his steak, cutting into it again. "But not anymore. My wife and daughter are everything to me."

"I'm not scared of being a father." Max was thrilled about that. It was being Lizzie's husband that freaked him out. To combat those fears, he admitted, "I am a little anxious about the wedding." Before either of his brothers could question him, he chalked up his anxiety to being a rushed groom. "There's just so much to do in such a short amount of time. I'm glad you guys will be there, standing up for me." They'd already agreed to be his best men. He addressed Garrett. "Can you recommend a wedding planner? Maybe someone you use at the hotel or an associate of theirs?"

"Sure. I'll email you a list of names. And don't worry, it'll turn out great."

"It definitely will," Jake agreed. "But don't forget about the honeymoon, too."

Max quickly replied, "That's already been worked out. We'll be going back to Nulah to start the adoption proceedings. But we'll still get to hang out at the resort where we stayed before and enjoy the beach." Only on this trip, they would have to share a bungalow, like a husband and wife would be expected to do. And that was the part about being married that petrified him the most. Wanting Lizzie, he thought, more than he ever had before. But not being able to have her.

Within a week after getting engaged, Max and Lizzie hired a whirlwind of a planner who would be consulting with them at every turn. And if that wasn't enough to keep them busy, Max had decided to revamp his yard for the ceremony, with a custom gazebo surrounded by a garden. Lizzie already thought his yard made a stunning statement, with its parklike acreage, but now it was going to be even prettier. She walked beside him as he explained work that would soon be underway.

He said, "I told the landscaper I wanted something tropical. I showed him pictures of the private gardens at the resort in Nulah to give him a feel for what I'm after.

I assumed that you would approve, since you incorporated that style onto your patio."

"I only dabbled with a few extra plants." Nonetheless, she was impressed that he'd noticed her effort.

He gestured in the distance. "They're going to build a stone walkway from the back of the house that curves around to the gazebo and serves as part of the wedding aisle. Then all the way around that will be the garden, with a waterfall fountain and some intricate little pathways."

"So essentially, we'll be getting married in the middle of the garden?" She gazed at the lawn, imagining the changes in her mind. Clearly, the landscaper and his crew would be working around the clock to complete the job. "It sounds spectacular."

"I figured if we're going to do it, we might as well do it right. I also thought it would make a nice spot for Tokoni later, for when he plays out here. It's too bad that coconut trees don't grow in this environment or I would add some of those, too."

"To give Tokoni a sense of home? We're going to have to take him back to Nulah for vacations so he doesn't lose his connection to it."

"We'll definitely do that, as often as we can." Max smiled. "I can't wait until he's our son."

"Me, too. It makes all this wedding stuff worthwhile." She breathed in the late-spring air. It would be summer by the time the ceremony took place. "I haven't talked to my dad yet. I haven't even told him that I'm getting married."

"You're going to have to do that soon, Lizzie."

"I know. But I haven't been completely remiss. I called my friends. Not everyone I associate with, but the ones I asked to be my bridesmaids. I spent an entire day on the phone, chatting with my gal pals and pretending to be in love." But she knew Max had done the same thing when he'd dined with his brothers. "It was interesting, how mixed the reactions were. Some of my friends were surprised, but others claimed that they knew all along that something was going on between us."

He checked her out, softly, slowly. "Funny, how people can't tell lust from love."

Her skin turned warm, her blood tingling in her body. "At least it's working in our favor."

He didn't respond. Instead, his stare got bolder, hungrier, as if he couldn't seem to help himself.

Lizzie's mouth went dry. If they were a real couple, heading into a genuine marriage, would they pull each other to the ground right here and now, desperate to make love on their future wedding site?

Pushing those dangerous thoughts out of her mind, she glanced away from him, breaking his stare.

He walked closer to where the gazebo was going to be, and she fell into step with him, eager to get past the heat that warmed her blood. But nonetheless, an inferno ensued. Clearly, he was still feeling it, too.

Finally, she started a new conversation by saying, "I chose blue, green and purple for the colors, with shades ranging from turquoise to magenta."

He squinted. "Colors?"

"For the wedding. It's called a peacock palette." She envisioned it being deep and rich and vibrant. "I spent hours on the net, looking at color combinations and kept coming back to that one. I hope that's all right with you."

"Sure." He stopped walking. "It sounds beautiful. I wonder what peacock symbolism is. I'm always interested in the spiritual meaning connected to animals."

She noticed how the sun shone upon his hair, creating blue-black effects. "That's the Lakota in you."

"Yes, I suppose it is." He removed his phone from his pocket. "Why don't I look it up right now?"

Still studying him, she waited while he did an internet search.

He shared the results with her. "First off, they're birds in the pheasant family, and only the male is referred to as a peacock. The female is a peahen, and both are peafowl. In terms of spirituality, some of the peacock and peahen's gifts include beauty, integrity and the ability to see into the past, present and future."

Fascinated by it all, she said, "That's quite a résumé."

"It's the eye shape on the feathers that gives them the gift of sight." He kept reading, explaining the meanings. "In relation to human spirituality, beauty and integrity is achieved when someone shows his or her true colors, so that's where all those colors come into play."

Suddenly Lizzie took pause, concerned about what he was saying and how it related to them. "Maybe we shouldn't use the peacock palette."

He glanced up from his phone. "Why not?"

"Because we're not showing our true colors. This whole thing is a lie."

"No, it isn't. Not if you look at it on a deeper scale. What we feel for Tokoni is our truth, our true colors, and adopting him is what our wedding is about to us." He glanced at his phone again. "It also says that peacocks have an association to resurrection, like the phoenix that rises out of the ashes. And isn't that what we're doing? Rising out of the ashes of our pasts and creating new lives for ourselves by becoming Tokoni's parents?"

When he lifted his gaze, she got caught up in the feeling, looking deeply into his eyes. "I'm so glad I'm going to share a child with you."

"Me, too, with you." He fell silent for a moment, looking as intently at her as she was at him. Then he asked, "So you're keeping the peacock palette, right?"

"Yes." She broke eye contact, needing to free herself from his spell. "I'm going to keep it."

"Do you think you could add a bit of gold?"

"Gold?" she parroted.

"To the color scheme. It would be cool if your dress had some gold on it."

He was putting in a special wardrobe request? Then it hit her. Lady Ari was wearing a gold dress in the painting he'd bought. "Do you want me to wear my hair loose, too?" Long and free and wild, like the goddess's?

"It would certainly look pretty that way." He reached out as if he meant to run his fingers through her hair, but he lowered his hand without doing it. "But that's up to you."

"I'll talk to my stylist about it and decide when the time comes." She didn't want to sound too eager to please him, not with how romantic he was making her feel. "What do you think of Ivy and Nita as the flower girls?" she asked, moving the discussion away from her and onto the people who would be part of procession. "Meagan and Carol could walk down the aisle with them. Meagan could hold Ivy's hand, and Carol could carry Nita."

"That's a great idea, having them participate in the ceremony, especially since my brothers are going to be in it, too."

"I'm having lunch with Meagan and Carol tomorrow, so I'll talk to them about it then. Meagan invited us to her house." No men, she thought, only women and children. But Max and his brothers had already had their meeting.

"So, what should we do about a ring bearer?" he asked. "Who should we get to do that?"

"I wish it could be Tokoni." Her heart swelled just

thinking about him. "But Losa would never let us bring him to the States to be in our wedding." Tokoni didn't even know that she and Max planned to adopt him. He wouldn't be informed about his prospective parents until everything was approved.

"I wish it could be him, too," Max said.

"So maybe we'll just skip having a ring bearer?" She couldn't fathom having another boy in place of him.

Max agreed, then said, "We can have an adoption party for Tokoni later, like Garrett and Meagan did for Ivy. Also, I think in lieu of wedding gifts, we should ask our guests to donate to the orphanage."

"That's perfect." Exactly as it should be. Not only would their marriage serve as the catalyst for adopting Tokoni, it would benefit all the other children there, too.

Meagan, Carol and Lizzie gathered around a coffee table in the living room of the residence where Meagan lived with Garrett. The elegant beachfront home was located on a cliff that overlooked the hotel and resort he owned.

They'd already had lunch, a taco feast Meagan had cooked, and now Lizzie was analyzing her companions and thinking about what she'd learned about them so far.

Meagan looked soft and natural in a chambray shirt, faded jeans and pale beige cowboy boots. Her long silky hair was plaited into a single braid, hanging down the center of her back. Little Ivy was dressed in western wear, too, but her outfit was much fancier and in shades of pink.

Both mother and daughter loved horses. Garrett's resort offered horseback riding along the beach, making the activity easily accessible to them. In fact, Meagan still worked as a stable hand in the original job Garrett had given her when she was first released from prison, even though she was engaged to him now. She'd kept the job to pay back the restitution she owed and meet the requirements of her parole.

Lizzie glanced over at Carol, who was a lovely strawberry blonde with a curvy figure and sparkling green eyes. She still worked in her original job, too, as Jake's personal assistant. But nowadays, she and Jake had baby Nita to consider, so they took the infant with them to the office, where Jake had built an on-site nursery especially for their daughter. A nanny was also on hand to help. Lizzie thought it sounded like a wonderful setup.

Carol was a former foster kid who'd lost her family. In that sense, she and her husband shared tragic histories. But as youths, they'd handled their grief in opposing ways. While Jake was running wild, Carol compensated by being a bit too well behaved. Lizzie understood. She'd become an overly proper person herself.

She turned her attention to Carol's daughter. The baby was asleep in a carrier, with two-and-a-half-year-old Ivy sitting on the floor, watching her like a mother hen. Even if they weren't blood related, the children looked like cousins, with their dark hair, chubby cheeks and golden-brown skin.

Tokoni would fit right in, Lizzie thought. He was tailor-made for this group. She was certain that he was going to love being part of Max's foster family.

Even Lizzie was beginning to love it, with how warm and welcoming Meagan and Carol were being to her.

Would that change after the divorce, creating a divide between Lizzie and the other women, or wouldn't it matter, since she and Max intended to remain close once the marriage was over?

"Did Max take you shopping for your ring?" Carol

asked, drawing her into conversation. "Or did he choose it by himself?"

"We were together when he bought it," she replied. "But he picked it out."

"It's absolutely gorgeous." Carol leaned over to get a closer look. They were seated side by side on a comfy sofa, with a sweeping view of the ocean. "It's sexy for an engagement ring."

Fire and passion, Lizzie thought, burning deep within. "Max said it reminded him of my hair."

"I can see why." Carol smiled. "That ruby is perfect for you. I think all of our men did a great job of picking out our rings." She held out her hand. "Jake had mine made in the style of a Claddagh ring because my great-grandparents were from Ireland, and he wanted to honor my heritage. He gave it to me before I'd agreed to marry him because Claddagh rings can be worn if you're single, in a relationship, engaged or married. It depends which hand you wear it on and which way the crown at the top is facing. Mine is obviously in the married position now."

"What an interesting concept." Lizzie gazed at the ring. Along with the gold crown, it boasted a dazzling pink diamond in the shape of a heart being held by two engraved hands. The band itself was etched like a feather, a Native American detail that appeared to be woven into the Irish design. "It's very romantic."

Carol replied, "I didn't want to marry Jake at first because he was so opposed to falling in love. I loved him before he realized that he loved me."

"That happened to me, too," Meagan said. "I became aware of my feelings for Garrett before he recognized his for me. But with how complex our relationship was, we were both struggling with it."

Lizzie shifted on the sofa. According to the lie she

and Max had concocted, they'd embraced their feelings at the same time.

Meagan continued by saying, "Garrett gave me a blue diamond in my engagement ring because I'm fascinated with blue roses. I learned about them through my sister-in-law. She studied a Victorian practice called the language of flowers, where couples used to send each other messages by using plants and flowers. Blue roses aren't found in nature, so they aren't part of the Victorian practice, but they've been introduced into the modern language of flowers."

Lizzie asked, "How did the people in the Victorian era know what the plants and flowers meant?"

"There were dictionaries on the subject. But there were different versions, so it could get confusing if they weren't using the same one."

Lizzie remarked, "Max hired a landscaper to plant a big beautiful garden for the wedding. We're having the ceremony in his backyard and the reception in his ball-room."

Meagan said, "You should research the language of flowers and have the landscaper plant some flowers that have meanings that would be special to you and Max."

Lizzie thought about Tokoni. He was the most special thing between her and Max. "Do you think there are flowers or plants that represent parenthood?"

"Oh, I'm sure there are. I'll bet you can find the information online. It's so exciting that you'll be adopting that little boy." Meagan grinned. "And I was right about you and Max becoming more than just friends."

Lizzie, of course, nodded in agreement, protecting the lie. But even so, the lie was starting to seem real, with how badly she wanted to kiss him. And hold him. And feel his body pressed tightly to hers.

Before she delved too deeply into that, she said to Carol and Meagan, "I would love to have your children in my wedding." She explained her idea about having Ivy and Nita as flowers girls, with their mothers accompanying them.

Both women accepted with joyful reactions, excited about the upcoming nuptials.

Afterward, Meagan said, "This will be the second time Ivy will be a flower girl. She was in my brother Tanner's wedding. But she's going to love sharing this one with Nita."

Ivy didn't bat an eye. She continued watching the baby sleep, even tucking a fluffy yellow teddy bear close to the infant.

"Nita means bear in Jake's ancestral tongue," Carol interjected. "We picked it because of all the teddy bears we've been given as gifts for her."

"She's a beautiful baby," Lizzie said, turning to study the kids again. "And so is Ivy's connection to her." It was such a tender scene, so sweet and loving that she knew she'd made the right choice by including the children and their mothers in the ceremony.

But Lizzie wasn't out of the woods yet. She still had to marry Max and fight her touchy-feely urges for him.

Eight

Lizzie glanced around her condo. Everything was in order, neat as a pin. The decorative pillows on her sofa were plumped. The magazines on the end tables were angled just so. She had a platter of fresh-cut fruit and gourmet cheeses in the fridge, along with a liter bottle of her dad's favorite soda. She'd invited him over today.

"I hate seeing you like this," Max said.

She turned to look at him. He'd come by for moral support, but he wasn't staying. He would be leaving before her dad arrived. "I'll be all right."

"Are you sure you don't want me to hang around?" He stood in the middle of her living room, his thumbs hooked in his jeans pockets. "We can both tell him about the wedding. After all, I am the guy you're going to marry."

"I think it's better for me to do this alone." She couldn't handle sitting there, pretending to be Max's fiancée in front of her father, not with how uncomfortably romantic this wedding was beginning to make her feel. "Besides, what's the point of you expending the energy to try to become his son-in-law when we'll just be getting divorced later?"

"We've been expending that type of energy for everyone else. And at least he already knows me." He crinkled his forehead. "I'll never forget the first time I met him."

"And how awkward it was?" When they were teenagers, she'd invited Max to the house for Christmas dinner, and the three of them had stumbled through a stilted conversation, with a big professionally decorated tree in the background. After Mama died, Dad always hired someone to dress the tree. But for Lizzie that just made the glittery ornaments and twinkling lights seem fake and lonely.

Sometimes, even now, she brought Max with her on that dreaded holiday, just so she didn't have to suffer through it by herself. Last Christmas was particularly odd. Rather than going to the house, they'd dined on a catered meal at Dad's high-rise office, before he'd jetted off for an overseas business trip, leaving her and Max alone for the rest of the day.

"Yeah, it's always awkward with your dad," he said. "But how often do you see him? Once, maybe twice a year?"

"I wish I didn't feel obligated to spend every dang Christmas with him." But it had become a painful ritual neither of them had broken.

Max sent her a concerned look. "Have you decided what you're going to do?"

"If I'm going to ask him to give me away?" She released an audible breath. It was a loaded question, filled with jittery bullets. "I have mixed feelings about it."

Mixed and shaken. "I'm nervous about walking down the aisle by myself, so in that respect, it will be nice to have someone by my side. But with how distant my relationship is with him, will it even make a difference?"

"Whatever you choose to do, just remember that I'll be waiting for you at the altar."

Her temporary groom? Just thinking about kissing him at the wedding was already filling her with a flood of unwelcome warmth. She bit down on her bottom lip. This biting thing was becoming a habit.

Silent, he watched her.

She quickly said, "You'd better go. My dad will be here at two." And it was already one thirty. If anything, her father was highly punctual.

She walked Max outside, and when he leaned toward her, she panicked, her pulse pounding in her ears. He wasn't going to jump the gun and kiss her, was he? Now, like this?

She hurriedly asked, "What are you doing?"

"There's a ladybug behind you, and I want to see if it'll climb onto my finger. They're supposed to bring luck."

Good God. She glanced over her shoulder and saw the spotted beetle in question, perched on a shrub beside her door. "Sorry. I thought you were…"

"I was what?"

She turned back to face him, admitting the truth. "Going to kiss me."

"Today? While your dad is on his way over?" He glanced at her mouth, looking hot and restless and hungry. "Is that what you want me to do? Will that make it easier for you?"

She bit her lip again, chewing on her lipstick, struggling to contain her desire for him. "I think we should wait until the ceremony like we're supposed to."

He stepped back, away from the ladybug, away from her. "The gazebo. The garden. You in a long white gown."

The wedding that was messing with their heads, she thought. "I have an appointment later this week to try on dresses. It's at an exclusive bridal salon some of my friends have used. I told the owner that you want me to wear a dress with gold embellishments, so they've been gathering gowns from designers all over the world to fulfill your request."

"Really? That's awesome, Lizzie. But remember that I'm paying for everything, okay? So don't spare any expense."

And buy the best gown she could find? "I'm going to try to look the way you want me to look."

"You're always beautiful to me. I think about you all the time. In the morning when I wake up. When I'm in the shower. When I'm working. When I go to bed at night. It's frustrating, knowing you're going to be my bride."

He meant sexually frustrating, she thought. And she understood exactly how he felt. "I think about you all the time, too."

"The way I've been thinking about you?"

"Yes." She crossed her arms over her chest, trying to stop her heart from leaping into her throat.

He shifted his stance, the air between them getting thicker. "This is wrong, isn't it?"

To be torturing themselves this way? To be pushing the boundaries of their friendship? "We're supposed to know better."

He glanced toward his car, a luxury hybrid parked on the street. "I should leave now and let you get on with your day."

She nodded. They certainly couldn't remain where they were, saying intimate things to each other.

But instead of shutting him out of her thoughts, she watched him walk away, dazed by her appetite for him.

Forcing air into her lungs, Lizzie returned to the house to wait for her dad.

He arrived sharply at two. Stiff and formal, David McQueen was a tall, trim man with an impeccable posture. As always, his short graying red hair was neatly trimmed. He wore a conservative blue suit and pin-striped tie. She assumed that he'd just come from a business meeting. Even before Lizzie's mom died, he was a workaholic. But at least they'd been a family then. Sometimes he even waltzed around the parlor with Mama, bowing to her after each dance. Lizzie used to sneak down the stairs and watch her parents, fascinated by how good they looked together.

Clearing her mind, she placed the snack tray on the coffee table, with small serving plates and paper napkins. She offered him a glass of soda, over ice. He used a coaster for his drink. He always did. Dad wouldn't think of leaving damp marks on a table.

He thanked her and said, "You didn't have to go to all this trouble for me."

He put a few bite-size pieces of cheese on a plate. He took a handful of grapes, too, and some watermelon balls. A polite amount of food, she thought.

She sat across from him. Since he'd claimed the sofa, she went for a leather recliner. When she'd invited him to come over, she told him that she had something important to discuss with him. Most likely, he was waiting for her to get started. Dad wasn't one for small talk. Mama had been. She could chat about insignificant things for hours.

But at the very end, Mama's words were few. The only thing she'd written on the notepad beside her bed on that fateful day was *I'm sorry. Please be happy without me.*

Lizzie gazed across the coffee table at her dad. *Happy* wasn't part of his vocabulary. It hadn't been part of hers, either, not after she'd become a motherless child.

Their housekeeper had found the body and the note. Mama had done the deed while Dad was at work and Lizzie was at school.

"I'm getting married," she said, going right for her news.

Dad calmly replied, "I noticed the ruby on your finger when I first got here, but I didn't want to say anything in case it wasn't an engagement ring. But apparently it is." He paused. "Who's the lucky man?"

"It's Max."

"I'm glad to hear it."

"You are?" She hadn't expected him to express his opinion, least of all his approval. Normally, Dad remained neutral when it came to Lizzie's life. Then again, he'd said it in his usual cut-and-dried way.

"It never made sense to me that you weren't dating him. You two seem so suited. But it appears you both figured that out."

Lizzie nodded, playing her part as Max's fiancée. But still, she'd never suspected that her father had been analyzing her friendship with Max all this time. "It's going to be at his house, on the second Saturday in June. I'm sorry for the short notice, but we're anxious to make it happen. I hope the date isn't a problem for you, with your work schedule," she clarified.

He sat back in his seat. "Of course not. I wouldn't miss my daughter's wedding."

Well, okay, then. At least he'd confirmed that he would be there. Now on to the next phase, she thought, the next question. "Do you want to walk me down the aisle?"

"Certainly." He sipped his soda. "I'd be honored."

Did he mean that? Or was it merely the proper thing to say? With him, it was hard to tell. "Just so you know, Dad, there's a child who's part of this."

His eyes went wide. The most emotion he'd showed yet. "You're pregnant?"

"Oh, my goodness. No. I didn't mean…" Based on the fact that she'd never even slept with Max, she thought about how impossible that would have been. "We're adopting a child. A five-year-old boy from Nulah."

"The one you wrote about on your blog?"

She angled her head. "You read my blog?"

"Sometimes."

They barely communicated, but he took the time to read her work? Her father was full of surprises.

"So is he the one?" he asked again.

"Yes. It's the same child who was featured on my blog." She explained how Max had gotten close to Tokoni when he volunteered at the orphanage last year. "Then he brought me to meet Tokoni and I bonded with him, too. We're excited about making him our son." She backtracked a little. "We haven't started the adoption proceedings, but we're going to do that after the wedding."

He studied her, with eyes the same shade of blue as hers. "You'll be a good mother, Elizabeth." He quietly added, "A good wife to Max, too."

Her father was buying into her marriage, just as everyone else had done. But lying to him seemed worse. Was it because he was the only human connection she had to her mom?

I'm so sorry. Be happy without me.

Now wasn't the time to think about Mama's final farewell. But she couldn't seem to stop herself from feeling the brunt of it. "Max has always been there when I need him," she heard herself say.

Dad reached for a piece of fruit off his plate, lifting it slowly, methodically, before he ate it. "The man you marry should be there for you."

His words struck a chord. Was he blaming himself for not being there for Mama? She wanted to know what he was thinking and feeling, but she didn't have the strength to ask him. And especially not while she was sitting there, pretending that her marriage was going to be real.

Dad didn't stay long. Within no time, they wrapped things up and she walked him outside, just as she'd done with Max earlier.

"I'll keep in touch about the wedding," she said as they stood in her courtyard. "Your tuxedo, the rehearsal dinner, all that stuff."

"Tell Max how pleased I am that you two got together."

"I will." She forced a smile. "Take care."

"You, too." He gave her a pat-on-the-back hug, which was about as affectionate as he got.

After they parted ways, she returned to the house, steeped in the complications of becoming Max's wife.

Lizzie's appointment at the bridal salon was private. Being as upscale as it was, it catered to a high-end clientele and offered preferential treatment.

She'd asked Meagan and Carol to join her, and now the three of them gathered in the lavishly decorated salon, sipping Dom Pérignon from crystal flutes. They'd been offered caviar and crackers, too, but they'd declined the salty appetizer. Personally, Lizzie had never acquired a taste for it.

She glanced at her companions, glad they were here. She couldn't do this alone, not with how overwhelmed she was. She wanted them to accompany her because they were part of Max's family, and, today of all days,

she needed a family connection, with as often as she'd
been thinking about her mom. Her father saying that she
would make a good wife triggered her emotions, too,
making everything seem far too real.

The salon had arranged for a showing, with models
wearing the gowns that had been selected for her. She'd
already been given a keepsake pen and a printed pro-
gram, so she could checkmark the styles that appealed
to her.

She sat in a wingback chair, with Meagan and Carol
by her side, and watched the models emerge.

Every dress was exquisite in its own way, but there
was one that drew Lizzie into its long, flowing silk-and-
lace allure. The creation offered a magical silhouette, embellished with crystal jewels and iridescent gold beads.
A richly appliquéd bodice and chapel train with a French
bustle lent the gown a sensual appeal.

Even Meagan and Carol gasped when they saw it.

Lizzie imagined it with a peacock-palette bouquet and
her hair tumbling in thick red waves.

"Look how romantic that is," Carol said.

Yes, Lizzie thought. It was like something out of a
wedding night fantasy. She even envisioned Max sweeping her into his arms and carrying her straight to his bed.

His bed?

She shivered from the forbidden thought. She wasn't
supposed to be dwelling on her desire for Max. But she
couldn't seem to control the ache it caused.

She drank more champagne, trying to cool off. But
it didn't do any good. Daydreaming about the man she
was going to marry swirled through her blood, heating
her from the inside out.

"Are you going to mark that dress?" Meagan asked her.

Lizzie snapped to attention. "Yes." She was eager to

try it on, hoping it looked as enchanting on her as it did on the model.

She marked other gowns, as well. But her mind kept drifting back to the fantasy one.

Finally, after the show ended, she was escorted to a luxurious fitting room. Meagan and Carol came with her.

The fantasy gown was incredible. With the beautiful way the gold beads reflected the light, she looked like a princess.

Or a fire-tinged goddess, she surmised, like the painting of Lady Ari. But that was the point. The reason Max wanted her gown to be marked with gold.

"You look absolutely radiant," Meagan said. "Like a bride should."

A bride who was desperate for her groom. Lizzie squeezed her eyes shut, making her reflection disappear. But when she opened her eyes, the hungry woman in the glittering gown was still there.

Suddenly, she was afraid of how easily she'd found a dress, of how it seemed to be made just for her. "This is how it was when Max chose my ring for me."

Too right, she thought. Too perfect.

Meagan and Carol smiled, assuming she meant it in a good way. But there was nothing good about how badly she wanted to be with Max.

Two weeks before the wedding, Max awakened in a cold sweat. He sat up in bed and dragged a hand through his hair.

The closer he got to saying, "I do," the more restless he became. Hunger. Desire. Lust. He had it bad, so damned bad. Getting naked with Lizzie was all he thought about, dreamed about, fantasized about.

He blew out the breath in his lungs. He knew what she

looked like in a bikini, with her tantalizing cleavage and pierced navel. But he'd never seen her completely bare.

Were her nipples a soft shade of pink? Did they arouse easily? Would she sigh and moan if he rolled his tongue across them? He wondered all sorts of erotic things about her. Was she smooth between her legs or did she have a strip of fiery red hair? And what would she do if he kissed her there?

Right *there*, all warm and soft and wet.

He longed to kiss her everywhere, to hold her unbearably close, to feel the silkiness of her skin next to his.

He'd wanted her for years, and now that they were getting married, the wanting had taken on a new meaning.

The romance of making love with his wife.

Cripes, he thought. Since when did he care about romance? Max was out of his clement, with the effect the impending marriage was having on him. But it would be over soon enough. After they adopted Tokoni, they would get happily divorced and everything would go back to normal.

But in the meantime...

He squinted at the light peeking through the blinds. It was the crack of dawn and he needed to get up and get moving. Lizzie was coming by later this morning to see the garden. The work was finished, the gazebo built and ready.

Was it any wonder he was stressed? A day hadn't passed where there wasn't something related to the wedding. Sure, the planner was doing a bang-up job of getting everything done. But it was still consuming Max's life.

And so was his yearning for Lizzie.

He climbed out of bed and put his running clothes on, anxious to hightail it out of his house.

And that was exactly what he did. He ran through the

canyons, taking in the crisp morning air. He worked up an even bigger sweat than the one that had drenched him during the night.

By the time he was done, he was ready for a long, water-pummeling, soap-sudsy shower. Of course, once he was naked, he thought about Lizzie again. But at least he didn't touch himself. That would have made the wanting so much worse.

After he got dressed and ate breakfast, he went out to the garden to wait for Lizzie. He'd already opened the security gate so she could let herself onto the property.

She arrived with her hair falling over her shoulders and a breezy blouse flowing over a pair of slim-fitting jeans. He wanted to ravish her right then and there.

"Look at this place," she said as she approached him. "It's absolutely gorgeous."

"Glad you like it."

"Like it? I love it. It's like the Garden of Eden."

The last thing he wanted to think about was a biblical paradise, where temptation ran amok. If Lizzie presented him with an apple, he would devour every luscious bite.

"Max?"

He blinked at her. "What?"

"Are we going to walk through it so I can see everything up close?"

"Yes, of course." The design was lush and dense, surrounded by stately palms and giant birds of paradise. Vertical layers of plants and flowers created a jungle-like appearance within a bold, brightly colored interior.

They wandered the variegated pathways, then stopped to admire the fountain, listening to the rainlike sound it made.

Next, they headed for the gazebo and stood inside the

custom-built structure. It wasn't decorated for the wedding yet, but when the time came, it would be adorned with flowers and sheer linen drapes.

"This is where it's going to happen," she said.

Yeah, he thought. Where he would marry the woman he longed to bed. But at least he would get to kiss her.

"So, how are things going on your end?" he asked, trying to shake the anticipated kiss from his mind. "Do all the women in the bridal party have their dresses and whatnot?"

"Yes, they do. I decided on mismatched dresses, with each of them choosing what looked best on them. I wanted them to express their individuality instead of putting everyone in the same style. My only stipulation was that they remained within the color theme."

"Are you pleased with the dress you got for yourself?" With as much time as they'd spent talking about it, he was eager to see her in it.

"Truthfully, it makes me feel a little strange."

He angled his head. "Strange?"

She winced. "Just sort of wedding nightish, with how soft and pretty it is."

Damn, he thought. *Damn.* "I guess it's too late to trade it in for an ugly one, huh?"

She smiled, laughed a little. "Now, why didn't I think of that?"

He doubted that it would make a difference. He slid his gaze over her and asked, "Did you have to get special lingerie to go with it?" He didn't have a clue what brides wore under their gowns.

She flushed in the sunlight, her fair skin going far too pink. "We're doing it again, Max."

He frowned. "Doing what?"

"Saying things to each other we shouldn't say." She

fussed with the buttons on her blouse, as if they might accidentally come undone. "We need to change the subject."

His brain went blank. "To what?"

"I don't know."

He hurriedly thought of something. He gestured to a small section of the garden. "See that area over there?"

She glanced in the direction of where he pointed. "Yes."

"Those are the plants that were added for the language of flowers you told me about. I asked the landscaper to research it and he worked up a collection of flowers that pertain to joy and parenthood and welcoming a new son."

"Oh." She made a soft sound. "That's wonderful. Thank you."

"You're welcome. We'll have to tell Tokoni about it when he comes here."

"He's going to love this garden." She gasped. "Oh, my goodness, look. It's a ladybug." She showed him where the little creature was crawling on a railing of the gazebo. "Do you want to see if it'll come to you?"

"Sure." He went over to the ladybug and held his hand close to it. Sure enough, it crawled onto his finger.

She watched the exchange. "I wondered if they bring a specific type of luck or if it's general goodwill."

"I don't know. I'll look it up after it flies away."

Just then the ladybug winged its way toward Lizzie and landed on the back of her hand.

She smiled and glanced down at it. "This has to be a good omen, right?"

Finally the beetle took off, disappearing into the garden. Curious, Max got on his phone to research the luck they'd just been given.

"What does it say?" she asked.

"There's lots of information. They mean different

things in different cultures. But get this—in one of the old myths, if a ladybug lands on a woman's hand, it means she is going to be married soon."

"Oh, wow. Imagine that? Does it say anything about a ladybug landing on a man's hand?"

He scanned the material. "There is something here about…" Oh, shit, he thought, as he read the contents. "Never mind. It doesn't matter."

She scrunched up her face. "It's not something about the wedding night, is it?"

"No." He frowned at his phone. "It's about love. It says, 'The direction in which a ladybug flies away from a man's hand is where his true love will be.'"

He glanced up, and they gazed at each other with disturbed expressions. The ladybug hadn't just flown in Lizzie's direction. It had gone right to her, making her his supposed true love.

But Max refused to believe a message like that, especially when there were other ways to analyze it.

"I'll bet the ladybug is part of our lie," he said. "That it's aware of the reason we've been pretending to be in love and is playing along with us."

A strand of hair blew across her cheek. She batted it away without saying anything. She still seemed a little dazed.

He prodded her for a response. "Don't you think my theory sounds logical, Lizzie?"

"Yes." She walked out of the gazebo, her hair still blowing. "That has to be it. It's the only thing that makes sense."

"Definitely," he said as they left the garden. They both knew that neither of them had the capacity to fall in love for real.

Nine

On the day of the wedding, Lizzie clutched her father's arm. Within a matter of minutes, she would be walking down the garden-path aisle, heading toward her groom.

Max Marquez. Her best friend. The man with whom she would be adopting a child.

She glanced over at her dad. Surprisingly, his strong and silent presence helped keep her limbs from shaking. But the storm that raged through her mind was a whole other matter.

Ever since the ladybug incident, she'd been struggling with the dangling, tangling heartstrings of love. Max's explanation that the ladybug's message was part of their lie should have satisfied her. But instead she'd begun worrying about love, fearful that it could happen to her.

Anxious, Lizzie looked down at her bouquet. At the moment, she was wearing blue, green and purple diamond earrings that complemented the colors of the flowers. Max had given the earrings to her as a wedding gift. They'd been specially made for this occasion.

She'd given him a jewelry gift, too: antique gold cuff links to wear with his tuxedo. Of course, once the ceremony was underway, she would be placing the band she'd chosen for him on his finger.

As for her rings, her engagement ruby and diamond pavé band had been soldered together to create one shimmering piece, and that was what Max would be marrying her with today.

She shifted her gaze to the elegantly decorated gazebo, where he waited for her. Soon, so very soon, she would be his legally wedded wife. She'd never believed herself capable of love, and now she was fretting over it. But given how long she'd known Max and as close as they'd always been, weren't those types of feelings possible?

As the opening notes of "Here Comes the Bride" began to play, signaling her entrance, she lifted her chin, determined to stay strong.

Her father glanced over and said, "It's time."

She nodded. Everyone, including Max, turned to watch her come down the aisle. But she doubted that he was worried about love. He seemed fixated on how she looked, his appreciative gaze sweeping the long, silky, white-and-gold length of her.

She shouldn't have told him that her dress made her feel "wedding nightish." But she couldn't take those words back. She couldn't take any of this back. She was marrying Max and afraid that she might fall hopelessly in love with him.

Would she know the moment it occurred? Would it pierce her like a warrior's arrow? Or would it be a gradual wound, a slow bleeding with an eventual loss of consciousness?

Lizzie held her breath, praying that her heart remained intact. Because nothing would tear her apart more than loving a man she was destined to divorce.

As her dad turned her over to Max, she wished that she'd worn a veil to cover her face. She felt terribly exposed, with the passion-steeped way Max was looking at her.

She gazed longingly at him, too, mesmerized by his tall, dark beauty. He wore his hair in its usual style, as thick and shiny and straight as it naturally was. His designer tuxedo featured satin details and notched lapels, and his boutonniere was attached on the left side, above his heart, where it was supposed to be.

He recited his vows first, as instructed to do. As he promised to love and honor her for all eternity, a soft rattle sounded in his voice. She recited hers just as quietly, just as shakily. Only her vows were rife with fear.

They exchanged rings, and when the time came for him to kiss her, Lizzie refrained from running her tongue across her lips. But that didn't ease the romantic restlessness that baited her soul. She was wearing red lipstick, as hot and fiery as the rubies in their rings.

"Are you ready?" he whispered.

"Yes," she said. She was more than ready.

He leaned forward and put his hands in her hair. His lips touched hers, and her eyes fluttered closed. This was the kiss she'd been thinking about, fantasizing about, waiting for. He pulled her closer, and the elements flowed through her.

The sun. The wind. The bloom of flowers.

Was she becoming part of her surroundings? Or did she feel this way because she was becoming part of him?

Lizzie couldn't think clearly, not while she was in the dreamy midst of wanting him. He didn't use his tongue and neither did she, but it still felt beautifully forbidden.

It ended far too soon, with him separating himself from her. She opened her eyes. His were open now, too.

Her mind went hazy. Was her lipstick smeared? Max didn't have any on him, so it must be okay. It was supposed to be the long-lasting, non-smudge kind. For infinite kisses, she thought.

The ceremony came to a close, with the man officiating it introducing them as husband and wife.

"We did it," Max said to her, his voice seductively quiet.

"Yes, we did," she murmured back. They were married now, first kiss and all.

As they descended the aisle, they were celebrated with cheers and the fragrant tossing of dried lavender. It dusted them like confetti, purple buds sprinkling the air. The wedding planner had recommended it, providing little mesh bags to their guests. Lizzie hadn't thought to check on what lavender meant in the language of flowers until last night, discovering that, among other things, it was said to soothe passions of the heart.

But as Max held her hand, his fingers threaded through hers, she wasn't the least bit soothed.

His touch only heightened her fears about falling in love.

The chandeliers in the ballroom had been altered, the original crystals replaced to reflect the colors of the wedding. Also enriching the décor were fancy linens, glittering candles and big, bold flower arrangements trimmed in peacock feathers.

The cake was outstanding, too. Max could see it from where he sat, displayed on a dessert cart, the four-tiered creation a frothily iced masterpiece. But for now he and Lizzie and their guests dined on their meals, prepared by a renowned chef and served on shiny gold plates.

Their table consisted of the wedding party. The best men and maid of honor had already made their toasts, and the flower girls and their mothers looked exceptional in their feminine finery. Baby Nita's nanny was part of the group, ready to whisk her off to a makeshift nursery that had been provided, in case the wee one needed a nap. A playroom for the older kids was also available, with child-care attendants standing by.

Lizzie's father fit naturally into the high-society gathering. He didn't seem as detached as he normally was, and for that Max was grateful. He wanted Lizzie to feel protected by her one and only parent, especially today. Watching her come down the aisle with her dad had left Max with a lump in his throat.

Becoming Lizzie's husband was confusing. The weight of the ring on his finger. The fake vows. The bachelorhood he'd lost. The make-believe wife he'd gained.

Earlier someone had imposed a "kiss and clink" ritual, where the bride and groom had to kiss whenever glasses were clinked together. So far, at the reception, Max and Lizzie had locked lips at least ten times. But he could have kissed her a thousand times and not gotten enough.

He leaned over and said to her, "Is it okay if I tell you again how beautiful you look?" He'd already told her how breathtaking she was, but he thought it bore repeating.

She softly replied, "You can say whatever you want, as often as you want."

"Then I'm going to say it every chance I get." With her sparkling gown and wild red hair, she was a seductive sight to behold. He wanted to haul her off to bed tonight, to strip her bare and relish every part of her. But that wasn't part of the arrangement.

In the next alluring moment, a whole bunch of glasses clinked in the background. Max hastily obliged. He cupped Lizzie's face and slanted his mouth over hers.

He'd yet to use his tongue. He wanted to, but it didn't seem appropriate with everyone watching. Still, he made sure that his lips were parted, just enough to entice a sigh from Lizzie.

No one would ever suspect that they weren't lovers. But Max knew. He craved her with every breath in his body.

Later, they engaged in their first husband-and-wife dance, with a well-known DJ spinning records. They'd chosen Queen's "You're my Best Friend," a classic soft rock ballad, for the opening song. Some of the lyrics included professions of love. But this was a wedding, and they were supposed to be projecting that type of sentiment, even if it wasn't true. Mostly, though, the song made sense, with how deep their friendship was.

As they swayed to the beat, holding each other close, Max ran his hand along the back of her gown, where it laced like an old-fashioned corset.

"Was it hard getting into your dress?" he asked.

She shook her head. "Sheila helped me."

Of course, he thought, her maid of honor, who was one of her old sorority sisters, a high-society girl, much like Lizzie. "She's probably used to dealing with these types of events."

"Yes, she is. But I had a team of assistants, too, a hairdresser, a makeup artist, a manicurist."

Max had gotten ready by himself. He hadn't wanted anyone, not even his brothers, straightening his tie or pinning his boutonniere to his lapel. He'd needed to spend his last few hours of being single alone. "Who's going to help you get out of your dress?"

"I can do it myself." She spoke quietly, with the colors from the chandeliers raining down on her. "I just have to be careful not to damage it."

He looked into her eyes, curious about what she had on under it—the mysterious lingerie that kept invading his mind. "You can come to me if the laces give you any trouble."

She nearly stumbled against him. "Do you think that's a good idea?"

"I don't know." He steadied her in his arms, wondering what the hell he was doing. He'd just invited her to his room, crossing a line that wasn't meant to be crossed. "I honestly don't." He couldn't be sure what would happen if they gave in to the temptation of being together. Would they regret it afterward, would they survive the heat? They'd been so careful not to jeopardize their friendship, and now they were drowning in a sea of unholy matrimony. "Maybe we should both forget that I ever suggested it."

"Yes," she agreed. "We should block it out."

He was trying. But the back of her dress kept getting in the way. He couldn't seem to stop from touching it.

The reception continued, with dancing and drinking and party merriment. During the removal of the garter, Max knelt beside Lizzie's chair, asking the Creator to give him the strength to endure it.

He'd been obsessing about her lingerie, and now he was getting to cop a husbandly feel of her sheer white stockings. They were the kind that stayed up all by themselves.

No hooks, no fasteners.

While he was still on the floor, with his hand lingering

on her thigh, Jake called out, "Hey, Max, did you know that in earlier, bawdier times, wedding guests used to follow the couple to their bedchamber and wait for them to undress so they could steal the bride's stockings and toss them at her and the groom until they hit one of them in the head?"

"That's not funny," Max called back, even if he and Lizzie laughed right along with everyone else.

"It was for luck," Jake assured him.

Yeah, Max thought, because at least the old-time groom had been lucky enough to bed his bride, even if one of them had gotten softly pelted in the head.

As he looked up to meet Lizzie's gaze, preparing to slide the garter down, a group of jovial guests clinked glasses, daring him to kiss the graceful sweep of her leg.

Accepting the challenge, he pressed his lips to her ankle, being as gentlemanly as the moment would allow. But damned if he still didn't want to peel off every jeweled-and-beaded stitch of fabric she wore.

By the time Max and Lizzie cut the cake, the sexy tone had already been set. He fed her a piece of the frothy white dessert, and when some banana-cream filling stuck lusciously to her lips, he leaned forward and kissed it right off her mouth.

Holy. Mercy. Hell.

She returned his salacious kiss, with camera phones flashing and recording every detail. For better or worse, Max felt wildly, sinfully married, their tongues meeting and mating.

Logic flew straight out the door. Desperate to have her, he whispered hotly in her ear, "Come to my room later and let me undo your dress," repeating his earlier offer and meaning every word of it.

Although Lizzie went beautifully breathy, she didn't

respond, leaving Max waiting and wondering if his wife would succumb to his request.

Or leave him hanging.

The mansion was empty, the guests and staff gone. There was no one left, except Max and Lizzie. They stood on the second-floor landing, silence between them. In one direction was the master suite and in the other were her accommodations. She stalled, not knowing which way to go.

He watched her through pitch-dark eyes. In the low-level light, they looked as black as his licorice-toned hair.

So deep. So intense.

She struggled to tame her desire. "Sleeping with you wasn't supposed to be an option."

His gaze didn't waver. "It doesn't have to affect our friendship, not if we don't let it."

"How?" she asked. "By only doing it this one time and never again?"

"That seems like the safest way to handle it." He moved a little closer. "But it's up to you, Lizzie."

There was nothing safe about how much she wanted him. Or about the fear of love that kept burrowing its way into her thoughts. If she told him what was going on in her mind, would he still be willing to go through with it?

"I can't," she said, fighting the feeling. "No matter how much I want to."

"Are you sure?" Roughness edged his voice: loss, disappointment.

She nodded, trying her darnedest to be certain.

He said, "Then sleep well and think of me, and I'll think of you, too."

She imagined him, alone in his bed, fantasizing about her. "I better go." Before she crawled all over him. She could still taste the cake they'd kissed from each other's lips.

The sweet creaminess.

Lizzie turned away, but he didn't. She sensed him, standing in the same spot, tall and sharp in his tuxedo.

She headed toward the guest wing. Again, there was no movement behind her, no masculine footsteps, echoing in her ears. He remained as motionless as a statue.

She stopped to breathe, and when she glanced over her shoulder, she lost her reason.

He was still there.

Lizzie ran to him, her dress swishing with every beat of her bride-in-jeopardy heart. He pulled her tight against him, lifted her up and carried her the rest of the way to his room.

She kept her arms looped around his neck, hoping she survived the night without falling in love with him.

He took her into his suite, past a royal blue sitting room and into the area where a big brass bed took precedence. This was the place where he slept each night, she thought, where he dreamed, where they would be together.

"Just this once," she said, stating the rules, making sure she repeated them. "Then never again."

"Yes," he replied, putting her on her feet. "This is the only time it's going to happen." He moved to stand behind her. "On our wedding night."

She felt his hands on the back of her dress, working the ties. Wonderfully dizzy, her vision nearly blurred.

He loosened more of the fabric. "It's so soft and pretty."

"The material between my skin and the dress is called a modesty panel." But she wasn't feeling very modest. Soon she would be half-naked. The only garments she had on underneath were lace panties and the thigh-high stockings he'd run his hands over earlier. Her gown had been structured so she didn't need a bra.

Still standing behind her, he helped her remove the dress, allowing her to step out of it. She didn't turn around, and he didn't ask her to. But she heard his sharp intake of breath as he closed in on her. Lizzie shivered, immersed in his nearness, while he skimmed his fingers along her spine.

"Look how bare you are," he said, following the line of her tailbone.

Yes, she thought. With her upper half clothes-free and only a wisp of lower lingerie, she was mostly bare.

Remaining where he was, directly behind her, Max circled her waist and reach around to the front of her panties. When he slipped a hand inside to cup her mound, she gasped on contact.

"You're smooth," he said, his voice raspy against her ear. "I've thought a lot about…"

The style of bikini wax she favored? She leaned back against him, stunned by how detailed his curiosity was. "You wondered about that?"

"All the time." He kept touching her, moving farther down, until he spread her open with the tips of his fingers.

Lizzie nearly came on the spot.

He rubbed her, teasing her, making her warm and slick and wet. He used his other arm to hold her in place, pressing it firmly across her breasts. Her nipples went unbearably hard.

There was something dominantly provocative about what he was doing and how he was doing it. He had all the power.

Her groom. Her husband.

She couldn't see his expression or the flashes of heat that she suspected were in his eyes. But she felt every insistent touch.

"Are you going to come for me, Lizzie?"

She gulped her next breath. "I almost did."

"Yes, but are you going to do it for real?"

She nodded, as he continued his intimate quest, using her as his bridal plaything.

"This is just the beginning," he said.

"Of what?" she asked, feeling deliciously dazed.

"Of how many times tonight I'm going to make you come."

Her heart raced, spinning through her body like a top. "When am I going to get to do things to you?"

"You already are." He bumped his fly against her rear, showing her how aroused he was. "But I'm not anywhere near being done with you, so that will have to wait."

She closed her eyes. Every second of his stimulation brought her closer to the countless times he promised to invoke pleasure.

Lizzie moaned. Was the arm around her breasts getting tighter? Were his fingers strumming harder and faster? He kept his hand inside her panties, creating massive amounts of friction.

Her dress was on the floor beside their feet, so close they could have stepped on it. But neither of them did, not even when she came.

She convulsed in a flood of carnal bliss, shimmering and shaking, the back of her body banded against the front of his.

He nuzzled her neck and said, "Let's take these off now, shall we?"

She wondered what he meant, until she realized that

he was talking about her panties. Blinking through the haze, she did her shaky best to recover.

He divested her of what remained: the panties in question, her shoes, her stockings, even the colorful diamond earrings he'd given her. He did all that while he was still standing behind her.

After there was nothing left to remove, he turned her around so he could view her nakedness.

"Damn," he said. "You're even more gorgeous than I imagined."

She couldn't think of a response, at least not one that wouldn't leave her mewling like a kitten at his feet. He was still fully clothed. If this was strip poker, she would have lost the moment he'd unlaced her gown.

He spoke once again. "I want you to turn down the covers and get into bed."

So he could finish what he started? She was eager to do his bidding, but nervous about it, too. He was looking at her as if he meant to hold her captive for the rest of her life.

But she knew that wasn't the case. Tonight was their only night. The only time they'd agreed to be together.

Wondering what it would be like to stay with him, to be his forever wife, she fought her fears, reminding herself that this was just sex—hot, dreamy sex—where love had nothing to do with it.

Ten

Max gazed at Lizzie, gloriously naked in his bed, with her hair tumbling over her shoulders and the soldered ring set that sealed their union glinting on her finger. She looked as much like a bride now as when she'd walked down the aisle. Wilder, he thought, more sensual, but a bride just the same.

He picked up her dress and placed it on a nearby chair, along with her panties and stockings and earrings. The only item left on the floor was her shoes. They weren't glass slippers, but they had a fairy-tale quality nonetheless. The entire wedding had seemed that way. Which was part of its allure, part of how it had been designed, he thought, fooling their guests into believing it was going to last forever.

And now he and Lizzie were alone, immersed in one married night of romance. The anticipation in her eyes excited him. And so did her ladylike moments of shyness.

"Don't cover up," he told her, when she began to pull the sheet over her body.

She released it, giving him an unobstructed view once again. Mesmerized, he stood where he was, drinking in every beautifully bare part of her. Her nipples were as pink and pretty as he'd imagined, and his fingers were still warm from where he'd touched her.

Finally, Max removed his tux and draped it over the back of the same chair where he'd placed her dress.

"I never knew you were so meticulous," she said.

"Normally, I'm not." By tomorrow, the careful placement of their clothes wouldn't matter. But for now it did.

Once he was naked, he joined her in bed and took her in his arms. He kissed her with gentle passion, and she roamed her hands over him, her glitter-polished nails skimming the ridged planes and sinewy muscles that formed his body.

She paused when she came to a scar, a cigarette burn—a pale circular mark of childhood torture. Although the majority of them had disappeared, some of the deeper ones, mostly on his chest, remained visible.

"Max?" Still lingering over the scar, she lifted her gaze to his, her voice soft and compassionate. "Have other women asked you about these?"

"Yes." Other women, other lovers. "But I've never told them what they are. I just tell them what I tell everyone who is curious enough to question me about them. That I had a bad case of measles when I was a kid that left me scarred."

"Oh, yes, of course. Your measles tale. I always thought that seemed like a believable story, even if I knew the truth."

Max nodded. Lizzie was privy to the pain his mother

had inflicted on him because he'd shared those gut-wrenching secrets with her.

"I'm so sorry for what she did to you," she said.

"I know you are." She'd told him that many times before. But hearing her say it now distressed him. He didn't want to be reminded of the abuse, not while they were being intimate. He moved her hand away from his scar, imploring her to stop touching it, letting her know it was off-limits.

A wounded look came into her eyes. Clearly, she wanted to comfort him, to do what she'd always done before. But Max couldn't bear to accept what she was offering.

When he turned down the bedside lamp, trying to shift gears and create a softer ambience, she asked, "Are you sure that being together like this isn't going to affect our friendship?"

"We can't let it," he said, even if a change was happening already. A discomfort he couldn't deny. But there was more at stake, he thought, than just the two of them. "We're going to co-parent a child. He's going to need us to stay close."

"But not this close," she said.

He climbed on top of her, preparing to kiss his way down her body, to turn their troubled closeness into mindless pleasure. "Everything will be okay, Lizzie."

"Promise?"

"Yes." Max licked her nipples, going back and forth, exploring each one. After tonight, they would do whatever was necessary to resume friendship.

But for now...

For now...

He moved languidly, enjoying the taste of her skin. He flicked his tongue over the delicate gold piercing in her navel. She'd gotten it while they were still in high school. It was the only rebellious thing she'd ever done, other than becoming friends with a nerdy kid like him.

He said, "I should buy you a ruby for here. Or a colored diamond, like what's in the earrings I gave you."

"No, you shouldn't."

"Why not?"

"Because it will only remind us of what we did tonight."

Damn, he thought. She was right. Giving her another jewel would be a mistake. "I won't do it. I won't buy you anything else." He thought about the cuff links she'd given him and the groomlike way they'd made him feel. "You can't buy me anything else, either."

She played with the ends of his hair. "I don't intend to."

"Good." He pushed her legs open and went down on her, kissing and licking and swirling his tongue.

She gasped and arched her hips, watching him through the misty light, telling him how much she liked it.

How good it felt.

How she never wanted it to end.

But it did end, with her shaking and shivering and coming all over his mouth.

She insisted on doing it to him, too, on giving him the same kind of lethal pleasure he'd just given her. He let her work her magic, his body responding in thick, hard greed.

But when it became too much for him to handle, he grabbed a condom, anxious to thrust inside.

He entered her, and they kissed warmly and fully, the sweetness of her lips drawing him deeper.

Locked together, they rolled over the sheets, and within no time, Lizzie was straddling him, her hair falling forward and framing her face. He gripped her waist as she traveled up and down, riding him quickly, fiercely.

They shifted again, bending and moving. He was behind her now, nibbling her neck and pumping like a stallion.

It didn't stop there. They swiveled onto their sides, kissed like crazy, then returned to where they'd begun, with Max braced above her.

Driving her toward a skyrocketing orgasm, he pushed her to the limit, making sure she came again.

And finally, *finally*, when she was in the throes of making primal sounds and clawing his back, he let himself fall.

Into the hot, hammering thrill of his wedding night.

In the morning, Lizzie awakened next to her husband. He was still asleep, the sheet bunched around his hips.

Should she gather her things and tiptoe off to her room? No, she thought. That would make her feel cheap, dashing down the hall, clutching her wedding gown.

The least she could do was find something to wear. She climbed out of bed and put on her panties. From there, she went to Max's giant walk-in closet, where his dresser was, and rummaged through the drawers.

The only belongings Lizzie had brought with her were in a suitcase that she'd left in her room. Later today, they were leaving on their honeymoon, jetting off to Nulah to start the adoption proceedings, and she wasn't moving into Max's mansion, not officially, until they got back.

She kept digging through his dresser, trying to decide what to borrow. Keeping it simple, she went for a black T-shirt and gray sweat shorts. She had to roll the waistband of the shorts down to her hips to make them fit, but it was better than just being in her panties. Rather than leave the hem of the T-shirt hanging, she twisted the material into a center knot and tied it below her bust.

Lizzie gazed at her reflection in the closet mirror, enjoying the way his clothes felt against her skin.

She frowned at her seductively smudged eye makeup and sleep-tousled hair. Nothing had changed in the light of day. She was still afraid of falling in love with him.

Determined to sneak off as quickly as she could, she exited his closet, hoping he remained asleep. But he was awake and was sitting up in bed.

He squinted at her. "What are you doing, pretty Lizard?"

"I borrowed some of your clothes." She stated the obvious, wishing her nickname didn't sound so endearing on his lips.

"So I see." He swept his gaze over her. "And how stylish you look in them, too."

While he studied her, she glanced at the scars on his chest, trapped in the memory of the well-intentioned touch he'd rebuffed. The solace he'd refused. She forced herself to look away from the scars, not wanting him to catch her doing it.

Would he rebuff her love, too? She hoped that she never had to find out.

He said, "I could use some breakfast. How about you?"

She wasn't the least bit hungry, but she replied, "Sure. I can fix it while you shower or whatever." She needed to bathe, too, but she wasn't ready to strip off her clothes. Or his clothes, as it were. She wanted to wear them a little longer.

"I'll shower after we eat." He got out of bed and took his tuxedo pants from the chair where he'd left them. Same chair where her dress was. "I can help you make the food."

He climbed into the pants, sans underwear. Of all things he could have worn this morning, he'd chosen to go commando in his wedding attire? He threw on the formal shirt, too, leaving it unbuttoned with the tails loose.

"No point in wasting a perfectly good suit," he said. "After all, I did buy the dang thing."

"Yes, you did." But most men wouldn't treat a pricey tuxedo as if it was casual gear. But Max wasn't most men.

He glanced toward his bathroom. "I'm going to brush my teeth before we go downstairs."

She tried for a smile. "So you can be minty fresh before breakfast? I should do that, too."

He smiled, as well. "I'll meet you in the kitchen."

When he was gone, Lizzie scooped up her gown, wrapping her shoes and stockings and jewelry inside it.

Once she was in her room, she deposited the bundle on her bed and went into her bathroom to brush her teeth. She washed her face, too, removing the remnants of her makeup. She also tamed her hair, taking a few minutes to get her emotional bearing.

Still wearing Max's clothes, she ventured downstairs and entered the kitchen. He was already there, removing pots and pans from cabinets. He had a carafe of coffee going, too.

She pitched in, and with minimal conversation they fixed ham, eggs and steel-cut oatmeal.

They sat across from each other at the main dining table, and Max drizzled honey over his cereal. Lizzie preferred hers with milk. But what struck her was how intently they were watching each other eat.

"Are you ready for our trip?" he asked.

Their big, fat, fake honeymoon, she thought. "Yes," she replied. "Are you?"

He nodded, but he didn't look any more ready than she was.

* * *

Since Nulah was twenty hours ahead of Los Angeles, Max and Lizzie arrived in time to hang out on the beach and swim in the crystal-blue sea. They tried to behave like newlyweds whenever other people were around. But mostly they kept to themselves, so they didn't have to make it harder than it already was. But either way, being in each other's company was absolute torture.

And so were their accommodations, Max thought.

Their bungalow was similar to the ones they'd stayed in before, with wonderful island amenities. The only difference this time was that they were sharing the same space.

Bedtime rolled around far too soon. Lizzie changed in the bathroom, putting on a long cotton nightgown. Max suspected it was the most modest thing she owned. But that didn't stop him from noticing how gracefully it flowed over her body.

"I can sleep on the couch," he said.

The couch was adjacent to the bed, as the main area of the bungalow was basically one big room. Even if he wasn't sleeping with her, he would be within tempting distance. But there was nothing either of them could do about that.

"All I need is a sheet," he said. "Sometimes I get hot when I sleep." He didn't mean "hot" in a sexual way, but it triggered sweet, slick memories of their wedding night.

Apparently for her, too. She shot him a dicey look.

A second later, she composed herself and removed the top sheet from the bed, gathering it for him. He took it from her, and she handed him a pillow, as well.

"We've got a big day ahead of us tomorrow," she said.

Max nodded. In the morning they would be going to the orphanage. "I hope Losa lets us see Tokoni. When I spoke with her earlier she said that she wasn't sure if we should see him on this trip."

Lizzie frowned. "Why not?"

"Typically she waits until the process is further along before she lets applicants spend more time with the child they are trying to adopt. She says it can get too emotional later if something goes wrong or if the applicants change their minds."

"We would never change our minds." She got into bed, but she didn't lie down. She sat forward and pulled the covers over her legs.

"I know. But that's just how she does it."

He settled onto the couch, plumping the pillow behind him. Neither of them turned out the light. They gazed at each other from across the room. The windows were open, with a tropical breeze stirring the curtains.

"Why didn't you tell me this before now?" Lizzie asked.

"I didn't want to disappoint you. I know how badly you want to see Tokoni. How you were looking forward to his big, bright smile and giving him a hug. I want to do that, too."

Concern etched her brow, signaling another frown. "I hope she lets us see him. We've been waiting all this time."

"Yeah, planning a wedding, getting married. We've been to hell and back to become his parents." He made a tight face. "Sorry, that didn't sound very nice."

"I knew what you meant. It would have been so much easier if we could have stayed single and still adopted him."

"But that isn't how it worked out." He glanced down at his hand. "It's strange wearing a ring."

"You think you've got troubles?" She waggled her

fingers, showing off her ruby. "Look at me, hauling this gigantic bauble around."

He laughed a little. "I'm surprised you didn't sink to the bottom of the ocean today."

A laugh erupted from her, too. "Good thing I didn't or you would've had to rescue me."

"Me performing CPR on you would have been a disaster." He smiled, winked, made another joke. "Mouth-to-mouth and all that."

She shook her head, and in the next uncomfortable instant, they both went silent. No more smiles. No more laughter. Their silly banter wasn't helping.

"We should try to sleep now," she said. "I just hope that I don't keep you awake, with the way I might be tossing and turning."

"I'm probably going to be restless, too." Being in the same room with her, knowing she was just a forbidden kiss away. But in the morning, they would get past it. Because all that mattered was doing what they'd come here to do.

To make Tokoni their son.

Lizzie and Max sat across from Losa in her office, but their meeting wasn't going well. Something didn't feel right, Lizzie thought. Even though she and Max had been prattling on about their wedding and how excited they were to adopt Tokoni, Losa seemed cautious of them.

In fact, she watched their every move, as if she were analyzing their body language. By now, Lizzie was so nervous that she kept glancing out the window, avoiding eye contact. Max seemed anxious, too. He shifted in his seat, like a kid who'd gotten called into the principal's office for committing a schoolyard crime.

Did Losa suspect that their marriage was a ruse? And

if she did, why hadn't she said something before now? Why had she allowed them to continue the charade, letting them believe that they were being considered for the adoption?

Losa asked Lizzie, "Do you remember what I told you when you first interviewed me for your blog?"

"You told me a lot of things," she responded, getting more nervous by the minute. "I used a lot of it in the articles I wrote."

"Yes, you did. But what did I say about our guidelines and what's the most important character trait we look for in prospective parents?"

Lizzie's heart dropped to her stomach. "That they must be honorable people."

Max spoke up. "Are you questioning our character, Losa?"

The older woman turned toward him. "Yes, unfortunately, I am. When you first called me and said that you'd fallen in love and were getting married, I was concerned about the speed in which it seemed to be happening. But I gave you the benefit of the doubt, wanting to believe that your feelings were genuine and you weren't just playacting so you could adopt Tokoni."

Max's dark skin paled a little. But he said, "We're going to be the best parents we can be. We intend to devote the rest of our lives to Tokoni."

"Yes, but you don't intend to devote the rest of your lives to each other, do you?" She turned her attention to Lizzie. "I could tell from the moment you walked into my office today that you weren't a true bride. I know the difference between a happily married woman and one who is finding it difficult. You can barely look at your husband without having shadows in your eyes."

Lizzie gripped the edge of the desk. Not only were

she and Max on the verge of losing Tokoni, but Losa was calling her out, baiting her to admit that the marriage wasn't real. But she couldn't do it. She couldn't say it out loud, not when she was so painfully afraid of falling in love with Max. "Please don't take Tokoni away from us."

"How can I allow you to adopt him," Losa replied, "when your actions haven't been honorable?"

Max interjected. "It isn't fair of you to say that."

"Isn't it?" Losa asked, challenging him to come clean. "Tell me, what were you going to do once the adoption was approved? Were you going to divorce your wife and create a broken home for your son? I want to know the truth, Max, and I want it now."

"All right," he said. "We are going to split up. But we aren't creating a broken home, not in the way you're implying. After the divorce, Lizzie and I planned to raise Tokoni in separate households, but we also planned to co-parent him with love and devotion. Both of us, together, as friends."

Losa blew out a heavy sigh. "That's not what Tokoni's mother wanted for him."

"I know." Max continued to defend their position. "But we couldn't bear to lose him, so we devised a way to make him our son. We can make the divorce work and still give Tokoni everything he needs."

Losa asked Lizzie, "Are you as certain about the divorce as Max is?"

Lizzie's grip on the desk tightened. She'd been wondering what it would be like to stay with her husband, to be the only woman in his life, and now she was being asked if dismantling their marriage was the right thing to do. She couldn't think, couldn't rationalize, not with him watching her from the corner of his eye. When he reached over, drawing her hand away from the desk and encouraging her to support the divorce, she knew that her worst fear had just come true.

That she loved him.

Absolutely, positively loved him.

What an awful time to figure it out, to see through the veil of her own heart. But she couldn't admit how she felt, not without destroying what was left of their friendship, so she lied and said, "Yes, I'm as certain about the divorce as he is."

Losa measured her. "So you honestly believe that it won't cause any problems later?"

"Yes," Lizzie lied again.

The older woman shook her head. "I'm sorry, but I disagree." She then told Max, "Neither of you is ready to be a parent."

His expression all but splintered. But in spite of his distress, Lizzie could tell that he wasn't giving up without a fight.

He said to Losa, "I understand how upset you are about our deception, and I apologize for leading you on. But we are ready to be Tokoni's parents. We love him and believe that he's meant to be our son."

Losa adjusted her glasses. "I'm not denying that either of you loves the boy. I know you do." She spoke with strength and careful diction. "I wish things could be different, but I won't go against his mother's wishes or subject him to a broken home. There's another couple who's interested in him, and I'm going to consider their application in place of yours."

Oh, God. Lizzie pitched forward in her chair. Losa wasn't just denying their application. She was thinking of giving Tokoni to someone else.

"Who are they?" Max asked, firing a round of questions at her. "And how long ago did they apply? Do we know them? Are they someone who contacted you through our efforts to find Tokoni a home? Or are they a local couple?"

"I can't discuss them with you," Losa said. She sounded weary now, troubled that she was hurting Max and Lizzie, but determined to abide by her decision.

"Whoever they are, they won't be us," he said. He looked at Lizzie, his voice quaking. "They'll never be us."

She could see that his heart was breaking. Hers was, too. Everything inside her was shattering, cutting her in two.

Lizzie got up and ran out of the orphanage. Once she was outside, she burst into tears.

No child. No husband to keep. Only fractured love.

Max soon followed her. He wasn't crying. But he was shaking, his chest heaving through ragged breaths. He reached for her, and she collapsed in his arms.

More lost than she'd ever been.

Eleven

Feeling horribly, sickeningly numb, Max stared at the beach, where the sky met the sea, where peace and beauty were supposed to reign. But all he saw was emptiness.

He glanced over at Lizzie. She sat beside him on their bungalow deck, curled up in her chair, her knees drawn to her chest. After they'd left the orphanage, she'd dried her tears, but her eyes were still swollen, her mascara still softly smudged.

"We got married for nothing," he said, the hope of becoming a father crushed beneath the weight of his heart.

Her voice hitched. "Our wedding night didn't seem like nothing."

"No, but it was something we shouldn't have done." The glittering warmth, the romance, the sex. Even now he longed to do it all over again, even if he knew it would only make matters worse. Taking fulfillment in Lizzie's body, holding her close, burying his face in her hair—

none of those things was the answer. "We messed up." Mired in his grief, he kept looking at her. "If we hadn't slept together, we wouldn't have been so uncomfortable around each other, and then Losa wouldn't have figured us out."

Lizzie's voice hitched again. "She said that she was suspicious of us from the beginning."

"I know, but with the way we were acting, we gave ourselves away. We didn't seem like a real couple to her."

Still wrapped in the fetal position, she rocked in her chair. "We aren't a real couple."

"Everyone else believed that we were. Everyone except Losa." The person who had the power to take Tokoni away from them. "I can't believe that she turned us down. That Tokoni is never going to be ours. I wish she would have told us who the other applicants are. At least then—"

"We'd know who we're losing him to? How is that going to help?"

"I don't know. But they must be happily married or she wouldn't be considering them." He analyzed the strangers who might become Tokoni's parents. "What if their marriage breaks apart at some point? What if they end up divorced, too? It isn't fair that she's blaming us for not being in love. Who even knows what it means, anyway?"

A choked sound escaped from Lizzie's lips. "I don't want to talk about the definition of love."

"I'm just saying that—"

"Please, I can't do this…" She unfolded her arms and put her feet on the ground. Then, as quick as that, she ran toward the beach, on the verge of crying again.

Max's gut wrenched. Should he leave her alone? Or should he chase after her? He knew how fiercely she was hurting. He hurt, too, so damned badly.

He took a chance and headed toward her. She looked so lost, facing the water, the hem of her pale summer dress fluttering in the breeze. Was she blaming herself because Losa had put the initial burden on her? Did she think that she'd botched their phony presentation of love more than he had?

He came up behind her. The air smelled of salt and sea and sand, of tropical flowers and leafy foliage, of everything that reminded him of this trip they'd taken together. Their phony honeymoon, he thought.

"Lizzie?" He said her name, letting her know he was there.

She turned around, drew a breath. "Yes?"

He gently asked, "Do you think it's your fault because of what Losa said to you about not seeming like a true bride?"

She nodded. "Yes, but it's more than that, so much more."

"Tell me."

"I can't." Behind her, the ocean turned a foamy shade of blue, rolling its way onto the picture-perfect shore.

"Yes, you can. I'm your BFF, remember? You can tell me anything."

"You won't understand."

"Yes, I will. You can confide in me." If not him, then who would she reveal herself to? "That's what we do, Lizzie. Tell each other our secrets."

"Then here it is. I want to be what Losa said I wasn't."

Too confused to make the connection, to let it sink in, he blinked at her. "That doesn't make sense."

"Yes, it does," she said, in a ghost of a whisper. "I want to be your true bride."

He shook his head, shook it so hard his brain rattled.

"You don't know what you're saying. You're sad, you're agonizing over Tokoni, you're—"

"I'm in love with you, Max."

Recoiling from her words, he flinched. His mother used to tell him that she loved him after every beating, every cigarette burn, every painful punishment.

Trapped in his memories, he pushed his feet into the sand. Beneath the surface of the thick white grains, something pierced his skin. The edges of a broken shell, maybe. Or a tiny shard of glass or something else that didn't belong in a beach environment.

"I knew it was going to freak you out." Lizzie spoke quietly, cautiously. "It freaks me out, too. I was so afraid I was going to fall in love with you, and I did."

He snapped back into the conversation. "You've been afraid of this? For how long?"

"Since the day when you first showed me the garden."

Her deception punched him straight in the gut. "You've been stressing about this since before we got married, before you slept with me?"

"Yes. But I've been fighting my fears. On the night we were together, I prayed to survive it."

Max wasn't surviving it. Already he could feel the monsters coming to get him. The two-faced creatures lurking in the closet with the door barred shut.

"I think my fear of loving you is what Losa was seeing in my eyes," Lizzie said. "The shadows she mentioned. I doubt she knew that's why I didn't seem like a true bride, but she still sensed that something wasn't right."

Shadows, he thought. Monsters. He glanced up at the sun, then back at Lizzie. "My mother could have been her. *Anog Ite*."

She squinted at him. "Double-Faced Woman?"

He nodded. The being who was condemned to wear

two faces for seducing the *Wi*, the sun. He gestured to
the sky. The setting sun was turning red, as if it was
fused with fire, as bright as Lizzie's hair. "My mother
had two faces. She was beautiful like *Anog Ite*, but ugly,
too. Some people say that *Anog Ite* isn't evil. That she's
just a figure of disharmony. But to me, she'll always be
evil, like my mother, like the love she used against me."

"Love isn't evil, Max."

"No, but it makes people hurt." He reached out to
touch Lizzie's hair. The beautiful redness. The fire.
"Look what happened with Tokoni. We lost him, even
though we loved him." He lowered his hand. "But maybe
it's all just a smokescreen, this love that you think you
feel for me. Maybe it isn't even real."

"It's real." Her voice broke. "What I feel is real."

"I don't think it is." He didn't want to believe it,
couldn't let himself believe it. "You just think you love
me because you got caught up in the fantasy of being
a wife. But that's not you. You aren't the wifely type."

"My dad said that I was going to make a good wife."

"Your dad? He barely knows you. But I know you,
Lizzie." He thumped a hand against his chest. "I know
who you are."

"You don't know me anymore." She argued with him,
defending the person she claimed to be. "I'm different.
I'm changed."

He fought the urge to grab her, to shake her until she
admitted that she didn't love him. But he wanted to hold
her and kiss her, too. Max was a mess, more emotionally wrought than he'd ever been. "You were supposed to
be my friend, my partner in parenthood. I trusted you."

"But you don't trust me now?"

"I don't know." He didn't know anything anymore.

"You can do whatever you want," she said. "But I'm

going to pack my bags and catch the last boat to the mainland, before it gets dark."

He tried to stop her. "You don't have to do that."

"Yes, I do. I'll get a room on the mainland and take a commercial flight back to the States in the morning or whenever I can arrange it."

"I understand that you want to go back early. I do, too." The pretense of being on a honeymoon was over. "But we can take my jet and return together."

"What for? So you can keep trying to convince me that I don't love you? I need for you to believe me, to trust me." She turned and walked away, leaving him alone.

As he watched her go, he knew it was just a matter of time before the monsters reappeared.

Smothering him in the dark.

It took Lizzie three days to get a flight, and by then she suspected that Max was already home.

While riding in an airport limo, en route to her condo, she thought about the wedding dress she'd left in the guest room at his house. She couldn't bear for it to be in his possession.

So what was she going to do? Text him and ask him if she could come and get it? Oh, sure, she thought, just pop over to his mansion to collect her gown, as if there was nothing weird or painful or foolish about that.

Nonetheless, she did it. She fired off a text. Deep down, she knew this was just an excuse to see him. She could have sent a delivery service for the dress.

Max replied quickly, accepting her excuse and agreeing it was okay for her to stop by. But they didn't keep texting. Their communication was brief and choppy.

She gave the driver Max's address, and he plugged it into his GPS and headed for their new destination.

When they reached the security gate, Lizzie squeezed the handles on her purse, clutching the leather between her fingers, her nerves skittering beneath her skin.

After they were admitted onto the property, the car glided up the circular driveway and parked out front.

The chauffeur opened her door, and she said, "I won't be long. I just have to pick something up."

"Take all the time you need," he said.

What she needed was her husband to accept that she loved him. But she couldn't say that to the stranger who'd brought her here. So she merely smiled and thanked him. He was an older man, probably around her dad's age.

He returned to the limo, and she took the courtyard path to the front door. Lizzie rang the bell, trapped in a situation that she'd created. Was coming here a mistake? Or would it make things easier?

Max opened the door, and they gazed awkwardly at each other. He wore a pair of faded jeans with one of his prized *Star Wars* T-shirts. She almost smiled in spite of herself, but then she noticed the depiction was of Luke Skywalker battling Darth Vader, the latter with a blood-like redness behind his black-helmeted eyes.

Good versus evil. Love versus pain.

"Come in," Max said.

Silent, she entered the mansion. She wanted to take him in her arms and make his pain go away. But she couldn't mend his ache, any more than she could cure her own.

She noticed that he was still wearing his wedding band. But she suspected that he was keeping up appearances and protecting his privacy, rather than face the questions people were going to throw at him if they saw him without his ring. He'd probably even told his pilot a phony story about why he'd returned from their honeymoon without her, citing a business emergency or something.

Lizzie hadn't taken off her ring yet, either. But she wanted to stay married. Her reason was better than his.

"I'll just go get my dress," she said, crossing the foyer and heading for the staircase.

He fell into step with her. "I'll go with you."

They made their way to the second floor, and once they reached the landing, she glanced in both directions, remembering the choice she'd made on their wedding night.

He appeared to be thinking the same thing. But neither of them said anything. They continued to the guest wing.

They entered the room where she'd left her dress. Her gown was on the bed, with the accessories that went with it, including the earrings Max had given her.

He stood off to the side, looking dark and brooding.

"It's as pretty as the day you wore it," he said, about her dress. "With all its silk and lace and shiny beads." After a long pause, he added, "If everything hadn't gotten so messed up, you would have been moving into my house instead of dashing over here to grab your gown."

She wasn't running out the door yet. For now she was having a painful discussion with him. "Even if the adoption would have gone through, I would have left eventually with us getting divorced."

"That's what we agreed on."

"Until I bent the rules and fell in love with you?"

"It's not love, Lizzie. You just think it is."

"I can't see you again after this." It hurt too much to be near him, to keep hearing him deny her. "I shouldn't have even come here today." It was definitely a mistake.

He pulled a restless hand through his hair. "I know

that we need to stay away from each other. But damn it, I'm going to miss you."

She couldn't begin to express how much she was going to miss him. She sat on the edge of the bed and touched a lace panel of her dress. "Nothing is ever going to be the same again."

He came forward and lifted one of the earrings, turning it toward the light. "Love was never supposed to be part of the deal. That's why our marriage and divorce was supposed to work."

But none of it had worked, not even the adoption. "When are you going to tell your family and friends about us?" Eventually he would have to remove his ring and face the music.

"I don't know. I just need a bit more time for now."

"Me, too." To hole up in her condo and cry. "When you're ready to deal with it, you can file for the divorce." She couldn't bring herself to end their marriage. They'd already lost the child who was supposed to be their son, and now they were losing each other, too. Just thinking about it made her want to crumble.

Turning away from him, she headed for the closet to retrieve the garment bag that had come with her wedding dress.

While he stood silently by, she placed everything inside the bag, zipping it up, shutting out the memory. The broken dream, she thought, of a marriage that never really was.

Max walked through his garden. He'd been spending countless hours here. He'd been going to the gym every night, too, but he always increased his workouts when he was stressed. Of course, immersing himself in plants and flowers was a whole other form of therapy. Or torture or whatever the hell it was.

Two weeks had passed since he saw Lizzie, since she collected her wedding dress, and he couldn't get her out of his mind. This was the worst era of his life, the absolute worst. And he'd been through some horrendous stuff when he was younger.

Yeah, he thought wryly, like the time his mom had abandoned him in their rathole of an apartment for three excruciating days. He'd survived on a half-empty box of cereal. No milk. No juice. No loving, caring parent. The TV had kept him company: cartoons in the morning, game shows in the afternoon, sitcoms and whatever else he could find that didn't scare him at night. Being alone was scary enough. And now he lived in a gigantic mansion, all by himself.

Hoorah for the nerd. The rich, single bachelor.

The monsters were back with a vengeance, just as he'd suspected they would be, keeping him awake at night, creeping and crawling into his brain. Hideous shadows in the dark. He couldn't shake them, no matter how hard he tried.

He kept walking through the garden, and as he approached the foliage that had been planted in honor of Tokoni, he stopped in midtrack. Mired in his loss, he wanted to pull every damned one of those plants out by their roots. But he would let them thrive instead, hoping and praying that Tokoni thrived in his new life, too. But it still tore him to shreds that the Creator had taken the boy away from him and Lizzie.

Lizzie. Elizabeth McQueen, his beautiful, faded friend. Even her name suggested her station in her life. She'd always been royalty, even before she'd become a high school homecoming queen or a grown-up likeness to Lady Ari.

Why did she have to misconstrue her feelings into what she thought was love? Why did she have to fall into that kind of trap?

He strode over to the gazebo and went inside, thinking about the moment they'd first kissed. He envisioned her with that luscious red lipstick, her mouth warm and pliant against his.

He missed her beyond reason. But why wouldn't he? Normally when Max needed someone to ease him out of an emotional jam, he called her. She was his go-to, his dearest, closest friend, his comrade in arms. Sure, he had his brothers, but he always chose Lizzie first. He'd shared his secrets with her, things he'd never even talked to his brothers about. Garrett and Jake knew that Max had been abused as a kid, but he'd never opened up to them about it, not like he had with Lizzie. He'd told her everything, how it felt to be beaten and burned and scorned by his mother, how he used to cower in the closet, how he'd cried himself to sleep, but most of all, how his mother had insisted that she loved him.

Sharp, jagged, bloodthirsty love.

Lizzie knew that he'd never wanted to hear another woman say those words to him again. And now she claimed to love him, feeding the monsters and making his heart hurt from it.

Max twisted the ring on his finger, warning himself to remove it, to let Lizzie go, to divorce his wife, as soon as he could summon the willpower to do it.

Twelve

Lizzie couldn't stop thinking about Max, every minute of the day, every hour of the night.

She glanced at the microwave clock and saw that it was almost 7:00 p.m. On a Wednesday, she noted to herself. But that didn't matter because one day blurred into the next.

God, she was lonely without him.

She prepared a cup of hot tea and carried it into the living room. She hadn't been out of the house since they broke apart. But being a recluse wasn't all that tough. For food, she ordered groceries online and had them delivered. She'd had a few take-out meals brought over, too. But mostly, she didn't feel like eating.

Her dad, of all people, had texted her this morning. He'd wanted to know if she was back from her honeymoon and how the adoption proceedings had gone. Since she couldn't get away with another lie, she'd typed out the truth. Not in detail, but enough to convey that the adoption had fallen through, triggering a painful separation between her and Max.

She'd also told her father that she wanted to be alone. Not that he'd offered to rush over and comfort her. But she'd made it clear that she needed her space.

So far, there was no word from Max about the divorce. But she figured it was only a matter of time before he took legal action. Lizzie still hadn't removed the ruby and diamonds from her finger. For now she was still emotionally attached to being Max's wife, even if it was killing her inside.

She contemplated where he was at this early evening hour. She suspected that he was at the rough-and-tumble gym he frequented, letting off some steam. He took his workouts seriously, especially his boxing routines.

Her doorbell rang, and she nearly knocked over her tea. Was this the final countdown? Was it someone delivering the divorce papers? Was she being served?

She didn't want to answer it, but that would only prolong the inevitable. She opened the door, preparing for the worst.

Lizzie started. The person on the other side was her dad. What part of her needing to be alone didn't he understand?

"I just wanted to check on you," he said. He wore a dark gray business suit and a concerned expression.

She glanced away. "I'm okay. I'm handling it."

"You don't look okay."

If she broke down, would he know what to do or how to comfort her? She almost pitched forward, just to see if he would catch her. But she maintained her composure.

"This isn't necessary, Dad."

"Please, let me visit with you."

Lizzie gave in to his persistence, hoping it was going to be quick. Like a bullet to the head, she thought. The last thing she wanted was to feel like a sad and lonely child, longing for her daddy's affection.

"May I get you some tea?" she asked, playing the hostess, doing what came naturally. "I already brewed a cup for myself. Or I can make you coffee or something stronger, if you prefer." She knew that he sometimes enjoyed a martini after work.

"I'm fine, Elizabeth. I don't want anything."

"Then have a seat." She gestured to the sofa. He never called her Lizzie. That name had come from Mama.

They settled into the living room, and she clutched the armrests of her chair.

He asked, "What happened to cause all this? Why did the adoption fall through and why is it keeping you and Max apart?"

She'd already given him a condensed version in her texts, but that wasn't going to suffice, not face-to-face. So Lizzie took a deep breath and explained why she and Max had gotten married, how they'd lost Tokoni and why they were separated now, including the achy part about her falling in love with Max.

"I'm so sorry," her father said. "I never would have guessed that you weren't a true couple."

"Losa certainly figured it out."

"That's her job, I suppose, to be more observant than the rest of us. Maybe I didn't see through your charade because I always thought you were meant for each other."

She fought the threat of tears, forcing herself to keep her eyes clear and dry. "I'm never going to stop loving him."

"I never stopped loving your mother, either, even after

she was gone." He paused, frowned, straightened his tie. "I just couldn't get over the loss."

"Mama dying was my loss, too."

"I know. And I should have been a better parent to you."

Yes, she thought. He should have. "Is that what you're trying to do now, Dad? Be an attentive parent?"

He nodded, making one last pull at the knot in his tie. "How I am doing so far?"

She managed a smile. Suddenly she was grateful that he was here, attempting to be the kind of father she'd always longed to have. "Pretty good, actually."

He blew out a relieved sigh. "Really?"

"Yes, really."

He finally smiled, too. "Did your mother ever tell you how she and I met?"

Curious, she shook her head. "No. No one ever told me."

"It was at a charity ball, a big, stuffy Savannah soiree. It was the first function of that type that I'd ever been to. My family was new money, nouveau riche, as they say, and this was an old-money crowd."

Lizzie leaned forward in her chair. "When was this? How old were you?"

"It was the summer before I left for university. Your mother was still in high school then, in her senior year at an all-girls' academy. That's who was hosting the ball. I was invited by a buddy of mine. He was dating one of the students and asked me to come along to meet her friend."

"And that friend was Mama?"

He nodded. "She was such a strange delight, the most eccentric person I'd ever known. We dated that summer, and even after I left for university, we stayed in touch. She used to write me the most fascinating letters. Later she went off to college, too, but we continued to correspond and see each other when we came home on breaks."

"When did you get engaged?"

"A year after she graduated. And two years later we were married. I wanted to wait until I was more established in my career. Her parents accepted me, but I still felt the new money stigma. They were such old-world people, so refined in their breeding. To me, they were like royalty."

"I wish I could have known them. And your parents, too."

"It was a tragedy that your mother and I shared, with both of us being only children and both of our families passing on so early in our lives—my father with heart failure when you were a baby, my mother with cancer when you were a toddler, and her parents in a helicopter crash, before you were even born. You'd think we were cursed."

Maybe they were, Lizzie thought. Being rich hadn't saved them, not old or new money.

He said, "Your mother never quite recovered from losing her parents. But she was already having bouts of depression before they died. It was always a part of who she was, being happy, then sad, then happy again. She had dramatic impulses, too, to do over-the-top things."

"Did you ever encourage her to seek help?"

"No. I thought that if I loved her enough, she would be okay. I didn't understand how depression worked. She might have been bipolar. Or maybe she had another type of disorder. I don't know. She never saw a doctor about it, so she was never diagnosed with anything."

Lizzie had to ask, "You never suspected that she was suicidal?"

His features tightened. "Sometimes she said odd things about death, about how freeing she thought it was going to be. But I didn't attribute that to her being suicidal." Another tight look came over him. "Even with as much as I loved her, sometimes she was just too much to handle. The moodier she got, the more time I spent at work." He lowered his head. "But I should have been there. I should have saved her."

Her heart went out to him, the father she'd barely known until now, the man struggling with his guilt. "You couldn't have, not without knowing how truly ill she was."

He glanced up. "If I'd gotten her the help she needed, she might be alive today."

"You can't go back and change it. You can only move forward."

"I'd like to do that, with you." He met her gaze. "But I have to admit that when you were a teenager and you brought Max home for the first time, I was impressed with how close you two seemed. I didn't know how to be a father to you, but he knew how to be your friend, just as you knew how to be his. It made me feel better, with him being part of your life."

Her emotions whirled, her breath lodging in her throat. "He went through some horrible things when he was a kid. Things he shared only with me, and now he's probably alone with his turmoil. He doesn't confide in people very easily, not even his brothers."

"If that's the case, then don't you think he needs you? More than he's ever needed you before?"

Yes, she thought. Heavens, yes. This wasn't the time to give up on Max. Even if he refused to believe that she loved him, she could still do what she'd always done.

Be his friend.

* * *

Max had been at the gym for hours, trying to knock the crap out of his past, throwing power punches at a heavy bag.

Why couldn't he let go of what his mother had done to him? Why did those memories have to be there, lurking in the dark? He should be better than that; he should be stronger than the monsters.

As he threw another punch, a warm, hazy feeling came over him. He sensed a presence behind him.

An immortal, he thought, a spirit helper. The Lakota called them *Tunkasila*. Although it translated to Grandfather, it applied to all guardians. In that regard, the term was genderless. Sprit helpers came in many forms, and he could tell that his guardian was female. He could feel her whisper-soft energy.

Max had never seen one before. None had ever appeared to him. But now a guardian was here, offering to help him banish the monsters, to get rid of them for good.

He turned around, startled by what he saw. His guardian looked just like Lizzie: bright blue eyes, long, fiery red hair.

Confused, he shook his head. Had a spirit helper borrowed her form? Or was it Lady Ari dressed in street clothes? Had *Tunkasila* called upon her to intervene?

He felt as if he were in the middle of a dream. Maybe he was. Maybe he wasn't even at the gym at all.

She moved a little closer, this beautiful, oddly alluring spirit who mimicked Lizzie.

"I'm sorry I didn't call," she said. "But I figured you'd be here, so I came on over."

He blinked, told himself to get a grip. The female standing before him wasn't an immortal. She was flesh and blood. She was human. She *was* Lizzie.

Tunkasila help him, he thought. He longed to pull her into his arms, to tell her how miserable he'd been without her. But he stood motionless instead, dripping with sweat, still wearing his boxing gloves. What if he touched her, what if he held her and the monsters still didn't go away?

He glanced down, taking a quick inventory of her hand. She was wearing her wedding ring. So was he, under his left glove.

"My dad came to see me," she told him.

Max finally spoke. "He did? When?"

"Today. This evening. We had a meaningful conversation, mostly about my mother. But he stopped by to make sure I was all right. He knows that you and I aren't together anymore." Her gaze lingered on him. "I'm sorry for taking my friendship away from you."

"Are you offering to be my friend again?"

She nodded. "Yes."

"Even if we get divorced?"

She nodded again, tender, determined, true. "I'll be your friend, no matter what."

He glanced at her ring again and noticed that her nail polish was chipped. He'd never seen her without a flawless manicure before. It made her seem fragile, but somehow powerful, too. "You'd do that to yourself? You'd deliberately put yourself in a painful situation for me?"

"I can't turn my back on you. I love you too much to do that."

His heart thumped in his chest. She wasn't *Tunkasila*. But she was still his guardian, his helper. He removed his gloves, setting them aside.

He held out his hand to show her his ring. "I couldn't bear to take it off. I haven't filed the papers yet, either. I kept telling myself that I should, but I just couldn't bring myself to do it." He studied her, with her gauzy blouse and long, floral-printed skirt. He appreciated how it looked on her. Flowers were becoming her signature to him. He imagined them raining down from the ceiling like petals from the gods. "Since we split up, I must have walked through the garden at my house a hundred times, going into the gazebo and thinking about our wedding. It's been torture, Lizzie, not having you in my life."

She reached for him. "I'm here now."

As soon as he hugged her, her blouse stuck to his bare skin. "I'm getting you all sweaty."

"I don't care." She held him tighter. "It feels good."

"I'm sorry for punishing you for loving me, for turning a deaf ear to it. But you know how badly it scared me."

She stepped back to look at him. "I'm not trying to push you into more than you're ready for."

"I know. But I want to be ready. I want to stop being afraid of love, to accept that I'm worthy of it." He explained the feelings rattling around inside him. "Whenever my mother used those words, they diminished me, as if I didn't deserve to be loved. They made me feel small and insignificant. A shell of the boy I was, of the man I was going to be. But that's not what you're doing. That's not what love is."

She touched his cheek, skimming her fingers along the hollowed area beneath the bone. "This is a huge step for you. For both of us." Tears welled in her eyes. "I love you, Max."

For the first time in his life, he wanted to hear a woman say those words to him. But in this case, she wasn't just any woman. She was his wife. "I love you, too," he said. He knew now that he did. That maybe somewhere in the depths of his angst-ridden soul, he always had loved her.

She kissed him, creating a fusion of warmth and comfort and strength. If the monsters tried to come back, Max would slay them. He would slice them to bits, with his guardian by his side.

Lizzie wasn't an immortal, but *Tunkasila* had sent her to him just the same. She'd been there all these years. The friend he needed, the lover he craved, the fiery-haired, tender, loving, supportive partner who'd turned his heart around.

When the kiss ended, he took both of her hands and held them in his. "There's something we need to do, besides resume our marriage."

"We have to try to get Tokoni back," she replied, clearly aware of where his mind was at.

He nodded. "Even if Losa already started processing the other couple's application, we have to try. It's only been a few weeks. There's still time for her to change her mind."

"What if she won't budge?"

"Then we'll have to keep trying. We can't give up, Lizzie. Tokoni is a part of us. He belongs to us as much as we belong to each other."

"Yes, he does." She put her head against his shoulder. "We're supposed to be a family, the three of us."

"I'll call Losa and make the arrangements for us to go to Nulah as soon as we can." He wrapped his arms around her. "But for now I want to take you home with me." And be together, he thought, as husband and wife.

Lizzie stripped off her clothes, her heart reeling. Max loved her the way she loved him. He'd said it openly, with a truth she'd seen in his eyes. And now they were in the master bath at his house. He hadn't showered at the gym. But she was glad that he'd waited, so they could get cleaned up together.

Clean and naked and wet.

He adjusted the water temperature, and she joined him in the clear glass enclosure. There was plenty of room for two people. But to her, it felt warm and cozy.

He took her in his arms, and they stood that way for the longest time, just holding each other, letting the water rain over them.

As steam fogged up the glass, Lizzie turned to face the enclosure door and drew a Valentine-type heart on it, using the tip of her finger. With a look of fascination, Max added their initials.

M + L, in his masculine script.

She smiled, laughed a little, felt her own heart go bump. "How wonderfully teenage of us."

"We're making up for lost time. Or I am, anyway. I still can't believe you had a crush on me when we were kids."

"Just like you had trouble believing that my love was real?"

"I believe it now." He kissed her, strong and deep, his tongue making its way into her mouth.

Her body flexed, her mind swirled. She pulled him closer, the taste of passion between them. The kiss went on and on.

And on some more.

Finally, when they came up for air, she realized that her eyes were still closed. She opened them, water dotting her lashes.

Max pumped liquid soap into his hands and began washing her breasts. He thumbed her nipples, making them peak from his warm, slick, sudsy touch.

Sweet love. Sweet marriage.

Lizzie relished every wondrous thing he was doing to her. "I like the scent of your soap." The sandalwood that often lingered on him.

"And I like touching you this way."

He bathed her entire body, front to back. He washed her hair, too, with his shampoo. Everything in the shower belonged to him, including her.

He massaged her scalp, his fingers kneading her skin. She'd always enjoyed going to the salon, but this, this...

He used a conditioner, then moved out of the way, en couraging her to step under the spray so she could rinse, completing the task herself. But it didn't end there. He watched her, like a voyeur taking forbidden thrills.

Within a heartbeat, he came forward, kissing her again. She nearly lost her breath, especially when he dropped to his knees. She gazed down at him, and he glanced up at her, a carnal warning in his eyes.

Lizzie didn't know if she was going to make it out of this situation alive. He used his mouth in wicked ways, relentless in his pursuit—an intense journey, hot and thorough.

The orgasm that rocked her body sent her into a state of erotic shock. She moaned in the midst of it.

"Max... Max... Maxwell..."

She rarely used his full name, but she was doing it now, slipping into the sound of it. She gripped his shoulders to keep from falling over, her knees going weak, her pulse thumping in intimate places.

In the afterglow, he stood and smiled, obviously pleased by what he'd done to her. Then, leaving her staring after him, he lathered his own body and washed his own hair.

As the steam thickened, she blinked through the haze. Her husband looked like a modern-day god, a contemporary warrior, every muscle in its place.

Needing him more than ever, she approached him. As she moved into his arms, he obliged her, pulling her tight against him. She wedged a hand between their bodies. He was already half-hard.

Lizzie took it all the way, giving him a full-blown erection with a rhythm that rippled through both of them.

He grabbed the condom that he'd brought into the shower and tore into it. She was just as eager, just as wanting.

Having sex while standing up wasn't an easy feat, but they managed just fine—in lip-biting, nail-clawing, body-twisting ways.

He rasped, "If we weren't already married, I would ask you to marry me, right now, just like this."

"And I would say yes." A thousand, hard-driving, hip-thrusting times yes.

They feasted on each other, mating like animals. Max came in a burst of male heat, and Lizzie held him while he shuddered, held him until she lost the battle and exploded into a soul-shattering orgasm, too.

Seconds passed before either of them had the stamina to move. When they did, it was to put their foreheads together and glance over at the mist-drawn heart.

Although it was melting, dripping down the glass, the sentiment remained.

M + L. Forever.

Thirteen

Three days later, Max and Lizzie arrived in Nulah, ready to fight for the adoption. Losa agreed to see them and hear what they had to say, but, as usual, she wasn't making any promises.

On this summer afternoon, they gathered in the picnic area of the orphanage. The sun was shining, with a fresh, clean, grassy scent in the air.

None of the kids were outside. Max wished they were. He was desperate for a glimpse of Tokoni. He knew Lizzie was, too.

She sat next to him, with Losa seated across from them, a wooden tabletop between them.

Max decided to start the conversation with an emotional tone since that's how he was feeling. "I love my wife," he told Losa. "And she loves me. She loved me on the day you denied our application, but she was struggling with her feelings then."

The older woman squinted beneath her glasses, narrowing her gaze at him. "This better not be another fake attempt at trying to make me think you're a couple."

"It's real." He reached for Lizzie's hand and held it, threading his fingers through hers. "We're not pretending to be together. We *are* together. On the day our application was denied, we returned to the resort where we were staying and had a breakdown. But it was worse for Lizzie because she admitted that she loved me, and I turned her away."

Lizzie didn't interject. She remained silent, listening to him recount their story. Losa was listening, too.

Max continued. "I was afraid of being loved by Lizzie, afraid of hearing her say those words. It relates back to my childhood and the terrible things my mother did to me."

Losa didn't reply. But she was no longer squinting at Max. Her expression had softened. Of course she already knew that he'd come from an abusive environment. He'd mentioned it when he first volunteered at the orphanage, but not to the degree he was speaking of it now.

He went on to say, "I accepted being loved by other people. My foster brothers love me, and I love them. I love Tokoni, too. That kid has been part of me since the moment I met him." He glanced at his wife, and she squeezed his hand, giving him her support. "But it was different with Lizzie because she knew all my secrets. When we were teenagers, I told her every painful detail, things I never told anyone else. That brought us together as friends. But now that I'm able to look back on it, I think it created a wall between us, too. I built that wall around other women, as well, insisting that I was incapable of falling in love. Yet all along, I think I was having those types of feelings for Lizzie, even though I was too mixed up to recognize them." He paused, giving himself a second to breathe. "I'm sorry if this sounds like psychobabble, but it's the only way I know how to describe it."

"I understand," Losa said. "We have children here who've been abused. I know how it can affect them. But we do everything in our power to get them the help they need."

"That didn't happen for me. I got lost in the foster care system, with social workers who were overwrought with work, with caseloads they couldn't handle. But I was glad that they left me alone. I didn't want to be singled out. Once my brothers took me under their protective wings, I felt a little better. But I was still guarded. I've always been that way." He turned toward the beautiful redhead by his side. "But not anymore."

Lizzie scooted even closer to him. "Max isn't the only one who's been working through his issues. I was just as afraid of loving him as he was of loving me. Those are the shadows you saw in my eyes the last time we were here." She softly added, "But I'm stronger now, and I'm ready to be a wife and mother."

Max quickly added, "You were right when you told us before that we weren't ready to be Tokoni's parents. We deceived you and ourselves in our effort to adopt him, but now we want to do it in the right way. We love Tokoni, and we want the opportunity to make him our son, to devote ourselves to him and each other." He implored her. "Will you consider our application in place of the other couple you told us about? Will you give us a chance?"

Losa didn't reply. She only shifted in her seat.

Max hurriedly said, "I guarantee that everything we just told you is true. But if you want us to sign an affidavit to attest to our feelings, we will. We'll sign it in blood if we have to."

"You don't need to go that far." Losa removed her glasses, cleaning them on the hem of her blouse. She put them back on and sighed. "I have a confession to make." A beat later, she said, "I lied to you about the other couple. They aren't real. They don't exist."

Max jerked his head in surprise. Lizzie did, too.

Losa explained, "I was concerned that if you thought Tokoni was still available, it would be harder for you to move on with your lives. I didn't want you holding on to false hope. Also, it was easier to deceive you once I surmised that you were deceiving me." She frowned. "I'm not prone to lies. That isn't my nature, and I'm sorry I used that tactic on you. You deserved the truth from me, just as I deserved it from you."

Max's thoughts spun inside his head: relief, confusion, new hope. Beside him, Lizzie's hand began to tremble. Their fingers were still interlocked.

He asked Losa, "Is this your way of telling us that you're reconsidering us for the adoption, that we have a chance? Or are you just making amends for deceiving us?"

"Both," she replied, her frown morphing into a smile. "You told me everything I needed to hear, and now I'm able to look past your former lies and see the love and care and devotion between you. The kind of devotion Tokoni's mother wanted his adoptive parents to have."

Lizzie burst into a grateful sob, and Max thanked Losa and drew his wife into his arms, inhaling the sweet scent of her skin, this beautiful, perfect woman who was going to be the mother of his child.

He turned back to Losa. "May we see Tokoni? Just for a minute or so? You don't have to tell him that we're going to adopt him. You can wait until we've been approved." Max knew that he and Lizzie still had a ton of paperwork ahead of them. "But it would be wonderful if we could at least visit with him."

Losa smiled again. "I think that would be all right. I'm certain that he's going to be as thrilled to see you as you are to see him." Short and stout, she came to her feet and moved away from the bench. "Stay here, and I'll bring him to you."

Max and Lizzie waited together, holding hands, anxious to see their boy. Nearly three months had passed since the last time they saw him, but it seemed like an eternity.

When they spotted him crossing the lawn with Losa, they stood and exchanged a smile. He was just as they remembered him, with his bangs flopping across his forehead and a wide grin splitting across his face. The older woman let Tokoni go, and he raced through the grass, heading for Max and Lizzie.

They knelt to greet him, and Tokoni barreled straight into them. The three of them toppled to the ground, arms and legs akimbo. Peals of laughter ensued, rumbling into breathless, mindless joy.

Max helped Lizzie up and pulled Tokoni toward them for a group hug: this crazy, beautiful family in the making.

After leaving the orphanage and returning to the island where they'd stayed before, Lizzie enjoyed a cozy evening with her husband. This was the trip of a lifetime and the original honeymoon they should've had.

For dinner, they ordered room service. And now that they'd finished their meals, they shared a dessert designed for two: a fruit tart, smothered in vanilla cream and laden with kiwis, bananas, berries and figs. They ate from the same plate, both with their own fork.

Lizzie gazed admiringly at her man. He sat cross-legged on the bed, wearing nothing but a pair of boxer-briefs. She was in her underwear, too. It just seemed like the thing to do on this warm summer night.

"What an amazing day," he said.

She nodded her agreement. "Yes, it was. But I can't wait until the day comes when we can bring Tokoni back to the States with us. Can you imagine how excited he's going to be?"

Max smiled and dipped in to the tart. "He'll be able to finish the drawings in his booklet, filling in the color of his parents' hair. His mother is going to be a beautiful redhead, and his father is going to have black hair."

"His gorgeous father, you mean."

He smiled again. "If you say so."

"I do." She took a creamy, fruity bite and moaned. Then she laughed and covered her mouth. "This is so darned good. I probably have it all over my face."

"You don't, actually. But it kind of reminds me of feeding you our wedding cake and kissing it off your lips. That was the sexiest thing I've ever done in a room full of people."

She suspected that this dessert session was headed in a sexy direction, too. That once they finished pigging out on the tart, they would be kissing like mad. But for now she asked, "What happened to the top tier of our cake?"

"I don't know. What's supposed to happen to it?"

"There's a tradition where brides and grooms freeze it and then eat it on their first anniversary."

"If that's the case, then the chef or someone in the catering staff probably kept it for us, putting it in the freezer in the ballroom kitchen."

She hoped they did. "We'll have to check when we

get home. It would be fun celebrating with you next year with our cake."

As Max speared his next bite, some of the crust crumbled onto his lap. He grinned, shrugged it off. "You know what I love, besides you?"

"What?" she asked, mesmerized by him.

"I love hearing you refer to the mansion as home. I love that my place is your home now, too."

She leaned over and nabbed another forkful. "I wonder what Tokoni is going to think of it. I'll bet he's going to be overwhelmed with how big it is."

"Once we're able to tell him about the adoption, we should show him pictures of it so he knows ahead of time where he'll be living."

"I hope the adoption goes quickly." Lizzie was anxious for them to become Tokoni's parents, to make that dream come true.

"It could happen as quickly as three months. We could have him home by Halloween. That could be our first official holiday, with the three of us together."

She glanced toward the window, where an ocean breeze was stirring. "Do they celebrate Halloween here?"

"I don't think so. But once we take the online classes that are required for the adoption, we'll know a lot more about how to blend Tokoni's traditions with ours." He shifted his legs, keeping them crossed, but moving his knees a little. "Remember when we talked about bringing Tokoni back for vacations so he can visit his homeland? I was thinking we should take it a step further and buy a summer house in Nulah."

"I love that idea. Maybe we can find a home near the orphanage, so Tokoni can play with the other kids and we can volunteer our time."

"That sounds good to me." He polished off his section of the tart. "Maybe, at some point, we could even adopt more kids."

Oh, wow. Lizzie widened her eyes. "You want more children?"

"Sure. Why not? If we're going to be a family, then we might as well share the love. We could adopt them from here and from the States, too, from foster care. Is that okay with you, to have more kids?"

"I hadn't thought about it until now. But yes, I would love to have a big family with you." She imagined them with a house full. "I think it would thrill Tokoni, too, to have siblings to call his own, to be part of something so meaningful."

"Then it's a deal. A future plan." He watched her take the last bite of the tart.

As she licked a dollop of the cream filling off her lips, he took the empty plate away, along with their forks. Was he preparing for the fast, mad kissing?

Once the area was clear, Max nudged her onto the bed. But he didn't rush her into it. He took his time, kissing her languidly, making her sigh like the dreamy new bride that she was.

He was warm and giving, gentle and passionate. There was no reason to hurry, she realized. No reason to get frantic on this soft, sweet island day. They had all the time in the world to be together.

She ran her hands over his body, over his scars, over the pain from his past. He looked into her eyes without the slightest flinch.

He caressed her, peeling off her bra and panties. Naked, with her heart fluttering, she moaned from the pleasure. The foreplay was as light and breezy as the ocean air.

He ditched his underwear and climbed on top of her. She felt the beats of his heart, tapping against her own.

He used protection, and they made love in a stream of consciousness, of tender awareness, with him being deep inside her. Deep, deep inside, just where she wanted him.

They moved in unison, her body becoming part of his, rolling over the bed, kissing as they tumbled. Lizzie had never had sex this magical before. But she was with Max, her husband, her dearest friend, the man she'd known for nearly half of her life.

He rocked his hips, filling her up, sliding back down, creating a motion that took her to the edge—and beyond.

Lizzie came, shuddering in silky warmth. And so did Max. She felt him, falling, drifting, spilling into her.

At the very same time.

The adoption was final in mid-October, and now it was Halloween, the holiday Lizzie and Max had talked about.

With the joy of motherhood in her heart, Lizzie studied the people that surrounded her. Jake and Carol were here with their daughter and Garrett and Meagan with theirs. Everyone gathered in the living room of the mansion, preparing to take the kids trick-or-treating.

Tokoni was dressed as a superhero, and he looked darned fine in his red-and-blue outfit and fly-through-the-air cape. Lizzie's mind drifted back to the first day she'd met him in the library of the orphanage. She'd told him that she was writing an article about the kids there, and he'd asked her then if he could be a superhero in her story.

And now he was. Lizzie had her very own superhero son.

She smiled at him, then glanced at her husband. He was as excited as she was. Tokoni had transitioned beautifully into their lives. He loved being their child and living in his big, fancy home in America. Halloween was new and exciting for him, too. Already, he adored sharing the spotlight with his cousins.

Ivy was costumed as a fairy, with glitter and sequins and colorful prettiness. Only she called herself an "Ella" instead of a "fairy." Meagan explained that it was because Ivy had a toy fairy, a tiny statue, named Ella, which also meant fairy. But it meant more than that to Meagan. When she was a child, she'd had a baby sister named Ella who'd died of SIDS. An angel in heaven.

Speaking of angels...

Nita was dressed as an angel, in a frilly white dress with gossamer wings. She was ten months old now and holding on to tables to walk. She babbled, too, in pre-toddler speak, saying things that no one understood except her. She was a darling child, a combination of her mother and father.

"I guess it'll be my sworn chocolate duty to eat her candy," Jake said as he caught Lizzie admiring his little angel. "Since she's too young for it."

"Yeah," Garrett chimed in. "That's probably just what the devil himself would do."

Jake flashed a mischievous grin. He sported a shiny red tuxedo and a set of pointy horns. He was the only parent out of the bunch who'd gotten dressed up. "Nita likes my costume."

Carol laughed. "That's just because she knows her daddy has always been a bit of a demon."

Lizzie couldn't ask for a nicer group of people. She loved Max's family. They were her family now, too, hers and Tokoni's.

She walked over to Max. "My dad is coming by later," she told him. "After we get back from trick-or-treating."

"Really? That's great." He leaned into her. "I'm glad he's taking the time to get to know Tokoni."

"I think he wants to learn to be a grandpa."

"He's welcome to see Tokoni anytime. Besides, we're going to keep him busy with the brood we're going to adopt. Just think of how many superheroes there will be around here in the future. And whatever else they decide to be."

Lizzie nodded, turning to look at the kids who were here today, pleased with how happy all of them were. They sat in a circle on the floor, all with their own plastic jack-o'-lantern candy bucket. Halloween was fast becoming her favorite holiday. But Christmas was going to be spectacular, too. She couldn't wait for it to arrive.

Jake adjusted his horns and asked, "So, is it time to get this show on the road?"

"Definitely." Max dashed over to Tokoni and picked him up. He spun him around, making him fly. "We're ready."

Yes, they were, Lizzie thought, as their son squealed in delight. They were ready.

For everything.

* * * * *

MILLS & BOON®

Desire™

PASSIONATE AND DRAMATIC LOVE STORIES

sneak peek at next month's titles...

In stores from 9th March 2017:

The Ten-Day Baby Takeover – Karen Booth *and*
Pride and Pregnancy – Sarah M. Anderson

Expecting the Billionaire's Baby – Andrea Laurence
and **The Magnate's Mail-Order Bride** – Joanne Rock

A Beauty for the Billionaire – Elizabeth Bevarly *and*
His Ex's Well-Kept Secret – Joss Wood

Just can't wait?
Buy our books online before they hit the shops!
www.millsandboon.co.uk

Also available as eBooks.

The perfect gift for Mother's Day...

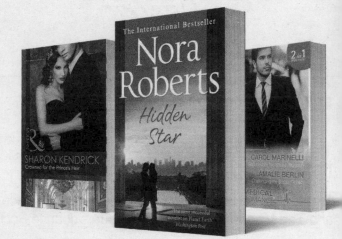

a Mills & Boon subscription

Call Customer Services on
0844 844 1358*

or visit
millsandboon.co.uk/subscription

MILLS & BOON®

Read on for an exclusive extract

How did she walk away? Lydia wondered.

How did she go over and kiss that sulky mouth and say goodbye when really she wanted to climb back into bed?

But rather than reveal her thoughts she flicked that internal default switch which had been permanently set to 'polite'.

'Thank you so much for last night.'

'I haven't finished being your tour guide yet.'

He stretched out his arm and held out his hand but Lydia didn't go over. She did not want to let in hope, so she just stood there as Raul spoke.

'It would be remiss of me to let you go home without seeing Venice as it should be seen.'

'Venice?'

'I'm heading there today. Why don't you come with me? Fly home tomorrow instead.'

There was another night between now and then, and Lydia knew that even while he offered her an extension he made it clear there was a cut-off.

Time added on for good behaviour.

And Raul's version of 'good behaviour' was that there would

be no tears or drama as she walked away. Lydia knew that. If she were to accept his offer then she had to remember that.

'I'd like that.' The calm of her voice belied the trembling she felt inside. 'It sounds wonderful.'

'Only if you're sure?' Raul added.

'Of course.'

But how could she be sure of anything now she had set foot in Raul's world?

He made her dizzy.

Disorientated.

Not just her head, but every cell in her body seemed to be spinning as he hauled himself from the bed and unlike Lydia, with her sheet-covered dash to the bathroom, his body was hers to view.

And that blasted default switch was stuck, because Lydia did the right thing and averted her eyes.

Yet he didn't walk past. Instead Raul walked right over to her and stood in front of her.

She could feel the heat—not just from his naked body but her own—and it felt as if her dress might disintegrate.

He put his fingers on her chin, tilted her head so that she met his eyes, and it killed that he did not kiss her, nor drag her back to his bed. Instead he checked again. 'Are you sure?'

'Of course,' Lydia said, and tried to make light of it. 'I never say no to a free trip.'

It was a joke but it put her in an unflattering light. She was about to correct herself, to say that it hadn't come out as she had meant, but then she saw his slight smile and it spelt approval.

A gold-digger he could handle, Lydia realised.

Her emerging feelings for him—perhaps not.

At every turn her world changed, and she fought for a semblance of control. Fought to convince not just Raul but herself that she could handle this.

Don't miss
THE INNOCENT'S SECRET BABY
by Carol Marinelli
OUT NOW

BUY YOUR COPY TODAY
www.millsandboon.co.uk

Join Britain's BIGGEST Romance Book Club

- **EXCLUSIVE offers every month**

- **FREE delivery direct to your door**

- **NEVER MISS a title**

- **EARN Bonus Book points**

Call Customer Services
0844 844 1358*

or visit
illsandboon.co.uk/subscriptions